The Alex Craft Novels

Grave Witch
Grave Dance
Grave Memory
Grave Visions
Grave Ransom
Grave Destiny
Grave War

Praise for the Alex Craft novels

Grave Destiny

"An exciting, action-packed, interesting, and wild adventure." —The Reading Cafe

"With a robust cast of characters and plenty of danger, Price's *Grave Destiny* weaves an enthralling tale of intrigue and intrepid sleuthing." —Fresh Fiction

Grave Ransom

"Dark urban fantasy fans will delight in Price's fifth Alex Craft, Grave Witch novel. . . . The story is filled with fast-paced action and creepy, immersive world-building." —*Publishers Weekly*

"Over the course of this transfixing series, Price has built a uniquely compelling world and made sure her characters were truly unforgettable!" —RT Book Reviews

Grave Visions

"*Grave Visions* has been a long-waited-for read, and it certainly delivers." —A Great Read

"If you love urban fantasy, DO NOT miss out on this series." —Kings River Life Magazine

Grave Memory

"A truly original and compelling urban fantasy series." —RT Book Reviews

"An incredible urban fantasy. . . . This is a series I love." —Nocturne Romance Reads

"An action-packed roller-coaster ride. . . . An absolute must-read!"
—A Book Obsession

Grave Dance

"A dense and vibrant tour de force."
—All Things Urban Fantasy

"An enticing mix of humor and paranormal thrills."
—Fresh Fiction

Grave Witch

"Fascinating magic, a delicious heartthrob, and a fresh, inventive world."
—*New York Times* bestselling author Chloe Neill

"A rare treat, intriguing and original. Don't miss this one."
—#1 *New York Times* bestselling author Patricia Briggs

"Edgy, intense . . . a promising kickoff to a series with potential."
—RT Book Reviews

"This series is more addictive than chocolate."
—Huntress Book Reviews

Grave War

An Alex Craft Novel

KALAYNA PRICE

ACE
New York

ACE
Published by Berkley
An imprint of Penguin Random House LLC
penguinrandomhouse.com

ISBN: 9781984805959

First Edition: November 2020

Printed in the United States of America
1   3   5   7   9   10   8   6   4   2

Cover art by Aleta Rafton
Cover design by Katie Anderson

To the readers who have gone on this journey with Alex and me. I can't believe we are reaching the end. I hope you've enjoyed this tale.

Grave War

Chapter 1

The first time a blade pressed menacingly against my throat, I experienced the obligatory life-flashing-before-my-eyes panic reaction. The hundredth time, as my back hit the wall and the cold edge of the dagger pressed against my skin, all I felt was annoyed. And exhausted.

"Yield," I said, huffing out the word and letting my own dagger drop to my side as I tried to catch my breath.

The man wielding the offending dagger frowned at me, his icy blue eyes narrowing in displeasure. "You can't yield, Alex."

I glared at him. He didn't even have the decency to look winded, and there wasn't a single white-blond hair out of place under the thin shimmering circlet on his brow. I, on the other hand, was a hot mess after spending the last hour getting my ass handed to me. *This* had not been what I'd been expecting for the evening. Which was why the little black dress I'd worn was currently riding up to an almost indecent level on my thighs. Not that my date had noticed. He was far too busy kicking my butt. Sorry, I mean *teaching me self-defense*.

My name is Alex Craft, and my specialty is raising shades, not hand-to-hand combat. Or any kind of combat, for that matter. For most of my life, that fact hadn't been an issue. I was a private investigator, but until about seven months ago, most of my clients needed nothing more than a graveside conversation with the deceased. Since then? Well, life had been considerably more dangerous, and I was set to start my probationary trial as lead investigator for the local Fae Investigation Bureau, so I needed more than mere self-defense sparring. But come on, I'd worn pantyhose for this date.

"I'm exhausted. Yield."

"If this were a true fight, you'd be dead. Now get your dagger up and figure out how to get out of this position."

I sighed. It was my own fault. I'd been the one who'd agreed to date a Faerie king. Currently that relationship was on the down low because in Faerie, the strongest took what they wanted and being perceived as standing between some other fae and the potential affection of a king? That could be deadly.

I gave a disparaging glance at the dagger in my hand. Like the one at my throat, the blade was dull, the tip rounded. Then I sucked in one more deep breath and kicked out, aiming for my opponent's knee as I angled the dagger toward his ribs. I missed both strikes when he stepped to the side. The pressure of the blade at my throat increased.

"And your throat has been slashed. Again."

Of course it had.

Falin Andrews, formerly the Winter Knight and quite newly the king of the winter court, stepped back, shaking his head as he withdrew the dull dagger. I blew air through my lips hard enough to dislodge the curls that had slipped in front of my eyes. Despite the ice coating the walls and floor around us, and the snow that fell above us, vanishing before it ever reached me, sweat beaded on my skin, making the already clingy black dress stick to me. My arms were sore, my legs aching, and even though I knew Falin was holding back, I would have bruises on top of bruises tomorrow.

Falin took several steps backward, ending with his legs slightly spread, his weight distributed evenly as he lifted his dagger. "Again."

"How long are we going to keep this up?"

"Until you score a hit."

One hit. It didn't sound like much. Except that it was.

"We'll die of old age first," I muttered, earning another downward twitch of his mouth. Of course, we were both fae so were theoretically slotted to live a very long time, but with him being Faerie's youngest ruler and me being, well, me with my propensity for near-death experiences, either one of us would do well to live to something fae considered middle age.

"This is totally not why I shaved my legs."

That statement made him pause. His eyes raked down my body, finally noticing how high our sparring had lifted my skirt. A wicked smile that did funny things to my stomach crossed his face, and he lifted an eyebrow. "And I will make sure to show my appreciation for that selfless act later. But first," he said, lifting his free hand and flexing his fingers in a *come at me* motion, "you need to score one hit."

Damn. I slunk forward, practice dagger raised. My own dagger would have served me better—I might have even stood a chance as the enchanted blade possessed an intelligence that guided my hand. But Falin had insisted I learn to duel without the enchanted dagger. I'd increase my chances of surviving if I had skill to back up the blade's magic, or so he claimed. The problem was, I had absolutely no skill at combat.

Falin's foot shot out in a sweeping blow. I was expecting it; the move was one of the attacks we'd been

practicing all night. I leapt to the side, but not fast
enough. My feet flew out from under me and my ass
slammed into the ground, the air bursting from my
lungs. Before I could blink, Falin followed me down,
and my back hit the ice, his knee planted in my sternum. Not hard—he avoided knocking the air out of me
a second time—but the move effectively pinned me to
the ice. I jerked my arm up, trying to block the blade I
knew was coming next.

The rasp and clang of metal colliding filled the air,
and for an elated moment, I thought I'd actually succeeded in stopping his dagger. Then the bite of dull
steel pressed at my throat.

Falin lifted one pale eyebrow. "Better."

"But I'm still dead," I said with a huff as he removed
the tip of his dagger from the hollow of my throat.

"Yes, but you're getting faster. You got your dagger
up in time to try to defend. That's progress."

"*Try*" being the key word in that sentence. *Yay
me. Not.*

"Again," he said as he stood with effortless grace. I
just glared from where I was sprawled on the floor. He
didn't even have the decency to look abashed, but at
least he held out a hand to help me up.

I accepted, letting him haul me to my feet, but as I
straightened, I feigned a stumble. He, of course, didn't
let me fall. Knock my ass to the floor while training?
Not an issue. But he wouldn't let me trip. Keeper,
right?

As he caught my arm, I moved into him. The fingers
of my empty hand skittered up the front of his shirt,
and I felt him tense, as if trying to determine if this was
an attack. I flashed him a smile, and then took a very
deliberate gaze down his body. While I was out of
breath, sweaty, and likely flushed from sparring, he
looked amazing. The top few buttons of his shirt were
open, flashing the lean muscles of his chest. The lightest glimmer of perspiration dusted that exposed skin,

making it look absolutely lickable. My eyes continued their wandering perusal, taking in his perfectly chiseled features, full lips, sharp cheekbones, and intense blue eyes.

I let my appreciation show in my face as I looked back up at him and bit my bottom lip. His gaze shot to my mouth, and the tension in his body changed. His arms slid around me, drawing me even closer. Then his mouth met mine.

Our history was complicated. We slept together months ago in a coupling that was probably more emotional than it should have been for how short we'd known each other at the time and for how many secrets we'd both been holding. But it had been a one-time event. Circumstances—and by that, I mostly mean the fact that Falin had been sworn to obey an insane queen—had prevented any further exploration of a relationship. Well, that and the fact that I'd briefly dated Death, a soul collector whose real name I still didn't know. Death and I broke up nearly two months ago, and the Winter Queen was dead, so theoretically nothing stood between Falin and me. But we seemed to be taking things slow. Frustratingly slow, even for someone with my commitment issues. Not that we were doing it intentionally. In the two weeks since the doors to Faerie had reopened, we hadn't managed to secure much uninterrupted time together.

The sexual tension had been building, and it was palpable on our lips, on the thrust of his tongue as my mouth parted for him. I wrapped my arms around the back of his neck and his hands slid a warm line up my back, pulling me closer. I was even more out of breath by the time we broke apart.

"You were supposed to score a hit before we took a break," Falin said, his voice amused and his lips so close they brushed against mine as he spoke.

I lifted a shoulder, but changed the angle of my hand that held the practice dagger. We were so close. The cheap shot should have been simple, a bend of my wrist to tap my blade on his throat and claim a win. Instead my blade clinked against metal, his hand suddenly not on my waist, but blocking his throat instead.

He cocked an eyebrow. "That's cheating. And that distraction is unlikely to work on most opponents."

"Didn't exactly work on you either." Not that I was sparing much thought for the hit I needed to stop this sparring match. My lips were still tingling from the bruising kiss we'd just shared, and Falin's blue eyes held enough heat to melt the ice around us.

I opened my fist and let the dagger fall harmlessly to the floor. It thunked against the frosted floor. "Yield," I whispered, dropping my hand to touch the flesh exposed in the opening of his shirt.

"You can't yield." But there was no weight to the words this time, his attention clearly no longer on training. His fingers trailed along my jaw before tangling in the hair at the base of my head.

He leaned forward, and our lips met again. A sparring of a very different sort began. One of tongues and breath, and hands that roamed. I had most of the buttons of his shirt undone when the sound of a distinctly feminine throat cleared behind us.

"Your Majesty," she said, and from her tone, I guessed it was the second time she had said it.

Falin broke the kiss with an almost inaudible groan. My huff of annoyance was considerably louder.

"A moment," he barked at the visitor where she waited on the other side of the privacy screen that cordoned the doorway and blocked the view of the rest of the room. I tugged my dress back into place while Falin rebuttoned his shirt. Once I was sure I wasn't indecent, I snatched my dagger from the ground, as if it would explain any remaining disarray of my clothing. Falin gave me a knowing look before turning toward the screen and saying, "Enter."

A willowy woman in a moss-green dress swept into

the main part of the room. Her lips pressed into a disapproving line as her gaze took us in, but she hid it quickly by dipping low into a curtsy, her head bowed so that all I could see was her brown hair tied up elaborately with mistletoe vines.

"Rise," Falin said, crossing his arms over his chest and leaning back slightly, as if her presence was of little concern beyond an annoyance.

Maeve stood from her curtsy gracefully, her features carefully pleasant, lacking any of the censure I'd caught when she'd entered. "My king, the delegates from spring and fall have arrived. They await your pleasure in the great hall." Her smile turned sharper, her gaze flickering to me for a moment before she continued by saying, "Between them, they brought three consort prospects. One can be dismissed out of hand, but two are very good candidates, either of whom would shore up your power base nicely."

My fingers clenched around my practice dagger, but I worked to keep my expression neutral. Maeve had made it clear she thought Falin needed to take a strong consort—if not a full queen—if he wanted to hold the winter court. He had a fearsome reputation as well as a significant amount of skill and lethal knowledge that had been passed to him, along with the blood on his hands, from his former job as knight, enforcer, and assassin. Both served him well as king and made him far more powerful than other fae his age, but he lacked the centuries of other court rulers—or even most of the courtiers.

Falin had appointed no knight of his own, so he fought every challenge brought to his throne. As the former queen's knight, he'd been fighting her challengers for years, but she'd been old. Powerful. There hadn't been that many challengers until her deceitful nephew's poisons had sent her into a spiral of madness. Falin was young, and though he'd proven he was deadly in a dueling circle, he was untested as a ruler, and the winter court was still recovering from the damage the former queen had caused as her sanity slipped. If the other courts thought him weak, how many duels could he fight before they wore him down? Or a challenger got lucky?

I wanted him safe. Strong alliances and more power behind the winter throne would help him stay that way. Maeve had lectured ad nauseam on the importance of a political union. So far he'd refused to consider any candidates. He wanted me to take the role. He'd told me as much, though he hadn't actually asked me to be his consort. I had commitment issues. I was still adjusting to terms like "boyfriend" and "dating," so "consort" was not on the table—not that I was powerful or fearsome enough to add anything to his claim on the throne. In the meantime, though, he'd been fighting duels every few days since the doors to winter reopened. The idea of him taking one of Maeve's suggested unions made me sick to my stomach, but him dying was worse, so I remained quiet, my features schooled as neutral as I could manage.

For his part, Falin glowered at Maeve. "I've told you before that I will not entertain consort prospects."

Maeve bowed her head but made the smallest shrug as if this was all out of her control. "Of course, my king. I have spread the word that you are not accepting offers, but that has done little to stop the applicants. I have offered you my advice as the head of your council. I'm afraid the other courts have noted the deficit in your court. They will continue to send prospects in hopes of securing the position. Or they will send challengers."

"Noted," Falin said, his voice cold. This was a conversation they'd had before. "I'll see the delegates shortly. I'll not see the consort prospects. If there is nothing else, you are dismissed."

She dipped into a quick curtsy before turning and sweeping gracefully out of the room, but I didn't miss the way her smile seemed to cut a cruel line as she shot one last glance at me. I wasn't sure why she didn't like me. If she had a problem with my part in the former queen's fall, you would think she'd hold an even bigger grudge against Falin, who'd been the one to behead the queen. Instead Maeve had made several attempts to seduce him, and had even offered herself as the first prospect of consort. Of course, I might have just answered my own question. Not that I thought Maeve had strong feelings for Falin—or likely any feelings, as she'd barely noticed him when he was the Winter Knight—but she was attracted to power and I was standing between her and queenship.

Which was why I was learning how to duel. Not because of Maeve in particular, but because I could be challenged by anyone who perceived me as an obstacle to clawing their way higher on the Faerie power ladder. That was also why my relationship with Falin, while not exactly secret, wasn't something we were advertising.

With a scowl, Falin watched Maeve go, and then he ran a hand through his hair. Or at least, he tried to. His long hair caught on the thin circlet of ice on his brow and he shook his hand free with a grimace.

When he turned back to me, his expression softened. He reached out and cupped my face, his thumb running lightly over my cheekbone. "Rain check on where that kiss was headed?"

I shrugged, trying not to show my disappointment, but in truth, the moment had passed. Between Maeve's brief appearance and the reminder about Falin's consort candidates—even if he didn't actually want said candidates—the mood was well and truly broken.

"How many rain checks does that make?"

He grimaced, because we were racking them up. I was starting to suspect Faerie didn't want us together with the way we were always interrupted whenever anything took a turn toward the romantic.

"Come to court with me, and we will pick up where we left off as soon as these blasted introductions are over."

That sounded awesome—okay, well, not really. Picking up where we left off sounded great. Court? No, I hated attending court.

I glanced at my watch. Digital watches were unreliable in Faerie, and anything battery powered was suspect, but windups worked well—as long as I remembered to wind it. It was only nine currently, but these meetings with representatives from other courts tended to drag on for hours.

"I should head back. First day at the FIB tomorrow and all. I need to get a good night's sleep." It sounded like a weak excuse, and the look Falin gave me said he wasn't buying it. Likely because regardless of how long I spent in Faerie, the door back to mortal reality should drop me in the mortal realm within minutes to an hour or two of when I'd left. Or at least that was how the door used to work. Recently the doors had not been functioning predictably. Or maybe it was that they'd been functioning too predictably. Regardless of how meticulously I filled out the ledger at the Eternal Bloom, time passed at an identical rate on either side of the door. For me, at least. I hadn't heard anyone else complain about the phenomenon.

Maybe it was just a run of bad luck—though typically bad luck with the doors resulted in me losing hours or days, not time being consistent on both sides. My hand moved to the locket on my throat. It wasn't actually a locket, but a ball of compressed realities. It was also what I suspected had caused the change in the door's behavior.

"I should go."

Falin frowned and stepped closer. He wrapped his arms around me, narrowing the world to just the warmth of his body pressed against mine. His lips brushed against mine, just a taste of a kiss, nothing compared to the kiss Maeve had interrupted. I wanted to deepen that kiss, but he did have to greet the emissaries. He was a new king, and he needed to make allies.

"Tomorrow?" he asked after our lips parted.

"Yeah." I started to nod and then stopped. "Oh, no. I can't tomorrow. I have plans."

He cocked an eyebrow. I shrugged.

"Tamara is on bed rest until the baby comes. Holly and I promised to go over and binge-watch the seventh season of *Curse Breakers*."

"That's a horrible show," he said, but he was smiling.

Before this whole "ascending to the winter throne" thing had occurred, he'd sat through more than a couple marathon sessions of the show, laughing at how flabbergasted I got over the improbability of most of the spells used by the cast. We weren't even dating then, just friends throwing popcorn at my television. Okay, I'd been the one throwing popcorn.

"You could join us. I'm sure Tam wouldn't mind."

The smile faded from his face. "I wish I could."

He pressed a kiss to the top of my forehead. There was sadness in the gesture, a weight of responsibility. He hadn't wanted to be king. He didn't want to hold court. He'd been protecting me when he'd killed the queen. And now he was in the precarious position of king.

"You could give up the court." I whispered the words, even though we were alone and there was no one to overhear them.

He sighed and pulled me in tighter. I leaned my cheek against his chest as his fingers slid along my back, ghost-light, leaving goose bumps of awareness in their wake.

"That, I wish I could do as well." His voice was also a whisper. If his mouth weren't inches from my ear, I wouldn't have heard him at all. "But who would I trust the court to? Who wouldn't have me killed as a potential threat and try to leverage your planeweaving abilities? Who would leave us in peace?"

And weren't those all million-dollar questions.

"Heavy is the head that wears the crown," I muttered, adding my own sigh. "You probably shouldn't keep them waiting much longer." I stepped out of his arms, though it took a force of will. "I'll try to stop by for a few minutes tomorrow and give you a briefing on my first day."

"And should I listen to this briefing as a boss or a boyfriend?"

I must have made a face at his question because he cocked an eyebrow and asked, "What?"

I gave a dismissive shrug. "I'm nervous about tomorrow. I'm still not sure I'm cut out for this job." It was a misdirection. All true, of course, but what I'd actually been thinking was that Faerie needed worker unions. The entire society was run by favoritism and nepotism. My appointment as probationary head of the FIB when I'd never even been an agent was case in point. Also, the fact that I was stepping into Falin's old job, which in matters regarding the mortal realm in winter's territory made me the most powerful authority figure second to the king himself, was terrifying. Oh, and my boyfriend being my boss was weird. Of course, having a boyfriend was weird . . . and that sounded terribly juvenile.

"If I didn't think you were suited for the job, I wouldn't have appointed you. I need someone I trust protecting my interests as well as representing my subjects in the mortal realm. You're observant, you're quick-witted, and I've witnessed you stubbornly pursue your cases as a PI. You'll be great in this role."

He was considerably more confident in my abilities than I was. I'd list my skills more along the lines of stumbling into the most dangerous situation possible and then managing to insert myself into the thick of it.

At least my track record for surviving such situations was pretty good . . .

I forced a weak smile. "I should go," I said, and then stepped closer to give him one last kiss. This one I kept chaste, just a quick brush of the lips so neither of us got distracted—he had places to be, after all. Then I made my good-byes, handed my practice dagger back to him, and headed back to mortal reality.

Chapter 2

As I'd expected, the door dumped me back into the mortal realm at a time consistent with how long I'd spent inside Faerie. It seemed silly to be upset about not being able to cheat a few extra hours into a day, but I couldn't deny my disappointment. I'd found very few perks to my recently discovered fae nature, and now I'd apparently lost one of them.

At least I'd anticipated it this time and hadn't driven to the Bloom. Years of using my gravesight—not to mention the extra damage that had been caused by peering across planes with my planeweaving—had left much to be desired in my night vision. If I'd driven, my car would be stuck here for the night, as I was going to have to get a ride home.

I reclaimed the items I'd checked before entering Faerie. Iron was the only item I was required to check, but Faerie didn't tend to get along well with technology, so I'd made a habit of not bringing my phone into the VIP room of the Eternal Bloom. The bouncer handed it back to me, and maybe he smiled, but I wasn't sure around the mouthful of jagged teeth protruding around his calloused-looking lips. I decided to err on the side of polite and gave him a small smile and nod as I accepted the phone. Then I headed out the front door of the Bloom, searching for a taxi.

Some nights, several idled outside the Eternal Bloom, hoping for a quick fare, but not tonight. It was a Sunday, so I wasn't all that surprised. I pulled up a ride-share app to summon a car. After I'd provided all the pertinent information and got an estimate of the cost, the app informed me that I had a fourteen-minute wait. Not terrible, but I didn't relish the idea of spending nearly fifteen minutes in the cold. While I'd been perfectly comfortable in the winter halls of ice and snow in just my skimpy black dress, January in Nekros on the mortal side of the door was far less pleasant. No snow or ice, but the night held that wet cold that sank right through my heavy coat and straight into my bones, chilling me with the first gust of wind that tore down the street of the Magic Quarter.

I headed back into the Bloom, but not the VIP room this time—while my phone would probably be fine in the pocket of Faerie that housed the door to the winter court, cell service was spotty at best and I actually wanted to catch my ride when it arrived. Instead I headed into the public part of the bar, which I typically avoided, as it was an overpriced tourist trap where humans went to stare at unglamoured fae. The bar was comfortably busy, most tables taken but not standing room only like I'd seen it at times. Still, a decent crowd for a Sunday.

I kept my head down as I claimed a table in the back, trying not to draw attention. Until recently, I'd had a chameleon charm that hid my few fae traits, like the telltale glow that seemed to light my skin from within. But the same magical shift that had made the doors behave differently for me had also canceled out the chameleon charm's ability to hide my nature. The bar was dim enough that my slight glow was noticeable, so a few heads looked up with curiosity as I settled into a seat, but I was far from the most interesting fae in the room. The whole purpose of this tourist trap was to allow mortals to gawk at fae. From the human perspective, it was a rare novelty. For the fae, it helped cement human belief, and mortal belief was what fueled Faerie magic. The fae who worked in the bar tended to be the more flamboyant and obvious kinds. Like the satyr who pranced on hooves as he retrieved drinks, or the green-skinned woman who waited tables, her feet barely seeming to touch the floor. A singer performed on the stage on the far side of the room, gills flashing at her throat as she took deep breaths between lines and holding her microphone with fingers joined by membranous webbing. I couldn't understand the words to the song she sang, but her sweet voice called up a longing for the sea in me, and I guessed she was some sort of siren. Looking at some of the enthralled faces around the room—most of them male—I wondered how safe it was for a siren to perform for humans. None seemed particularly inclined to run off and drown themselves, but now that I was going to be head of the Fae Investigation Bureau, maybe that would be a question I'd look into.

The siren had just finished her third song when the cocktail waitress, a fae with a shock of brambles for hair, waltzed over to my table. I'd declined to order a drink when I first sat down, hoping I'd be out of here before she made another round. Apparently my time had run out.

"I'm about to leave," I said, glancing at my phone. Fourteen minutes had passed already; the car had to be here soon.

The waitress smiled. "Well, then I'm sure your admirer will be disappointed. He sent this." She held out a rose so deeply red it was nearly the color of blood.

I frowned, not taking the offered rose. "Who sent it?" It couldn't have been Falin. He was tied up in court. Of course, the doors were acting funny for me, not him. It was possible he could have spent several hours with the delegates and then managed to slip into the mortal realm only minutes after I arrived.

The briar fae turned, lifting a willowy hand to point out my admirer, but the motion faltered before landing on anyone. "Oh. He is gone."

Definitely not Falin then.

My phone pinged, an alert from the ride-share app letting me know my car had arrived. Thank goodness. I stood, shrugging into my heavy coat.

"You keep the rose," I said as I grabbed my purse and headed for the door. She made a sound of protest behind me, but I didn't stop.

The car at the curb matched the model my app said would be picking me up so I leaned down to peer into the passenger-side window. The driver lowered it automatically.

"Ms. Craft?" he asked and I nodded before climbing into the backseat. Nausea twisted in my stomach as I pulled the door closed behind me, but that wasn't the driver's fault. It was the iron in the car. Unfortunately the ride-share app didn't have an option to request fae-friendly vehicles. But it wouldn't be a long drive. I could stomach the discomfort from the Bloom to my house. I just hoped the driver wasn't chatty.

Unfortunately, he was.

He confirmed the address I was headed to, and then immediately began telling me about the fact that he was actually a full-time college student studying something to do with magical convergences—I tuned him out pretty quick as he rambled without pausing to breathe.

"So what do you do, Lexi?" he asked as he pulled to a stop at a red light.

I'd been focusing on not getting sick in the backseat, but at that, my head shot up. The sick feeling in me turned cold.

"What did you call me?"

"Uh, Lexi? The guy who came out before you said you were a friend and that your name was Lexi. And he—holy shit, your eyes are glowing! I mean, you were kind of glowy before, but now . . . geez."

I didn't doubt my eyes had just lit up like lanterns. I'd opened my shields so that I could gaze across planes. I'd almost expected the man's features to change, to reveal a different face hidden under a glamour, despite the sickening amount of iron in the car around us. But he didn't change, and from the look of his cheery yellow soul, he was human.

Behind us, a car honked several angry beeps. With my psyche gazing across multiple planes of existence, I couldn't make out the color of the traffic light, as it now looked rusted and broken, but I guessed it must have turned green. Still the driver was staring at me, his eyes a little too wide.

"It's, uh, not Lexi then?" he asked.

I shook my head. Only two people had ever used that nickname for me: the insane—and now deceased—Winter Queen, and her treacherous and maniacal nephew, Ryese.

"What did the guy who told you that was my name look like?"

"Uh, I don't know. Short blond hair? Tall? Normal?"

The last time I'd seen Ryese, "normal" wouldn't have been a description I would have applied to him, as he'd been badly disfigured from iron poisoning. From what I'd been told, glamour couldn't hide scars caused by iron. But if it hadn't been Ryese, who else would have called me Lexi?

"He, uh, he told me to give you these when we reached your house." The driver lifted two bloodred roses from the passenger seat beside him. Roses just like the one the briar fae had said an admirer had sent.

"I don't want them." In fact, I didn't want to be in this car anymore. How far was I from the house?

Would it be smarter to get out and walk? Or would that be a really dumb idea if Ryese or one of his associates was out there in the night?

The horn blasted behind us again, and the driver jumped, only now seeming to notice the sound. He twisted back around in his seat, letting off the brakes and hitting the gas a little too fast, making the car lurch. I considered closing my shields again, as my glowing gaze was clearly freaking him out and I didn't want to die in a flaming car accident. But if Ryese was in Nekros, I didn't want to be blind.

I settled for staring out the window, the world flashing by in a chaotic mix of colors and planes of existence with my shields open. The driver, who had been so chatty before, now remained completely silent, exceeding every speed limit, clearly as ready to have me out of his car as I was to get out.

I'd already paid him through the app, so when he stopped in front of the house address I'd given him, I simply opened the car door and stepped outside, drawing the dagger from my boot as discreetly as I could. Maybe it was not quite discreet enough, or maybe he was still freaking out about my glowing eyes and the awkwardness of the drive, because the driver peeled out as soon as I slammed the car door, his tires squealing and leaving the scent of burnt rubber behind.

I scanned the yard and house in front of me, but nothing seemed out of place. The quiet suburban neighborhood had all the normal sounds of everyday life, and the magic in the air felt the same as it always did. Still, I kept my dagger out as I walked up the drive to the front stoop. There, on the doormat, sat what appeared to be three withered bloodred roses.

One at the bar, two in the car, and now three at my door. In Faerie, three was a significant number. Something bad was coming. I nudged the roses off the stoop with the toe of my boot, not daring to touch them. I couldn't see or sense any magic in them, even with my shields open, but Ryese was a sneaky bastard and there had to be a reason he was sending me roses. I seriously doubted it was an apology for his multiple attempts on my life.

But what the hell was he up to?

Chapter 3

$\rightarrowtail \Longrightarrow \; \Longleftarrow \longleftarrowtail$

No more roses appeared in the night, thank goodness. By the next morning, I was half wondering if
I'd overreacted. Not that I planned to let my guard
down, but maybe I'd jumped to the conclusion it was
Ryese prematurely. Most of the winter court had heard
the queen call me Lexi at some point or another. It was
entirely possible some courtier thought that was my
name and this was some really awkward—and a little
creepy—courting attempt. My relationship with Falin
wasn't exactly public, so maybe some other fae was
playing secret admirer.

I'd definitely stay alert, but for now I needed to focus on my first day at the FIB.

I was waiting by the front door nursing my third cup
of coffee by the time a knock filled the small one-room
loft. Technically, I didn't live in the loft anymore—in
fact, the entire house was vacant most of the time—but
the fact that a folded space with an honest-to-goodness
fairy-tale castle tucked inside it had opened up in my
landlord's backyard wasn't a fact I wanted advertised.
Though I guess Caleb wasn't actually my landlord anymore, seeing as how he lived inside my castle, but the

door to the castle connected to his house, so we called it a wash and all enjoyed being castlemates.

Punctuality wasn't my strongest skill, and the walk from the castle to the house was a good ten-minute jaunt, so I'd arrived at the house with plenty of time to spare. Which was a good thing, as the knock came ten minutes before I'd been told to expect it. It seemed Agent Nori did not have any punctuality issues. That didn't surprise me. I opened the door before her hand had time to drop.

"Morning," I said, offering a feeble smile held in place only by the copious amounts of caffeine I'd consumed. PC, my Chinese Crested dog who'd promptly curled up on my old bed and fallen back asleep as soon as we'd arrived at the house, now flung himself off the bed and charged the door, barking. He growled, his entire six-pound frame shaking with the sound as he pressed himself against my boots, staring at the fae at the door with his small teeth bared. PC apparently didn't like Nori much.

I couldn't fault his taste, but I did need to create a working relationship with Nori.

For her part, Nori ignored the small dog. She also didn't bother returning my smile. Her narrow gaze raked over me, disapproval dripping off her starched outfit. "Didn't the king issue you a credit card for miscellaneous expenses?" she asked, but didn't wait for me to confirm before she continued. "You should use it to buy a more professional wardrobe."

I stiffened, the already thin smile I'd managed turning brittle, but I resisted glancing down at myself. I knew what I was wearing. I'd picked it out two days ago in preparation for my first day. The black leather pants were an old favorite, and I thought looked rather nice tucked into my equally black boots. I had added a collared red top, as well as a black blazer—which was new, though I'd used my own money, not Falin's, thank you very much. All in all, I thought I looked pretty sharp.

Maybe I would let PC bite her; though, my luck, her skin would be poisonous . . .

"New dress code option for the whole team," I said, as if I couldn't care less. I was theoretically the boss, after all. Well, probationary boss. Falin had offered me the position without any trial period, but he had more confidence in my ability to lead the FIB than I did. I wasn't ready to accept the position as head of the Fae Investigation Bureau for the entire winter court until I was sure I could actually cut it. In the meantime, though, if Falin had an issue with my wardrobe, he could let me know.

I snagged my purse from the chair, glanced back to make sure the inner door was open so PC could get downstairs to Caleb's studio, and then stepped around Nori without another word. I wanted to march right down the stairs without a backward glance, but I had to turn to lock up the house. It rather ruined the effect.

Nori didn't wait as I locked up, but took the stairs in a clipped but efficient stride. When she reached the bottom, I caught the slight hesitation to her step, as if she was trying to decide if she should stop and wait. She didn't, but marched around to the drive in the front of the house. Once she'd disappeared from sight, I allowed myself a single sigh. Then I rolled my shoulders back and lifted my chin, lengthening my own stride.

Today would be interesting. I was entering the FIB at the top. Nori was my second in command, but until I got up to speed with the intricacies of the organization, she was also my guide and teacher. There was a power play going on, and if I wanted to protect the people I cared about, I needed to come out on top.

I rounded the side of the house, trying to look authoritative. And then stopped. Nori was waiting beside a shiny black sedan. That wasn't surprising. She'd told me she'd be picking me up in an agency vehicle and the car had the plastic-like look of all fae-favored vehicles—

no fae liked to be trapped inside a metal box. No, the surprising part was that she wasn't alone.

A man, well, a troll, towered behind her and I had to wonder where he shopped for black suits in his enormous size. More than that, though, I wondered what he was doing here.

I stopped, eyeing the pair.

"Craft, this is Tem. He is an agent," Nori said with a toss of her head to indicate the large troll.

The troll stepped forward, holding out his hand. "It is nice to meet you, ma'am."

Ma'am, huh? Well, at least he wasn't pulling the cocky power play Nori seemed to be running. Also, it surprised me that he spoke with a thick accent. Something European, his words crisp and shockingly well articulated around the two large tusks protruding from his mouth.

I plastered a smile on my face and stepped forward to accept his offered handshake. I'd never actually shaken hands with a creature as large as a troll before, and there was an awkward moment of trying to figure out how I was supposed to accomplish the task. His palm engulfed my entire hand, his thick fingers wrapping up my forearm halfway to my elbow. I tried not to grimace as I shook my entire arm in a strange parody of a handshake.

"Would Tem be a first or a last name?" I asked by way of pleasantries, though in truth I was still wondering what he was doing here. Nori had told me she would be picking me up for my first day—she hadn't mentioned bringing backup.

The large troll lifted one shoulder without letting go of my arm. "Little of both, I suppose. It's the only name I got. Is this your first time shaking hands with a troll? Most folk Sleagh Maith size opt to shake just a finger." He lifted his other hand and wiggled one very large finger for emphasis. "'Fraid I'll break their arm, I think."

That possibility had crossed my mind, and my teeth gritted behind my smile, but I didn't jerk my arm away. He released me with a grin that made his scaly yellow lips slide over his tusks, and I wasn't sure if he was happy I hadn't flinched away or if he was enjoying making me uncomfortable. Not even off my own property yet and I was already questioning my life choices.

"And which handshake do you prefer?" I asked, placing my hands on my hips to prevent myself from crossing my arms.

The troll smiled even broader, showing an impressive number of teeth, which I was surprised to see were rather square and blunt aside from the two large tusks. "Amongst my own kind? Nothing that wouldn't snap *your* bones. With the frailer folks like yourself, I don't much mind either way, but I do like having a boss who isn't afraid of me."

He gave me an approving nod. So, I guessed the handshake was a test. At least I'd apparently passed? It was a good thing troll ears weren't sharp enough that he could hear my heart hammering in my chest.

Nori rolled her narrow eyes and opened the driver's-side door of her black sedan. Small talk was apparently over. I slid into the passenger side, and then lifted an eyebrow when Tem opened the back door. The troll was at least eight feet tall, and while the sedan was bigger than my little convertible, I wasn't sure how he was going to fold his huge bulk into the backseat.

Tem had introduced himself free of his glamour, which, now that I thought about it, was odd. Very few fae walked around in the mortal realm without a protective coat of glamour. For starters, glamour helped them blend into humanity more, but it also provided an extra layer of insulation from the metals and technology that didn't agree with fae physiology. I'd been spending a considerable amount of time in Faerie of late, and few fae glamoured their appearance while there, so it hadn't immediately struck me as odd. As he ducked into the car, though, his glamour folded around him, shrinking his frame by at least two feet and changing his skin from a leathery yellow to a more human tone. He still didn't look comfortable cramped in the backseat, but he did fit, which wouldn't have been true in his unglamoured troll form. Presumably he'd arrived in the car, which meant he'd intentionally dropped his glamour to meet me. Was that a form of respect by showing his true face? Or was it another test, to see if I would spook?

It was going to be a long day.

"Tem, this doesn't seem like your kind of transportation," I said as Nori reversed out of my driveway. Even glamoured, the troll hunched slightly, and he sat in the middle seat so that his elbows would have room.

The troll grunted; he might have even shrugged, though it was hard to tell in his current position. "The king wanted to make sure you had some muscle at your back."

So, a bodyguard. I should have guessed. Falin had always worked alone when he'd headed the FIB. Considering I was learning the ropes of the organization as well as fae culture, I understood why he'd partnered me with Nori. But a bodyguard as well? So much for his confidence in my ability to do this job. What had I signed myself up for?

Chapter 4

"So all of these areas belong to winter?" I asked, staring at the map spread out before me. It was roughly similar to world maps I'd seen back in school, but this one was shaded in only four colors, which covered all continents and oceans in amorphous and seemingly haphazard blotches of color. Winter's territories were icy blue, spring's pastel pink, summer's grass green, and fall's a golden brown. There seemed to be little rhyme or reason to where the colors covered, only that there was only one of each seasonal color on each continent.

There were also discrepancies in landmass shapes from what I'd learned in school, as this map took into account folded spaces. The Organization of Magically Inclined Humans—OMIH, pronounced "oh me" with a groan by most of us—had been trying to produce a map that showed the folded spaces for years but had struggled to chart them. The fact that most folded spaces could only be entered or exited from very particular passageways, and were places between other places, made it extra difficult. Such as Nekros, which was between Georgia and Alabama. Take the one highway that led into Nekros, and it took several hours to drive through the wilds surrounding the city, the city itself, more wilds, and then out into the neighboring state. But, if you instead turned off before reaching the folded space and took the road a mile or two south or north, you could cross from one state to the other, turn and drive over the highway that exited Nekros, and make a full circle around the folded space in about fifteen minutes. I knew that for a fact—Casey and I had done it one summer when we were teenagers. For that reason, most official maps were updated with only the entrances of folded spaces. This map, though, seemed to shimmer and move as my gaze swept over it. When I focused on the entrance to Nekros's folded space, it unfolded before me, the city named with a small dot floating inside a massive wild space. The Sionan River, which ran through Nekros City but didn't exist outside the folded space, was clearly delineated on the map. I followed the thin snaking line of the river up until it vanished into a mountain range I'd never seen before, but then the map seemed to blur and I was instead staring at the state line of Georgia. All of Nekros was depicted in icy blue, as was most of the southeast of America.

"This is as close an approximation of the borders as even magic can track," Nori said. Her hand flittered over the top of the map, not quite touching the surface as she outlined the edge of the blue area in North America. "The borders waver a bit from day to day, and of course our territory is at its largest right now, seeing as our season currently reigns. At the Spring Equinox, our borders will shrink back a bit, and then become the smallest they ever are after the Summer Solstice."

I'd had no idea the borders moved with the seasons, only that the territories changed when the doors moved. Two hours into my first day and I was both fascinated by how much I'd learned and developing a stress headache. Also, I'd just learned that every continent had a territory belonging to winter on it, and oh yeah, me being head of the FIB meant I was head of the whole thing. Each continent had an office and they all reported to me. Not all the fae spoke English either—English was just one of many human languages. They all spoke the common language of the fae, but *I* didn't. I was scheduled to be introduced to all the branch heads later in the week. A meeting set up inside Faerie since we all could gather there with ease and be back on our respective continents in the same afternoon. A convenient way to bridge the world for sure, but the language issue? That was going to be a problem.

I rubbed my temples and stared at the map, watching it shimmer and subtly shift. I'd thought I was taking over as head of an agency that policed Nekros City and the surrounding wilds. I'd never considered how much farther winter spread beyond that, or that winter's territories would touch other continents. Hell, there was even territory in Antarctica. But just the amount of territory on this continent was daunting. And from what I could tell, there was only one door in each territory.

"What is this?" I asked, peering closer at a small area in the middle of Florida. Everything around it was blue, but it was colorless. "Is this not part of winter's territory?"

Nori leaned down to see what I was pointing at and then frowned. "That's Disney. The belief magic there is so strong, it reshapes Faerie. No court can hold it."

"So there are no fae there?"

"Oh, there are fae. It truly is one of the most magical places in the human world. There is enough belief magic there to sustain an entire court, but the fae who live there are changed. They become lost princesses and happy dwarves and enchanted beasts. It is . . . terrifying."

I smirked, but moved on without further comment.

"So what happens to fae living on the borders if the edges are in constant flux?"

The look Nori gave me suggested even a child would know the answer to that question. As I'd grown up believing I was human, and had only discovered any different a little over half a year ago, I didn't know the answer. It wasn't like the fae were all that open about their world or society. They wanted human belief, not human understanding.

I did know—from painful firsthand experience—that even those independent fae living in the human realm had to pledge to a seasonal court and live inside that season's territory or they would begin to fade, growing weaker until they eventually died. So were fae near the border nomads? Constantly on the move if the territory shifted?

The shrill sound of Nori's wings rubbing together betrayed her annoyance. The wings were currently hidden with glamour, and she couldn't fly this wrapped up in her human disguise, but they still occasionally announced her mood. "Few fae live that far from the door to Faerie—the magic is too thin. Those that do have adapted to the point that they are nearly human. Few fae even venture outside of the folded spaces for extended periods."

"Oh." It made sense. The fae had come out of the mushroom ring seventy-odd years ago because human belief had dwindled to the point that the courts were fading. Their reemergence had set off the Magical Awakening. Nearly a quarter of all humans discovered they were witches, able to manipulate magic. The wilds began emerging. The folded spaces opened. Wyrd magic appeared in families that had never had a hint of magic before. It was not a peaceful time, and many of the magically inclined had resettled into the newly unfolded spaces. I'd grown up in a city founded in one such folded space, and the boarding school I'd been shipped off to when my wyrd power emerged was in another folded space. Nekros boasted higher than the national average of magic users, and for most people, some aspect of magic—be it a charm to keep food fresh, a potion to cure wrinkles, or a bandage enriched with a healing spell—was part of day-to-day life. That wasn't the case in other parts of the country, and certainly not everywhere in the world. In some countries, practicing magic was strictly forbidden. Looking at the map, I noticed that the cities and countries least tolerant to magic were farthest from the doors.

"So what is the winter fae population on this continent outside of Nekros?" I asked.

Nori shrugged. "There are a few wild spaces where fae frequent." She pointed to various points on the map. "And a scattering of fae inhabit the territory's major cities for short sabbaticals either by choice or because they are compelled to do so, but the majority are in the folded space closest to the door."

"Compelled to do so?" I lifted an eyebrow. "Compelled by the former queen or by their own desires?" Though wouldn't the latter fall under "by choice"?

"By the High King, ultimately, but yes, by the seasonal rulers directly." Nori had that tone like she was instructing a rather dense toddler, but when I continued to stare at her, she sighed and said, "Faerie runs on belief magic. Humans forget very easily, especially those who are not exposed to as much magic as those inside folded spaces. Fae are sent out into the world to remind humans we are real."

"Ah. And how often are the FIB contacted about cases outside of Nekros?"

Nori shrugged again. "Humans who are not accustomed to interacting with magic tend to be more prickly. They report on minor grievances more often—in which case we typically solve the problem by removing the fae in question. Disappearances resulting from human violence against fae are the bigger problem. That will usually demand an agent's actual presence."

"Is that common?"

"It happens. The largest cities have a field office where a single agent is stationed. They serve there for three- to four-month assignments. You will be in charge of creating the rotation."

Well, wouldn't that make me popular. It probably also explained the attitude of the law enforcement personnel I'd met at the conference I'd attended the previous week. When I'd introduced myself as a PI turned FIB agent most had dismissed me out of hand. I'd thought it was my background—PIs were rarely taken seriously by real cops. But over the course of the weekend, I'd found that the general attitude tended to be that the entire FIB organization was worthless. It had shocked me, because in Nekros, while I wouldn't say the FIB were respected by the local cops, they were at least acknowledged as a legitimate agency and one to be taken seriously. The conference had been in Texas, though, pretty damn far from the door to Faerie. If most big cities only had a single FIB agent who was responsible for the entire surrounding area, and that agent rotated out three to four times a year . . . Yeah, I could see why agencies outside Nekros thought they were a joke.

We discussed how many agents were in North America's FIB team, both in Nekros and serving in cities across winter's territory. Then Nori hauled a large stack of manila envelopes onto the desk in front of me.

"These are the reports from our field agents since the king's reign began. Some are cases they've marked as closed and others are more general reports," she said, and I eyed the daunting stack of files. Falin had only been king for about a month.

Nori wasn't finished yet. She next retrieved a nearly equally large stack, but this one was loose paper. "And these are queries, complaints, and requests from the territories outside of Nekros. A few are from law enforcement, some are from independent or stationed fae, but most are from humans. And this stack is composed of the reports from our local agents." She dropped a third pile of manila folders in front of me. It rivaled the first two, despite being for only Nekros. "Here are the queries, complaints, and requests for our local office. And finally, here are the files on our active open cases." She put a fifth pile on my desk. This one at least was only a handful of folders. "We'll address the foreign offices later."

I stared at the piles of files and papers in front of me. Had Falin really done so much paperwork when he'd been head of the FIB? I'd always seen him more as an action guy, but then that was typically the role he played when we were together on a case. I never saw him in the office, though now that I thought about it, he did spend a fair number of late nights on his laptop. Between the paperwork, the cases he worked, and the fact that he'd spent a significant amount of time fighting the former queen's duels, I wasn't sure how he'd been keeping up with everything. Had he really gone through every complaint and request personally, or was Nori trying to overwhelm me?

I picked up the stack of local current cases first. It was the smallest stack, which made it a little less intimidating. I thumbed through the top few quickly, noting that each started with a request or complaint form on which someone—I was guessing Nori, as the handwriting wasn't Falin's—had scratched out a few notes as well as an agent assignment. The next few pages were mostly handwritten daily reports from the assigned agent on what had been accomplished.

The first case involved searching for who had carved their initials into a dryad's tree trunk. That seemed like a fairly trivial crime until I realized the case being built was for aggravated assault. Right, dryads didn't just live in trees—they were trees. The next case involved a dispute between two fae over ownership of a flower. I stopped and read that again. The agent run-

ning the case had been interviewing neighbors and
attempting to establish which fae held rightful ownership of the flower.

A flower.

Then I realized the fae in question were diminutive
sprites, and the flower was where they lived. This was
a home ownership/squatter issue.

I was so out of my depth here. My knowledge of
fae—or really my lack thereof—was going to be a major
stumbling block.

I quickly scanned the rest of the active files, multiple
times having to check my perspective and try to puzzle
out why the case was a case. Then I grabbed the stack
of outstanding requests, complaints, and queries and
flipped through them quickly, knowing I was going to
have to get Nori to help me prioritize them. Some of
the forms were complete, with all the boxes filled in.
Other forms had clearly been transcribed from a message, with barely any information provided at all, just
a short summary of the problem and the source of the
complaint or request. Most seemed trivial, but so had
the flower and the carved initials at first blush. Some
of the files already had notes jotted on them marking
them as not a priority or waiting for confirmation before further investigation. The handwriting was the
same as I'd seen on the assigned cases, which I was
guessing meant the notes were written by Nori. Some
of the forms were older than a month, a few considerably older, and while I spotted a couple with Falin's
penmanship, most were Nori's. Which I guessed meant
Falin hadn't gone through all these files himself.

Nori was hazing me.

I pressed my lips together to keep from calling her
on it, and kept scanning the pile of paperwork. After
all, even if it was some sort of dominance play, I was
learning something. A request from the Nekros City
Police Department caught my eye. It referenced a
file—which wasn't attached and I had no idea where to

find it—but the brief summary mentioned disturbances inside a home in Nekros City in which fae involvement was possible. Not suspected, just listed as possible. From what I could gather, the original owner had died, and after probate, the house was put up for rent. No renters would stay more than a few weeks, most claiming the house was haunted. I frowned. That sounded more like a job for Tongues for the Dead, my PI firm, than for the FIB. I was surprised the cops hadn't contacted me to look into the case. I'd been on retainer for the local PD for years, and while usually they called me in to raise shades, I had been asked to investigate a haunting or two. Of course, I wasn't on the best terms with the police department currently. Too many of my recent cases had landed me in the middle of their murder investigations, and as some of the bad guys had ended up dust, there were questions I couldn't answer.

At the bottom of the request for assistance page, Nori had jotted a note that it might be a boggart and the priority was low. I frowned at the note. I'd read through dozens of complaints and requests, and this was one of the few that came from the PD—shouldn't it have been prioritized, if just for law enforcement relations?

I held up the sheet. "Why is this low priority?"

Nori's lips twitched downward, but she walked over and took the paper from me, scanning it quickly before shaking her head. "Because if it is a fae, it is likely a boggart."

"And he or she is apparently damaging personal property and driving humans out of their home. Shouldn't that warrant a little more investigation?"

Nori rolled her eyes, as if terribly put upon that I was asking her to explain herself. "Brownies only transform into boggarts when they are really pissed. If it is a boggart, most likely the brownie is attached to the house and was upset when the owner died and strangers started showing up and moving stuff around. While not impossible to relocate a brownie, it's a pain in the ass and complicated. Brownies rarely remain in full-on boggart mode long, so waiting for it to calm down is more expedient than relocating it."

I knew a couple brownies, but they were attached to people, not places. I had heard stories of the tenacity and dedication the small fae tended to display, so while I didn't doubt that moving an angry one would be complicated, I also didn't think it would be a waste to check out the site. I put the request to the side, planning to have the mentioned file located and check out the house myself. At least I would be able to determine if it was an angry ghost or a pissed fae causing the trouble.

I continued through the stack of papers, reading quickly. A few I separated, intending to discuss further with Nori and have agents assigned to look into them. Others I left in the main pile, not sure what to make of them, or trusting Nori's triage notes denoting them as low priority. One report made me pause. It was short, the form scarcely completed, as if the fae who'd filed the request hadn't done so in person and someone in the agency had simply jotted down the most pertinent information. The summary was short, just a single sentence:

The nixies in the swamp south of Nekros have reported one of their ponds has fouled.

That and a date three weeks past was all the information listed. At the bottom, in the space reserved for internal use only, Nori had noted the complaint as a low priority.

I stared at the form, as if it would reveal more than the few words it held. Months ago, Falin and I'd had a nearly deadly run-in with a water hag named Jenny Greenteeth in the swamp below Nekros. She'd been part of a conspiracy to destabilize the winter court that had resulted in the deaths of many fae and quite a few humans, but she'd escaped, and was presumed to have fled winter's territory. We'd located her last time because she fouled the bodies of water where she made her home. Was she back? The report was already nearly a month old and didn't say exactly where the fouled water was—the swamp was a big place—but I put the form aside to follow up on as soon as possible.

I was slowly working my way through the first of the stacks when a knock sounded on my office door. The door wasn't actually closed, so the woman outside had knocked on the frame only in an attempt to be polite.

"This was delivered for you," she said in a dreamy voice that didn't match the girl-next-door glamour she wore.

The "this" she'd mentioned wasn't immediately obvious. Then she stepped aside, and a man walked in carrying an enormous bouquet of red roses.

The blood drained from my face at the sight of the flowers.

"Where would you like them?" he asked. He wore one of those stretchy athletic jackets cyclists favored, so I guessed he worked for a courier company, or maybe the flower company, not the FIB.

I nudged the small trash bin next to my desk toward him. "In there."

The guy looked down at the bin and then back up at me. "Excuse me?"

I opened my mouth, and then closed it and cleared my throat. Acting like I was afraid of a bouquet of flowers was not going to earn me points with my agents, and Nori and Tem were both watching me. So was the agent who had led in the delivery guy, and everyone looked bewildered by my actions.

I forced myself to smile, but judging by the way the guy shrank back a step, maybe it wasn't my best attempt. "Do you know who sent them?"

"I'm just the delivery guy," he said, dropping the flowers on the corner of my desk. "You might check the card."

Right. I glanced at the bouquet. There was a small

card attached to a plastic pole bound in with the flowers. The outside was simple ivory with silver embossing around the edges. I'd have to touch it to see if it said anything inside. I opened my senses, just a crack, searching both with my ability to sense magic and visibly looking with my psyche at the flowers and card, scouring them for any hidden spells.

Nothing.

I'd removed my gloves to flip through the piles of paperwork Nori had given me, but now I retrieved them, pulling them on before reaching for the card. I plucked it from its post and flipped it open. I was hoping I'd see Falin's neat cursive, that he'd sent me flowers because I'd been nervous and this had nothing to do with the roses the night before.

No such luck.

In tight, unfamiliar block print, the card read:

Lexi, congratulations on your big promotion.

No signature. No stamp or mention of the florist they'd been ordered from. Nothing overtly menacing, and yet a cold chill crawled down my spine. Who the hell was sending me flowers?

I dropped the unhelpful note and looked back up at the delivery guy. "You're a bike courier?" I asked, again noting his athletic wear and lack of uniform. "Did you pick these up at a flower shop or . . . ?"

The courier glanced down at his phone. "It was a private pickup. Guy met me at the park in the Quarter with the flowers. Listen, I have another job, if you're not going to tip me . . ." He started backing out of the room.

Shit. I hadn't even considered that he was waiting for a tip. Do you tip someone for delivering what might be a threat? Not that it was his fault. I reached for my purse and he paused when he saw me move, obviously anticipating some money.

"What did the guy look like?" I asked as I dug out my wallet. I had all of two dollars in cash. I poked around searching for more as I waited for him to answer.

The courier shrugged. "Tall. Dressed like he had money."

Which told me nothing. "Do you have his customer information?"

"Uh, I know you are kind of like a cop, but if you want that, you'll have to go through the company. I just pick up and deliver."

Right. I handed him the two dollars and he made a face like it wasn't enough. I didn't care. It wasn't like I'd wanted the flowers and he hadn't been super helpful. Besides, based on the way he assessed the guy he'd picked up the flowers from, I was guessing he was tipped on both ends.

"That's not a normal reaction to receiving flowers, boss," Tem said after the courier left the room, the female agent who'd shown him in escorting him out of the building again. Tem's tone was conversational, but there were questions under the surface.

I shrugged. I wasn't going to go into why the flowers bugged me. There was nothing overtly threatening about them. They really might be from some admirer who didn't know me by anything but the planeweaver the former queen had been trying to add to her court. Hell, it might not even be a romantic admirer, but a courtier simply trying to gain a foot up by entangling themselves with someone—me—they thought the new king had interest in tying tighter to his court.

I swiped the flowers into the bin beside my desk and then turned back to the files I'd been digging through. I had other things to focus on than a secret admirer.

Chapter 5

❦ ⟶ ⟶ ❦

So, how was the first day?" Tamara asked, reaching for the bowl of popcorn Rianna had just set on the TV table beside the couch. She couldn't quite reach and did this odd rolling, straining thing until Holly took pity on her and nudged the entire stand closer. "Thanks," she said, balancing the bowl on her enormously pregnant belly like it was a table. Then she looked over at me, waiting for my answer.

"Uh . . . it was . . . really long."

"That's seriously not all the information you're getting away with giving us," Holly said, staring rather longingly at Tamara's popcorn. "Dish. We want all the details."

I shrugged. "Truly, it was boring. I spent most of the day doing paperwork," I said as I queued up an episode of *Curse Breakers* on Tamara's big-screen TV. The opening credits began rolling, but I knew I wouldn't get out of the questions that easy.

"And how did it go stepping up as a superior to the fae that once arrested you?" Rianna asked, settling down on the couch with her own bowl of popcorn.

Holly watched Rianna toss a kernel of popcorn,

gleaming yellow with a heavy covering of butter, into her mouth and shook her head. "How can you eat that?"

Rianna examined another smothered piece and then shrugged, tossing it in her mouth. "I like the motions. It brings back memories."

And only memories, I guessed. Holly hadn't questioned Rianna because of the health ramifications of the heavily buttered popcorn, but because Rianna was a changeling and as such, couldn't gain any nutrition from mortal food. It turned to ash on her tongue, which sounded rather disgusting, but Rianna just picked up another piece, tossing it high and tilting her head back to catch it in midair.

"I've always enjoyed popcorn and movies," she said.

Holly wrinkled her nose. She wasn't a changeling, but she was addicted to Faerie food so mortal food turned to ash for her as well. Unlike Rianna, she didn't enjoy going through the motions, so she had no popcorn in front of her. On the floor beside Rianna, Desmond, who in appearance looked to be a huge black dog with red eyes, huffed. He clearly disapproved of Rianna's actions, but I guessed the popcorn wouldn't actually hurt her, or he probably would have insisted she stop.

The huge barghest turned and placed his front paws on the couch, about to jump onto the seat.

"No. No. No dogs on the furniture," Tamara said, snapping her fingers at Desmond.

Desmond huffed again, his large jowls blowing outward, and he stared at Tamara.

"You know the rules. You're lucky I let you come inside," she said.

His lips curled, ever so slightly, not yet showing teeth, but looking like he wanted to. Then he looked at Rianna. She gave him an apologetic smile and reached up to scratch behind one of his large ears. "Her house, her rules."

He kept staring at her, front feet still planted on the couch beside her, then he twisted and looked at where

I was sitting cross-legged on the La-Z-Boy with PC curled in my lap. Yeah, my dog was sort of on the furniture. Oops.

Tamara seemed to follow the barghest's gaze as well because she said, "PC is all of six pounds and hairless. Also, he's on Alex, not the actual furniture. Plus, *oh-em-gee* that sweater is too cute on him."

I laughed, running a hand down PC's head. He did have *some* hair. Mostly just a white tuft on his tail, feet, and the crest of his head, but yeah, as was typical for Chinese Crested dogs, he was mostly hairless. Which was why he was wearing a little blue knit sweater, since going without a coat in January was a bad idea. And Tam was right, it was adorable.

Desmond's head swung back around, and he seemed to consider Rianna's lap for a moment.

"Oh, no, you don't," she said, shaking her head vigorously enough to make her red curls fly. "You weigh more than me."

The barghest huffed again.

"You didn't have to come with me. It's girls' night."

Another disgruntled huff.

"Oh, fine." Rianna slid off the couch and settled on the floor. The barghest plopped down beside her, rested his front legs in her lap, and then gave a pointed look at her bowl of popcorn. "Girls' night," she said again, putting emphasis on the words, but she tossed him a kernel of popcorn.

His head jerked, his jaws snapping, but he missed. He looked at where it had fallen on the floor. Then he looked up at Rianna again, expectant.

"You *are* going to pick that up, right?" Tamara said.

Rianna tossed him another piece, which he caught this time, before she said, "I'll get it, don't worry."

Tamara shook her head. "What kind of dog refuses to eat food that touches the ground?"

I stifled a grin. I knew the answer to that question. The type that isn't really a dog. Desmond was fae. Not just a fae-dog, but a fae with both a dog and a human-oid form. I had no idea why he remained in the dog form at all times. I'd seen him in his human form only twice, once at a revelry and another time in the realm of dreams and nightmares. I assumed Rianna knew he had another form, as they'd looked pretty close when I saw them at the revelry, but when I'd tried to talk to her about it, Desmond had very nearly bitten my head off. Literally, like with his giant barghest teeth. She seemed content with his constant dog-shaped companionship, so I hadn't pressed the issue.

"You never answered my question about the fly," Rianna said from her spot on the floor.

That was because I'd thought I'd avoided it.

"Fly?" Holly asked, frowning.

"Nori," I said. "She shares features with a dragonfly if you see her without her glamour. And she hates me. I can do no right in her opinion. I can't even dress right for the job."

Holly and Tamara exchanged a long look before Holly turned back and asked, "Is that what you wore to the office today?"

I glanced down at my outfit. I'd left the blazer at the castle after dinner, but everything else, yeah. They must have seen the answer on my face.

"Oh, Al," Tam said, shaking her head. "Don't look like that. It's not like there is anything *wrong* with the outfit. It was great when you were your own boss as a PI. But you're, what, director of the FIB?"

"Agent in charge." But considering that the only higher authority in my line of command was a king, I got her point. I sighed. "Fine. I'll go buy some stuffed-shirt suits this weekend."

"Hey, they aren't that bad; I wear power suits daily," Holly said, but then she sat up straight and pretended a tie she wasn't wearing was choking her. The effect was rather lost in that she'd changed into an oversize sweatshirt after work, but it still made everyone laugh.

"Are we going to actually watch *Curse Breakers*, because I have no idea what is happening in this episode," I said.

"Oh yeah, we are doing this. Back it up, I'm lost too," Tamara said, and then placed a hand on her belly, her brow furrowing. "And you settle down in there. You're kicking my popcorn bowl."

"What's the latest word?" I asked as Holly jumped up to grab the remote.

Tamara rubbed her hand over her belly again, and her baby bump moved in response. "He's more than caught up at this point. They now think we might have our dates wrong by as many as five weeks."

"Five? Is that possible?" Holly sank back onto the couch, the remote in hand, but she only paused the show. "You said you thought you were in Faerie about a week."

Tamara shrugged. "At this point, he might be coming real soon."

That earned silence all around the room. Last fall, Tamara had been attacked by a ghoul. To stop her from transforming into a ghoul herself, I'd sent her to Faerie while we dealt with the source of the issue on this side of the door. It had worked, and in mortal reality, only a day or two passed before we were able to safely bring her back. But in Faerie? Time could be funny in Faerie to start with, but the fact that we sent her to limbo where there was apparently no day or night and time was more or less impossible to track . . . Yeah, we really had no idea how long she'd spent there.

"The latest scan shows that he looks perfectly healthy, though. They don't know why my fluid is so low, and we are working on my iron still, but now they are saying he might get too big. Isn't that a change?" Her tone was light, purposefully jovial, but her hand kept running over her baby bump, as if reassuring herself he was still okay in there.

We all smiled, making light comments, discussing when we should move the baby shower up to, if the baby was likely to arrive a month or more earlier than expected. The mood was heavier, though.

"Hey, Al, man, it took me a while to find you," a new voice said as the owner of said voice walked through the front door. Literally through it. In his defense, the door didn't exist on his plane, so he probably barely considered how disturbing it was when people walked through seemingly solid objects.

Not that anyone else could see the ghost who'd just walked into the room.

"Girls' night," I said, frowning at Roy as he shuffled over to my side.

"I know, that's why I'm here." He pushed his translucent glasses higher up his nose. "Can you make me visible? I really need some girl opinions."

"Girls' night means it is for girls."

"Who just joined us?" Rianna asked, looking over at me, but she sounded more curious than alarmed. In fact, everyone in the room took it as a given that I was talking *to* someone even though they couldn't see him. And not that I'd just gone crazy and was talking to myself.

This was why I loved my friends.

"Roy just walked in."

"Tell him hi," Holly said cheerily, as she backed out of the *Curse Breakers* episode so she could start it back from the beginning.

Rianna gave her a funny look. "He can hear you. We just can't hear him."

Well, technically Rianna could have seen and heard him if she'd expended some magic, but she and Roy had a bit of a rocky relationship, so she tended to intentionally ignore him.

"Which one is Roy again?" Tamara asked. She had the least experience with the ghosts and other unusual characters my life tended to get entangled with. Rianna and Holly were my roommates—well, castlemates—so they tended to get a whole lot more exposure.

"Geeky-looking ghost," Rianna said, her tone flippant. "Glasses. Flannel. Slumps all the time."

"No I don't!" Roy sounded downright offended as he rolled back his shoulders.

"You kind of do," I told him. "Now, like I said, this is girls' night. We're going to veg out in front of a couple episodes of *Curse Breakers* and make fun of the bad spellwork they use."

"But, Al, I really need a female perspective here. Come on, just make me visible for a couple minutes."

I frowned at him. Roy hadn't asked me to make him visible in quite a while. In fact, in the last few months, he'd been pretty preoccupied by the fae ghost who had started haunting my castle. Something clicked with that thought.

"You want dating advice, don't you?"

Roy hunched forward a little, as if trying to curl in on himself to hide his embarrassment, but he nodded. "Yeah. I mean, I just want to bounce some ideas off your friends. I don't have a lot of people I could ask, and, well, the two grave witches I have access to . . . Well, neither of you have very normal relationships."

My gaze cut to Rianna, where Desmond lay with his big doglike head in her lap. Yeah, that probably didn't count as normal. And me? Well, between my commitment issues and the fact that I had feelings for two different guys, neither of whom it was practical or particularly safe to date . . . Yeah, I likely wasn't a good source either, even if Falin and I were giving a relationship a go.

"Roy wants some advice on his relationship with Icelynne," I said, looking around the room. "Any objections?"

None came, so I sent a tendril of power in Roy's direction. A few months ago, I would have had to have physical contact to make a ghost manifest on the physical plane. Now I had a radius of nearly a dozen feet.

Roy looked around, his gaze widening. I wasn't sure how different things looked for him when I bridged reality for him, but it was obviously something noticeable. Everyone else in the room noticed too, as the ghost was now visible to them.

"So what's the problem?" Holly asked, smiling helpfully at the ghost.

Roy started off on a long spiel. In his stumbling, overexcited narration, it was clear that the root of his issue was that he wanted to do something special for Icelynne because their three-months-dating anniversary was coming up—*uh, do people really celebrate that?*—but he had no idea what to do because, well, they were both dead. It kind of limited their options.

Holly and Tamara tried to make useful suggestions, but the ghost dismissed most of them out of hand, his shoulders slumping further as he grew discouraged.

"It's so hard," he said. "I can't just bring a bouquet of flowers like someone delivered you."

"Me?" Tamara laughed. "I don't remember the last time I received flowers. Though in truth, I prefer live ones I can plant to dead ones that rot in a few days."

"Then are the flowers on the porch not yours?" he asked, nodding toward the front door he'd floated through a few minutes earlier.

A cold chill shot through me. "There are flowers on the porch?"

"Yeah, I saw them when I came in."

I jumped to my feet, the motion dislodging PC from my lap. He gave a disgruntled bark as he hopped to the floor.

"Al, what's wrong?" Holly asked, climbing to her feet. Rianna was rising as well. I was already dashing toward the front door.

As Roy had said, there were flowers on the stoop. Bloodred roses.

I stared at the bouquet. How . . . ? This was getting too creepy. If this was an admirer, they were a stalker. And if it was Ryese?

But why would he be sending me flowers?

"Whoa. Those are gorgeous," Holly said from where she'd come up behind me. "Tam, do you think Ethan—?"

"They're not from Ethan." My voice sounded hard, distant, and Holly, who had leaned down to gather up the flowers, paused, shooting me a startled glance. Then she snatched the card sticking out of the top.

"You're right," she said, giving a low whistle. "It says, 'My dearest Lexi, we need to talk.' Alex, I guess that means they're yours. Lexi? Is that what Falin calls you?"

"No."

I bent to grab the offending bouquet. I hadn't told my friends about the weird flowers. I hadn't wanted to get them caught up in anything—the last few months most of my friends had been dragged through enough because of me. And yet, here were the flowers, on the doorstep of my friend's house. I wanted to hurl the bouquet into the street, but Tamara's compost bin would be sufficient.

None of the other flowers had hidden traps. I was so flustered I didn't even think to look for one in this bouquet. Which, of course, meant it contained a spell.

As soon as I touched the stems of the flowers, fae magic tickled across my mind, followed half a heartbeat later by a surge that crawled over my skin. A tendril of silver magic shot out of the bouquet, attaching itself to my arm. The chain of magic was so cold it burned as it coiled around my wrist and then began to sink into my flesh.

"Fuck!"

I dropped the flowers, jumping backward. The chain already had me. It dug into the skin of my wrist, sinking straight through my sweater as if it wasn't there.

But that wasn't the real threat. I could already feel the chain attacking my mind. My will. I'd seen a spell like this before.

This was a soul chain.

I dug my dagger from my boot—this might be girls' night, but I never went anywhere unarmed anymore. My fingers felt too thick as they closed around the hilt. I needed to cut the chain, but already that need was starting to fade. It wasn't really that bad, having the chain. Kind of comfortable. Like a warm bath.

The blade urged my hand up, and I frowned at it. Why was I holding a dagger?

Oh, yes, the chain. That soft, cold, shiny chain. It was kind of pretty.

The dagger sliced through the magic, severing it. Reality crashed back into me, piercing the fog in my mind like an ice pick to my skull. My friends were yelling. Rianna's eyes were glowing, an enchanted spear having appeared in her hand. Holly had summoned magic, though she hadn't directed it yet. Even Tamara had hauled herself to her feet.

"Light up the roses," I gritted out between clenched teeth.

Holly didn't hesitate. She was one of the best damn fire witches I'd ever seen, and the roses burst into flames as she released her magic. The fae magic I'd felt in the bouquet sputtered and then sizzled, burning away with the flowers.

Within moments, nothing was left of the bouquet but a sooty pile of ash on the front stoop.

"What just happened?" Tamara asked, breathing heavy as she joined us at the door.

Someone had just made a damn good attempt at binding my soul. I stared at what had been the flowers. The last time someone bound me with a soul chain, they'd commanded me to merge reality, and I'd hemorrhaged so much magic, I'd unintentionally torn reality apart and rewoven it in a mad conglomeration that

created its own pocket of Faerie spliced with the land
of the dead, the Aetheric, and dozens of other realities
I couldn't name. I hadn't even known I was a planeweaver then. I'd grown into my powers a lot since then.
What would happen if that were to happen again? I
shuddered.

"Was that a soul chain?" Rianna asked, stepping
forward and staring at my wrist where I'd been snared.

I nodded, glancing at the spear she still carried—a
spear she hadn't been carrying earlier. I recognized it.
It was an artifact that allowed the user to reach other
planes. I hadn't realized she still had it, let alone that
she'd been carrying it around. It was supposed to be
locked away, as it was dangerous as hell. Of course,
considering I touched other planes naturally, maybe
that was a hypocritical thing to think.

"Who . . . ?"

"Ryese." It had to be. Which meant I needed to talk
to Falin. Now. "I think we'll have to cut girls' night
short."

Chapter 6

❧⟶⟺⟵❧

I had Holly take me to the Eternal Bloom after we left Tamara's. Unfortunately, after some wandering around and being passed between guards, I was finally informed that Falin was not presently in the winter court. I was hoping that meant he'd received my message and was waiting for me back home, but when we reached my castle tucked away in the small pocket of Faerie attached to Caleb's house, he wasn't there either.

I waited up most of the night, but he didn't show.

"What took so long?" Nori asked as I pulled open the door of my loft the next morning. I was sweaty and out of breath from running from the castle to this room, hoping to beat Nori to what was supposed to be my front door. Clearly, I hadn't been successful.

"Didn't have time to shop, I see," she said as I locked the door, the sneer in her voice obvious.

I chose to simply ignore the comment. Yeah, I was wearing the same blazer as the day before, paired with a different sweater and my second-best pair of pants as I'd worn my best for my first day. It was what I had and I rather liked the outfit, but after talking to Tamara and Holly I had decided I'd get some more professional clothes. I wasn't going to admit that to Nori, though.

"So what is on the agenda today?" I asked as we made our way to her car. I nodded to Tem, who had waited in the backseat today, thankfully not deciding to put me through any more tests.

"You still have the rest of the paperwork to go through this morning. And the king has recommended you start firearms training this afternoon."

I didn't groan. It was a near thing, but hey, I was an adult, right? Of course, when we reached the office and I saw that the mountain of papers appeared to have grown, a tiny disgruntled sigh might have hissed out. Wasn't my fault. It was the fact that I could barely even see the desk under the papers.

My gaze landed on the small stack of files I'd set to the side the previous day. I scooped them up, flipping through them. "I think we should take a closer look at these," I said, pulling the one from the floodplains and moving it to the top. Walking around a swamp in January didn't sound like a ton of fun, but cold and mud were still better than spending the day wanting to claw out my eyes while reading through paperwork.

Nori glanced at the file. "That is not a priority."

"I know Falin had people searching for traces of the bogeyman Jenny Greenteeth. This"—I held up the first file—"is a potential lead on that case as she tends to foul any body of water she inhabits for long."

Nori's lips pursed, pulling slightly to the side as she considered that. "It's a thin lead at best, but perhaps it was an oversight not to look into the report more closely," she admitted.

I very nearly fist-pumped, but resisted. "Then let's go," I said, hiking the strap of my purse up higher on my shoulder.

"Like I said, it is only a thin lead. Probably nothing." She crossed her arms over her chest and gave the file a disgusted look before meeting my eyes. "We should assign some agents to look into it. Something this flimsy in a case that is months cold is not the top priority for an agent in charge."

Well, crap.

I considered pulling rank and insisting, but she was probably right. Devoting the travel time, not to mention the hours or days it would take to search based on the vague description in the report, was probably not the most responsible use of my time. Though digging through paperwork didn't seem that great either.

I sighed, but took her recommendations of which agents should be assigned to which cases. Once they were briefed and on their way, I had no other way to avoid the mountain of paperwork. Nori watched me settle in, then she went off to her own office to do whatever it was she was doing. Tem stood in the corner of my office, leaning against the wall and staring down at his phone. I wasn't sure what exactly he expected to guard me from inside my own office, but apparently he was sticking by my side. I really had to talk to Falin about this whole bodyguard thing.

I worked through all the local files and then moved on to the reports from the agents stationed outside Nekros. After an hour or two, I stood and stretched, working the kinks out of my back. Tem looked up from his phone, his hand still hovering from where he'd been punching at the screen. I wondered how well that worked for him. He was glamoured currently, and his phone was larger than most, but his hands were still huge and goodness knew I fat-fingered a lot of texts.

As if summoned by the fact that I'd moved, Nori stepped into the room. She gave a look at the piles of files still on my desk, as if disturbed that I hadn't made my way through all of them yet. Screw that noise.

"We really need to work on digitizing some of this," I said, thumbing open the file in front of me.

She cocked her head to the side. "Most of the files are scanned and in the database."

My head shot up. "You mean I could have been doing this on my laptop?" And she'd just chosen to bury
me in physical files instead.

"I prefer paper." She shrugged.

I stared at her. I should have realized there were
digital files somewhere—Falin used a laptop all the
time. But fae tended to resist technology, so I hadn't
even questioned it.

I was about to tell her to haul all this paper back out,
when a knock sounded on the doorframe of my office,
making us all turn.

"Someone apparently didn't think you liked your
first flowers enough," Nori said, as one of the agents led
in a woman in a simple uniform. "Looks like you received two bouquets this time."

The deliverywoman smiled, stepping forward with
the two very large bouquets of bloodred roses. I scrambled backward, putting the desk between us.

"No. I refuse them. Take them back."

The deliverywoman frowned at me. "Uh, I'm not the
postal service, you can't just refuse shipment. These
were paid for. I'm just dropping them off." She set the
two enormous bouquets on my desk, nearly knocking
over one of the piles of paperwork in the process.

I took another step back. I didn't even care that my
agents were staring at me. After the soul chain hidden
in the flowers at Tamara's, I wasn't getting near these
flowers.

"That's fine," Nori said to the deliverywoman.
"Tem, see her out."

She turned to me, frowning. "What is going on,
Craft?"

I didn't answer but stared at the flowers for a moment, opening my shields as I searched for anything
malicious. Nothing jumped out at me, no trace of spells
or any magic that I could see, though sometimes I
missed fae spells. I'd only recently become sensitive to
the magic and it was often easy for me to overlook.

Nori made an agitated sound and said, "Who is sending you flowers, Craft? And why are you so freaked out about them?"

I opened my mouth, not sure what I would answer, but I had to say something. Then the floor seemed to roll under me. The ground leapt, knocking me from my feet.

I yelped as I dropped to my knees, but it wasn't just me. The building shook, jolted, and rumbled. My coffee mug lurched from my desk, shattering beside me. Files and papers careened over the desk's edge, scattering. The roses skittered over the edge, hitting the floor. Nori screamed and vaulted into the air, her glamour evaporating as she freed her wings.

I curled into a ball, my hands covering my head. Yells came from elsewhere in the building, the sounds of crashing and banging filling the air as furniture toppled. If the ceiling gave way . . .

As fast as the tremor began, it ended. The world stilled. There was one last crash as something fell, and then there was silence broken only by the annoyed rhythmic beeping of some disturbed electronic device.

I remained tucked tight, waiting for the world to jump again. It didn't. I opened my eyes. I was surrounded by papers and roses. A silver-embossed card lay a few inches before my nose, splayed open so that the increasingly familiar script was visible.

My dearest Lexi, are you having an exciting first week?

I swallowed hard, pushing up to my elbows. What had happened? Had something in the roses caused that? It had felt like an earthquake. I hadn't sensed any spells. What the hell could cause an earthquake? Nekros wasn't exactly on a fault line. The only other earthquake I'd ever experienced had been in Faerie just a few weeks back, when the Winter Queen had fallen . . .

I uncurled from my protective ball and shot to my

feet. My breathing was fast, my heart pounding in my ears nearly loud enough to drown out the incessant electronic beeping from somewhere in the building. My gaze shot around the room, searching for my purse. Had it been on the desk before the quake? The room was in shambles. The chairs were toppled; drawers hung open; the contents of my desk were strewn across the floor. But the walls and ceiling were intact, so while the floor jolting had felt intense, it couldn't have been that bad, right? Surely not as violent as when Faerie had reshaped itself after the queen's fall.

Of course, this building had survived that as well.

I spotted my purse peeking out from behind the far side of the desk and all but dove for it. I dug my phone out of the bag, not caring that I knocked even more of the contents onto the already cluttered floor. Across the room, the door burst open, clattering against the wall and making me jump. Tem burst into the room, his eyes sweeping over me as if assessing me for damage.

"Are you hurt?"

I shook my head. "I'm fine," I said, barely glancing at him as I pulled up Falin's number and hit dial. The phone rang. And rang.

The troll moved faster than I would have thought possible considering his size. Before the next ring, he was kneeling at my side, his pink eyes searching me as if I might be hiding some injury. His concern didn't seem personal, but it was insistent.

I forced a tight-lipped smile as the phone in my hand continued to ring. "Like I said, I'm fine. Besides, I don't think a bodyguard could shield me from an earthquake." My gaze shot to Nori's still-hovering form. "That was an earthquake, wasn't it?"

"It appeared to be." Her feet touched the ground and her form shimmered as her glamour cloaked her again, dulling her blue skin to a pale flesh tone and making her features more human and less other. "Has anyone contacted the Bloom yet?" Nori called out the open doorway to whoever might be listening beyond. Without waiting for a response, she pulled her phone from her pocket and began dialing.

My phone clicked, Falin's voice mail answering. Not that surprising—Faerie had no phone reception and he'd barely left since becoming king. The electronic voice instructing me to leave a message did nothing to reassure me. I didn't leave a message.

"No one is answering at the Bloom," Nori said, glaring at her phone as if the electronic device was at fault.

"Do you suppose—" Tem began before startling, as if pricked by an invisible knife.

The look Nori shot him certainly contained daggers, and I wondered if she'd done something to him that I hadn't seen. Her head jerked ever so slightly in my direction, not to look at me, but as if she was trying to slyly indicate me.

"Do you suppose what?" I asked as I straightened from where I'd been crouched over my phone. I could guess how the sentence might have ended. Did she suppose Falin had fallen in a duel? Did she suppose Faerie was reshaping again? Dread clawed at my throat, slicing painful gashes as it slid to land heavy and hard in my stomach. That couldn't be it. Maybe I was on the wrong track. Maybe Tem had been going to ask if she supposed the doors were moving? Of if she supposed it was a natural occurrence?

Two pairs of eyes turned to look at me. Nori's were assessing and guarded. Tem's were wide and sympathetic. His were the more painful to see, because the kind pity in his eyes meant he suspected the worst.

What had all the notes attached to the flowers said? The first had congratulated me on my promotion. The second said we needed to talk—right before soul chains tried to remove my free will. And this one asked if I was having an exciting first week. Well, I certainly was now, but not in any good ways. None of the notes were overtly threatening toward me. Or toward Falin. And yet Nekros had just shook.

I hit redial on my phone, even though I knew it wouldn't make a difference, and grabbed my purse, shoving the spilled contents back in haphazardly before slinging it over my shoulder. Was I the lead investigator here or wasn't I? Well, I was going to go investigate, damn it. "I'm headed to Faerie."

I'd made it halfway across the room when I remembered I hadn't driven today, and while the FIB headquarters and the door to Faerie hidden inside the VIP room of the Eternal Bloom were both in the Magic Quarter, they were dozens of blocks apart and I'd waste a lot of time walking. I turned to Nori, intending to ask for—demand—a ride, but before I opened my mouth, a fae rushed through the open door.

Her head swung between Nori and me before her focus settled on the more familiar authority figure, ignoring me. "The human authorities just contacted us," she said, her voice taut with panic. "There has been an explosion at the Eternal Bloom."

Chapter 7

Despite our quick response, the blockades around the Eternal Bloom were already in place. I hadn't expected to roll right up to the crime scene, but I was surprised to discover they had set up a three-block perimeter around the Bloom and were actively evacuating a thousand-yard circumference around the building. Our FIB badges would get us beyond the barricades, but not our car, as the streets closest to the explosion had to remain clear for essential fire and medical vehicles.

Nori parked our car more or less on the sidewalk just beyond the barricades, nearly scraping a news van that had beaten us to the scene and was already illegally parked on the curb. I slid out of the car before it had even jolted to a full stop, all but running toward the barricades.

Nori caught up to me a moment later, her hand catching my shoulder and pulling me to a stop.

"Don't run," she said, her eyes hard. "You cannot show panic or uncertainty. You are in charge, and since this explosion happened in a fae establishment, you have the most authority on the scene, but that doesn't

mean the other law enforcement agencies will just
hand it to you, so you must demand their respect from
the moment we arrive."

"Right," I said, squaring my shoulders. It was good
advice, and something to remember, as I still felt like a
PI sneaking onto a crime scene and not like a special
agent in charge of the entire winter branch of the FIB.
I brushed my palms down the front of my pants, taking
a deep breath and checking the pocket holding my
badge folder.

I set a brisk—but not frantic—pace to the barricades. Already a crowd was forming outside the barricades. Some no doubt those who'd been evacuated
from the surrounding buildings or who had been in the
area, but a shocking amount of press were already
present, more arriving right behind us.

The officer manning the barricade gave us more
than one skeptical look as he recorded our entry into
the scene. Actually, maybe it was just me he studied a
little too closely. Of course, in his dark suit, Tem looked
like a secret agent from a movie and Nori certainly
looked slick and professional. In my leather pants and
boots, and with my blond curls no doubt an unruly
mess, I looked like a tagalong—not like the person in
charge. Maybe Nori's dig on my wardrobe had been
warranted. It was also possible the officer recognized
my name—likely as someone with a history of ques-
tionably accessing crime scenes—but I had a badge, so
after jotting down our pertinent information he let us
through. Still, the whole thing took far too long, and I
was doing my best not to break into a run again when
he finally handed back my badge and stepped aside.

We hurried through an area that had been set up as
a medical triage. People stood or sat wrapped in blan-
kets, soot and dust covering their hair and faces. I saw
more than one person with clean streaks cutting
through the grime where tears had washed paths down
their cheeks. Paramedics and uniformed officers hur-

ried between these small huddled groups, but these were the survivors who hadn't been hurt bad enough to need immediate emergency attention. Not everyone had been so lucky. We'd passed several ambulances with their sirens blaring on our way to the scene, and even though I couldn't see the Bloom yet, I could already feel the distant tug of the grave. That chilled brush of death that feathered over my skin in a way that only human—or humanoid—bodies could. I was too far away to feel anything specific, at least without opening my shields, but I already knew that we would discover casualties.

What had happened? I didn't know. We were still too far away to see the Bloom yet, but the brush of the grave had me chewing at my bottom lip, faces flashing through my mind of the fae I regularly saw when I passed through the Bloom. It was the middle of the day, probably not one of the busiest times, but there were definitely bodies up ahead.

My steps felt heavy and yet I kept pushing my feet to move faster without actually breaking into a run again. We passed a few more clusters of people. They didn't have the dirty and shell-shocked expressions of the survivors in triage, so I was guessing these were individuals the cops had detained as witnesses. They were being questioned not too far beyond the barricades, still quite a distance from the Bloom. Then we passed that flurry of activity and entered a type of dead zone where there was no activity. The street and buildings were cleared, the noise and bustle of the paramedics and cops left behind us, but we hadn't yet reached the chaos of sirens and fire trucks a couple blocks ahead of us.

With each step, the chill of the grave grew stronger. I couldn't see anything beyond the emergency vehicles, but I felt the death staining the air. Human. Fae too. And more than just a few. Whatever had happened, a lot of people had died. I shivered, fighting the urge to wrap my arms around myself.

·

I wove between fire trucks and around a bomb squad van and then I stopped. My jaw dropped as I caught my first sight of the Eternal Bloom.

Or at least, what had been the Bloom.

The entire facade of the building had collapsed. The roof was more or less gone. Some interior walls still stood, at least partially, but much of the building was little more than rubble. Glass and debris covered the sidewalk as well as half the street in front of the building. One car that must have been parked on the street was on its side. Two others had clearly been on fire but were already extinguished. The buildings on either side of the Bloom were blackened on their closest sides, the walls cracked, windows busted from the blast.

A charred pillar rose from somewhere in the center of the Bloom. Fire licked up its dark surface, defying the jets of water firefighters on trucks were angling into the ruined building. The enormous pillar towered over the surrounding buildings, standing at least three stories tall. The Bloom had been a single-story building.

No, it wasn't a pillar, I realized. There were smoldering protrusions jutting from it at random locations. It had been a tree.

The amaranthine tree.

"Oh, that can't be good," I whispered, coming to a complete stop.

The amaranthine tree typically was covered in hundreds of blooming flowers, regardless of season. It also typically wasn't in human reality, but in the pocket of Faerie that existed between here and the winter court, the tree acting as the doorway. If that was the tree . . .

Beside me, Nori stood in similar shock, her eyes wide as she absorbed the destruction. Tem didn't waste time staring, but took off at a run as soon as he saw the building. Firefighters and a man in a uniform with BOMB SQUAD emblazoned on the back attempted to block him as he lunged toward the building, but he shoved them aside without breaking stride, his troll strength enough to throw all three grown men back several yards.

"You can't go in there!"

"That structure isn't stable!"

"Who the hell is that? Where is his superior?"

Shit. That superior would be me.

I glanced at Nori, hoping for some help. She was still staring at the building. A high-pitched keening sound trilled through the air, emanating from her unseen wings. Her eyes bled to black, becoming larger and multifaceted as her glamour slipped.

Great. Tem had dashed headlong into a burning building and Nori was losing her shit. Which meant for the moment I was on my own. I let my shocked gaze sweep over the scene, trying to absorb it all. To wrap my head around what had happened.

Aside from a small team of firefighters manning the hoses aimed at the roof and amaranthine tree, everyone was keeping their distance from the Eternal Bloom. No vehicles were closer than three hundred feet, and for the most part, no people either. Just Tem, who'd disappeared into the gloom of the destroyed structure already. The men who'd tried to stop him from getting close to the building hadn't followed once he'd breached that three-hundred-foot perimeter.

I caught movement in the rubble. Tem? Rescuers searching for survivors? I peered harder, trying to force my bad eyes to sift through the shadows of the building.

A figure stepped out from behind a ruined wall and stopped, looking up as if he felt me looking. He wore no safety gear, only a dark T-shirt and worn jeans against the frigid January air. I was too far away to make out his eyes, but I knew they were hazel—I'd seen them hundreds of times before, sometimes quite intimately.

Death.

Grim Reaper, angel of death, soul collector—
whatever you wanted to call him, I shouldn't have been
surprised to see him in a place where so many had
died. But his presence caught me off guard. I'd barely
seen him in the two months since we'd both conceded
that a relationship wasn't going to work. I still stood by
that decision, but damn, I missed my friend.

He lifted a hand, a small wave. Then he turned, vanishing from sight. I didn't bother calling out or chasing
after him—I'd only find him if he wanted me to, and if
he wanted to talk, he'd find me.

Faces flashed in my mind again. I didn't know many
of the fae who frequented the Bloom by name, but
there were a lot of faces I saw nearly every trip I took
through it to the winter court. How many of those familiar faces had been inside when . . . whatever
happened . . . happened?

My gaze moved to the still-burning amaranthine
tree. How the hell was the tree even visible from outside the building? How badly damaged was the pocket
of Faerie? Was the door to winter still there? Would it
still work with this much damage to the tree?

And had the door been the target?

"Nori, do you think—" I started, turning toward her.

Her glamour had completely fallen, her large, multifaceted eyes riveted on the destruction in front of us.
As if her name had been a catalyst, she launched herself into the air. Before I could so much as call out to
her, she zipped forward, her wings taking her higher as
she shot toward the remains of the Eternal Bloom.
Shouts erupted as Nori soared over the crumbled remains of walls and dodged around the spray from fire
hoses, headed straight for the burning trunk of the amaranthine tree.

And now I'd lost both my agents.

I frowned, looking around again. I needed to locate
the command tent and find out what had been learned

about the explosion. My brain kept circling back to the note on the flowers delivered directly before the earthquake that coincided with the explosion. It had wished me an exciting first week. If the flowers were from Ryese, had he bombed the Bloom? Just to fuck with me? Not that there was any love lost between him and Falin, or hell, he might hate the entire winter court, as the former queen had thrust him out of it. So maybe the roses were to get in my head, but this was an attack on the court. And if it was an attack, was Nekros's door the only one targeted?

I dug out my phone and dialed the main number for the FIB office. The noise around me was deafening— sirens, emergency responders calling out to each other, the jetting water, and the roar of the flames as they consumed the door to Faerie.

I started talking as soon as an agent answered. "This is Special Agent Alex Craft. I need someone to contact the other FIB offices and find out if there were any other explosions at the other doors to winter."

"Yes, sir, er, ma'am," the agent said, the anxiety evident in his voice increasing.

I started to disengage, but then added, "If the other doors are intact, increase security around them." Another thought occurred to me. Standing in front of the destruction of the Bloom, I'd been working on the assumption that the damage had taken place on this side of the door. But what if this was spillover from the other side? "And someone get me a status update on what is happening inside the winter court and the well-being of the king. Update me immediately as soon as contact is established."

"Of course," he said, his voice more of a panicked squeak. I doubted I sounded any better. It was all I could do not to rush into the burning building myself, but I wasn't a troll with near-impenetrable skin and the ability to heal quickly, nor did I have wings to flit down through the roof. Even standing across the street, the heat licked at the exposed skin of my face from the still-burning tree.

Falin was okay. He had to be.

"The king needs to be apprised of the fact that the Nekros door might be damaged," I said, unwilling to accept the possibility that Falin might not be able to receive that message. "Now, start making those calls."

"Y-yes, sir," the fae said again, shock dulling his voice.

I disconnected and shoved my phone back in my purse, then I turned from the building. I needed answers, and I wasn't going to get any standing here gawking.

Officers, agents, paramedics, firefighters, first responders, men and women in suits, people in uniforms emblazoned with large letters proclaiming ABS, ABMU, NCPD, MCIB—the entire alphabet soup of public safety were gathering in clusters in the street a distance from the Bloom. Everyone seemed busy, and yet none were entering the building. Had they cleared it of survivors already? Even if I hadn't seen Death among the rubble, I knew there were still casualties inside. I could feel them, the grave essence lifting from them a constant pressure against my mental shields. I could have opened myself and known exactly how many dead were inside, but I couldn't help the dead. I needed to focus on the living. And to do that, I needed more information.

I spotted a hastily erected canopy on the far side of the perimeter and headed toward it. That had to be the command tent, which was where I was most likely to find answers. Also, as agent in charge, it was probably where I was supposed to be.

A few people glanced my way as I marched over to the command tent, but no one stopped me, all too involved with their own tasks. I'd just reached the edge of the tent when a loud booming crack sounded from the remains of the Bloom. I whirled around as a plume of dust and flame erupted from somewhere inside the unstable building, and the ground shook with the impact of part of the ceiling collapsing. My heart, already erratic in my chest with the panic I was barely controlling, seemed to stutter, and I held my breath, watching for movement inside the ruined building.

For a long moment, the only sounds on the street were the sirens, the fire hoses, and the crackling fire that refused to extinguish. No one on the street seemed to move, all of us waiting, watching to see if more of the structure would collapse. The dust plume settled quickly under the spray from the hoses. No one emerged from the building. Slowly people began to turn away and return to the tasks they'd been focused on before this newest collapse. No one attempted to go into the building. I kept watching, but seconds stretched. No sign of movement from inside. No sign of Tem or Nori . . .

Had they been caught in the collapse? Had they made it to the door and stepped through to the winter court? My feet itched to race forward, to go search through the rubble, but I fought against that instinct. *They* had rushed into the building. *I* needed to keep my head.

After another moment, I turned back to the command tent I'd nearly reached and crossed the distance to step into the shadow cast from the sunshade. Five people stood inside, locked in what sounded like an animated conversation, but they fell silent as I stepped into the tent opening, all eyes turning toward me.

"Can we help you?" asked a woman with blond hair slicked back into a high bun.

I held up my badge, flipping it open to show my ID once again. "Alex Craft, FIB. What can you tell me about the explosion?"

The woman lifted a sharply angled eyebrow so that it arched over the narrow, red-rimmed glasses perched on her nose. She gave me an appraising once-over, taking in my no-name blazer and big boots, which were a world apart from her expensive-looking pencil-skirt suit and three-inch heels. Okay, yeah, she looked more professional, but if we both had to run into that building, I'd not only reach it first in my more sensible footwear, but my leather pants would provide a lot more protection and my heels wouldn't get caught in piles of rubble, so she could take her judgment and shove it. Her gaze moved to the man beside her, exchanging a look that I ignored.

This man was at least more sensibly dressed than the woman, wearing what I guessed was a dark uniform under a heavy flak jacket with the initials ABS on the right breast area. *Arson Bomb Squad unit*. The man beside him must have been the fire chief, based on the heavy fire coat he wore. The only other woman in the group wore a dark uniform. Because of the position of the group, I couldn't see if she had any identifying letters on her uniform, but I could feel the assortments of charms on her person, so I guessed she was either Anti-Black Magic Unit or Magical Crimes Investigation Bureau. The last man wore a plain suit, but him I knew—the police commissioner of Nekros City.

After a tense moment, the judgy blonde stepped forward. "Hello, Ms. Craft. I'm Hilda Larine with the Office of the Ambassador of Fae and Human Relations." She held out her hand. "Will Agent Andrews be joining us?"

I reached out to accept her hand, and her gaze darted momentarily to my gloves. She loosely grasped just my fingers, and then retrieved her hand quickly, as if I might have some communicable disease she hoped to avoid.

Yeah, I didn't like her. This was the local representative for the ambassador of fae and human relations? That did not bode well. Still, I gritted out my smile.

"*Agent* Craft, actually. And no. Falin Andrews will not be joining us. He has . . . accepted a higher position." That was putting it mildly. "I have replaced him as special agent in charge."

Her red painted lips made a small O, and she once again gave me a disparaging appraisal. I ignored her, turning to look over the rest of the group.

"Do we know the source of the explosion yet? Where the bomb was located when it detonated?"

The man in the Arson Bomb Squad vest took the lead, stepping forward and holding out his hand. "Captain Oliver, ma'am." His handshake was firm and professional. He looked young to have risen all the way to the rank of captain, maybe midthirties, and had dark hair cut short and deep brown eyes that were both intense but approachable. "No. We don't know the source yet. And we aren't ruling out anything. This explosion could have been caused by a gas leak, an incendiary device, or magic. Reports suggest an earthquake hit the Quarter at about the same time, so it is possible that contributed. We won't know until we get inside and I can't send my guys in there while the fire is still burning. Once it's out, and the structural engineer has approved our entry, we'll begin processing."

I nodded, not really surprised by the news. Oliver flashed a smile, and while it was a nice smile, even friendly, it was a smile that expected something, so I wasn't surprised when he followed up with a question.

"Is there anything *you* can tell us about the explosion?"

I glanced out the open side of the tent to the devastated building. This didn't feel accidental. The damage was too catastrophic, but also contained to the Bloom with only a little spillover to the surrounding structures. So the real question was, if this was an attack, had it been planned by enemies on this side of the door or in Faerie?

"I just got to the scene, Captain," I said, committing

to nothing. His smile dimmed only slightly as he gave me an accepting nod. First impression? He was some-one I was going to be able to work with a whole lot easier than Hilda Larine. I turned toward the fire chief. "Were you able to evacuate all the survivors?"

The chief twisted his lips and didn't quite meet my eyes. "Civilians were rushing in and out of the building when first responders arrived. We secured the build-ing, made sure no more civilians could rush in. Once the fire is out, my men will start shoring up the building and do a thorough search."

I frowned. "So you didn't clear the building? Search for trapped survivors?"

The older man's face reddened, and his hand made an aggressive sweep to encompass the Bloom. "There is a bloody three-story tree that appeared out of no-where, a fire that won't go out, and when I briefly en-tered to do a cursory sweep, I found out the space beyond the first doorway is impossible and couldn't exist in the building. We got several people out of the bar area. But that magical, impossible space? I'm not sending my men in to die from magic they can't fight. Once we have a better understanding of the situation, they'll begin searching for survivors." He lifted a meaty finger and pointed it at me. "And until the build-ing gets a complete walk-through for structural integ-rity, a sweep for secondary explosives, and a magic evaluation, no one is authorized to enter. I'm the inci-dent commander on the scene as long as a fire is pres-ent, not you, so if those were your people who barreled in there right before you barged into this tent, you need to call them out of there."

Well, I definitely hadn't made a friend. I opened my mouth, unsure how to salvage this situation or what to say about my agents rushing into the building. Admit-ting I had no control of the situation didn't seem like a good idea. I was saved from having to figure out what to say by the chirping of my phone. I dug it out of my purse, noting the agency number on the display before holding up my hand to the people in front of me. "I have to take this."

I turned my back and took a step or two away, though I knew the small space afforded me no more privacy. "This is Alex," I said, and then mentally berated myself for using my first name and not my last.

The agent on the other end didn't seem to notice. "This is Agent Bleek. I've reached every winter territory except the one on Antarctica—they don't have phone reception, but an agent from the territory in South America will be traveling there through Faerie and getting back to us. No one reported any other explosions. I'm waiting to hear back from the agents relaying your information to the king."

"Good. Let me know as soon as you hear something. And, Agent Bleek, try to find out if any of the other doors on this continent were attacked."

There was a pause on the other end of the line. Finally he said, "But there are no other doors to winter on this continent."

I pressed a hand to my temple, staring out at the ruined remains of the Bloom. "I'm aware." I'd stared at that weird map long enough the previous day. "But let's eliminate possibilities. It sounds like no other doors to winter were targeted. But were any of the other courts? Was this an attack against the fae in Nekros? Or is it something bigger?"

The agent on the other side of the line was quiet a moment too long, like he didn't want to again disagree with the new boss but didn't know what to say. Something moved in the building, catching my eye, and I looked up, squinting in the late morning sun and blazing fire. A figure emerged from the ruined facade of the building, flying slowly over the crumbled rubble as if weighed down. Nori. It had to be her.

"Just make the calls, Agent," I said, already striding toward the building.

He mumbled his assurances, and I disconnected and pocketed my phone without ever looking away from Nori's approaching figure. She carried something large and limp in her arms. A body? No, there was no grave essence reaching for me. A survivor, and fae, based on the pale purple hair.

Nori landed a few feet from me, sagging to the ground as she lowered the fae she carried to the sidewalk. Paramedics rushed forward, but then hesitated as they noticed the inhuman features of the rescued victim. She was small, no bigger than a child, but her skin was as purple as her hair, except where it was stained with soot and blood.

"I'm sure oxygen and healing charms will be just as effective on her as anyone else," I snapped to the closest paramedic. He startled and then jumped into motion, sliding a mask over the fae's face and beginning to assess her injuries.

I moved closer to Nori, who was still on her knees beside the smaller fae, but she wasn't looking at her. Nori's inhuman expression was hard to read, but she seemed dazed, unfocused.

"Did you see Tem inside? Is he okay?" I asked.

Her head twisted toward me, but her eyes didn't focus. She nodded slowly. "He's right behind me." She turned, the movement stiff, and looked around. She seemed confused for a moment before mumbling, "The ledger . . . must have been destroyed."

Shit. That was going to make things tricky. The ledger kept the door to the VIP room mostly in sync with the time in mortal reality. Without it, well, Tem might have been right behind Nori, but he could emerge at any time.

Nori shook her head as if to clear it. "Tem has more survivors, but even he couldn't carry all of them. Agent Mabel is a healer. Has she reached the scene yet?" She fumbled her phone from a case on her waistband, but then stared at the blank screen.

"How many more people are trapped inside?" I asked. The fire chief had said he'd cleared the human side. The fae had been left behind—and the VIP section was where the fire was still raging, so they were in the greatest danger. I stared at the ruined building, again considering going in to look for survivors. I'd run into a burning building once before, but I'd known the fire was only glamour then, and I'd been able to See through it. This fire was very real.

As if to highlight the danger, something inside the building cracked, more of the roof caving in. I swallowed. Not moving. *Coward.*

"You said Tem couldn't carry out all the survivors. How many more are trapped inside? Can we get reinforcements from court?"

Nori looked up and blinked, the membrane of her eyelids sliding sideways. She stared at me as if she couldn't quite place me or process my words, and then she twisted to stare over her shoulder at the burning amaranthine tree.

"It's gone." That didn't answer the question I'd asked, and I frowned at her. Her voice was soft, distant, and it held a note of helplessness I would never have expected to hear from the strong-willed fae. "The door to Faerie. It is just . . . gone. We're stranded."

Chapter 8

※──◎　◎──※

Stranded.

A few months ago, I probably wouldn't have cared. Direct access to Faerie being severed might have even been a relief, as that would have meant the courts couldn't mess with my life as readily. Now the confirmation that the door was gone rocked me.

My tongue felt too thick and dry in my mouth to speak, so I nodded, staring at the still-raging fire. If this was an attack on the winter court, Falin was in danger. Damaging an amaranthine tree was forbidden in Faerie. If this had been done by another court, it was an act of war.

Ryese.

I almost asked Nori if there had been roses inside, but that seemed like a ridiculous question. Besides, she was too unfocused to answer my question about Tem; she was unlikely to have noticed if a bouquet of roses had been left behind. But someone calling me Lexi had been stalking me the last two days, taunting me, had even tried to catch me in a soul chain. I couldn't prove Ryese was behind the flowers or the explosion, but he and the Winter Queen were the only people who ever called me Lexi. Ryese had been the growing poisonous thorn in my side for months and my gut instinct was that he was behind this.

Still, I should probably examine other possibilities as well. If I became too focused on Ryese, I might miss something that was right under my nose. That could be a deadly mistake. Also, the ABS wasn't even committing to the explosion being caused by a bomb yet. This could be an accident or it could be a hate crime by an extremist in the Humans First Party. But most humans didn't know the Eternal Bloom was anything more than a tourist trap where humans could buy overpriced beer while gawking at fae on display. Humans couldn't see the outer door to the VIP section—the true heart of the Bloom and where the amaranthine tree grew—unless they knew it was there. A chameleon glamour hid the door from casual observers.

Fire continued to lick up the blackened bark of the tree. No other fires still burned. Would an explosion on the tourist side of the Bloom have done so much damage to a pocket of Faerie? By its nature, the VIP section was grounded in this realm, a type of transition area between here and Faerie. Or was the fire still consuming the tree proof that the attack had originated in the VIP section? We were going to have to get in there if I wanted to learn more. And if there were still survivors inside, they needed that fire out now.

I turned back to Nori. "When you were inside, could you see what is causing the fire to rage on? Is it a spell?"

She did that strange sideways blink again, not looking away from the Bloom as she spoke. "The water isn't reaching the tree. Part of the tree is manifesting in the human realm, but as you get closer to ground level, the bubble is still in place. I tried to fly in from the top but ended up outside the door. The water is pooling at the entrance."

Well, that would explain why nothing was working. The firefighters spraying water through what looked like the ruined roof wasn't going to cut it.

I turned to head back to the command tent and talk to the fire chief, but caught sight of four black-suited people running up the street. FIB agents that had approached the scene from the opposite cross street. Took them long enough. They must have gotten held up at the outer barricades.

I called Nori's name as I moved to intercept the agents. Tem still hadn't emerged from the building. I didn't need anyone else rushing in until we had a plan. I stepped in front of the four running agents, lifting both my hands in front of me. Their glamours were currently holding, though the panic on their faces was clear, but I knew at least one of these agents was a troll. If she ran straight into me, I was going to be hurting.

"Nori's already scouted inside. The door is gone." I shouted the words, not caring that the humans milling around the scene could hear. The words created the effect I wanted. All four agents ground to a halt.

Jaws fell slack. Glamour began to slip. One fae fell to his knees, staring at the burning tree. But they stopped, and for now that was enough. I gave them a moment to absorb the news.

Nori stepped up to my side. She still hadn't gotten her glamour back under control, but her eyes looked focused now, so that was a good start. "Agent Mabel, there are quite a few injured fae who will need your attention," Nori said, pulling the lapels of her jacket straight before brushing at a large smear of concrete dust on her sleeve.

One of the agents in front of me snapped to attention at Nori's words. Mabel, apparently. She looked over, nodding slightly. Her glamour had only just begun to slip, leaving her eyes looking like large pools in the center of her face. Not being metaphoric there. Literal pools of liquid shimmered where eyes should have been.

The energy and noise level around us changed as the human emergency workers responded to something behind me. I turned, peering into the darkened depths of the crumbling Bloom. It took me a moment, but I caught sight of an enormous form lumbering over collapsed walls and piles of rubble. *Tem.*

The troll had dropped his glamour, and he looked like an enormous yellow hulk appearing from the gloom. His suit was now more gray than black, at least what I could see of it. He was carrying multiple people, one slung over each shoulder, another in each arm. I hoped there were no neck injuries, because they were being violently jostled. Of course, that was probably preferable to burning to death, or dying of smoke inhalation, or being crushed by a collapsing building.

Yeah . . . I wasn't going to criticize Tem's methods.

Two smaller figures followed behind Tem, one holding on to his huge arm for support and nearly dragging the other. They looked like children compared to Tem, but as they cleared the last of the rubble, I realized they were both grown men, and human from the look of it.

Tem's gaze landed on our clustered group, and he picked up speed, heading straight for us. "Mabel, we're going to need your skills."

The water fae was already moving to intercept him, as were several EMTs pushing gurneys. Good, they weren't hesitating this time. I waited until the last person had been handed off before stepping closer to Tem.

"How many more are inside?"

"Alive? Not sure. The ones I pulled out were conscious and crying out. How many are unconscious but buried? I don't know. I saw more while I was inside, but I'm not sure how many are beyond helping. The damage is . . . it's bad." He stared down at his hands. His formerly white gloves were coated in ash and dust. "There might be some humans too. Would-be rescuers must have rushed in. Some made it into the pocket of Faerie. Those two got caught in a secondary collapse."

He jerked his head toward the two humans who'd hobbled out with him. One was being lifted onto the closest gurney, looking pale and ashen as a paramedic stabilized his mangled leg.

Tem straightened and turned back toward the building. "Lea, you coming?" he asked as he started walking again. At least it wasn't a mad sprint this time.

One of the female agents straightened—the other troll, if I had to guess, though her glamour made her appear no taller than me. She did look a whole hell of a lot more buff than me, though. Even with her glamour she looked like she could bench-press me. In truth she could probably bench-press a car.

"Wait," I said, holding up a hand as if I could have physically held back either troll.

Tem turned. Without his glamour, he had no eyebrows, but the way the rough yellow skin over his large forehead bunched made me guess that the look he gave me was quizzical. Damn but it was hard to read inhuman faces when you'd spent most your life around people who all more or less looked relatively similar.

"Nori said the reason they can't get the fire out is that the water isn't reaching the pocket of Faerie. Is the building stable enough that you could lead in firefighters?"

Tem's thick lips tugged down around his protruding tusks. "I'm not going to be responsible for leading a bunch of humans into a collapsing, burning pocket of Faerie that can't decide if it exists in the mortal realm or not. But the Bloom not being on fire would make getting survivors out a whole lot easier, so I'm not opposed to carrying in one of those fire hoses."

Well, that was better than nothing. Now to talk to the fire chief.

Chapter 9

"Absolutely not." The fire chief's cheeks and forehead were bright red, his eyes hard. "This may be a fae-owned property, but I'm the incident commander. There is an active fire of unknown source, an explosion caused by suspected incendiary devices, and unknown magic at hand. No one is authorized to enter the building. You shouldn't have sent your people in to start with, and there is no way they are going back in now that they are clear."

I didn't correct his assumption that I'd been the one to send my people in. "There are still survivors inside, and your efforts to extinguish the flames from outside are not working. We know why they aren't working. Let my agents put out the fire from the inside." I almost added that I wasn't asking permission, just giving him a heads-up on our plans, but I didn't actually know how far my authority extended on this scene. If I overstepped, would I get thrown out? Arrested? That wouldn't speed up the process of getting help to those inside nor answer any of the questions about what had happened.

Outside the command tent, I could see Tem pacing.

He wouldn't wait much longer. With or without permission, he was going back inside. *It would be nice if I could secure him some official backup.*

"She's right." This from the anti-black magic task force leader. She looked from the fire chief to me and then back again. "The fire isn't going out. My team hasn't been able to isolate a magical reason—at least not from out here. And your team hasn't made any progress in extinguishing the fire. Civilian lives are always a priority. We need to get to those trapped inside. If her team knows how to fight the fire more efficiently, we should give it a try."

The fire chief's cheeks puffed out in his outrage, and he shook his head. But after a silent moment he gritted out the word "fine." Then he turned on his heels and marched out of the command tent. "Let's get your team suited up."

I followed the chief toward one of the fire rescue vehicles. Nori, Tem, Lea, and a fourth agent whose name I'd already forgotten trailed close behind. Mabel had opted to remain with the survivors who had already been pulled from the rubble, and the last agent who'd accompanied us to the scene was interviewing witnesses. It wasn't until we reached the vehicle that I realized we weren't alone. The ABMU task leader had followed us, two of her officers bringing up the rear of the group. The chief gathered several helmets and fire jackets before turning, his arms overloaded. He gave a disparaging glance over my small crew and then noticed the ABMU agents. His scowl deepened.

"Not you too," he said, staring at the task force leader.

"The magic at the scene needs a closer inspection. My team isn't making much headway from the outside. We will get a better understanding inside," she said, holding out her hand to accept some of the protective gear.

He stared at her a moment, and then tossed a helmet in her direction, shaking his head but not fighting her.

Beside me, Tem crossed his massive arms over his chest.

"No," he said, his deep voice causing every eye to move to him. I cocked an eyebrow, but he just shook his head. "No humans. I don't mind walking in there and fighting the fire. I can carry people out. But I'm not leading humans in."

"You don't have to lead me or my team anywhere," the task force leader said. She was an inch or two shorter than me, which made her at least three feet shorter than Tem, but she glared up at him with enough confidence in her spine that it seemed to equalize them. "We are going in." She turned toward me as she said these last words, the challenge clear in her face.

I considered it a moment. The dangers of the fire and collapsing building aside, taking them with us meant leading them into a pocket of Faerie. Of course, Nori said the doorway was down, and with the destruction, most of the inherent dangers of the Bloom to humans were likely not an issue. If she planned to take her team in regardless, they would be safer going with us than going in alone.

I nodded, and the hardness in the ABMU leader's face softened slightly. Tem opened his mouth to argue, but I met his gaze and said, "They go."

We stared at each other a moment, Tem's lips pressed tight around his tusks. "I can't protect them," he mumbled.

"We aren't asking you to," the task leader snapped back, sliding into a heavy fire jacket.

Tem glared at her, but the argument seemed to be over, so I turned and accepted the helmet and flame-retardant jacket the fire chief handed to me. Tem continued to grumble as I shrugged into the heavy coat—the thing had to weigh thirty pounds. He did not approve of my decision to enter the building, but we'd already had this argument. I wasn't sending my team in somewhere that I wasn't willing to go myself.

"I don't need that," Lea said as the chief attempted to hand her a helmet.

"You're not going in that building without some protection."

"That hat would crack before my skull." She stepped backward, as if repulsed by the helmet.

The fire chief made a disgusted sound. "Fine. You're not my responsibility and you won't weigh on my conscience."

As I wasn't impervious to collapsing walls, I donned all the gear the chief had given me, double-checking all my straps and buckles as I walked. Two firemen met us at the edge of the sidewalk in front of the Bloom. They handed off the hose to Tem, giving us a brisk but succinct rundown of how to operate the hose and valves. Then they retreated back behind the three-hundred-foot safety perimeter that had been established across the street.

I glanced around at our group of five fae and three witches—or at least I assumed all the humans were witches; all three carried enough charms to stock one of the shop displays here in the Quarter. The humans were all wearing full protective gear, and as I watched, the male witch in the back clipped a small token to the front of his jacket and activated the spell inside it. I was close enough to feel that it was a heat resistance spell. There were already several such spells active in the gear we wore, but I guessed one more wouldn't hurt. My team was far less protectively dressed. Nori had accepted a helmet but not a jacket as the heavy coat would interfere with her wings. Lea and Tem had rejected both. The final fae—was his name Moor? I thought that was what he'd introduced himself as—was dressed in full gear. I guessed whatever type of fae he was, he didn't have a ton of natural armor like the trolls.

"Ready?" I asked, stepping forward into the shadow of the building. I received a chorus of grunts and affirmatives in response, but when I started forward, Tem stepped into my path.

"I'll take point—I'm the one with the hose," he said, and then he leaned down so that only I could hear his next words. "Stay close to me. If this building starts collapsing, I need to know where you are. You're the one the king tasked me with."

Right. Which meant the rest of the team and the humans were on their own. Still, it was good to know I probably wouldn't be crushed to death. Not by a building at least. Maybe by a troll shielding me from said collapsing building, so yeah . . .

Tem led the way into the building. At first it was just a matter of stepping over bits of debris that had been blown clear, but soon we were climbing over what remained of the facade. Lea dropped her glamour. She wasn't quite as tall as Tem, but she still had a good two feet on me, and that extra height gave her an advantage in scrambling over debris piles. Nori simply flew over them. Moor proved to be a satyr, and while I would have thought his hooved feet would have been a detriment, he moved like a mountain goat, easily finding steady footing on the shifting rubble.

The person scrambling beside me tottered, and I threw out my hand, catching her elbow and steadying her. The ABMU task leader glanced at me and gave a small nod of thanks as she straightened. Through the plastic of her face shield, she gave me the briefest smile.

"I don't think we were introduced earlier," she said once she had her footing under her. "I'm Lieutenant Martinez." She held out her hand.

It was a bit of an awkward angle for a handshake, with us among the rubble and nearly side by side, but I accepted her hand. The handshake was quick but firm and friendly. I'd already liked her direct, logical assessments, but my respect for her increased.

"Alex Craft," I said. Probably should have added "special agent in charge," but she knew that and it

didn't exactly roll off the tongue. Besides, I didn't want
to waste the breath. Finding my footing in the rubble
had me breathing hard already.

The January air was hot from the fire, and under the
heavy fire jacket, I was sweating by the time we reached
the door that normally would have led to the VIP area.
Water pooled everywhere, filling every crevice and churn-
ing in muddy swirls of ash and dust around my boots.

Half the wall had collapsed here, transforming
where the door had been into a jagged opening. A limp
arm hung out of one of the nearly submerged piles of
rubble. One of the witches rushed forward, kneeling in
the water to check the wrist for a pulse.

"Dead," I said, not moving any closer to the body. I
was shielding hard against the press of the grave, but
seeing the body gave it an extra push as it raked against
my mind. A shiver ran over me even under my heavy
fire coat. I wasn't sure if the man had been crushed in
the initial explosion or drowned under the torrent of
water, but the impression sliding against my mind was
that he had been fae and old. Very old.

"We should move on," I said, sloshing through the
water toward the opening in the mostly missing wall.

The agent searching for a pulse didn't say anything,
but he didn't move either. After a moment, he nodded
to Martinez as if confirming what I'd already said. The
body was a corpse. In a case like this, the living were
rescued. Bodies remained in place as evidence.

Tem motioned for me, shooting suspicious glances
up at the ceiling. Sections of it had already fallen, but
others sagged and bowed, likely to collapse at any
point. I didn't need any more incentive, but hurried
toward the former doorway. Without the ledger, time
might get a little funny. Even if the ledger had survived
the blast, would the magic that tied it to the doorway
have still functioned without, well, a door?

Once I passed through what had been a doorway,
the water that had flooded the entry vanished. The

floors of the VIP room had been rough hardwoods, but were now nothing more than ash. Visibility dropped, smoke filling the air. Thick, but not deadly. More like when a bonfire blows in your direction. If the VIP room had been a true room, I'd have likely needed to drop to my stomach and hope for a layer of air under the smoke. Instead this "room" had no ceiling, and the smoke still pouring off the burning tree dispersed at least a little as it filled an open sky.

The air was hot, dry, like the fire had sapped every drop of moisture. Pieces of charred furniture littered the ground where it had been blasted backward during the explosion. The real hazards were the massive twisted and blackened branches that littered the ground. Some still burned; others had apparently already burned themselves out, making me wonder how much time had passed in this pocket of Faerie since the explosion. It had been maybe two hours in the mortal realm, but here enough time had passed that many of the fallen branches were nothing but husks of ash. There was no rubble here—with no ceiling to cave in and the room so massively large, the bomb hadn't done much structural damage, unlike on the mortal side. But the massive limbs created an obstacle course.

Tem doused any actively burning limbs as we passed them, but he didn't linger on them, and many still glowed with burning embers. I understood why—we didn't know where fae might be pinned under the huge branches and he didn't want to drown them. Not that cooking under a fire sounded any better.

Lea set to work clearing some of the larger branches, lifting limbs thicker around than my waist without effort. She seemed to be impervious to the angry orange embers. Nori flew over the branches, heading deeper into the room at a fast clip. Moor followed her, leaping nimbly over the burning branches. The witches and I were not nearly as fast. I wove around the largest branches, wary of the hotter patches, but I had to clamber over some. Several times I had to stop and brush burning embers from my pants and boots when I brushed against a charred branch that still burned under the blackened bark.

Ash fell like snow all around me. There had been snow falling in the Bloom the last time I'd been here, but this was different. This wasn't magic, or at least it wasn't only magic. I held up my palm and caught one of the larger chunks floating about. The silvery pink petal still shimmered, even with its edges withered and charred. I glanced up. In the thick haze of smoke, the sky was absolutely filled with the drifting but charred petals of the amaranthine tree's flowers.

Ahead, I could make out the hazy shape of Tem, silhouetted against the fire still consuming the trunk of the tree. The hose had reached its limits, falling short by several yards. Tem's deep voice cursed. Despite the fact that the fire had been raging long enough that the fallen branches had nearly burned themselves out, the fire along the trunk of the tree blazed hot. Tem opened the valve the way the firefighter had shown him and released a jet of water.

My first instinct was to hold my breath; something about the fire made me doubt the water would work, but I hoped I was wrong. While the smoke was not too thick to breathe, it burned my lungs when I held it too long. I ducked down, sucking in cleaner air near the ground.

"What is this place?" Martinez said from somewhere behind me, her voice breathy from either the smoke, the exertion of scrambling over burning branches, or simply awe.

"Somewhere humans rarely see." At least not without being changed by it in some way. The lucky ones only lost a little time to Faerie. The unlucky ones? Well, they likely ended up addicted to Faerie food, changelings, indebted to a fae, or enslaved in Faerie. Even just a pocket of Faerie wasn't a particularly safe place for mortals. "Don't eat anything. And if you hear music, don't follow it."

Martinez gave me a strange look, which probably had to do with the fact that we were at the scene of a bombing and this place didn't look exactly enchanting right now, but better safe than sorry.

I glanced to where Tem was still dousing the flames. Were they getting any smaller? I couldn't tell, but it didn't look like it. Nori, Lea, and Moor had scattered. I couldn't see them in the smoke, but I guessed they were searching for survivors. The land of the dead was thinner here; it did still exist—unlike in Faerie, where souls never moved on—but the realms only barely touched. Even still, I could feel the death around me. The grave essence was light, brushing barely there fingertips across my mind. I had a sense that the essence reached for me from several sources, but I couldn't even tell the gender of the victims—the land of the dead simply wasn't strong enough here for my grave witch abilities to discern much, not with my shields in place. Outside the bubble of Faerie, I'd struggled to ignore the dead I'd sensed, but here, I had to concentrate just to differentiate the thin traces of grave essence.

There were a lot of victims. I wasn't sure how many, but I was sure I sensed multiples. Maybe some could be recovered. Death wasn't as permanent in Faerie as it was in the mortal realm. But we weren't completely in Faerie right now, and in this space in between, the taint of the grave loomed. No soul collectors would come here, but the tie between body and soul was surely damaged. There was likely no helping those who had died in the explosion. But we could help the survivors, and that would be easier if there wasn't a giant bonfire in the middle of the Bloom.

"Can your people do anything to help put out the fire?" I asked, gesturing from Martinez to where Tem still held the huge fire hose.

Martinez nodded and then looked at one of her people. The male witch she'd brought stepped forward. He must have attempted to reach the Aetheric plane—the source of magic—because shock registered over his face for a moment and his jaw fell open. The Aetheric plane did exist here, but only thinly and at a distance, much like the plane for the land of the dead. After a stunned moment, he reached down and twisted a ring on his finger. I could feel the raw Aetheric energy he'd stored there as he tapped it, then he held his hands out in front of him, channeling the energy between his palms. After a moment, an orb of floating water appeared in the space between his hands. It grew as he walked, though his progress was slow as his attention was divided between crafting his spell and scrambling over the charred branches. Once he stumbled, falling to one knee, and I was sure he'd lose the spell, but he maintained it, reclaiming his footing. By the time he'd made it the last yard to stand next to Tem, the orb of water was wider than he was. He threw his arms wide, and the orb hurtled toward the tree.

I expected it to pop like a water balloon upon contact, but it instead spread as it reached the tree, thinning and elongating to wrap around the trunk. The fire hissed, and steam sizzled off the amorphous glob of water. The flames fizzled where the magic water touched them, dying out.

Neat trick.

The fire hose hadn't made much of a dent, but the witch's strange congealed water blob smothered the flames it covered. It was evaporating quickly, though. Tem seemed to notice, and focused his hose in the area with the water. Considering the magic involved, I wasn't sure that would help, but after a moment, it appeared the hose fed the blob. The witch turned toward Tem, giving him an approving nod before tapping into his stored magic again and beginning to create a second orb.

I had little magic that would be useful in fighting a
fire, but I was a sensitive and I could see witch spells,
pierce glamour, and sometimes even get a sense of fae
magics. If the explosion had some magical compo-
nents, or the fire was magical in nature, maybe I could
get a sense of the cause and help unravel it.

I cracked my shields. Not far, just enough that I
could gaze across the planes. Beside me, I heard Martinez gasp as my eyes began to glow. With the face
shield an inch in front of my nose, the green light from
my eyes reflected off the plastic, blinding me to anything happening past the shield. I cursed under my
breath and pushed the face shield up, out of the way.
Smoke stung my eyes, but at least I could see.

With the land of the dead being so thin here, and the
Bloom already in ashes and cinders around me, there
wasn't much change to the scenery. Thin wisps of
Aetheric energy swirled here and there, trailing bits of
green, pink, blue, and yellow through the air, but even
that was sparse and easy to ignore. Magic clung to
Martinez, as well as to the two witches she'd brought
with her, but underneath that, they glowed a pale yellow. Human souls. My team all glowed a faint silver, as
they were fae. The soul light was harder to discern in a
pocket of Faerie, but it was there, noticeable.

The water spell the witch fighting the fire was using
looked like a densely woven web of green Aetheric energy now that my shields were open. The spell clung to
the tree, the fire eating away at the Aetheric energy as
it evaporated the water binding the magic. The ABMU
witch's spell was the only magic I could see on the tree,
and the fire didn't change in my gravesight, which
meant it wasn't glamour—not that I'd been holding out
hope for that chance. But just on the edge of my senses,
I thought I could *feel* another magic.

I wasn't good at sensing fae magic. I'd only begun
picking it up at all when my fae nature had emerged
around the Blood Moon half a year ago, but the part

of me that sensed magic had a hard time focusing on it. I turned away from the tree, trying to glance at the fire only from the corner of my eye. Yes. *There.* I could just, almost, see silver lines of magic snaking up the left side of the tree.

"The fire is being fed by a spell," I said, taking a step closer to the tree. I was still several yards farther away than Tem and the male witch, but the heat billowing off the fire was intense, even with the spells worked into my jacket.

Lieutenant Martinez stepped closer to me, and I could see her frown through the plastic of her visor. "I'm not sensing anything we didn't bring in here."

So she was a sensitive as well. Not all that surprising for an Anti-Black Magic Unit lieutenant. She likely wouldn't be able to pick up this magic, though, unless she had some skeletons—okay, well, fae—in her genetic closet. Based on the color of her soul, I was guessing she was purely human.

"It's not witch magic," I said, trying to get a better look at the spell, or at least the source of the spell, but every time I looked harder, the traces of magic slipped away.

Martinez looked back at the other witch she'd brought with her. The woman was short, the heavy fire gear making her look a lot wider than she actually was. She carried an odd instrument in her hands. It looked like a huge brick of a tablet, but with multiple antennae and several protrusions that glowed with embedded magic.

The woman looked up and shook her head at her lieutenant. "This thing started going haywire the moment we stepped into this room. It's spitting out max-level readings for fae magic pretty much everywhere."

"That reads magic?" I asked, staring at the weird, half-tech, half-magic device the woman carried. I'd seen plenty of spellcheckers before, and I could sense at least one spellchecker worked into the machine. But spellcheckers gave an alert—typically by changing color—if a spell was malicious. They didn't determine anything more specific about the magic, and I'd certainly never heard of one that could detect fae magic. In fact, I regularly snuck fae spells past spellcheckers. The fact that spellcheckers could only be cast to check very specific things and relay only the most basic information was why sensitives were so highly valued.

"It's experimental. We're still working out the bugs," Martinez said, climbing over a branch to move closer to her officer so she could glance at the display screen. She frowned at whatever reading it was spitting out. "That isn't going to help much." She turned back to me. "Where are you sensing the magic? Maybe we can isolate it if we have a better idea."

I tried to look at the tree again with only my peripheral vision, though it was hard to look and not look at the same time, especially since the fire was continuing to rage. The water witch's original spell had already shattered, and his second spell was dissipating rapidly, despite the fact that he was reinforcing it with more magic and Tem was adding extra water from his hose. From the look of him, he didn't have enough stored magic on him to form a third water bubble. He clearly was accustomed to grabbing the raw Aetheric energy he needed at will, and had minimal reserved backup magic stored.

It took a moment for the spell I'd seen earlier to pop into focus again. I could just barely make it out if I didn't look too hard, but when I let my gaze unfocus, I could see the white lines snaking through the fire, wrapping up the tree. The magic retreated from the witch's water spell as the fire was smothered, but as soon as the water gave ground, the fae magic shoved forward, pushing the fire back into the vacated space. At this rate, the fire would never extinguish. At least not until the tree was little more than charred dust.

But where was the spell fueling the fire tethered?

Was it on the tree itself? I clambered over burning branches, circling the tree without getting any closer to the flames. I couldn't get too close; the radiant heat blasting off the fire felt like an oven. Every few feet I had to stop and work on unfocusing to catch a glimpse of the spell again. As I rounded the back of the tree, I finally saw that the silver lines of fae magic snaked off the tree, down to the soil around the roots.

"Can you direct your water spell this way?" I asked, gesturing toward the spot.

The water witch's spell was no larger than a pizza now, and sweat poured down the lines etching his face. He tore his gaze away from his spell long enough to look not at me, but at his boss, who had followed me as I searched for the fire's source. Martinez gave a nod of approval, and the witch flared his fingers. He'd positively glowed with magic when we'd walked into the Bloom. In the last few minutes, he'd depleted his stored magic and apparently cannibalized his charms for traces of Aetheric energy, because they were all dark and dormant now. Even the spell in his fire jacket—which wasn't even his charm—had been drained. He used the little he had left to direct the rapidly shrinking water spell toward the spot I'd indicated. I hoped I was right about this, because if I wasn't, this witch was tapped out and wouldn't be doing anything else.

The water spell was barely the size of a dinner plate by the time it reached the area where the fire spell originated. With the witch's spell so small now, placement needed to be fairly precise if we were going to neutralize the fire. Not an easy feat as I could only focus on the magic by *not* focusing on it.

"Left and down," I said, frowning as I lost sight of the white lines of magic again.

The water spell sloshed into the spot that seemed to have been glowing the brightest when I had been able to see it. The fire there sputtered, crackled, and then abruptly died down. I tried to see the fae magic again, to see if anything changed, but I couldn't catch it. Was I trying too hard or . . .

Tem's fire hose was still drenching the trunk of the tree, and the fire sizzled and then suddenly snuffed out all along the wet base. Tem blinked in surprise, then repositioned the hose, spraying more of the tree. The fire, which hadn't responded to the water at all a moment before, died out.

"Lea, take over here," Tem called out, and the other troll ran toward him, knocking aside the heavy branches as she bustled through them. She reached Tem, and then seemed to be at a loss at what to do with the unconscious fae in her arms, whom she must have extracted from the debris. After only a brief hesitation, she slung him over her shoulder and accepted the hose. The force of the water seemed to surprise her for a moment, causing her to take a step back, but then she braced her legs and took control, spraying the water higher up the tree, soaking the still-burning branches.

"Where was the fire spell?" Tem asked, running to where I was standing.

I opened my mouth to tell him it had been directly under where the witch's spell was now, but while I could still see the web of glowing green magic, no larger than my palm, it likely looked like nothing more than one more puddle to everyone else. And water was puddling everywhere around the amaranthine tree.

"Here," I said, rushing forward. Now that the fire was out in the bottom half of the tree, the air wasn't quite as oppressive, but the charred tree still radiated heat. I pointed to the spot the witch's spell covered, and could feel the heat pulsing up from the ground through my gloves.

Tem shoved his hand into the water pooling at the base of the tree. I gasped, yelping out a warning about the heat. The troll didn't pay me any mind, but fished around in the mud and soot.

His hand squelched as he jerked it from the puddle,

something faintly glowing clutched in his massive fist.
The moment the object cleared the water, flames burst
over Tem's hand.

"Shit!" Tem shook his arm, only succeeding in allowing the flames to travel up his sleeve. But he didn't
let go.

Someone screamed. I cursed, stepping forward like
I would do something. But what the hell was I sup-
posed to do? I couldn't summon a water spell like the
ABMU witch had done.

"Drop it in here," Martinez yelled, rushing forward
with a box the size of a loaf of bread.

Tem didn't ask questions, but dropped the item into
the open box. Then he turned and plunged his arm
back into the water as Martinez snapped the lid shut
on the box. I could feel the magic-canceling charms
worked into the small box. They were good. Some of
the strongest I'd felt. But they were witch charms.
Would they be enough against the fae charm?

I held my breath, waiting to see if the charms could
hold the fire spell. I think everyone else was wondering
the same thing, because we all stared at the box, the
only sound the water bursting from the fire hose and
the moans of the wounded from deeper in the Bloom.

No fire erupted from the box, and I let out a breath
that had too much smoke in it, and ended up coughing
as my lungs emptied.

"I think that's that, then," Martinez said, snapping
another seal on the box before accepting a third from
the female witch who'd accompanied her. The woman
rooted through the bag at her feet, possibly looking for
a fourth seal, but Martinez shook her head. "This
should hold. Well, I guess we can safely say this is a
crime scene—unless that fire spell was in a hearth or
something and the explosion just knocked it into the
tree?"

A never-ending hearth fire? That actually wasn't
impossible in Faerie, but I'd never seen one in the

Bloom. I glanced around for Nori, but she wasn't in sight, so I looked to Tem instead. He shook his head.

"That was intentional."

"Well then," Martinez said, nodding. "That is that, then. Looks like the fire is under control now. We should let the fire chief know and get some help in here to get the survivors out."

Chapter 10

I did what I could to help locate and move the survivors. I'd originally thought looking with my grave-sight would be clever—I'd used it in the past to search out living souls—but with no land of the dead here, the physical objects didn't disintegrate in my sight, and my grave magic wasn't exactly infrared heat vision. If no part of the body was visible, I couldn't see the glow of a soul. Then there was the fact that the glow wasn't bright like in mortal reality.

I did great at finding the dead. Not so helpful with finding the living.

When the firefighters finally joined us, I agreed to Tem's urging to leave the rescuing to those trained to do it. He didn't want to have to hover over me worrying about my safety, and I felt useless, like I was holding him back from actually helping people, so I left.

The VIP door was just as finicky even without a physical doorway, but as I expected, time passed for me at the exact rate as what I'd spent inside the Bloom. Not for everyone else, though. Nori beat me out, even though she hadn't technically left the Bloom yet when I'd exited.

My phone beeped as soon as I walked out of the VIP room, letting me know I'd missed a call while inside. The caller hadn't left a message, but I recognized the number as coming from the FIB office. I pressed the screen to return the call, and Agent Bleek answered on the second ring.

"Have you made contact with the king yet?" I asked as soon as he answered.

"Uh . . ." he started, and then stumbled on, the words speeding up, like he couldn't stem the flood of them. "We haven't contacted the king. No one has. The other doors are all intact but not working. The winter court is locked."

The last sentence slammed into me, dread gripping my lungs and squeezing out my air.

"Ma'am? Are you still there?" Agent Bleek asked when my silence had stretched too long.

I nodded, which he couldn't see through the phone. "Yes. Yes, I'm still here," I said, my voice coming out thin and hoarse. I cleared my throat and then forced air into my dread-frozen lungs before speaking again. "Have the other FIB offices continue trying the doors. I want to know as soon as the winter court opens."

I didn't wait for the agent to reply, but hit the disconnect button with a finger that felt too thick and clumsy. Then I stared at my phone.

The winter court was locked.

The last time the winter court went into lockdown, it was because the former queen had fallen and Faerie was giving Falin a chance to adjust to his new court. Now the doors were locked once again.

Damn it. You better be all right. Why was I stuck on the wrong side of the door? Again.

And when had the mortal realm become the wrong side to me?

Raised voices caught my attention. I didn't really care what was being yelled about, but I did need the distraction or I was going to spiral into a frenzy of panic that would be useless. There was no action I could take right now to help Falin. My most useful contribution at the moment would be figuring out who attacked the amaranthine tree.

I turned, searching out the source of the angry voices. It wasn't hard to find. Nori and Martinez appeared to be squaring off outside the command tent, surrounded by a small contingent of ABMU officers. My feet felt strange and bouncy from the shock of adrenaline rushing through me, but I managed not to trip over myself as I made my way toward the angry group. Go me.

"Going back in won't help," Nori said to a very pissed-off-looking Martinez as I approached.

"The hell it won't. He should have been right behind me. He was exhausted after using all that magic. Something must have happened."

"What's going on?" I asked, though I had a guess. It sounded like someone hadn't made it out of the VIP room yet.

"Halloway is missing," Martinez snapped. "My team all exited together, but when Callen and I emerged, Halloway wasn't behind us anymore."

She hadn't technically introduced me to her team, but I guessed Halloway was the water witch as she'd said *he* was exhausted and had used magic and the other witch she'd taken with her had been a woman. I gave her what I hoped would come off as a sympathetic smile and said, "Give him some time. The doors can be tricky."

She glared at me. "It's been over half an hour. Callen went back to check on him, and now she is missing too. I'm going back in there to secure my people, but your agent is getting in my way."

Oh, now that was a mess. I didn't remember seeing Callen when I'd left, which meant she hadn't made it through the door yet. With no magic to direct the door, this could get really complicated.

"Agent Nori is correct. You shouldn't go back in. It won't help. In fact"—I turned toward Nori even though I could feel Martinez's increasingly angry glare searing into the side of my head—"the doorway is a problem. Is there any way to get it working at least to the efficiency it did before the bombing?"

Nori's lips pressed into a thin line and she cocked her head to the side, considering it. "I'll put in a call, but I doubt anyone here is familiar enough with the magic to fix it. Not in its current state. We should probably restrict human access to it."

Oh yeah, that would go over well . . .

"The hell are you two talking about? How is a blasted-out doorway a danger and where are my people?" Martinez's accent had grown thicker with her anger, and she hurled the question at me as if it were a weapon.

"Your people are . . . between time, I guess would be the best way to put it," I said, lifting my hands in a slight shrug as I searched for the right words. She gave me an incredulous look and I stumbled on. "I told you when we entered that you were in a place humans rarely see. We weren't in Faerie, but we were in the next closest thing. That room—it isn't fully here. Which is why it was bigger than what should have fit in the building, and why that tree hasn't always been bursting out of the top of a single-story building. The doorway links the two places, but the connection isn't always the best. Sometimes you walk out in one moment, but the person behind you misses that connection, and the door spits them out at a later time."

She stared at me, her eyes studying me as if trying to decide if I was making this all up. After a moment she asked, "Then why don't we use the door to go back to before the bombs were set and make sure all those people don't die?"

Nori made an exasperated sound behind me. "It's not time travel. You can't go back along your same timeline. Once time has passed, it's gone. The past can't be changed. Sometimes the door just . . . jettisons people on a shortcut to a later time."

That was one way to put it.

Martinez considered this for a moment. "So how long will my people be missing?"

I glanced at Nori. She shrugged. "Usually people don't lose more than a few hours."

"Hours?" Martinez took a step back, as if the idea of that much lost time had come as a physical blow. She turned and stared at the darkened building. I wondered if she'd read any old folktales. They were full of stories of people losing days or even lifetimes to Faerie. That wasn't typical, but neither were the circumstances here. Still, I hoped her people emerged soon.

The door was definitely going to be an issue. Keeping the humans out would be a feat in and of itself, and one I doubted I'd succeed at enforcing. But I couldn't have my team losing hours or days either. Of course, if I was correct about the effect of the realities I was carrying with me, and they kept me tied to a continuous time, maybe there was something I could do about the Bloom door issue, at the very least. *If only I could do something about the door to Faerie.*

Chapter 11

The next few hours were long and exhausting. Dozens of trips through the door more or less proved my hypothesis correct. My reality was grounded in a continuous time, and because of my planeweaving, I naturally dragged anything I touched along with me. It wasn't that dissimilar to how ghosts could interact with the mortal realm while in physical contact with me. I was a conduit between the planes, and now that I carried several on my person, it forced time to remain consistent for me in both Faerie and the mortal realm. Pretty convenient for not losing huge swaths of time to the doors, but unfortunately it meant I had to personally escort everyone who passed through the doorway. And I had to be in physical contact with them as we walked through.

Because that wasn't awkward at all with a bunch of law enforcement types I didn't know.

Once the survivors were carried out, the building was once again evacuated until the structural engineer arrived. He walked through with his team and suggested places that would need to be shored up and reinforced before the investigation could continue. I

expected that to take a while, but the makeshift braces
and structures were erected quickly, all things considered. The Faerie side of the bar needed no structural
supports. The lack of a roof left little besides the tree
that could fall, and many of the branches had already
fallen. The fire had done much more damage than the
explosion on the VIP side, with the reverse being true
on the mortal side.

By late afternoon, the building was opened for investigation, and the bomb squad and arson investigators took over the scene. My team was also free to
enter at will to investigate. The problem was, I had no
idea what we should be looking for. I was in way over
my head in this investigation.

I spent a lot of my time escorting people through the
doorway. My team accepted the arrangement without
question, thankful I could control the door. Pretty
much every single human questioned my insistence on
escorting them, though many were more than happy to
leave the weird fae side of the bar to my team, which at
least cut down on traffic. Others were too curious or
dedicated to be dissuaded by my warnings that they
would be entering a pocket of Faerie. For some I was
thankful they still wanted to investigate, like Captain
Oliver and his bomb squad techs. Others I considered
arguing with—like the crime scene photographer.
Cameras didn't work in Faerie, and the VIP room was
more Faerie than not, but arguing over the necessity of
procedure was more than I felt up to, so I walked
her in.

I held a lot of hands. Most grudgingly accepted
when I explained the issue with the doorways. A few
refused. One of those lost about an hour, another
emerged in more or less the correct time, and a third
emerged confused because only about thirty seconds
had passed in the mortal realm even though he'd spent
over an hour in the VIP area. We were still waiting on
the fourth to return.

Callen returned two hours after the investigation went into full swing. Halloway still hadn't emerged. Martinez had me walk her in, but of course she hadn't been able to find her errant officer. I still hadn't managed to make her understand that he wasn't actually lost or lingering in limbo somewhere. We simply hadn't caught up to the time in which he would step out of the door yet.

The sun hung low behind the neighboring buildings, only a sliver of reddish-orange glow left on the horizon, when a car that wasn't an emergency vehicle rolled past the barricades and up to the cleared perimeter in front of the Bloom.

"Our preliminary analysis shows that there were two devices," Captain Oliver said. We were in the command tent for this briefing, and I was off to the side, wishing they'd brought in more light now that the sun was setting. Several heads turned as the vehicle approached, but Oliver didn't seem to notice, continuing without pause, "We have found a lot of shrapnel in the normal part of the bar, but the explosion on the fae side appears to have been—"

"Is that the governor's limo?" Hilda Larine asked, cutting off Oliver. She lifted a hand to her hair, patting it into place before glancing down at her immaculate suit skirt. She was the only one of us still in pristine shape. Martinez, Oliver, the fire chief, and I had all spent time in the bomb-wasted remains of the Bloom, but not Larine. Her impractical high heels didn't have a speck of soot or rubble on them.

"He'll be wanting an update," the fire chief said, straightening from where he'd been slumped in a foldable chair as he'd listened to Oliver.

The door to the limo opened, and a tall man in a simple brown suit stepped out. I wasn't sure if he was an aide or a bodyguard, but he took a slow glance around the scene before heading straight for the command tent.

Both Larine and the chief moved to intercept him. He smiled politely, but shook his head at whatever they said. Then he walked around them and ducked into the tent.

"The governor would like a briefing from the FIB agent in charge," he said, looking straight at me as he spoke. Well, word had certainly gotten around quickly about my new position.

I gave him a tight smile, but didn't say anything as I followed him out. I considered throwing Larine a smug smile as I passed her, since she clearly was dying to rub elbows with the governor, but the truth was, I didn't want to talk to him and would have gladly given her my spot. It's hard to be smug when you're dreading the coming confrontation.

Nori fell in step beside me as we walked. The tall aide/bodyguard didn't stop her, or even say anything to her, until we reached the door of the limo. Then he stepped between Nori and the limo door.

"The governor requested an audience only with the FIB special agent in charge," he said.

Nori frowned at him. She'd regained control of her glamour hours ago and once again looked like a cool, controlled FIB agent. She certainly looked more professional than me as her glamour covered not just her otherness, but also all the soot and mud she'd picked up inside the Bloom.

"This is Agent Craft's second day as agent in charge. I am her partner and mentor. I should help her brief the governor." Nori's voice was reasonable, no-nonsense, and her argument was a good one.

It was also doomed to fail. I didn't even need to see the man's face to know that.

I knew secrets about the governor that Nori was not privy to. Like that he was a fae in hiding. And also that he was my father. This was not a meeting he was likely to let outsiders overhear.

The man didn't bother smiling at Nori the way he

had Larine and the chief. He simply shook his head and said, "I'm following direct orders. Only the agent in charge." Then he turned his back on her and opened the door to the limo for me.

I stepped up to the door and leaned down, exhaustion and dread warring with the panic singing through me. I took one glance at the white leather seats and then hesitated before stepping inside.

"I'll ruin your upholstery," I called out to the shadow of a figure inside. Some days I might have taken twisted satisfaction in smearing ash and cement dust on his immaculate seats, but today I didn't want to waste the emotional energy on the barbed shaming that would be thrown my way if I did.

"Alexis," my father said in that vexing way that made me hate my own name. "Come inside and sit."

Beside me, I saw Nori's posture change. My full real name wasn't common knowledge, so in one sentence, the governor had just revealed that he knew me. That was a slip he rarely made, and the mistake, more than his words, urged me into the car.

The moment the aide shut the door behind me, the limo fell into a silence that could only be achieved through magic—fae magic most likely, though I couldn't sense it with my shields in place. Or maybe my father simply had the best noise-canceling tech built into his limo. Considering he'd been elected running under the Humans First Party banner, that would make more sense. Not that anything with my father seemed to make sense since I learned he was fae. The man was a mystery wrapped in contradictions and topped by a nice dollop of impossible. Not exactly who I wanted to talk to after my extremely stressful second day as an FIB agent.

Not that I had a choice.

He gestured to the seat across from him before steepling his hands and tapping his lips with his raised pointer fingers.

It was a simple movement, nothing notable from most people. But from my father? It was an unconscionable amount of fidgeting. He was the master of being as still as a poised ambush hunter, especially when he had someone in his crosshairs.

I sank into the seat, using the movement to cover a closer scrutiny of him. The face he presented the world was that of a man in his early fifties with clean-cut brown hair and the first set of wrinkles, which people tended to call distinguished as opposed to looking old. But today his eyes were a little too green, rather than the gray he normally wore, and his hair had streaks of his true pale blond showing through.

Was his glamour failing?

"What happened?" he asked, staring at me with those slightly too green, too bright eyes.

"The ABS unit could probably answer that better than me—" Though not if he was going to lose his shit and drop his glamour. I didn't know exactly why he hid the fact that he was fae, but it was a secret meticulously concealed. "It appears two bombs were detonated, one on the tourist side of the Bloom. One in the VIP room. The latter also had an attached fire spell, maximizing the damage."

"And the tree?" His hair was more blond than brown now, the ends lengthening from its clean-cut state to fall past his shoulders.

"Charred. The door is gone. I have no idea if it can be repaired. Agents are searching for druids or nymphs or any other fae who might specialize in working with flora to see if we can heal the tree."

My father turned his head, but not before I saw the almost pained grimace that cut across his face. He stared out the window, in the direction of the Bloom.

"It won't be enough. If the door is gone . . . the tree is beyond helping." He let out a breath, the sigh heavy and seeming to fill the limo. I almost thought I heard a mournful dirge playing just out of earshot, which could have happened in Faerie—the land reacted to all kinds of stimuli—but shouldn't happen in a limo in the middle of the mortal realm.

My shoulders stiffened, and I looked around, sure I was catching the lightest drifts of music, and the air suddenly smelled sweet. Like funeral lilies. My father's steepled hands dropped, clenching at his sides, and the sweet, sad scent turned acrid and harsh. I lifted an eyebrow, studying his profile, which no longer resembled the features of a man I'd known my entire life. Now he looked young, no older than me, and his features were sharper, his skin glowing with the same telltale Sleagh Maith light my own shone with. Was he causing the distant music? The sourceless scents? He'd dropped his glamour, or more likely his emotions had eroded his control—was he losing control of some other magic as well?

By the time he turned back to me a moment later, his glamour was back in place, not a dark hair on his head disheveled. The distant eerie music was gone, as were the misplaced scents, the limo once again smelling only of the polished leather seats. He gave me an empty smile that came nowhere near his eyes, and laid his loose hands in his lap.

"This is not a good thing," he said, once again a picture of calm reservation.

"I'm aware." Understatement. We had no direct route to Faerie, and this was almost certainly an attack on the winter court. I hadn't heard from Falin still. No one could even reach the winter court. The fact that this attack might have corresponded to one that caused Falin to lose the court—and death was the most common way for a court to change hands in Faerie—was something I was trying not to think about but that buzzed like a frantic bee around the inside of my skull. And then there was the fact that I'd never seen my father lose control before. Oh, I'd seen his calm break a few times—but his glamour fail? No. That was new.

And a little terrifying. It had only lasted a moment, but his reaction had my palms sweating in that cold clammy way that made me want to rub my hands on my pants, which wouldn't have helped through my gloves anyway.

"I don't think you are truly aware of how severe this is," he said in that same smooth, calm tone. Normally I would have chuffed under the implied condescension, but the contrast to his loss of control moments earlier made his calm now downright unnerving. I waited, saying nothing, because after a statement like that, there was no way he would fail to continue.

"Without the door," he said, steepling his fingers once again, "Faerie has no hold on this part of the mortal realm. *Winter* has no hold at all on this *continent*. The magic that sustains the fae living in this little oasis will soon dry up without the door to replenish it, leaving this place a magical desert. The surrounding courts' influence will eventually claim winter's lost land, but that will take time. Time in which no fae will be able to survive here."

I blinked. One of those long, slow blinks as your body stalls, waiting for your brain to process what you've just heard. My agents had freaked out at the loss of the door. I'd thought that was just because we'd lost easy access to Faerie. Hell, I was freaking out that I couldn't reach Falin, and my FIB agents were court fae, their families and loved ones were in Faerie. I hadn't considered that without the door, Faerie would have no tie to the land. That the belief magic that sustained the fae would dry up. "That . . ." I shook my head. "Can we fix it?"

My father turned and looked out the limo window at the Bloom again. People moved in and out of the ruined building, processing the scene; photographing, tagging, and collecting evidence; or monitoring the stability of the remaining structure. The human bodies were finally being removed from the mortal side of the Bloom. I'd helped the crime scene techs locate each body earlier, but they'd only marked the location for further processing. Now I saw the first black-bag-topped gurney roll out, and I could feel the whisper of grave essence as it drifted through the air. The fae bodies would not be removed tonight. Nori had suggested not removing them at all, but waiting until the door was repaired and taking them to Faerie in case any could be revived, as death wasn't always as permanent in Faerie.

If the door was permanently lost, and the connection to Faerie was going to wane as much as my father said, there would be no reviving any of those fae.

My father turned back to me. His eyes were once again unnaturally green, but his glamour was in place everywhere else, so maybe it was simply the last rays of sunlight catching his irises.

"You should leave," he said, his lips drawn tight.

I blinked again. "Okay." I slid across the seat, reaching for the door.

"Not the limo, Alexis," he said, sounding exasperated. "Leave Nekros City. Hell, the entire mortal plane. I very neatly arranged for you to have a prominent spot in the shadow court. You should go there."

"Pass. Prince Dugan agreed to back me up in refusing our betrothal."

Now it was my father's turn to look surprised. Then he scowled. "He wouldn't . . . What have you done now, you foolish girl? How did you get him to agree to that?"

Oh, just saved the entire shadow court and cured the king of a deadly magical infection. I wasn't going to go into all of that now, though. I was never going to willingly become part of my father's planeweaver breeding program. He'd told me once he was playing the long game—but I sure as hell wasn't going to be an obedient pawn.

"Is there a way to save Nekros?" I asked, redirecting the conversation.

My father stared at me, waiting, as if he thought that

if he watched me long enough I'd spill all the secrets I held. Not likely. He may have shipped me off to a wyrd boarding school for all my formative years, but I'd spent every summer at home, and I'd grown immune to his stare of silence.

The limo grew darker as the sun sank lower. With my night blindness, I could no longer read my father's expression clearly. On the plus side, his silent glare was far less effective, but as the silence grew, the urge to squirm in my seat did as well.

I didn't get a chance to see which of us would break first. James Hetfield of Metallica began belting out that we were off to never-never land from somewhere inside my purse. I startled, and then dug through my bag, retrieving my singing phone. The display showed an unknown number, so apparently "Enter Sandman" was my new generic ringtone. The ghost haunting my castle had quite a sense of humor.

Without glancing at my father, I hit the engage button and lifted my phone to my ear.

"Alex Craft, it's been a while," a bubbly but only vaguely familiar female voice said on the other side of the line.

I glanced at the number again. I didn't recognize it, but this was a relatively new phone—my phones kept getting irrevocably destroyed—so I had only a handful of numbers saved in my contact list.

"So, funny story," the woman on the other end said as if she hadn't noticed my silence. "I was watching some B-roll we shot this afternoon, and I'm positive I caught sight of your unruly blond curls heading beyond the barricades in the Quarter. Are you at the Eternal Bloom? Can you confirm it was a bombing?"

The voice finally clicked with a face. "Lusa Duncan," I said, not hiding my inward cringe that was surely audible in my tone. If I'd recognized the number as the star reporter for Witch Watch, I wouldn't have answered the phone. Not that Lusa was that horrible.

We'd found common goals in the past, but she was still a hungry reporter and I was at a crime scene.

"No comment, Lusa. Now I need to keep this line clear."

"Wait," she called out through the phone. "Come on, Craft. At least tell me if you suspect this is connected to the explosions at the other fae establishments today."

I stopped, my finger hovering over the end button. My father, who had returned to staring at the ruined Bloom, whirled around, his piercing gaze locking on my phone. Clearly he'd overheard her as well. I jerked the phone back up to my ear.

"What other explosions? Where?" I asked.

"Oh, so now I have your attention. You scratch my back, I'll scratch yours."

I rolled my eyes, not that she could see me. "If you know about it, others do too. Do you really think it will be hard for me to find out?"

She huffed on the other end of the line and I almost hung up, but then she said, "A small town in a folded space in Alaska, I can't remember the name, but it was a private fae establishment. Also the fae bar in Terraville. Both experienced explosions around the same time as the one that rocked the Magic Quarter here in Nekros. I don't think it is a coincidence."

"Neither do I," I muttered, and then winced at her excited exclamation of "Aha!"

"So are you confirming the explosion in Nekros was a bombing?"

"No comment," I said, and this time I did hang up. I didn't want to say more than I meant with Lusa on the line. The phone immediately began ringing again, Lusa's number showing on the display. I turned it to silent mode and sent her to voice mail as I wracked my brain to remember the details of the map I'd been looking at the day before. It felt like that morning in the FIB office had been a week ago, but it had been only slightly more than twenty-four hours. I knew there was a door somewhere in Alaska, and Terraville . . . I was pretty sure that was a folded space near North Dakota, and the site of another door to Faerie.

"Those are the sites of the doors to summer and spring, aren't they?" I asked, looking at my father.

"Yes." The word was a strangled whisper. His glamour had fallen again, and that awful, acrid scent filled the car. His fingers moved over his phone in a flash, sending a text, likely because he didn't trust himself to speak to whomever he was contacting.

I sank back into the leather seat, processing this news. I'd been sure Ryese was behind the attack on Nekros—he had a grudge against winter. But if it were him, why would he attack spring and summer? The light court was growing in power, but surely they wouldn't want to alienate all the other courts. And what would cutting off all of North America from Faerie accomplish? Of course, Lusa hadn't mentioned the door to fall. Where was it located? Somewhere near Mexico, if I remembered clearly.

I picked up my phone and dialed the FIB office. "Were you able to find out anything about the other courts?" I asked as soon as Agent Bleek answered.

"Well . . . we don't actually have channels established to exchange information with the other seasonal courts," he said, the words coming out as a reluctant mumble.

I might have growled under my breath.

"Then turn on the news. Apparently spring and summer were also attacked and at least one news outlet in town already knows. Try to find out if fall was attacked as well."

I disconnected and looked at my father. He'd returned to staring at the Bloom, though I wasn't sure he actually saw it. He hadn't bothered reestablishing his glamour and his fingers drummed against his knees.

"How do we fix this?" I asked because I had no idea, but my father tended to be very well informed.

He turned and looked at me with his too bright, too green eyes. Now I knew how unnerving it was when I looked at people with my own power blazing through my eyes, because the weight of his gaze was downright creepy. If he hadn't been glowing, I wouldn't have been able to see him at all in the gloom that hung over the street as the sun vanished behind the horizon.

I braced myself for sunset. It was January, and it tended to come on quick and early. Since coming into my fae nature, I'd become incredibly aware of sunset and sunrise. Those times between were not particularly dangerous to fae—though they could be deadly to any changelings caught outside Faerie—but they were uncomfortable for about sixty seconds as the world transitioned from day to night and Faerie temporarily lost contact with the mortal realm. That was also the time most fae magics dissolved. It was unpleasant, but passed quickly.

Tonight was different.

Sunset hit like a fist to my guts and the air rushed out of me in a violent exhale. Outside the car, I saw Nori pitch forward, her glamour vanishing.

The magic of Faerie rushed out of the world, but it didn't immediately rush back in, and for a moment, I couldn't catch my breath, my very blood feeling like it was consuming itself. The sensations lasted nearly a minute before they passed, leaving me exhausted, as if the entire day had caught up with me in one fell swoop.

My father watched me, his features devoid of expression. He hadn't been wearing his glamour, so I couldn't tell if sunset hit him as hard as it had me and Nori, but there was a slight tightening around his eyes that made me suspect he'd felt something, even if it hadn't been as drastic as what I'd experienced.

"What *was* that?" I asked, my voice coming out raw, painful.

"That was sunset."

Like I hadn't figured that part out. I grimaced at

him more than frowned, and he reached down without a word and pulled a bottle of water out of some unseen cooler built into the side of the car. Then he tossed it to me. I accepted gratefully, twisting off the top and taking several large gulping swallows. The cold water helped, and I felt almost back to normal when I replaced the cap, half the bottle already gone.

"It's going to get worse every sunset and sunrise," my father said, watching me. "You are familiar with the right of open roads?"

I nodded. "It allows a fae to pass through another court's territory."

"Yes, but only for twelve hours. That time is significant. It prevents the fae in question from being away from their own land for too long, from experiencing too many sunsets or rises." He frowned. "Every fae in Nekros—on this continent—if the other seasons' doors are gone as well, is in danger of fading if they linger here."

I swallowed hard. "How long do they . . . we . . . have?"

"A week? Two at most? Everyone needs to return to their courts."

"That seems really fast. I wandered around a lot longer than two weeks before I established my tie to winter." I'd also started fading and nearly dragged my friends who were tied to me down with me. But it had taken more than a month from the time my full fae nature emerged before it became a noticeable issue.

"You had no court tie, but you were still surrounded by Faerie. The land is no longer tied to Faerie here. The magic that sustains the fae has been cut off. You now only have what ambient magic was left—most of which was lost during sunset—and what is in your own blood and bones."

Shit. That didn't sound good at all.

"How do we fix it? Can we plant a new amaranthine tree?"

"If the amaranthine trees are destroyed . . ."

"Can we replant them?"

He frowned, turning again to look out the window. Then his shoulders twitched ever so slightly backward, his fingers flexing in the slightest show of surprise. I glanced out the window as well, but in the gloom, I couldn't see much.

"What?" I asked, squinting. The temptation to open my shields and gaze across planes to try to see whatever it was that had startled him was there, but I had no idea how much longer I'd be at this scene, and I needed as much of my poor eyesight as I could manage. While gazing across planes would give me an immediate picture of the world around me, it would cost me at least part of my vision after.

"The tree . . ." my father said, his frown stretching downward. "It is no longer visible."

"That seems like a good thing. Maybe sunset reset whatever was wrong with the VIP area. It was unnerving with it half in, half out of the pocket of Faerie." Or perhaps it had been visible because of a spell we hadn't yet located, something malicious that had been planted alongside the bomb and fire spell, but that sunset degraded.

My father's frown didn't lessen. "Perhaps," he said, but his voice was empty, cold. Not a lot of hope to be found in that tone. He turned back toward me. "I should go. This conversation has gone on much longer than a briefing should have lasted."

He cared about his image as a Humans First Party member at a time like this? Screw that. "Is there a way to repair Nekros? Can we plant a new amaranthine tree? Is there some other way to establish a door?"

"There are no amaranthine trees to replace the lost ones with."

Fae can't lie, and there was no wiggle room in that statement. But fae can be wrong.

"I found one. A sapling. Just a few months ago." It

had also promptly disappeared after Falin and I had taken it to the former queen, but its existence at all proved that there was at least one spare tree somewhere.

Again surprise flitted across my father's face, his features so strange and foreign unglamoured, and yet also oddly familiar, as, while I'd never held much resemblance to the face he wore as Governor Caine, I could see hints of myself in his fae face. His eyes narrowed a moment, evaluating me.

"That's not possible. The High King created and planted the amaranthine trees. They can't be propagated. There are no spares."

I frowned. "I found one. It was here, in Nekros."

"Impossible. It must have only resembled the amaranthine."

I crossed my arms over my chest. "It was only a sapling, and it was sucking down belief magic already, but it hadn't formed a door yet. It was most definitely an amaranthine tree."

My father stared at me, and my back straightened in my seat as I met his glare head-on. Then he turned and pushed a button on a small control panel at his side.

"James, prepare to leave as soon as Agent Craft exits the vehicle."

"Yes, sir," a male voice said over an intercom I couldn't see, and then the car, which had been idling this entire conversation, shifted as the driver put it in gear.

Welp, I guess that was my dismissal. I slid across the seat, reaching for the door handle, but my father speaking again made me pause.

"Alexis, you need to get out of this city before you begin fading. You should go to Faerie, but even another winter territory would be better than staying here. There is nothing you can do in Nekros. Do not go looking for an amaranthine tree. Leave. Faerie needs planeweavers, and you are not enough as the only one."

I bristled, turning back toward him. "I'm not just abandoning all the fae in Nekros without at least trying to find a way to fix this."

"What can you do here, Alexis? Are you planning on raising the dead? Would they know anything the survivors do not? Are you an expert on bombs? Or destructive magic? No? Then return to Faerie."

I glared at him. "Even if I wanted to flee to Faerie, my agents are reporting that while all the other winter doors are intact, they are locked."

"Your Andrews was too young to hold a court. I'm surprised he survived this long." He waved a hand, dismissing the fact that Falin may be dead as if it didn't matter, and my jaw clenched. He didn't even notice, but continued by saying, "Invoke the right of open roads and walk through any other season's door. Hunker down in the shadow court until this all passes."

I glared, not even really seeing him through the haze of anger and pain washing over me. Then without a word, I slid across the seat and threw open the door, clambering out without another word—not that I could have uttered one through the grinding of my teeth.

"Get to the safety of Faerie, Alexis," he said, his voice following me out of the vehicle.

He must have used magic to ensure only I heard his words, because there were several people in the street around the limo who no doubt would have found that command very odd for the Humans First Party governor. But no one reacted. I didn't turn back and acknowledge his command. Slamming the limo door, I stepped back, and the limo rolled forward, toward the barricades, as soon as I was clear.

"That was a long briefing," Nori said as she approached, her eyebrows high in an implied question.

I glared at her before reining in the expression. Nori wasn't who I was infuriated with. Sucking in a deep breath and letting it back out, I forced my expression to soften. "I took a call in the middle of the briefing.

Winter's wasn't the only door bombed. Spring and summer were attacked as well. I'm waiting to hear about fall."

Nori didn't blanch, or if she did, it didn't translate through her glamour-created skin tone, but the sickly surprised expression that left her lips slightly parted and her eyes too wide made me guess that under the glamour, all the blood had just drained from her face. "That . . . Who would do this? And why?"

And wasn't that the question.

"Are their courts also locked?"

"I don't know," I said, heading back toward the command tent. "I heard the news from a human source."

Nori didn't say anything, but fell in step beside me. Her unseen wings once again were emitting that ear-splitting sound as she rubbed them together beneath her glamour.

My phone buzzed as I neared the glow of the command tent. I dug it out of my purse, hoping it was Agent Bleek with good news. It wasn't the FIB office, but one of my roommates, Caleb. He was fae, and no doubt had been hit as hard as the rest of us during sunset. Every fae on this continent likely had been, but most didn't know why. Yet.

"Hey, Caleb, you okay?" I asked by way of greeting.

"Something is wrong," he said, and I could hear the undercurrent of panic in his deep voice.

"I know. And it's bad. The amaranthine tree was destroyed. I'm at the crime scene. I . . . I don't know what we are going to do yet. We are working on it." That was as reassuring as I could be.

There was silence on the line for a long moment, and if I hadn't been able to hear his slightly ragged breaths, I might have thought I'd lost the call. Then he said, "Maybe that explains it. Al, the castle. It's gone."

I froze, one foot still hanging in the air, midstep. Then that foot dropped, awkward and unsteady.

"What? How? Where?"

"I don't know, Al." Panic laced Caleb's voice, making the words thready. "It's . . . just gone. The door just opens to the empty backyard."

Nori, who'd been walking beside me, turned to stare at me. I barely saw her.

How could the castle be gone? That was where I lived with a half dozen friends. It had superimposed itself into its own little pocket of folded space inside the mortal realm when I'd first aligned with the winter court. But now . . . the winter court had no hold on this land. And the castle, along with its mixed pocket of Faerie and reality, was gone.

"Who was inside when it vanished?" I asked, my voice sounding very far away. When had it vanished? When the amaranthine tree was destroyed, or during sunset? If it was this afternoon . . . Where was Rianna? She was a changeling. If she was caught outside of Faerie during sunset, she'd turn to dust.

"Rianna made it home earlier. I heard her and Desmond pass through the house about an hour ago. So, after that at some point?"

Sunset then. It had to be. But if Rianna was in the castle when it vanished, where was she now? Had the castle moved to Faerie? Or somewhere else in mortal reality? Somewhere winter still held? Or, hell, it could be back in limbo—it had spent several months there when I first inherited it. Wherever it was, I had to hope it had still shielded Rianna from the time *between* during sunset.

"Holly?" I asked.

"At Tamara's."

So, safe then.

"With Holly out, I was working late in my studio. PC is here with me," Caleb said, and I would have been embarrassed to admit how relieved I was to hear that my dog hadn't gotten whisked away to parts unknown.

Nope, just one of my best friends, probably a brownie, a garden gnome, dozens of gargoyles, and . . .

Shit. Roy and Icelynne, the two ghosts who'd moved in, were likely in the castle as well. The reality at the castle was blended, part the planes typical for the mortal realm, including the land of the dead, but with enough Faerie that it could sustain a changeling. But if the castle had returned to Faerie proper, there would be no land of the dead. What would happen to the ghosts?

I almost asked Caleb if he'd seen them, if they'd been at the castle or if they'd gone to Tongues for the Dead for the day. But of course, Caleb wouldn't have seen them. He wasn't a grave witch. He couldn't see ghosts.

Shit. This was bad. I paced back and forth, the phone clutched to my ear, but neither Caleb nor I speaking.

"Al, with the door gone . . . what are we going to do?" Caleb finally asked, his deep voice sounding lost. Caleb was an independent who held no love for the courts. But he was still fae. He needed Faerie to survive.

And Holly . . . she wasn't fae, wasn't even a changeling, but she was addicted to Faerie food. Mortal fares turned to dust on her tongue, providing her no nourishment. Without my enchanted castle serving up a feast daily, what would she eat? It wasn't like the Bloom was going to open back up its kitchen anytime soon.

My gaze fell on the spot where the charred amaranthine tree had darkened the skyline all afternoon. In the darkness, I wouldn't have been able to see it even if it were still visible, but my father had said it vanished at sunset. I stopped pacing. My castle apparently vanished at sunset as well.

"Caleb, I have to go," I said, already running toward the Bloom.

Running when you can see only a foot or so in front of you isn't the best idea, especially when the ground is littered with the remains of a blasted-out building. I brushed by several people and might have knocked over one. Lights had been brought into the Bloom, long extension cables snaking from them to huge generators outside the building. I was lucky I didn't trip and break something in my mad dash, but at least I could see by the time I started scrambling over crumbling walls.

I reached the misshapen opening where the VIP door had been and dashed through the jagged doorway. And dropped three feet down into the alley beside the Bloom.

The pocket of Faerie holding the VIP room and the remains of the amaranthine tree was gone.

Chapter 12

Chaos consumed the scene after my discovery that the VIP room had vanished with sunset. The humans didn't understand. The fae around me seemed to bounce back and forth between a state of numb horror and frantic panic, neither of which was conducive to, well, anything. I spent the time feeling more and more useless. My father had been right, there was nothing here I could contribute. That was especially true now that the bulk of the crime scene had vanished.

At nine I told Nori I was ready to leave. She offered no resistance. She'd been uncharacteristically quiet since the Bloom's disappearing act. She'd barely said anything aside from a short argument with Martinez over the fire spell we'd removed from the amaranthine tree. The charm, still contained in the Anti-Black Magic Unit's magic-dampening box, was more or less all the physical evidence that we still had. The bomb techs had removed a few fragments they thought might have been part of the detonation device, but everything else had vanished with the VIP room. Out of clues that might lead to who had caused the explosion, the spell was our best lead. Fae spell, fae location, and fae victims—at least of that particular magic—so we had clear jurisdiction. I agreed to allow Martinez's team to take a closer examination of the magic involved, but the charm was to remain in FIB custody. So, the charmed box was now resting on my lap as we drove in silence back to the FIB headquarters.

I was surprised to find the office still swarming with agents. The FIB office didn't close, of course, especially since there were some fae who were nocturnal either due to preference or photosensitivity, but I'd been under the impression that the night shift at headquarters was a skeleton crew. Tonight there were as many agents in house as when I'd left earlier. Maybe that should have been expected considering the events of the day, except that no one seemed to actually be doing anything.

Most of the agents were clustered in the small break room, sitting around the round table. A few sat on the floor along the wall. At least two were asleep.

"Do I need to send them home? Let them know it is okay to turn the case over to those working night shift?" I asked Nori in a hushed whisper.

She gave a wry laugh that held no humor in the sound. "If you can send them home, every fae in this room would offer you a boon."

I stared at her in confusion for half a heartbeat, and then the implication of her words sank in. "They live in Faerie? All of them? Not one has a home on this side of the door?"

I looked around the group. Every agent I'd met that day was accounted for except Moor, the satyr who'd gone to the bombing scene with us. He'd been inside the VIP room when sunset hit and we could only assume he was now wherever the rest of the Bloom had gone. I'd known that all the agents were court fae—I was the first independent in the history of winter's FIB organization post–Magical Awakening—but I hadn't really considered all the ramifications of that fact. After all, Falin had kept an apartment on this side of the door when I'd first met him. I'd just assumed that was standard for agents.

"Is there a safe house, guest house, or anything where we can lodge everyone?" I asked, studying the group.

Nori gave me an odd look, and I realized she was trying to parse out my phrases, as they were apparently not something she'd heard before.

"A place you would put guests or fae under your protection? An apartment or house the agency might own?" Hell, even holding cells would offer places for some of the agents to crash for the night, though that would be the least desirable option.

Nori shook her head. "Fae stationed outside of Nekros have mortal dwellings, but we are—were— close to the door."

So anyone taken into custody or visiting Nekros stayed in Faerie. Which didn't help house any of the agents until we fixed the door.

This might be the main office for winter's FIB on this continent, but it wasn't a huge organization. There were maybe twenty-two agents here, including Nori and Tem. Still, that was twenty-two displaced people who needed a place to go. If my castle hadn't vanished, I would have considered taking them home with me, but Caleb's house had even less space than the FIB office.

"What is the daily limit on the card Fa—the king— gave me? Do I have enough to rent hotel rooms for everyone? Are there other petty cash accounts we can use to make sure everyone has somewhere to stay tonight?"

Nori opened her mouth to answer, but a chair scraping across the floor as it pushed back cut her off.

"Ma'am, if it is all the same to you, I'd rather stay here with other courtiers," a male fae said. His skin was pale gray, which should have made him look sickly, but with his dark hair shifting in an unfelt breeze and his eyes glowing with an inner light, he came off more as eerie, like he would have been more in his essence stalking through a thick fogbank. His voice was familiar, though.

"Agent Bleek?" I asked, and he nodded, his hair defying gravity to float around him. Other fae nodded and murmured their agreement with his statement. Well, suit themselves. "You and anyone else who wishes to bed down here is of course welcome to until we can make other arrangements. Anyone who would rather have a real bed, we will rent a hotel room for. What supplies will you need for the night?"

In the end, only about five agents accepted the offer of a hotel room. With almost everyone staying, we needed to make a supply run for pillows and sleeping bags, as well as some basic groceries, though the office had only a mini-fridge and microwave, so there weren't a lot of options there. A long debate started on why not just glamour everything needed, but Nori pointed out the fact that with the local tie to Faerie gone, magic needed to be conserved as it might not be replenished. It was a sound argument, and Nori, Tem, and I ended up going on the supply run. I probably could have had Nori drop me off on the way, but these were my people now; I'd do what I could.

By the time everyone was set for the night, either with supplies or in one of the only hotels in the Magic Quarter, and the fire spell was stored securely in a safe in my office, I was dragging. It had been a long day. I considered bunking down in my office, but I did have a home to go back to, so I didn't need to add any more crowding to the office. I felt bad having Nori take yet another trip to drop me off—she'd had as long a day as I had—but I couldn't drive myself. Beyond not being able to see, I didn't have my car.

"Do any of the agents have the ability to contact Faerie through magical means?" I asked as we drove back to Caleb's house. "Through mirrors, perhaps?" Because I'd seen that done more than once, so I knew it was possible.

I couldn't see Nori in the darkness of the car, but I could feel her stare at me. "No," she said after several seconds passed. "That is primarily a Sleagh Maith magic."

Oh. Right. And I was the only Sleagh Maith in the FIB, but I certainly had no idea how to do it. Yeah, I was feeling more and more useless.

It was midnight when I trudged up the steps to my old loft. My heart raced as I scanned the landing, trying to force my bad eyes to pick out any misplaced shape that might indicate more roses had been left, but the porch was clear. I'd seen no more roses since the bouquets this morning. Maybe I wouldn't see any more. After all, we were cut off from Faerie, so unless my stalker had stranded himself as well, he was probably not even in the realm anymore.

I'd just inserted my key in the lock when a face appeared in the center of my door, startling me. The fact that I could see the face despite the darkness, and that the face moved *through* the solid wood of the door, should have tipped me off whose face it had to be, but I still jumped, stumbling back enough that I nearly tripped down the stairs.

Roy's eyes flew wide, his glasses slipping down his nose, and he grabbed my arm, steadying me. I guess, for once, it was a good thing ghosts were solid to me.

"Don't do that!" I hissed as I straightened, sucking down an unsteady breath. I moved farther from the edge to the step.

The ghost looked momentarily confused, his shoulders slumping as he pushed his glasses back into place. "Don't help you?"

"Don't startle me. You can't just pop out at me through a door like that. Give me some warning next time," I said, shoving my key back into the lock. Then

I turned and gave Roy a quick one-armed hug, which was awkward, because I really wasn't a hugger, but I'd spent most of the night thinking he'd probably gotten dragged to Faerie, where ghosts couldn't exist. "I'm glad you're okay."

Now the ghost looked even more startled, and he shoved his glasses up again, even though they hadn't slipped this time and if he kept pushing at them like that, they were going to go through his face.

"Uh, yeah. I'm okay, but Alex, something really weird is going on," he said, following me into the one-room loft. "The castle is gone. I mean, I know it just kind of appeared one day, so easy come easy go, but how does a castle vanish?"

"What has happened?" a gruff voice asked from farther inside my small one-room apartment. "I came home and there was no home."

Ms. B, who had been sitting on the lone barstool I owned, repositioned herself so she could stand on the stool. At barely two and a half feet tall, even adding the stool's height to hers, the small brownie wasn't quite as tall as me, but what she lacked in size, she made up for in personality. The small fae woman was an intimidating force to be reckoned with, and right now she was angry enough that her quill-like hair bristled and the items on the counter behind her rattled with her displeasure. I didn't think that anger was directed at me, but it was still there, below the surface and very close to erupting.

Unfortunately, I didn't have news that was likely to calm her. I just hoped she didn't go full boggart when I shared it. Judging by the way the cabinets closest to her kept clattering open and closed, I wasn't holding my breath.

Looking around the room, I spotted Icelynne, a ghost who had once been a handmaiden to the former queen. She'd been haunting my castle since I'd helped find her killer several months ago. She and Roy must

have both been out of the castle at sunset. Thank goodness. I had no idea what they'd been doing—Roy fan-
cied himself an unofficial PI at Tongues for the Dead,
but Icelynne rarely left the castle grounds. Wherever
they'd been, I was thankful they hadn't been dragged
to a place with no plane for them to exist upon.

"I'm not sure where the castle is," I said, and the
cabinet door behind Ms. B slammed hard enough that
the wood creaked, making me wince before I continued. "Someone bombed the Bloom today. The amaranthine tree was destroyed and at sunset, it seems all
the pockets of Faerie must have . . . moved. We are
currently cut off from Faerie."

The rattling and banging suddenly ceased, and the
silence in the room was almost worse. Ms. B stared at
me for a long moment, her dark eyes searching for
some other meaning to my words. Then she covered
her face with her small hands. She made no sound, but
her shoulders quivered as she sank down into a slump
on the stool. Roy paced the confined space of the small
kitchenette, his features pinched with his thoughts,
though he looked more intrigued than worried. Icelynne was the least affected by the news, her head
cocked slightly to the side, studying me as she hovered
silently on her snowflake wings.

"Who would do that?" she asked, sounding more
appalled by the fact that someone had dared attack
Faerie than concerned about the ramifications. Of
course, as a ghost, she'd already lost everything. My
castle had been as close to returning to Faerie as she'd
ever likely get.

I opened my mouth to answer. Closed it. Ryese was
still the first name that popped in my mind, but why
would he have attacked the other courts as well?
Maybe I was wrong. Could this be a terrorist act coming from outside Faerie?

"So what are we going to do to fix it?" Roy asked,
filling the silence.

And that was why I'd never exorcised Roy out of existence. Okay, I wouldn't have done that anyway, but out of everyone I'd talked to since the explosion who'd heard about the lost door, he was the first who asked how it could be fixed. The fae all seemed to already be mourning the loss of Nekros. My father had certainly not been any beacon of optimism. But Roy, my awkward ghostly sidekick, not only asked how to fix it, but said "we," including himself in whatever plan I might be formulating. I could have hugged him again.

I didn't. It had been weird enough the first time I did it. Once in a night was more than too many. Still, I appreciated the support. Now if only I had an answer or at least an idea. But I didn't.

"I'm not sure," I said and sank onto the edge of my bed because with Ms. B on my only stool, it was the only place to sit. "I need to reach Falin in Faerie. The winter court is apparently locked down again. I'm not sure about the other seasons. Spring's and summer's doors were also attacked. Maybe fall's as well," I added, realizing I'd never heard back from Agent Bleek on that front. "So I guess the first step is figuring out how to establish contact with Faerie. On this side of the door several courts suffered attacks to their doors. What happened inside? After that, well, I guess it depends on what we learn, but I think we need to find a new amaranthine tree." And regardless of what my father thought, I had found one before. It was out there; I just had to find it again. Or figure out how it had been propagated.

"That's not much of a plan," Icelynne said and I frowned at her. Not that I disagreed.

"Maybe the first part of the plan should be getting some sleep. You look beat, Al," Roy said.

He had a point there.

The ghosts didn't need sleep, so Roy and Icelynne said their good-byes and arm in arm sank deeper into the land of the dead because I'd long ago forbidden

Roy from hanging out in my room while I was getting ready for bed. Not that I had much getting ready to do. My little room-over-the-garage apartment hadn't been an actual residence in months. I'd left some things here, like my electronics since my castle didn't have electricity, and all my mismatched dishes and furniture as they hadn't been needed in the enchanted Faerie castle. But my clothes? Toiletries? Those had long ago been moved to the castle. Which meant they'd all vanished at sunset.

Ms. B was still crying silently on the stool, and I didn't know what to say or do to comfort the small brownie. I would have offered her chocolate if I had any, but my stash of candy was also in the castle. So I let her be and took the inner stairs down to the main part of the house.

The main floor was quiet and mostly dark. Caleb had left a lamp on in the living room, likely knowing I'd come downstairs. I found PC, my tiny Chinese Crested dog, curled up in a gray and white ball on the couch. He looked up as I walked close and then jumped to his feet, yipping happily.

"Shhh. You'll wake everyone," I whispered, picking him up.

He wiggled happily, tail wagging. I hugged him close, his hairless body almost too warm, but right now, that was exactly what I needed. After accepting at least a dozen dog kisses on my chin, I set him down and headed back for my loft, PC at my heels.

Ms. B was no longer on the stool when I reached the room. I looked around, alarmed. The small closet door stood open, and when I stepped around it, I found Ms. B standing on the edge of the middle shelf, shaking her head as she dug through the spare linens.

"They're all musty from disuse," she said, her voice somewhere between disgust and dismay. She snatched a thick comforter, pulling it free and giving it a vigorous shake all in one motion. A prickle of magic filled the air, and I guessed the comforter was now fresh and clean.

I considered repeating some of the points several of the fae had made on why magic and glamour needed to be conserved, but brownies were a tidy and fastidious lot. My musty linen closet not only provided a distraction from the events of the day, but I doubted she would bed down in anything less than brownie-approved clean.

"Do you want my bed?" I asked as she refolded the large comforter with a flick of her wrist, the heavy material defying gravity to arrange itself neatly. "I can head downstairs to the guest room."

Ms. B gave a dismissive wave of her hand. "Your bed is much too big and open for my liking," she said, hopping from the shelf with the folded comforter in her arms. She'd added a pillowcase as well, though no pillow, and the two-item stack was taller than she was. That didn't slow her down. She scurried across the small kitchenette, her green quill-like hair dragging behind her.

She stopped in front of one of the lower cabinets, and it opened on its own. Ms. B carried in her pile of linens, arranging the thick comforter on the bottom of the cabinet like she was creating a den. She didn't even have to rearrange anything to do it. While I'd left all my kitchen gear in the apartment, I hadn't actually ever owned much—I was a ramen noodles or nuked hot pocket kind of a chef.

Once the small brownie had arranged the comforter into a cushy nest, she tucked herself in with the pillowcase as a blanket. "Good night," she said in her gruff voice, and then the cabinet door closed without anyone touching it.

Okay then. A cabinet didn't look like somewhere I'd want to sleep, but then I wasn't a two-foot-tall brownie. I splashed some water on my face and made a mental note to buy some essentials. I should have picked some up while I'd been shopping for the FIB agents, but I hadn't thought about it. Then I slid off my boots, placed my dagger under my pillow, and settled into bed, as I didn't have anything to change into.

Then I lay there, staring at the darkness of the ceiling. It was late. The day had been more than exhausting, and yet my mind wouldn't stop. I had no idea what to do, but I needed to do something. How was I going to reach Falin? I considered calling my father and seeing if he would help me, but I doubted he would. If he'd been willing to contact Faerie for me, he likely would have offered when I'd seen him earlier. And even if he were willing, I doubted he'd contact Falin for me. He seemed to hate the knight-turned-king for reasons he'd never expounded upon and he'd been more than willing to accept the locked doors to mean Falin had lost the throne. No, my father would likely contact Dugan . . .

I sat up in bed. Dugan owed me no small amount of favors, and I didn't need my father's help to try to contact the Shadow Prince. He'd told me once that every secret made its way to the shadowed halls. That there were fae in the court who did nothing but listen to the secrets that were whispered in darkness. I'd tried calling for Dugan before, the last time the winter court had locked, and he hadn't come. But, to be fair, his own court was dealing with a lot at the time, and Nekros had been as locked as the door to Faerie. I had no idea if that was the case this time, or if Faerie pulling out of Nekros would also sever the ties from darkness to the shadow court, but it couldn't hurt to try.

I flipped on a lamp so that the room was cast in an artificial orange glow that made all the shadows grow long and dark. Then I climbed out of bed, looking for the deepest of the shadows. With my bad eyes, they all looked pretty deep, but the corner of the room, where the dresser and TV blocked the light of the small lamp, seemed my best option.

"Hello," I said, leaning into the dark shadow. "I need to speak to Prince Dugan of the shadow court."

I felt ridiculous, talking to the shadow, but I had to try. If this didn't work, I'd have to go to my father.

Several minutes passed with nothing happening except PC deciding I'd lost my mind and abandoning me for the comfort of the bed. Okay, maybe I needed to try something different. Maybe just talking to a shadow wouldn't gather the listeners' attention. Maybe it actually had to be a secret. They were the court of shadows and secrets, after all. Dreams too, though that part of their realm had been cut off.

"I have a secret. I'm in way too deep with this case, and I'm not sure what to do. I could use some help and I'm willing to trade one of the favors Prince Dugan owes me for some assistance." Okay, not much of a secret. Anyone who'd been paying attention would have picked up on the fact that I was floundering.

I waited, but nothing happened. After several minutes, I sighed and stepped back. What had I expected?

I trudged back to bed, but I didn't turn off the light. Not yet. My brain was still way too busy. Instead I dragged out my laptop and opened up an Internet browser. Searching for the latest news headlines from across the country proved that all four courts had suffered bombings today.

Humans tended to think of the FIB as some huge fae conglomeration. That was hardly the case. Each court policed its own territories, which included those in the mortal realm, but they didn't collaborate with other courts. The lack of any interagency communication meant my FIB agents could not provide me with any contacts to FIB offices in other courts.

But that was what the Internet was for.

A cursory search suggested that summer had no FIB offices in their territory, at least none that listed any contact information online. Fall had a single number listed for an office located in the folded space where their door was located, so I grabbed my phone and dialed the number. It was ridiculously late, but most likely someone was working the phones, especially if their day had gone like ours had.

"Hi, yes, this is Special Agent Alex Craft with the Nekros City–based FIB office. I'd like to speak to the special agent in charge," I said to the perky-sounding woman who answered the phone by asking how my call should be directed. Who was perky at nearly two in the morning?

There was a long pause on the other end of the line. I wondered for a moment if she'd redirected me without a word, but then, in a far less bubbly voice, she said, "Nekros is winter territory."

"I'm aware."

"You've reached an office in fall."

"I'm aware of that as well. May I speak to the agent in charge?"

There was another pause, and then, "This is *fall*." She put emphasis on the season, as if I hadn't heard her the first time.

"Yes. And the news reported that there was an explosion at a fae-owned establishment there today. Winter was also attacked today. Our door was destroyed. Did fall's door survive?"

The woman on the other end of the phone squeaked, a legitimate, high-pitched animal-like sound, and I wondered what type of fae she might be. "Winter agent, if you would like to speak to someone in fall, you will have to have your king contact ours for approval," she snapped, and then the line clicked.

She'd hung up on me.

I searched out a phone number for spring next, but no one answered. I saved the number to try again, but I didn't hold out a lot of hope after my interaction with the fall office. We were quite likely all stranded on this continent together. It would be better if we could all work together, but I seemed to be the only one of that opinion.

Chapter 13

◦──═◦ ◦═──◦

I woke to an explosion of pain in my head. I sat straight up, gasping as if I hadn't been breathing. The room around me was dark, and I blinked at the unfamiliar shadows before I remembered that I wasn't in the castle, I was in my old loft, in Caleb's house.

A weight seemed to press all the air out of me, even as I sucked down huge gulping breaths. At my side, PC looked up from the warm ball he'd tucked himself into beside my hip. He cocked his head, his eyes only half open but his ears up, erect and listening for danger. He clearly didn't hear anything that alarmed him, because he looked at me again, as if curious why I'd woken him.

Then the wards on the house fell. I stiffened. That pounding headache was still hammering at the back of my head, but the familiar feel of the house wards had vanished. They hadn't broken. There had been no feedback or snap of them overloading. They'd just stopped.

From the cabinets, I heard a gruff curse and a loud thump. PC jumped to his feet, but he just stared, not moving from his warm spot on the bed.

"Ms. B? You okay?"

"Why do I feel like I'm drowning?" her gruff voice asked from the depths of my cabinet.

Yeah, that was a good question as I was feeling it too. I started to answer that I didn't know, and then my gaze snapped toward my window. It was still pretty dark behind the blinds, but it was beginning to lighten.

"It's dawn."

But the wards were Aetheric magic. Not quite witch magic, as they'd been created by a fae, but they weren't glamour. So why had they failed?

Now that the actual moment of transition between night to day had passed, the headache was fading. Theoretically, there should have been a rush of magic flooding back into the world, but I'd never been able to feel it, and from what the fae around me had said at sunset, it hadn't happened then. I was guessing it wasn't happening now.

I waited, letting the lingering pain between my eyes dissipate. Soft snoring sounds drifted from the cabinet—Ms. B had fallen back asleep after dawn passed. But the wards weren't reactivated. The house was silent, still. There didn't seem to be anyone or anything attacking us. Was Caleb okay? Had something happened?

I pulled back the comforter and slid silently out of bed. Then I hesitated. The house was dark in the dawn light—far too dark for me to see much of anything. I grabbed my dagger from under my pillow and opened my senses. If there was someone lurking in the dark, my glowing eyes would make me an easy target, but at least I'd be able to see. A flashlight would have made me even more obvious, and wouldn't help me see nearly as well.

With my psyche seeing more than my physical eyes, I crept down the inner stairs, aware of every creak in the wood. PC didn't even try to follow me, just watched me leave from his spot on the bed.

The house was quiet in the early morning stillness

as I reached the main level. The stairs emptied me into the living room, near the door to the garage Caleb had transformed into a studio. The main controls for the wards were spelled into an ornately carved stone relief hanging on the wall beside the front door. Caleb was not only an acclaimed wardsmith, he was an artist, though with my mind peering across multiple planes, the sculpture looked very different. The intricate forest scene, with its mischievous sprites, dancing nymphs, and merrymaking green men, was chipped and cracked. The entire sculpture pulsed with a soft pink glow, not magic, but emotion. An emotion strong enough that it had imbued the entire sculpture as Caleb had carved it. I didn't fully understand that plane, I only caught glimpses of it occasionally. What I didn't see in the statue was any Aetheric energy. The thing should have been glowing with tightly woven spells that powered the house's ward network, but the rosy emotional glow was the only thing illuminating the statue. Magically, it was completely inert. Just marble.

I frowned as I walked across the room toward it. I'd made it halfway across the living room, no farther than the couch, when a door opened in the far hallway that led to the bedrooms. I froze, my hand clenching around my dagger, but other than the completely missing wards, there was nothing to suggest anything was wrong.

"Caleb? Holly?" I called out softly enough that I wouldn't wake anyone.

"Al?" Caleb's voice was rough, as if he was out of breath, and he kept a hand on the wall as he shuffled into the room.

I'd stepped wide, dropping my weight into something that at least felt like a defensive stance—Falin would be proud—my dagger clenched in my raised hand. Caleb's gaze took me in and a frown claimed his face as his eyes lingered on my weapon. Apparently he did not have any issues seeing in the early morning gloom. In my less-than-normal vision, he glowed a brilliant silver under his green skin. Among other things, my peering through the planes also let me see through glamour, so to me, he had the slightly wider features, green skin, and extra finger digits that he usually kept hidden. I wasn't sure if dawn had shattered his personal glamour and he hadn't reinstated it yet or if it was there but I couldn't see it. He looked tired, though, his shoulders slumped and his feet dragging.

"You okay?" I asked, dropping the hand holding my dagger.

"Dawn hit hard," he said, his frown lingering. I'd felt it too, but it seemed to still be draining Caleb. He seemed to realize that and made an effort to stand up straighter; it looked like it cost him, though. "Did you take the wards down?" he asked.

"No. I felt them fall and came down here thinking something may be wrong." I gave a half shrug. "How did dawn nuke the wards? Weren't they crafted with Aetheric spells?"

Caleb didn't answer, but shuffled over to the statue that should have held the wards. He placed his hand on the carved stone, closing his eyes and dipping his head as he concentrated on wards that were not there. I didn't tend to sit around watching magic while my shields were down; it made things a little too chaotic seeing emotional imprints, shimmering souls, twisting raw magic, and layers of decay as my mind tried to take in all the different planes on top of each other. Not to mention the fact that it allowed the chill of the grave to reach for me. I'd only had my psyche open a few minutes, but I was already shivering despite the heat being on in the house. But, with my shields cracked, I could see exactly how Caleb's magic reached out, poking at where the spells should have been inside the wards. It dissipated as soon as it hit the emptiness inside the statue and Caleb made a frustrated sound in his throat.

"What's happening?" Holly asked around a yawn as

she shuffled into the room. "Oh, hey, Alex." Her hand dropped to the edge of the shirt she was wearing. It was Caleb's shirt, and though it was the only thing she wore, on her petite form it was long enough that it was more modest than some dresses I saw on the street. "I didn't know you were down here. Are you okay? I heard about the explosion yesterday. Caleb said the door to Faerie is gone? What is going to happen now?"

"Everything in Nekros is going to get FUBARed, apparently," Caleb said, dropping his hand. "It's like the wards are gone."

"They are." Everyone turned to look at me at that. "There isn't a trace of magic left in the statue."

"That's . . ." Caleb stopped and then shook his head. He might have been about to say "impossible," but he was too fae to say that when the fact that it had happened was before his eyes.

"Great, so we have no wards. And probably every ward I've created under commission just failed too."

Holly walked over and slid her arms around his waist, hugging him from behind. He ran his hand over the empty statue one more time, and then turned so he could wrap his arms around her as well. He leaned forward, resting his green lips against the top of her flamered hair. It was a casually intimate gesture, one of familiarity, and it made me shuffle my feet and glance back at the door to my loft. It was still weird that my roommates were dating—oh, they were perfect for each other, even I could admit that. But that didn't make it less weird.

"So why did the door getting destroyed cause your wards to fail?" Holly asked without stepping out of Caleb's arms. "They were witch magic, weren't they?"

A good question. I'd been about to retreat back to my loft, and my bed—I'd stayed up way too late and didn't need to be at the FIB office for at least two more hours—but that question stopped me short because it was a good one. Would witch magic start failing in

Nekros? But that didn't make sense. Faerie and fae as a whole weren't typically compatible with Aetheric energy, with notable exceptions, like Caleb.

I turned back in time to see him grimace, his lips stretching down further than a human would have been able to manage. "I manipulate Aetheric energy, but that doesn't make me a witch. I'm still fae, and use fae magic to shape the Aetheric energy."

Now that made a lot more sense.

"So do you guys have a plan to fix this?" Holly asked, this time aiming the question at me.

I winced. I guessed by "you guys" she meant the FIB. And from what I could tell, no. The FIB had no idea how to even begin to address the issue.

At my silence, Holly frowned, her face turning from friendly-girl-next-door to a sterner expression, one I recognized from when I'd seen her in her element in the courtroom as an assistant DA. "That's not a sufficient response, Al. Surely you are working on something."

"I have some ideas," I said, because I had to say something. And I did have some ideas. I'd track down that sapling and get the door functioning again. Of course, the whole how that would work, or hell, how I would find the sapling was still a big question mark, but at least it was a possible direction. Yeah, okay, I was floundering.

"I should go back upstairs. I just came down because I felt the wards fall," I said, starting to step backward.

Caleb nodded, giving me the smallest of smiles. Then he turned back toward Holly. "We're going to have to leave the city," he said to her, his voice low.

"What? No. I can't leave." Holly stepped out of his arms. "I'm working two huge cases right now and I have court dates set for most of this week."

"How can we stay? You can't eat." Caleb's tone was

gentle, reasonable, but I could all but feel Holly's rising temper from across the room.

"No. No way. I can't take a vacation right now."

I'd reached the door to the inner stairs, but I glanced back. Part of me wanted to stay, to hear what decision they reached, maybe even to encourage them to stick it out a little longer. But my gaze moved from two of my best friends to the statue that had held some of the best ward magic in the city—until dawn. I couldn't encourage them to stay. Holly needed to find a source for Faerie food, and Caleb was fae. He needed an active tie to Faerie to avoid fading. No, I couldn't in good conscience ask them to trust that the FIB would fix this.

And I knew if they left, it wouldn't be a vacation.

They'd be leaving Nekros for good. Or at least until the door was reopened. They wouldn't be just leaving Nekros either, but the entire North American continent. This wasn't only an issue for two of my best friends either, but for all the fae. We all would have to leave.

I had to find a way to fix the door.

Chapter 14

I woke with a jolt for the second time that morning.
This time it was due to PC's furious barking. The six-pound dog might not be big, but he could make a lot of noise—most of it high-pitched and headache inducing. I hadn't exactly gone back to bed after dawn, but I'd drifted off while searching the Internet, my laptop still in my lap. Sunlight now filtered through the blinds, but according to the time stamp on my laptop screen, I couldn't have been asleep more than half an hour. It was one of those naps that was just long enough to leave you bleary but still exhausted.

PC bounced around at the foot of the bed, yipping as fiercely as a little dog could, and I squinted, looking around for the source of his agitation. With my bad eyes, shadows still claimed most of the room, despite the early morning light.

Then one of those shadows moved, and I jolted, fully alert now. I'd shoved my dagger back under my pillow, and I grabbed it, flicking off the small clip that kept it tucked safely in its hilt.

The shadow moved again, proving to be a small shape perched on the top of my television. It was oddly substantial for a shadow, thicker and darker than a shadow should have been in the morning sunlight. As it arched its back in a deep stretch that went all the way to its lifted tail, I realized it was the shadow of a cat.

I'd seen a displaced cat shadow before.

"Are you Dugan's cat?" I asked the shadow. Had he gotten my message last night after all?

The shadow cat cocked her head to the side, as if studying me. She had no visible eyes, but I was sure she took my measure. Then she jumped from the television and darted across the room. PC started to follow, his back legs bending in preparation of springing from the bed. I grabbed him.

"No," I said sternly, placing him back on the pillows at the head of the bed.

He gave a small whine, but I wasn't going to let him chase the shadow. Either she was Dugan's cat, and he'd sent her to contact me, or she was something else, and potentially a danger. Faerie shadows could be deadly.

"Do you have a message for me?" I asked the shadow, who had stopped by the edge of the counter separating my small kitchenette from the rest of the apartment.

The cat sat on her haunches. With no features on her face, I couldn't be sure where she looked, but I could swear I felt her unseen eyes on me, her gaze piercing and, in typical cat fashion, unimpressed. She licked a dark, insubstantial paw and ran it over her head.

What the hell does that mean? Was the cat a messenger? A spy? Just a random displaced shadow creature? With no wards, anything could get in the house, a thought that chilled me and made me grip my dagger tighter.

I slid off the bed, keeping the dagger in hand as I approached the small shadow. Before I got close enough to touch her—not that I planned to—the cat turned, darting farther into my apartment. This time she sat down directly in front of the bathroom doorway and stared at me.

Okay, I was pretty sure I was supposed to follow her.

As I stepped past the counter, a cabinet door opened and Ms. B stepped out, carrying the comforter she'd nested in during the night already neatly folded. Her gaze landed on the shadow cat, and she dropped her load of linens as her quill-like hair bristled, rustling. A miniature broom appeared in her hands, and she dashed forward.

"Out," she yelled, stopping a good two yards from the cat and waving her small broom in front of her.

"Ms. B!" I didn't dare chase after her in case the cat thought both of us were after her. "Leave the cat alone."

"It's a shadow spy!" Ms. B took another step forward, holding her broom like a jousting lance. "Never trust a shadow without a source."

"I think it's a messenger for Dugan," I said, stepping between the brownie and the cat.

"The Shadow Prince?" Ms. B sounded genuinely befuddled. "But he's shadow court."

Yeah, and I was winter. I was getting rather tired of all the hard lines fae seemed to draw between the different courts.

"He owes me a favor and I'm hoping he can help me access Faerie."

Her broom drooped and she stared at the cat for a moment. The cat hadn't moved this entire time, but her ears were no longer visible, so I guessed she had pressed them back against her head.

"Do you have a message for me?" I asked her once again.

Behind me, Ms. B gave a snort, which was quite a feat, as she didn't have a nose. "It's a shadow. It can't talk."

She had a point there. Though some shadows could, or at least they could scream—I'd witnessed that first-hand. But if this was Dugan's cat, he'd confirmed she couldn't speak. So why was the shadow here?

I took another step forward. The cat stood, circled

for a moment, and then trotted into my bathroom. There was nothing else to do but follow.

"I don't like this," Ms. B muttered as I trailed after the cat, but she stuck by my heels, her broom held aloft.

The cat shadow jumped from the floor to the bathroom counter. She paced along the edge, and then she turned, seemed to coil back, and sprang straight at the mirror behind the sink. I gasped at the sudden movement, sure she was about to bounce off the hard surface in pain, but the cat seemed to merge with her image in the mirror, leaving only a dark blotch behind. Then the blotch began expanding, the shadows spreading across the surface like spilled ink.

Ms. B made a sharp sound and scooted farther behind my legs as the darkness spread over the mirror. When the darkness covered the entire mirror, it seemed to thicken, growing even darker. Then a man appeared in the center of the darkness.

His dark hair and armor almost blended into the shadows around him, making his slightly glowing skin and light blue eyes stand out in stark contrast. He looked so solid and clear, it seemed I could have reached out and touched him. I expected him to step through the shadows consuming my mirror, but instead he gave a small bow, inclining his head toward me.

"My lady," he said as he straightened, and I found myself floundering for the proper etiquette in this situation.

Fae were big on showy etiquette. I'd seen Dugan show less deference to Faerie queens, and I wasn't royal. He, on the other hand, was a prince. Not a prince of the court I belonged to, but still a prince. Still half-hidden behind me, Ms. B dropped into an awkward but deep curtsy. That was probably expected of me as well.

My hesitating indecision was clearly noted, because a small smile touched Dugan's lips. Not a friendly smile, per se, but one that bespoke amusement.

"You look lovely this morning," he said, with that same silently laughing smile.

Now I stopped worrying about etiquette and rolled my eyes at the prince. "Oh, yes, bedhead and yesterday's sleep-rumpled outfit are simply the height of fashion in this new, Faerie-less Nekros. Drop the 'my lady' and compliments. You agreed to call off our betrothal, remember? No need to play false friendly."

He blinked at me, the amusement dropping from his face, replaced with a frown. "I was being genuine. I am perhaps rather out of practice at establishing friendships."

Now it was my turn to frown, because maybe it was me who was being an ass. I wasn't going to apologize and indebt myself, but I shook my head and said, "It's been a rough twenty-four hours. I might be ornery."

He stared at me a moment, assessing, and then he nodded, accepting my unspoken apology. Shadows moved around him, though with the darkness of the mirror, I'm not sure how I could even tell, but I saw the small shape as it darted for him, flinging itself in the air. I started to call out a warning, my hand lifting involuntarily as my mouth opened. Then the shadow of a cat landed on Dugan's shoulders. The cat traipsed across his shoulders before collapsing dramatically, draping herself around the back of Dugan's neck like a living scarf.

The prince barely reacted to the cat's sudden entrance. He simply lifted a hand and rubbed behind her ears. Large green eyes peered out at me from the black mass of shadow now draped across his shoulders, so apparently this was the more substantial shadow cat, not the shadow's shadow that had been in my bedroom.

"I heard whispers that you were looking to cash in some favors," Dugan said, still nonchalantly petting the cat. "I owe you an answer and a boon. Need I advise you not to waste either on foolish questions?"

Hopefully I didn't need that advice. I'd pondered

what I'd ask if he actually did respond. When I'd called him, I'd intended to ask after Falin. It was what I wanted to know most. But nothing about the current crisis changed regardless of the answer. Whether Faerie had locked the doors to winter because he had fallen or because of the attack on the tree, the issue still remained that Nekros was going to suffer if I didn't figure out how to reroot Faerie to the land. And for that, I needed an amaranthine tree.

"Several months ago I found an amaranthine sapling in the floodplains. We dug it up and took it to the winter court, but it vanished. Ryese was left alone with it, and I'm sure he secreted it away. I'd like shadow to locate and, if possible, secure it. Surely the tree's location must fall into the purview of secrets."

Dugan blinked at me, the surprise evident on his features. "I truly expected you to inquire after your ... king." His hesitation before the last word made me suspect he'd been going to say something else.

He lifted a hand and ran his thumb along his jaw, his eyes going distant in thought. Then his gaze sharpened, landing on me once more. "I do not know the location of the sapling, but I will make some inquiries and try to find it."

I nodded, not thanking him, as you don't thank a fae for repaying a boon.

"Is that all?" he asked, studying me again.

No. Not hardly. But I only had so many favors I could trade in. I could ask if he knew who was behind the explosions, but if he didn't, that would be his answer and the favor would be wasted. I'd look into it myself first.

At my silence, the prince nodded. "Well then, I will look for the sapling as your boon, but in the name of friendship, I will gift you this." He seemed to take a step closer, filling the mirror surface. "The Winter King lives. He is injured, but should heal. Light's most fearsome warrior cannot say the same."

Falin is alive.

My knees went soft, nearly dropping me to the ground as relief washed over me. My breath caught, my heart knocking against my rib cage, and I pressed a hand over my mouth to prevent any relieved gushing of thanks that threatened to bubble out. The news that he was still alive was like a weight falling from me. It changed nothing about the dangers to everyone else around me, but it still made everything inside me lighten, like everything else had just become slightly more manageable. And Dugan had given me more than just reassurance that Falin lived. If light's most fearsome warrior was dead, that implied it had been the light court that had attacked him, either in an official duel or otherwise. More and more indications that Ryese was behind this.

I took a deep breath, pressing my lips tight as I nodded to Dugan before finally babbling, "I would hug you if you were really here."

Dugan gave a faint, very small smile, but it was one of his rare genuine expressions. "That would be difficult as there is only one place on your entire continent that has enough of Faerie left that our planebender could reach the shadows."

I froze because that seemed like information he was once again gifting me. It confirmed the other trees had been destroyed. One spot on the entire continent still tied to Faerie . . . Where? If I could find it, would the planebender help me reach Faerie? I'd cashed in the favor Dugan himself owed me, but the shadow court as a whole also owed me a favor. I tucked this information away.

"Shadow Prince," Ms. B said, her gruff voice uncharacteristically thin. She'd never risen from her curtsy, likely because he'd never acknowledged her, so she addressed her words toward the floor as she spoke. "We've friends who vanished with the missing parts of Faerie. In all my history, I've heard of doors moving,

but never of doors being destroyed. Alex's castle, and
the people inside it, are they somewhere safe? Or . . . ?"

I blinked at her. Faerie moved things all the time.
I'd assumed everything that had vanished Faerie had
just relocated. But I'd be the first to admit I had no idea
how Faerie worked, and now fear wiggled through me
as well as guilt that I hadn't even considered the possibility.

"Are you looking to trade, little brownie?" Dugan
asked, considering the fae still half-hidden behind my
legs. The quills in her hair rattled softly. Usually that
was a sign of her anger, but now it was because she was
trembling.

"Yes, I—" she said, but I took a step forward and cut
her off.

"No, she's not, but I am."

Dugan frowned at me. I crossed my arms over my
chest and lifted my chin, meeting his gaze. My friends
had vanished too, so if anyone traded for information,
it was better for it to be me, not Ms. B, who was terrified of the prince. Not that I planned to use my question on it, but we could come to some new deal. Dugan
and I stared at each other for a moment, and then he
shook his head, not in negation but in wry amusement.

"And just yesterday you berated yourself as a coward," he said, reaching up to scratch behind the ears of
the shadow cat draped across his shoulders. I went
completely still. Had I said that aloud at the crime
scene? Somewhere shadows could have overheard me?
I'm not sure what my expression betrayed, but the
smallest of smiles touched his mouth before he said,
"My bargaining with the brownie has already begun,
but do not take up your sword and shield yet, my lady
champion. What she has asked is a very minor trade,
and for a friend of my friend, I shall offer a good deal."
He lowered his gaze toward Ms. B, who had actually
looked up during this exchange, her large dark eyes
wide. "For the answer you seek, I would take your

shadow to serve in my court for a single day—from now until sunset. Do you accept this trade?"

Her hair rattled louder, and the slits that served as nostrils on her noseless face flared with fear, but she nodded. "I agree to your terms, Shadow Prince."

I wanted to stop her, to intervene, but I knew enough about Faerie bargains to know that it was already done. She was scared, but she'd agreed without hesitation, so I guessed whatever it meant to have one's shadow serve in the shadow court for a day must not be too horrible.

"Your friends are safe. Faerie moved the castle into the winter court. The inhabitants who were inside the castle at the time of its relocation are locked inside the court like the rest of winter, but once the court re-opens, you should be able to locate the castle and your companions with ease."

At his words, a soft sigh of relief slipped from Ms. B's lips. While I had no doubt she was happy to hear Rianna and Desmond were all right, I guessed her true concern had been for the shy garden gnome who tended the grounds.

I cocked an eyebrow at the prince. "Knew that one off the top of your head, did you?"

He shrugged, jostling the shadow cat enough that she cracked open her emerald-green eyes. "I did attempt to anticipate what you might ask of me. The welfare of your lover, the location of your missing castle, and the closest point you could cross into Faerie were all possibilities I considered. I admit, your request to find a sapling took me rather off guard." Again, the smallest hint of amusement touched his features, but it faded quickly as he focused on Ms. B again. "Step forward, little brownie. It would not do for your shadow to be tangled with our planeweaver's." He held out a hand, beckoning her closer.

Ms. B shuffled forward. Not far—she wouldn't be able to see the mirror at her height if she moved too much closer—but she stepped up beside me. Dugan made a sweeping motion with his hand, and the brownie's shadow, which was being cast by the lights ringing the mirror, suddenly stretched and then jumped sideways. The shadow darted forward, leaping onto the sink before hurling itself into the darkness of the mirror. Ms. B shuddered as her shadow melted into the surface the same way the cat had.

"Your shadow will return at sunset," Dugan said, the words stiff and formal. Ms. B only nodded, not making a sound. Then Dugan turned back toward me. "I shall look into your sapling. I'll send Ciara again when I know something." He reached out and scritched the cat, who I guessed was Ciara.

I nodded and the shadows in the mirror began to swirl, the edges clearing as the darkness seemed to pull in, toward Dugan's form. When there was just a small ring left around the prince, he looked up, his eyes locking on mine.

"Good luck, my lady. But should you need it, remember that my court will always welcome you."

Then the shadows faded and I found myself staring at only my own reflection.

Chapter 15

After a quick shower—thankfully Caleb had some basic toiletries he let me borrow—I was feeling much more ready to face the rest of the day. With Dugan helping look for a sapling, I at least had some forward movement toward a plan. And Ms. B had worked some brownie cleaning magic on my clothes while I'd been showering—she'd even repaired the charred spots in my pants—so while I was back in the same outfit as the previous day, I was at least clean and no longer smelled like I'd spent too long at a barbecue serving scorched plastic.

Roy and Icelynne returned while I was getting ready. Even though the brownie couldn't actually see her, Icelynne volunteered to stay with Ms. B. The brownie was headed to Tongues for the Dead to mind the office. With me working with the FIB and Rianna stuck in Faerie, someone needed to man the office, and Ms. B had appointed herself office manager months ago, so it made sense. Roy seemed reluctant to separate from Icelynne, but ultimately decided to accompany me.

I picked up breakfast on my drive toward the FIB

office, taking a slight detour to drive by the Bloom on
the way. Most of the blockades were gone, though the
street immediately surrounding the bombed building
was taped off and official personnel were still working
through the scene. They were no longer maintaining a
thousand-yard perimeter, though, and it looked like the
surrounding businesses were reopened, so apparently
they were no longer concerned about the possibility of
a secondary explosion.

"Whoa, is this normal?" Roy asked as I approached
the FIB building.

"Not at all."

The grounds were absolutely crawling with fae. A
centaur galloped across the parking lot as I turned in,
making me slam on my brakes to avoid clipping him.
A group of nymphs gathered in the green space near
the lot entrance, three women wearing only feathers
despite the chill in the morning air not far behind
them. An entire contingent of goblins stood on the
lawn, none taller than four feet and with skin colors
that ranged from pale pink to mustard yellow to a few
such a deep purple they almost looked black. Fae
milled about the grounds, but even more were gathered
around the building entrance, like shoppers waiting for
the doors to open at a major chain store on Black
Friday.

Despite the crowd, the parking lot was oddly empty
of vehicles. I was sure it had been full the night before.
This morning I pulled in beside a sleek black sedan
and we were the only two cars in the lot.

Roy stood, the motion putting him through the roof
of my vehicle, because that wasn't disturbing. Not that
the ghost noticed.

"What are they all doing here?"

"I don't know," I said as I killed the engine and
climbed from the car.

A lot of stares landed on me as I shut the car door,
and I made a mental note to not talk to the ghost no

one else could see. Most of the looks I received appeared cautiously curious, some suspicious, and a few
downright hostile. I noted those looks, making sure to
take a path that didn't put me too close to them but
also didn't look like I was trying to avoid them. Roy
trailed behind me, gawking. He'd been hanging around
for over half a year now, but even I had never seen this
many unusual, unglamoured fae outside of Faerie.

A light-plum-colored goblin with four legs, three of
which he used to walk but one scrawny and short,
hanging limp from his side, scuttled up to me as I
reached the back of the crowd gathered around the entrance.

"Are you FIB?" he asked, his voice thin and sharp,
like nails on a chalkboard.

I nodded. "I am. I'm Alex Craft."

"Why are the doors locked? What is going on?"

I frowned. The doors? Did he mean the door to Faerie or the doors to the FIB office? But why would the
office be locked? I tried to catch Roy's gaze, to signal
him to check it out, but he was staring at all the people
around him.

Of course, while Roy was a solid-looking form I
couldn't see through, no one else could see him. Which
I sort of forgot until a very tall fae with two heads stood
up, giving me a strange look that I realized was in response to the fact that he'd thought I'd been motioning
to him. Oops.

"I'm looking into the doors," I muttered to the goblin before turning to work my way through the crowd.
That was easier said than done. Some of the fae were
made of living stone; others had rather deadly-looking
spikes, or thorns. It wasn't the kind of crowd I could
muscle my way through if polite excuse-mes and throat
clearing didn't work. And this crowd was in no mood
for politeness.

I heard the goblin's questions from other fae over
and over as I worked through the crowd. Tensions were

high, as were tempers. They didn't know what was happening, but something was wrong and their one place to go for recourse was locked. These fae didn't know me, but just from looking at me, they could tell I was Sleagh Maith, which, to most, made me not one of them. Sleagh Maith were never independent.

"What happened to my home?" one fae yelled at me as I tried to slide around her.

"What's going on?" a tall fae said, shoving past his neighbor to step into my path.

"I'm trying to find that out," I said, meeting some of his eyes. He had seven, so I wasn't exactly sure where to look.

"What did the queen do?" another fae muttered, not directly to me, just a general question.

That made me pause. It had been over a month since Falin took the throne, but these were not court fae. How many of them didn't even know who sat on the winter throne?

I finally reached the doors. They were, in fact, locked. Not that I doubted it at this point. A sheet of paper with the hand-scrawled word CLOSED had been taped onto the glass of the door. *Oh so helpful.* I was going to have to have a serious talk with the agents. Nori hadn't provided me with a key, an oversight I'd have to address, but the door was never supposed to be locked.

I dug my phone from my purse and pulled up Nori's contact information. It took her long enough to answer that I thought she wouldn't, but just before I was sure it would flip over to voice mail she answered with a curt "What?"

"Why are the front doors locked?"

"Craft? Are you at the office?" she asked, and then she said something in that musical language of the fae, but while it sounded pretty, I was rather sure she was cursing. "Go to the back door. I'll send Tem out to get you."

I wanted to argue, to tell her that if she was inside,

she needed to open up the front door so we could address the fae gathered on our doorstep, but she hung up before I could get a word in. I stared at my phone for a moment. Then I pocketed it and started making my way back through the crowd.

If I thought getting to the door was hard, getting back out was worse. Going against the crowd got me a lot more notice. And hostility.

A fae with a serpentine head wrapped a scaled hand around my upper arm, his talons pressing against my blazer hard enough that I could feel small pricks of pain blooming in my arm. "What is-s-s happening? My den vanished at s-s-suns-s-set. My mate and children were ins-s-side. But I am s-s-still here."

I stared into his glassy black eyes, unsure how much I should say. He deserved to know—they all needed to know what was going on. I'd been so wrapped up in my own concerns about the court being locked down, and with fixing the problem with the door being gone, that I hadn't considered the fact that most of the local fae had no idea the door had been destroyed. Things were happening around them, and they had no idea why. How many more were here because family and friends had vanished with the first sunset? No one had told them what was happening, or what they should do.

I probably needed to consult with Nori before saying anything; I didn't want to start a panic. Of course, she shouldn't have closed the FIB office. Whose brilliant idea had that been? Wasn't there some sort of protocol we should be following in a situation like this?

Probably not. From what Ms. B had said, there hadn't been a situation like this in fae memory. Doors to Faerie moved, but they weren't destroyed.

"Your den and family were likely relocated into the winter court. They should be safe," I said, trying to offer him comfort.

I couldn't read his serpentine expression, but the

way his tongue flickered bespoke agitation. "S-s-safe? In the court? I doubt that."

This confrontation had not gone unnoticed. All around me the gathered fae were pressing closer, eyes on me.

"What is happening?"

"Why did I feel like I was drowning at dawn?"

"Where is my home?"

"I couldn't walk for nearly an hour after dawn."

"What has the court done?"

All around me voices called out questions, and bodies pressed closer and closer, boxing me in. I'm not claustrophobic, but I was feeling rather panicked with fae all around me. All focused on me. All expecting answers.

I did have some. I just wasn't sure how many of them I should share.

How the hell did I get in this situation? I was so not qualified for this job. Who'd thought I'd be good at it?

Falin. I seriously wished he were here with me. He'd know what to do. I tried to imagine what he would do. *Probably look menacing enough that they all backed away, maybe at the point of his daggers.*

That wasn't me, though.

I took a deep breath and let it back out, looking at all the anxious faces around me. They looked angry. Violence wasn't impossible. But mostly they were scared, confused. I couldn't relieve those fears, but I could at least let them know what was happening.

I cleared my throat and then lifted my voice. "Yesterday morning, a magical attack was detonated at the Eternal Bloom. The amaranthine tree was damaged beyond repair, as was the door to Faerie. This territory was cut off from winter, and at sunset, parts of Faerie still attached to winter were relocated into territory still controlled by the court."

A low murmur coursed through the crowd, growing

louder as a hundred different voices repeated my words to neighbors, called out questions, or simply cried out.

"What is the queen doing?"

"What happens to us?"

"Now what?"

"Is this the new king's fault?"

"What is being done?"

"Where is the Winter Knight?"

Questions came at me from every direction. Overwhelming me. More hands reached for me. Someone grabbed my other arm, trying to drag me toward him, but the snake-headed fae still hadn't released my other arm. A small fae grabbed the edge of my jacket, tugging at the fabric to draw my attention.

At this rate I was going to be torn apart.

"Uh, Al . . . Can I help somehow?" Roy had finally caught up to me. Being a ghost most beings couldn't see could be useful at times. In this situation, though, not so much.

Talking to someone people couldn't see didn't seem like a good plan right now, not with tensions this high. I considered expending the magic to manifest Roy, but really, what would that help? If I had to fight my way out of the crowd, I was dead. Roy wouldn't be a ton of help even if I did make him physical. He was not a fighter.

I focused on the fae around me. Trying to keep my voice calm but authoritative.

"If you can leave the city, you should head to the closest winter territory." I tried to remember the map I'd seen earlier in the week, to recall exactly where the closest winter territory was. I frowned. With only one door per court on each continent, the closest winter territory was in the center of South America. That would be a hard journey, and they'd have to pass through at least two other courts' territories to reach it.

They clearly realized those facts.

"And how are we supposed to do that, little Sleagh

Maith?" one of the fae sneered. I wasn't even sure which one at this point.

I considered the fae around me. Typically when I saw fae in the mortal realm, they wore their glamour, but very few of these faces were glamoured. I didn't think it was because they were trying to be intimidating, but simply that these fae rarely glamoured themselves. The court fae working in the FIB office kept their glamour up as insulation against the tech and iron in the mortal realm. Independent fae like Caleb kept their glamour up because they lived and worked among humans. But the independents around me were likely not fae who lived in suburban neighborhoods and worked in Nekros. These were fae from the wilds, the untamed areas of the world where myths and legends roamed. These were the fae of fairy tales who led travelers astray when they journeyed too far off the beaten path or lent magical assistance for prices often hard to pay. These were the wolves who talked to little girls in the woods, and the women who could be heard singing from the depths of still waters. These were the helpers that toiled in the night, unseen, and the mischief-makers who played pranks on the unwary. They didn't have cars to jump in and drive to a new court. They weren't likely to board a plane and fly to some other winter territory.

"I . . . I will work on an evacuation plan for the fae," I said, because wasn't that my job? These were the people I'd taken this job to help.

"And who are you, Sleagh Maith, to help us?" This question from a woman with skin the texture of bark and naked twigs for hair, her foliage having fallen for winter. The way she said "Sleagh Maith" was practically a slur. Considering it was nearly synonymous with court fae, and not only that, but nobility among the court fae, I knew why she didn't think I'd help the wild independents. But she didn't know me.

I opened my mouth to say that I was the agent in charge, but I'd shown up here not knowing my agents had closed the damn FIB building. How in charge was I? Didn't seem like very in charge at all. And how the hell was I going to evacuate this many fae?

"Everyone out of my way!" a booming and accented voice said from the other side of the crowd. An accented voice I recognized.

Tem, unglamoured, pushed his way through the crowd. Even in this group, he was taller and wider than most of the gathered fae. Some grumbled, but everyone moved aside as he moved through.

"You all right there, Craft?" he asked as he reached my side.

I gave a small nod and followed him out, Roy on my heels. No one grabbed at me this time or got in my face, though several called out questions at our backs. A few of the fae looked ready to stop us, to demand more information. I had to force myself not to hold my breath—passing out while walking out of this throng would be bad—because if just one of the fae decided to make a scene, more would join in and there were a lot more of them. Tem was a big guy, and trolls had fearsome reputations, but he was still only one troll. I breathed a little easier once we broke free from the thickest part of the crowd, though I still felt gazes on us as Tem led me around the side of the building.

"Now would be a good time to be unseen," he whispered.

"Uh . . ." Crap. He meant he wanted me to glamour myself invisible, which should have been easy enough for pretty much any fae. Except me. I couldn't use glamour to save my life. "I can't do that."

Tem frowned at me, his wide mouth pulling downward around his tusks. Then his gaze flickered over my head, back the way we'd come. I knew what he was looking at; I could hear the movement of fae following us. Tem grabbed my hand—which actually meant his fingers wrapped around my hand and a portion of my wrist and arm as well. And then I felt his magic slide over me.

It wasn't a bad sensation, just weird. I hated the feeling of other people's magic on my skin, and glamour was a heavy magic. It crawled up my arm, attempting to cover me in the invisibility he desired. I tried to ignore it, to pretend I didn't even notice it, but my magic and glamour didn't mix.

The glamour had barely reached my shoulder when I felt the magic splinter, sloughing back off my skin.

"What the fuck, boss? My glamour just broke," Tem muttered, his jaw falling slack as he stared at me.

Yeah. That had been happening recently.

"Let's just get inside." I wasn't even sure where the back door was. If it was also glamoured, we might be in trouble.

Tem didn't argue or hesitate, but led me around the back of the building. The door was thankfully not hidden behind a glamour, simply out of the way. Tem unlocked it quickly and ushered me inside, flipping the bolt as soon as it shut behind us.

The sound of the fae outside cut off as soon as the door was closed, the dark room I'd been escorted to feeling too still and silent compared to all the frightened excitement. They'd asked who I was to help them. It was a good question. I'd ducked behind a troll bodyguard instead of even answering. Dugan was wrong. I was most definitely a coward.

Chapter 16

Tem led me through the silent FIB building. Far too silent. The bulk of the squad had slept here last night; the place should have been bustling. Instead it was still and quiet, the air having that undisturbed quality of an empty building.

"Where is everyone?" I asked as Tem headed for the hallway to my office.

"Gone."

"Gone?" I sounded incredulous, even to my own ears.

"Loaded up and took off just after dawn," Tem said, pausing as we rounded a corner. Someone had left a cart full of files pushed up against the wall. It wouldn't be a problem for most people, but Tem barely fit in the hallway as it was. He seemed to consider the cart for a moment, and then his glamour slid into place, changing him from hulking to simply a hugely big guy. He still had to turn sideways to step around the cart. "Nori and I are the only ones left."

I stopped. "You're the only two left out of the entire agency?" There had been nearly thirty agents here when I left. "Where did they go?"

"South. To winter territory," Nori said, stepping out of a doorway up ahead.

"Obviously. But they shouldn't have just taken off." I mean, I knew we needed to move all the nonessential fae to somewhere Faerie would actually keep them alive, but shouldn't my agents have, I don't know, checked in with me before they left? I was the agent in charge here, right? Some boss I'd turned out to be. Three days in and my entire squad had fled. "Abandoning Nekros won't fix the issue. And I'm sure more agents would have made the evacuation of the local fae easier."

Nori lifted a shoulder. "This land isn't tied to winter anymore, so they are no longer bound to serve it."

"The fae here are still our responsibility."

She just stared at me, and I twisted and pointed toward the mobs she'd locked the doors against.

"Independents have no true loyalty to crown or court," she said and it was my turn to stare at her, disbelief mixing with a rising anger.

"So you'll just abandon them?"

She made a sound in the back of her throat, something between derisive and dismissive. "What is it you think our job is, Craft?" she asked, but she didn't give me a chance to answer before continuing. "Let me give you a hint. We aren't here to make sure all fae live happy fairy-tale lives. Our job is to secure the interests of the winter court in the mortal realm. Most of the time that means making sure relationships with mortals remain positive and keeping the peace among the fae in our jurisdiction so that the crown does not have to deal with them directly. Independents are the hangers-on of our society. They contribute little to our court and are tolerated only because their presence in this realm reminds mortals of our existence and increases belief magic."

"Yeah?" I said, placing a fisted hand on my hip. "So then they do more than a lot of fae, because Faerie fades without belief. All those fae who can't be bothered to mix with mere mortals are the real leeches."

"That would accurately describe the Sleagh Maith," she said, her tone pure acid.

"Then how come I'm the only one who cares about all the fae gathered outside our door!"

"Because blooded true or not, *you are no fae.*"

"I'll take that as a compliment," I said and turned on my heel.

"Where are you going, Craft?" she called after me.

I didn't even know, but I wasn't going to get any help from Nori, that seemed certain. "If there is no reason to stay, then why are you still here? Shouldn't you run off like everyone else?" I called back over my shoulder.

"Because my loyalty was to Falin while he was still knight, not yet even the king, and he wouldn't want Nekros abandoned."

That made me hesitate.

"I know you've never held me in much regard, but I do care about my court," she said, and I could tell from her voice that she was moving closer to me.

I had the choice of continuing to storm away or to turn and face her. I turned slowly. She'd dropped her glamour and was hovering a foot off the ground, moving slowly forward. Her blue face and large insect eyes were alien, but not threatening. Once I would have found her frightening, but I no longer did. I met her multifaceted eyes.

"You're saying it's my fault we don't get on?"

She cocked her head to the side, her antennae twitching with the movement. She looked different without her glamour, but her voice was exactly the same. "I don't like you, Craft. I don't make any attempt to hide that fact. You don't fit in our world. But I admit you see things I don't see, and I don't mean your plane-weaving. You approach things more as a mortal than a fae, and that perspective is something the king appreciates. I hate to admit that I've seen the value of it, but

I've seen your results, and I understand his position. I still don't think you belong here, but here you are, when no one else is. And I admit, I would have left too if I hadn't thought you would show up here today, planning to fix things." She landed in front of me. The movement was awkward, the shape of her hips in her true form more suited for flying than standing upright. "But how do you plan to fix things?"

And wasn't that the question.

I turned to Tem. The big troll was staring pointedly away from us, looking like he wanted to be anywhere else but in the middle of this conversation.

"And what about you?" I asked. "Why are you still here?"

He lifted a large shoulder. "King charged me with watching over you. So I'm here. But you stay here too long, you start to fade, and I'll be dragging you out of here."

Good to know. So I had a babysitter who would also become my jailer if he deemed things too dangerous. It was a good warning to have. What went unsaid was that if Tem suspected Falin had lost the court, all bets were off. That was good to know as well. At least I knew the line of his loyalty.

"These are your new allies, Al?" Roy said, shoving his hands in his pockets and shaking his head. "I'm not saying turn them away, but, man . . ."

Yeah, not my ideal choice of who to have at my back. I found I was more happy that Roy was with me than the two fae, though the ghost definitely wouldn't be my first choice in a fight.

I walked to my office, stepping over files and roses still scattered across the floor from the earthquake. The safe where I'd stashed the fire spell we'd found on the remains of the amaranthine tree hid in the corner of the room. I placed the spell, still in its triple-sealed magic-dampening box, in my purse. Then I searched out the map I'd studied on my first day. Unrolling it, I spread it across the piles of scattered paperwork littering my desk. Then I stared.

I'd guessed what I would find, but my gut still twisted at the sight of the entire North American continent devoid of any color where the four seasonal court colors had stained it the last time I'd seen this map. So all four courts really had lost their doors. Rolling the map back up, I began to tuck that into my purse as well, but paused as a folder underneath it caught my attention. Pretty much all the other folders left on the desk were askew, their contents spilling in all directions, but this one was neatly placed on top of the chaos, dead center on the desk.

I snatched the file from the desk and flipped it open, my brow creasing as I read over the handwritten report. "The agents we sent to the floodplains, they found the fouled pond," I said as I scanned the short summary. Nori stepped into the room, walking over to glance around my shoulder at the file.

"It had a pocket dwelling under the water."

Which fit with Jenny Greenteeth's lair. "It won't be there now," I said, cursing under my breath. All the pockets of Faerie had moved at sunset. "She was in Nekros." But was she still?

"So what do we do now, boss?" Tem asked from the door.

I considered the file. If Jenny was—or had been—back in Nekros, that was further evidence that Ryese's scheming was behind the destruction of the door. Would he have stranded his ally on this side, though, or were they all safely tucked away back in Faerie? I shoved the file into my purse. I now had four aspects of this crisis vying for my attention, and as much as I was tempted to run out to the floodplains and search for Jenny, I had doubts she'd still be there. I should have done it before her lair vanished with the rest of the pockets of Faerie.

I did need to meet up with Martinez from the Anti-

Black Magic Unit and see if she could discern anything from the fire spell. Most likely the only thing her team would be able to learn was that it was fae magic—which I already knew—and if they tried to track it, the spell most likely wouldn't lead anywhere, as the caster was probably back in Faerie, but it was still worth looking into. My gut said Ryese was behind this, but solid proof would be good. Hell, maybe I could take that proof to the High King, or at least the other seasonal monarchs and we could chase Ryese out of his safe little hidey-hole in the light court and hold him accountable for his crimes.

The most important thing was to secure a new door for Nekros, but that was also the most complicated. I already had Dugan looking for the sapling. I had no clue what more to do on that front, or even where to go for advice. Was there a way I could get an audience with the High King? Of course, I'd likely need to be in Faerie to do that, if it was even possible. I wasn't foolish enough to think he was the Santa Claus of Faerie and I'd just ask him to fix the doors and show him any proof I'd gathered as to who was behind it and he'd magically fix everything. Real life didn't work that way, regardless of magic and legends.

My gaze moved to the front of the building where I knew the independents were still gathered, confused, scared, and angry. There was also the independents to consider. They were our responsibility and we'd been doing a piss-poor job with them during this crisis thus far. That needed to change.

"We need to evacuate the independents," I said. I almost asked Nori how fae normally traveled, but I knew the answer. They just used the doors to Faerie. That wasn't an option, so what else was there?

I had a moment of imagining booking several international planes and filling them with the fae, but I knew that wouldn't work. Even if the lot of wild fae could glamour their way through TSA to board the planes, I couldn't imagine they'd be able to stomach the flight. It was painful to spend time inside a regular vehicle because of the metal content. Flying in a huge metal cylinder in the sky? Yeah, that might kill fae.

How did my father travel? Surely as governor he had to from time to time. Did he have a private plane? Something made primarily with plastics and fae-safe materials?

I glanced between Nori and Tem. "Have either of you ever met the governor of Nekros?"

Chapter 17

—⋆⇒⊙ ⊙⇐⋆—

There is only so much mass displacement that reality will accept from glamour. Tem had glamoured himself as small as he could, but he still didn't fit comfortably in my little convertible. He should have ridden with Nori, but he insisted that he stick by me while we were on the job and I wanted to keep my car today. We ended up with the top down despite the cold January air because Tem had to keep most of his natural height to make himself narrow enough to fit in the passenger seat. He still ended up hunched forward, leaning over his phone as he tried to make himself short enough for the windshield to block some of the frigid air whipping around us. Roy, who couldn't actually feel the cold January air, thought it was great. He whooped and hollered from the tiny backseat while I shot him menacing looks in the rearview. It was not a fun trip out of the Magic Quarter.

I considered going straight to the statehouse, to make this frigid trip as short as possible, but ultimately I decided to first make a quick detour to Central Precinct to drop the fire spell off with Martinez and the ABMU team. Nori was opposed to turning over the spell, which she made vocal at every possible point, but what were we going to do with it? Neither Nori nor Tem had any magic that would help them track the caster. I did break the seals and try to feel out the spell, but the best I could do was get a sense of the caster's signature. Then the thing had started sparking and I'd slammed the lid back down on the box and put the magic-dampening seals back on. If I ran across other spells by the same caster, I'd likely recognize the signature, but that wouldn't help me track him. So I turned the spell over to the ABMU and hoped they got something more from it. Then we headed for the state-house.

The last time I'd stood inside the office of the governor, I'd snuck in after hours to search for evidence on a bodythief. This time I had a badge and an official title, but if I'd thought that would be an instant ticket inside, I was badly mistaken.

"I will relay any message you have to the governor," the aide standing in front of me said, clip pad at the ready, but he hadn't offered to shake our hands when he'd shown us from the receptionist's desk into this small closet of an office. Of course, he was an aide for the Humans First Party and in the dim fluorescent lights, I was very obviously not human.

"I need to discuss this directly with the governor," I said, not for the first time.

The aide only frowned at me. "He has a very busy schedule today. You are free to schedule an appointment." He glanced down at a calendar on his tablet. "We can probably work you in for a week from next Monday."

Considering it was Wednesday, that was a pretty shitty offer.

"Has he been told the FIB agent in charge is here to discuss a matter relating to yesterday's bombing?"

"As I said, the governor has a very busy schedule—"

"So then no. He hasn't been told," I said, cutting him off.

The aide jutted out his chin, his chest puffing out in his bluster. "Did you want to give me your message or schedule an appointment?"

Nori, who had been mostly silent, began listing off statutes that should have gotten us a prompt meeting with the governor, but the smug little aide continued stonewalling.

We clearly weren't going to get anywhere with this guy. I considered just marching out the door and down the hall—I knew where the governor's office was, after all. But that would probably end with security jumping me and all kinds of messy paperwork.

"Roy, go see if the governor is in his office," I whispered under my breath, trying not to move my lips as I spoke. Nori's heated debate with the aide kept either of them from noticing, but Tem shot me a confused look from where he stood off to one side.

"Sure thing," Roy said, practically dashing from the room. The ghost loved being able to contribute to a case, and I'd learned long ago that ghosts made excellent spies.

Roy made it back just as the aide began trying to dismiss us from his office. I ignored the short man and gave Roy an expectant look.

"That room is warded tight. I could peek in, but I couldn't actually enter. I hate wards like that."

I made a small hand motion, trying to hurry Roy along.

"He's here. He's not even with anyone. From what I could see, he is alone in his office looking over paperwork."

Perfect.

I pulled out my cell phone and scrolled through my contacts. I'd saved my father's private number with no other information, just the number. I didn't use it often, but I had called on him in emergencies before, so I always made sure I kept the number on file.

He picked up on the second ring. "Alexis, now is not a good time."

"Governor Caine, your staff are insufferable assholes who refuse to make me an appointment for any sooner than two weeks from now."

The aide's jaw went slack as he stared at me in stunned horror. On the other end of the line, my father was silent for a moment before saying, "Are you in the office currently?"

"I am. I'm with . . ." I looked at the aide. "What did you say your name was?"

The aide sputtered, but didn't actually supply an answer.

My father sighed.

"Wait there," he said and then hung up. Moments later he stepped into the doorway of the small office in which we stood. The aide had been holding open the door, insisting we leave—I don't think he really believed I'd called the governor.

"I'll take it from here, Henry," my father said, nodding to the flustered aide.

The other man just stammered for a moment, staring at me. Then he said, "But, sir, she—"

"I said I would see to it. Agent Craft, if you would follow me?"

I flashed some teeth at the aide and then turned on my heel, marching out of the room, Tem and Nori at my side. When we reached my father's office, he nodded to the two security types outside of it and then turned back to me. "Your associates will have to wait out here."

Tem looked about to protest, but Nori just narrowed her eyes. She wasn't an idiot. Between the little bit she'd overheard at the limo last night and the trick I'd just pulled, she'd clearly figured out I had some tie to the governor. Thankfully she was smart enough not to give voice to whatever questions she might have and only nodded when I said, "I'll be back in a moment."

The big troll clearly didn't like the arrangement, but he didn't argue. Roy, on the other hand, made several disparaging comments as the wards blocked him in the doorway.

"I guess I'll wait out here," he said with a sulk, slumping his shoulders.

My father shut the door behind us. Then he walked around his large executive-sized desk and settled himself before motioning for me to take one of the padded chairs across from him. He watched me as I sat, his elbows balanced on the desk, his hands neatly clasped. It was a power posture, both relaxed and authoritative at the same time. He studied me in perfect stillness, the edginess I'd seen last night now absent. He may have been unnerved yesterday, but here and now, he was perfectly in control.

I crossed my legs, and then thought better of it and uncrossed them. The chair, while it looked sleek and professional, was uncomfortable. The dimensions were wrong in some slight way so that I couldn't figure out where to put my arms to strike that balance between assertive and casual. Which left me fidgety. My father watched me, impersonating an angry statue.

"Was that really necessary?" he asked once I'd settled, his hand making the smallest gesture toward the door and, I guessed, the stunt I'd pulled to get in here.

With a shrug I said, "Your gatekeeper wouldn't let me pass." And while I could have waited until tonight, when he was home and out of the public eye, I did have a legitimate reason to be here in an official capacity.

"And what is so very urgent that you decided to make a scene?"

I stared at him. Surely he hadn't dismissed the bombing and all the potential ramifications this quickly. Or maybe he just didn't care. "You're governor of Nekros and a portion of the population needs help evacuating."

He blinked at me.

"The wild fae? I need to figure out how to relocate them while I try to fix the door. If I can't fix it in time, I don't want them fading."

"What is it you think I can do?"

"I don't know. Supply an airplane? Possibly several buses if we want to send them to South America, though I imagine land travel might be tricky as they'd have to pass through other courts."

He continued to stare at me as if he'd never seen me before.

"What?" Was I overlooking some obvious and simpler way to get the fae to the nearest winter territory?

"You want me to relocate all the fae in Nekros?"

"If this were a natural disaster, the government would create some sort of evacuation plan, right? I mean, really, coming to you is probably not a big enough response. With all the doors on this continent gone, the evacuation needs to be much larger. But I'm starting where I can."

A slow smile crawled over my father's face. This was not his normal politician's smile. This smile came from a different face, one I couldn't actually see with his glamour up. It was slightly creepy, as it looked misplaced, and yet it was a smile that went all the way to his eyes and made them light from within, not in a magical way, but in an expression I'd never seen before.

"Why, Alexis," he said, leaning forward, and I had the urge to shrink back from the sheer oddness of the way he looked at me. Not bad—in fact, it was probably the most genuine expression I'd ever seen on him—but it was alien, out of place. "I do believe what I am feeling is pride. I don't think I've ever been proud of you before."

Gee, thanks. "And that would be why you never won a Father of the Year award," I said, working hard to keep my voice flat and empty. I wasn't that little girl who'd searched for his approval anymore. I'd given up on that a long time ago, and this was far too little too late. "So does that mean you'll help evacuate the wild fae? And any other independents who might need help?"

"No."

His answer was immediate and caught me off guard, as just a moment before, he'd been beaming at me.

"But . . . you just said—"

"Alexis, I'm pleased you are thinking about the well-being of the fae as a whole, and not only the few you know personally and have decided are safe and friendly." His expression was back to that of the distant politician. "But what you are asking isn't feasible. Talk to the Shadow King about providing safe passage. Work out a negotiation with him, and I will allow the fae access to the private garden you created in my house."

I opened my mouth, and then closed it. "Private garden" had to refer to the room in which I'd accidentally merged realities under the Blood Moon over half a year ago. Chunks of Faerie had been woven right into mortal reality, as had patches of the land of the dead and other planes I didn't even have names for. I'd assumed when Faerie had withdrawn and taken all the other pockets of Faerie at sunset, that one would have been dissolved as well. But from his words . . .

"It's still there?"

My father nodded. "I checked on it this morning, after dawn. The edges have begun to fray, but your work is holding so far. Without an amaranthine tree to root Faerie into this world, even your planeweaving will not last, but for now, it is there. You should act fast, though, if you want the Shadow King's help. Once that bastion of Faerie falls, we will truly be cut off. Even I may have to leave."

I sank back into my seat, my mind going too fast to

worry about my body for the moment. Dugan had said there was one place left in all of North America that still had enough ties to Faerie that the planebender would be able to reach it. This had to be where. If I could negotiate with the Shadow King to use his planebender, I could walk all the fae in Nekros right into Faerie. But there was more to unpack here. If the area I had merged had survived, could we create a new door there? I had a vague memory of Falin once telling me that it was rumored planeweavers had created the original doors. My father had said the High King had planted the amaranthine trees, but until recently, he'd had planeweavers in his court to do his bidding.

"If there is nothing else . . ." my father said when my silence stretched.

My gaze snapped to him. "You still owe me an answer on how to get to the high court."

Shock crossed his features for half a moment before he schooled his face neutral once more. "Now what, Alexis? We did discuss this during the Winter Solstice."

"You told me a legend about how the courts were formed. You didn't tell me how to reach the court."

He rolled his eyes, looking exasperated. "Because there is no court. We've covered this. You wanted to find other planeweavers, but they are gone. Dead."

"Yeah, well, you said the High King is the one who planted the amaranthine trees initially. We kind of need more, so I'm guessing we will likely need the High King for that."

Again my father stared at me like he had no idea who I was. After a long pause he said in a tone like he might use when speaking to a young child, "Four amaranthine trees were destroyed in a single day. I promise you, the High King knows this and is taking action. But amaranthine trees do not grow overnight. Not even in Faerie." He stood. "You need to hurry now. You have negotiations to undertake, and then the actual rounding up of all the fae you wish to rescue. Do call before you start herding them to my home. I will have to make arrangements."

The dismissal was obvious. I rose to my feet slowly. He'd both given me a path and neatly sidestepped having to actually do anything himself. Well, except allowing droves of fae onto his estate, I guess that was something. Getting the fae directly to Faerie—assuming I could work out safe passage with the Shadow King—was far better than trying to figure out a way to ship them across the world. I considered pressing my father for information on the high court, but it sounded like I wouldn't find the amaranthine trees I needed there either. At least not for a while. I had to hope Dugan found the sapling from the swamp.

My father stepped around his desk to see me out, but my thoughts were already on how I was going to get in touch with the Shadow King, my feet following on autopilot. Dugan had responded when I'd whispered into shadows, but it had taken a while. How long would it take to gather the fae once I'd worked out passage? And how long would the merged pocket of Faerie last? If it was already fraying, how many sunsets, how many dawns, would it last?

We were halfway to the door when my father suddenly stopped, his back going rigid. Then he fell to his knees. His glamour dissolved as he pitched forward, catching himself with his hands a moment before his face would have slammed into the floor.

I yelped, rushing forward. "What happened? Are you okay?"

He coughed. Drops of liquid hit the floor in front of him, glittering like rubies lit from within for a heartbeat before losing their glow and turning dark red. *Blood.*

"Shit." I dropped to my own knees beside him. I reached out, but then hesitated, not sure if I should touch him. Not sure what the hell was going on.

"Help!" I screamed, looking up at the door. The security guards were just outside, as were Tem and Nori. "Someone help us!"

The door didn't open. Of course not. This office was likely both magically and structurally soundproof.

I laid a hand on his shoulder, unsure what to do. He looked up at me. Blood dribbled down the corner of his mouth. Whatever had just happened, he needed help.

"I'll be right back," I whispered, starting to climb to my feet.

My father's hand wrapped around my wrist, holding me in place. He took a breath, and it made a sucking, wet sound that left him coughing again, blood spraying from his lips. The blood wasn't only coming from his mouth. His shirt was covered in blood, a hole as big as my fist in his chest.

I gasped. Had he been shot? I hadn't heard anything. Hadn't seen anything. My gaze swung around the room, my shields dropping as I searched for some unseen enemy. Nothing. No one.

"I'm going to get help," I said again, trying to pull away.

He shook his head, his hand locking tighter around my wrist. Damn it. Was his secret so important that he would rather bleed to death on his office floor?

"Alexis . . ." His voice was a cracked whisper, my name barely discernible. "My blood . . . will open it. Go to . . . Shadow."

He released my wrist as another awful cough shook his entire body. I jumped to my feet, dashing for the door, for whatever help I could find beyond. But his cough cut off in midwheeze. I glanced back over my shoulder, afraid of the worst.

And found the room . . . empty.

There was a spattering of blood where he'd been and a pile of bloody clothing and his shoes. I still had my shields down, my psyche peering across the planes.

He wasn't hidden under a glamour. He was just gone. Vanished.

Fae don't just vanish.

And yet he had. And I was alone. In the governor's office. The only trace of my father some discarded clothing and blood on the wooden floor.

Chapter 18

I stood stunned, my heart pounding. *What just happened?* I blinked. My father had not just collapsed, bleeding from a gaping chest wound, and then vanished. That could *not* have happened.

But there was blood on the office floor. His clothes. His phone, which had fallen out of the pocket of his now empty pants. His polished shoes, one sitting upright, the other lying on its side.

I walked around the room, quickly scanning every crevice and corner without touching anything. There was no one here. No traps. No holes in the windows or walls to indicate a sniper attack. Bullets would have left a trace. Magic should have too, but while I could feel my father's wards, there was no trace of any foreign magic in the room, and the wards felt undisturbed.

So what the hell had just happened? And where had he vanished to? Had he teleported somewhere else, naked and bleeding? Was that possible? Soul collectors could translocate. Ghosts could sink deeper into the land of the dead, seeming to vanish but really only leaving the mortal plane. But fae had physical bodies.

They couldn't just—*poof*—disappear. Humans often thought they could, but if a fae vanished, it was a trick, like glamour, sometimes combined with superhuman speed or flight or something. But they didn't teleport.

So where was my father? With my shields down I should have seen through any glamour tricks. Hell, I probably could have seen if he'd managed to step into another plane. But he was just gone.

I didn't particularly *like* my father on most days, but I didn't want to see him hurt.

And he'd had a freaking hole in his chest.

This was bad. So, so bad.

I stopped walking because I realized I was now pacing, no longer searching, just moving because I couldn't stay still. So I forced myself to stop and take a deep breath. I'd been in here a while now. How long before someone would knock on the door to check that everything was okay? Not that things were okay . . .

Shit. Where had he gone? Was he alive?

I stared at the blood. There wasn't much on the floorboards considering how badly he'd been hurt. His shirt, though . . .

It was on my gloves too, as well as the cuff of the sleeve where he'd grabbed me. The black material mostly hid it, but I caught a bloody fingerprint on the skin of my wrist and smudged on my charm bracelet. I started to strip off my gloves—I had a backup pair in my purse. Then I hesitated.

Should I hide his clothes? Clean up the blood on the floor? If so, no point removing my soiled gloves yet. I couldn't exactly explain to security that their seemingly nonmagical governor had vanished without a trace. That would definitely get blamed on the glowing girl who'd come to visit him. This was bad on so many levels.

The last thing he'd told me was to go to shadow. Was that to find out what had happened to him? Or because he was trying to send me where he thought I'd be safe? Damn, he had too many secrets.

I considered the room again. The only thing out of place was the crumpled clothing. If I hid that, nothing about the scene would look amiss.

I grabbed the clothing and mopped up the more obvious drops of blood, but most blended in with the dark wood and I didn't want to create large smears, so after soaking up a few spots I hastily folded the clothes into a pile that, while not neat, at least hid the bloody sections. I carried the pile into the small attached bathroom in the back of the office. I'd once hid out in that bathroom, so I knew there was a standing shower and even a small closet where toiletries, towels, and a few spare clothes were stored. I dumped the badly folded clothing onto a shelf behind a stack of towels. Then I stripped off my gloves and washed my hands, careful not to touch anything that might pick up prints. Replacing my gloves with my spares, I went back out to the main office and retrieved the phone and shoes, adding them to the closet as well.

Leaving the light in the bathroom on, I locked and shut the door and then gave the main office a cursory once-over. It didn't look like anything unusual had happened. A close examination would no doubt find the blood and clothes, but at a quick glance, hopefully anyone checking in would assume my father had stepped out. It wouldn't buy me much time, but if I just walked out and said the governor had vanished and here are his bloody clothes, I'd be arrested.

Damn it, was I really covering up the fact that my father had maybe been murdered right in front of me? Could I really walk out of here? Was there anything else I could do? Getting questioned for his disappearance was not going to help anyone. Panic buzzed in the back of my brain and my vision fogged, not from my magic-damaged sight but from hot tears that threatened to break through. But I didn't have time for that.

I took a steadying breath, which sounded ragged so I did it again and then a third time until it came out smooth. Then I rolled back my shoulders and headed for the exit.

I opened the door only enough that my body blocked most of the room, but it didn't look like I was slinking out. I twisted slightly so that I was half looking into the room as I moved.

"Thank you for your time, sir," I called out in what I hoped came off as a chipper but professional tone, as if it was part of the end of an ongoing conversation. "I'll let you get to that, then."

I turned, pulling the door closed behind me. If I'd had the glamour, I'd have created a voice that followed me out, or fashioned a facsimile of my father to stand in the doorway. But I lacked the ability to do either, so I just hoped misdirection worked.

Tem and Nori were frowning at me as I turned toward the hall. Roy was staring, eyes wide, his lip clamped between his teeth, and I wondered how much he'd seen. He hadn't been able to get past the ward, but I knew he'd seen my father in his office earlier, so he might have watched that whole thing.

The two security guards were blissfully ignorant, though. Neither even turned toward the door as I stepped free. The aide was still in the hall, looking anxious and angry. He was going to be a problem. He was the most likely to enter the office.

"The governor just took a call," I said as I passed him, hoping the comment came off nonchalant. Hell, I didn't even care if he thought I was making a dig at him for telling me the governor was too busy earlier. As long as he didn't go in that room.

I kept walking, my pace casual but brisk, trusting that Nori and Tem would catch up with me. They didn't disappoint.

"Did you just *thank* the governor?" Nori asked under her breath as she met my stride, clearly distressed that I might have casually granted a human a debt to cash in.

"Not exactly," I said, and then fixed my eyes on Roy. Smiling and talking through my teeth I whispered, "If anyone goes in that room, pull the fire alarm."

"What?" Tem asked, grinding to a halt.

"Not either of you," I hissed without slowing down.

Roy, his eyes still too wide, nodded. "You got it, Al. Oh, man. This is so messed up."

Was it ever. And Nori and Tem were both staring at me, not moving.

"Come on," I said, my voice barely a whisper. "We have to get out of the building. Now."

We made it to the front steps of the statehouse before the fire alarm sounded.

I cursed, picking up speed as people began pouring out of the building. I'd really been hoping we would have made it farther away before anyone entered the governor's office. How long would it take before they went from trying to locate him to searching for me?

"We need to get to our cars." Because I had to get out of there.

I was walking fast enough to be considered jogging—which worked with the crowd around us. Half of the people were running from the building and the rest were doing more of a confused backward retreat trying to figure out if an actual emergency had occurred or if it was a false alarm.

Nori caught my arm, stopping me. "What the hell is going on, Craft?"

"It's a really complicated story. Suffice it to say I'm going to be in a lot of trouble if security finds me, and we don't have time for that, so let's move."

To her credit, Nori released me and started moving at a good clip. That didn't mean she stopped asking questions, though. "What happened in there? And who is Governor Caine to you?"

Yeah, I figured that second question was bound to come up. I considered Nori out of the corner of my eye without slowing. My relationship to the governor was buried—he'd made sure of that—but it wasn't impossible to find. Falin had unearthed it within days of my meeting him.

"He's my father," I said under my breath. Nori stumbled, but I didn't slow. She caught back up a moment later.

"And why are we running away?" she asked.

I was moving with enough speed that I was starting to feel winded, my voice breathy as I answered. "Because he is missing and I don't know when or if he is coming back and I don't want to be here when security discovers that fact." Which would be any second now.

Tem stopped me with a huge hand on my shoulder. "Shit. And you were alone with him. Where did he go? And how?"

Good questions. Unfortunately, I didn't have answers to either. Not that he waited for an answer.

"They are going to come for your head," he said, with a guttural sound that was very close to a growl. His gaze assessed me, and I could feel him weighing whether it was time to toss me in my car and get me out of Nekros. That wouldn't work for me.

"Which is why we need to keep moving," I said, breaking away from him and picking up my pace toward the car.

Most of the crowd that had evacuated for the fire alarm had stopped just before the street. Now that we'd passed them, heading farther down the sidewalk, our near run made us more noticeable. I bit my lip as I wondered if we should slow down to a more casual pace, but every second that passed felt like a countdown to the moment security would burst out of the building behind us. At least we'd parked on the street and not in the garage—less places to get trapped.

We'd almost reached my car when I stopped dead in my tracks. Tem didn't stop quite as fast. I stumbled forward as the troll bumped into me and remained on my feet only because he grabbed my shoulders.

"You okay? What's wrong?" he asked.

I didn't answer. I just stared at a bouquet of flowers lying on the hood of my car. Bloodred roses. A card stuck out of the bouquet. All the other flowers had included cards that were blank on the outside. Not this one. Even from a distance, the gold-embossed lettering clearly read:

Condolences on your loss.

I stared at those beautifully scripted, ugly little words. Pressure built in my chest, a still, silent scream. I bit my lips to keep that scream from bursting free.

How? How could the flowers be here? Who knew what had happened already?

Whoever maybe just killed my father. The thought came unbidden and the scream nearly won.

I clenched my fists until my nails bit into my palms. I'd thought the destruction of the door had trapped my stalker in Faerie. Apparently I was wrong.

I marched forward, toward the flowers. I wanted them to burn. To go up in a ball of fire that consumed them and their awful little note.

But I couldn't create fire like Holly. I didn't have that kind of magic.

I had a different kind.

I dropped my shields and the world around me changed. The Aetheric popped into focus as the land of the dead washed everything in a patina of decay. Unearthly wind ripped across from the land of the dead, whipping my hair around my face and sending sidewalk debris swirling down the street. Inside the bouquet, a glimmer of magic sparked, red and silver snaking through the flowers. The spell seemed to reach up, as if sensing my attention, but when I focused on it, it vanished from my vision. I could *feel* it, though. The magic felt aggressive, dangerous, and ready to spring if I touched those damn flowers. The magic also felt familiar, the signature the same as the spell from the Bloom.

Normally I kept a thin translucent shield between my mind and the layers of reality so that I didn't accidentally pull or push anything across. Now I popped that protective bubble.

I reached out with my magic and shoved the realities around the bouquet. The flowers withered, the gold lettering on the card flaked off, and the paper decayed. As they dissolved, a thin wooden rod that had been hiding inside the bouquet became visible. I had a moment to see the magical glyphs carved into the surface, to see the strands of blond hair wrapped around the wood, personalizing the spell, making sure it would spring only on the target. Me. Then the hair shriveled. The wood rotted. The spell dissipated as the item it had been focused on disintegrated. In a heartbeat, nothing was left but dust that shifted in the wind whirling around me.

"Shit. Craft. What are you doing?" Nori was yelling. How long had she been yelling? She grabbed my arm and then jerked back as the chill of the grave jumped to her. "Stop. Now."

I blinked. The flowers were gone. Hell, all trace that they'd ever existed was gone. And I was still on the street, doing weird magic that was no doubt drawing attention. Crap.

I closed my shields. The world immediately darkened despite the bright midday sun. Not incapacitatingly dark, but noticeable.

Roy, who I hadn't even seen arrive, moved to my side. "Uh, Alex. I'm not sure what you're doing, but they just broke down the door to the governor's bathroom and discovered no one was inside. You should get out of here."

He didn't have to tell me twice.

The top to my car was still down after the drive over, and I all but vaulted inside. I hit the button to start the car and threw it in gear in the same movement. I reversed without looking back, my tires squealing as I pulled into the street. A horn blared. An approaching car swerved. I blinked, trying to clear the darkness from my eyes, but I didn't have time to wait. I switched gears again.

Nori and Tem, who hadn't been privy to Roy's warning, both yelled, rushing forward.

Well, crap. I probably shouldn't leave my team behind.

Tem dashed toward the car, as if he planned to pull me back out of it. Then he passed through the space where the hood of my car—and the flowers—had been. The sleeve of his jacket disintegrated, the fine material rotting away as it passed through the exact spot where I'd dusted the flowers. He jerked back, his eyes widening.

Crap. I'd not only destroyed the flowers, I'd created a hole in reality. I hadn't done that in months. That . . . that was bad.

For a long moment, we all stared at the seemingly inconspicuous spot. Then another car horn blared behind me.

I had to get out of here. I didn't have time to try to fix reality. I didn't even want to think about the hole I'd just punched in it, the flowers, or the targeted spell they'd contained. I certainly didn't want to talk about it. And I couldn't risk Tem dragging me off for my own good. I had to contact shadow. I had to figure out what the hell had just happened to my father, and how my stalker even knew I was at the statehouse. I had to go. Somewhere. Now.

Nori had her own car. Tem would fit better in it anyway. Nori's gaze caught mine for half an instant, her lips pressed in a tight line. Then I pulled away, speeding down the road.

Chapter 19

"Where are we going?" Roy asked from the passenger seat of the car.

"I don't know." My hands gripped tighter on the wheel, my fingers stiff with cold because I hadn't stopped to put up the top.

"Are you going to answer that?" He motioned to my purse where my phone was singing. Again. It pretty much hadn't stopped ringing since I'd sped away from the statehouse ten minutes ago.

"No."

I kept driving, turning down streets at random. The phone kept ringing. Roy watched me, fidgeting in his seat.

"Do you want to talk about it?" he asked after I turned down another random street.

"No."

He shifted again. Tugging on his flannel shirt. I needed to get off the street. But where should I go? There would be an APB on me soon, no doubt.

"Your father ... I couldn't hear, but I saw when he—"

"I said I didn't want to talk about it." I'd been there

when he collapsed, suddenly covered in blood; I didn't need to rehash it right now. Heat seemed to gather around my eyes despite the frigid air, and my already iffy vision turned worse as moisture gathered in my eyes. I tried to blink it back.

It didn't work.

I pulled the car off the road, into a small alley between two buildings, and then turned to face Roy.

"Did you see something I didn't? See what attacked him?"

The ghost opened and closed his mouth like a fish gasping for air. Then he shook his head hard enough that his glasses slid down his face.

"How about the roses? Did you see who left them on my car? Where they went?"

"Roses?" Again, the gasping fish thing. His eyes were wide, and I realized I'd yelled the questions.

I could barely see now. The tears were going to break free. I couldn't stop them. I turned forward again and slammed my fists against the steering wheel. Who could attack someone without being in the room? Without leaving a physical or magical trace? How? And had they attacked him just because I was there? So that they could leave those flowers? Was it my fault?

I slammed my hands on the steering wheel again, and then leaned my forehead on my hands. The tears I'd been holding back streamed out, hot and ugly.

"I . . . Uh. I'm going to go check on Icelynne," Roy said, drawing down into the land of the dead.

I didn't try to stop him. Honestly, I barely noted his absence. I sat there with my head buried against my arms. This was a stupid waste of time. I knew that. I should have been doing . . . something. I couldn't even think what right now. Getting off the street for sure would be a good idea. Instead my brain kept running in circles.

My father. The bomb. The flowers. The wild fae

stuck and fading. Falin, injured. The door I had no idea
how to fix. The police likely looking for me.

"You're cold," a deep voice said, and I jolted, my
head jerking up.

Death sat beside me, his arms crossed over his chest
as he watched me with his deep hazel eyes.

"If you're here, am I about to die?" I asked as I
wiped my eyes with the back of my hand. It didn't help.
More tears streamed down my face. My stalker had
managed to follow me to the statehouse and attacked
my father from inside a heavily warded room without
leaving a trace. Maybe I was next. I didn't even know
where I was. An alley that smelled like a restaurant
dumpster.

Death frowned, his full lips pulling down as he
shook his head. "You know I can't see your timeline."
He reached out, but his hand hesitated before actually
touching me as if he had second thoughts. It hung there
a moment, and then he must have reached some conclusion because his hand finally alighted on my cheek,
his thumb wiping away a tear. "I'm here because you're
my friend and you're alone in a dirty alley crying."

Which only made me cry harder.

Death didn't try to get me to talk about it. He didn't
ask questions. Didn't offer advice. He just sat with me
as I ugly-cried, my face buried in my arms, his warm
hand firm and reassuring on my back. At some point
he found the controls for the convertible roof and got
it closed. By the time I'd cried myself out, Death had
cranked up the car's heat and I was no longer shivering.

"Better?" he asked as I dug through my purse
searching for a tissue.

"Not really." Crying hadn't solved anything. I still
didn't know how to fix the door to Faerie. I was no
closer to evacuating the independents. I didn't know if
my father was alive or dead, or where he'd vanished to.
I didn't know what spell had been inside the roses, but
it had contained my hair so it was a trap set specifically

for me. I was worried about Falin, injured and locked in his court in Faerie. I had no idea what to do about Ryese, if he was even behind all this. And I'd only lost time in evading the police as they were no doubt looking for me by now. But I did feel calmer after my cry. It was good to be with a friend, and right that it was Death.

He still had one hand on my back, but now that I'd stopped crying, it felt like a strange amount of contact. Either too stiff and standoffish for our level of friendship, or too much if we were keeping our distance. Personally, I was sick of the distance. I leaned over the middle console between us and leaned the side of my head on his shoulder. For a moment he went still. Then his hand slid up, across my back to my opposite shoulder, and he squeezed lightly, drawing me just a little closer. There was an awkward moment, as if we both held our breath, trying to determine if this level of contact was okay. He was my oldest and closest friend, and right now, that friendship was what I needed. We hadn't worked as lovers, but we'd always made good friends.

"You're an ass for staying away so long," I whispered.

He inclined his head, his dark hair falling forward. "I missed you too," he said, and I could hear the smile in his voice.

We sat like that, in comfortable silence. I thought I was cried out, but another tear slowly worked a hot trail down my cheek. "I don't know what I'm doing," I said, my voice sounding slightly strangled, as if even my throat resisted admitting the fact.

"That isn't atypical for you," Death said without hesitation.

"Hey!" I sat up, but despite myself, a small smile broke through.

At my fake outrage, a lazy smile crossed Death's lips and he lifted a dark eyebrow. "Am I wrong?"

"Yes! Well . . . okay, maybe not, but you don't have to rub it in." I crossed my arms over my chest, and Death only grinned wider.

He reached across and hugged me to him. It was awkward only because of the car's console, but it was a good hug. A comforting one, and I relaxed into his warmth. Unfortunately the lighthearted moment couldn't last, the desperation of the minutes before clawing back to the surface of my mind.

"In seriousness, though, I don't know what to do. This . . . this is all so much. It's too big."

"Who said you had to be the one to fix everything?" Death asked, still holding me in that comforting one-armed hug.

I frowned. I didn't actually think I had to be the one to fix everything. Hell, I knew I couldn't fix it all on my own. "I . . ."

I had been approaching it like it was all my responsibility, though.

"I can't do it all. But I do have to do something. I can't just say, oh well, guess I'll move to Europe!"

His chest moved in what must have been a sharp but silent laugh. "No. That's not your style." His thumb rubbed over my shoulder, the movement rhythmic and comforting. "What can you do right now?"

Hide in a smelly alley with a soul collector, apparently. I dragged in a breath, considering the question.

I had a long list of things I *shouldn't* have done in the last hour or two, like abandon my team, punch a hole in reality, or destroy the spell in the flowers before I knew what it did. I was still on the fence on if it was the right choice to try to cover up my father's disappearance. But those were all things already done. They affected what I could do next, but there wasn't a lot of point in dwelling on what was done.

So what could I do now?

Finding out who was stalking me had moved to the top of my list. The condolence note was too on the nose to not have been connected to whoever had attacked my father. Of course, tracing whoever was leaving the flowers was the issue. I'd disintegrated the evidence. I might have been able to use the flowers in a tracking spell since whoever left them on my car was clearly still on this side of the door. But no flowers meant nothing to trace. The spell that had been in the bouquet held the same signature as the fire spell from the Bloom. Maybe Martinez and her team had made some headway on tracing it. Of course, considering she was with the police and I was likely wanted by the police . . . Yeah, that might complicate things.

I made a frustrated sound, because I'd circled back to regrets about things I'd already done, instead of things I could do next. Death's hand slid into mine, and I realized I'd been fidgeting as I thought, clenching and unclenching my hands so hard that my palms were sore where my nails had been digging into the skin.

"I don't know," I said with a sigh that had a slight, frustrated catch to it. I'd cried myself out already, but I still felt like screaming at the world. Not that I thought it would be a good idea to start rage-yelling in an alley. I needed to keep a low profile, not have the police called on me. "I should probably get off the street."

But where would I go? Death offered no opinion, just sat with me as I mulled it over. I couldn't go home. If the police were looking for me, that would be the first place they checked. The FIB office was out for the same reason.

My father had said to go to shadow. That seemed my most viable next step. There were too many secrets, too many unknowns, and shadow was the court of secrets. Hopefully I could glean some of them without trading away anything too valuable. It was also the only court with a planebender, and I needed to talk to the king about evacuating the independents anyway.

The decision gave me some direction. While I could attempt to contact the king anywhere—hell, even this alley was an option, it had shadows—it made sense to head to my father's mansion. It was the only spot of Faerie left, so it was where the planebender would have to open his portal for the independents. Assuming, of course, I could negotiate passage to Faerie with the king. The shadow court did owe me a favor.

The bonus of heading to the estate was that the police would be unlikely to look for me there. Plus I had a higher chance of getting on the property now, before my sister or my father's staff heard he was missing. Once that news went public, I doubted I'd set foot on the Caine estate. I had no idea how I'd get the rest of the fae there later, but at least I could try to get access to the property now.

Nodding to myself, I sat up. Now that I had at least some idea of what I would do next, I did feel a little more sure of myself, or at least less likely to start screaming. Death gave my shoulder one more small squeeze before releasing me.

"Okay, I have . . . well, I have a first step, not really a plan."

"It's more than you had," he said. He was still holding my hand, and his thumb ran over the top of my knuckles. "I'm glad to see you are looking well."

"Well?" I cocked an eyebrow. Death wasn't prone to throwaway comments. "I just had a breakdown in my car. I'm sure my nose is red, my eyes swollen, and my face blotchy, so I'm guessing what you're looking at isn't my stunning beauty."

He smiled. "Well, the red does bring out the green in your eyes, but no." He hesitated, and I waited. There was something he wanted to say, I could feel it in the air between us, some secret he was weighing. Pressing Death for secrets never worked, so I waited, letting him decide if it was something he could share. "The other fae I've seen since dawn appear . . . less vital. You are not similarly afflicted."

I stared at him. "The other fae are fading . . ." I said

slowly, because he was trying to tell me something without actually saying it. "But I'm not fading." I frowned. "Why would I not be fading?" I'd definitely felt dawn harder than ever before, but thinking back to the way Caleb had been stumbling around, and the comments from some of the wild fae, maybe I hadn't been affected as much as others. But why?

Death's gaze shot down, and in another situation, I would have thought he was staring at my chest. There was too much purpose in that look, though. I lifted my hand. The heart-shaped amulet that wasn't truly an amulet sat against my sternum. I'd carried the ball of realities on me for over a month now, and I barely noticed it unless I focused my magic on it. When the Mender had forced it on me, it had contained only a few planes, namely the land of the dead and the plane the collectors existed on. I had noticed that it seemed to be denser the more I practiced with it, but I'd thought that was simply my own mastery. My first attempts at unraveling it had created a circle of blended realities around me only about eight feet wide. Now I could regularly extend the realities fifteen feet.

I mentally reached for the ball of compacted realities, not attempting to unravel it, just poking at the condensed strands. It could be hard to differentiate the ball from the surrounding strands of reality in the mortal plane because the ball contained planes that were already here, all around me. In Faerie it was a little more obvious, as the collectors' plane and the land of the dead didn't naturally occur there. Now as I mentally poked at it, I realized there were several planes that weren't around me in the mortal realm, including one that felt just like Faerie.

"I . . . I'm carrying around a sliver of Faerie." Like, more than just the magic of Faerie that fae normally carried around in their blood and bones—I had somehow gathered strands of the plane in with all the rest. How had that even happened? I still had so much to learn about my planeweaving. Unfortunately, teachers were in short supply. The Mender had given me enough instruction that at least I wasn't ripping my hands to shreds, but there was so much more I didn't know about how my magic worked. It was a dangerous position to be in. I fingered the locket. "So if I unfurl this ball of realities, will I have a fifteen-foot area of Faerie anytime I need it . . . ?" Which could change my plans as, in that case, the planebender might be able to open the portal to Faerie proper anywhere I needed it instead of only in the blended space in my father's house. "Or will the strands dissipate? Quickly destroyed by the harsh reality of the mortal plane without a connection to Faerie to sustain them?"

Death gave me a small shrug, shaking his head to show he didn't know. Which made two of us. So right now the strands of Faerie were keeping me from fading like the rest of the fae on this continent, but if I unfurled the realities, I might lose those strands I'd unintentionally bound. Which meant opening the locket was a gamble. Half of me wanted to unfurl the bound layers of reality right here and now in the car, to see if the collected strands were even dense enough that the planebender would be able to reach them, but if they instead started breaking down, that would be a terrible waste. I knew there was a pocket of Faerie left in my father's home. It made the most sense to go there first, and save my locket for an emergency.

As I looked back up at Death, the hazel in his eyes swirled, a kaleidoscope of spinning colors. I knew what that meant. "You have to go."

He nodded, squeezing my hand lightly, but when he released my fingers, I didn't let go as quickly.

"Don't stay away so long this time?" I said.

The smile that touched his lips was small, almost sad. "As long as you do not run away to Faerie forever."

"Hey, I'm trying to get the door reopened here, remember?"

"Not what I meant."

Yeah . . . He was talking about the fact that I was dating Falin. I gave an awkward shrug, because what do you say to something like that? I had feelings for Death, I probably always would, but we'd given it a shot and it hadn't worked. That didn't mean I wanted to lose my best friend. I needed him. But it also didn't mean I wouldn't explore what was between Falin and me, because I had feelings there too. A lot of them. And thinking about Falin made me feel instantly guilty for sitting here taking comfort from Death while Falin was badly injured and locked away in Faerie. Not that I could actually reach him right now.

I looked away from Death, my awkward shrug turning deeper, until it was more of a withdrawing cringe. "You know me. Commitment issues and stuff."

From the corner of my eye, I saw Death lift an eyebrow, and I glanced at him long enough to see him studying me. The kind of look that seemed to see deeper than the skin, and that small, sad smile continued to cling to him as he shook his head ever so slightly.

"If you say so," he said. "But my time is up. I must go to the soul that needs me." He lifted my hand, his lips grazing over my knuckles ever so lightly before his touch suddenly vanished, and my hand hung in empty air, his seat now empty.

I stared at the spot where he'd been for a moment, my hand falling to my lap. Then I twisted back around to face my steering wheel, because he was gone, off to collect a soul and send it wherever souls went. I had other things to do, like talk my way into my father's estate. I should probably also call Nori.

I dug my phone out of my purse and discovered that its silence wasn't due to the fact that she'd stopped calling, but that Death must have taken the time to put the phone on silent while I was crying. For a guy who could only interact with the mortal world while in physical contact with me, he'd proven to be rather good with technology today. Glancing at my screen, I saw that I'd missed dozens of calls from Tem, and another dozen from Nori. I also had quite a few calls from numbers I didn't recognize.

Nori was likely pissed I'd taken off, but that would hardly be noticeable beside her normal display of disdain for me. Tem . . . well, Tem was likely ready to drag me out for my own good. I'd have to be careful when I met back up with him. Nori and Tem were probably together, but I decided I'd rather deal with Nori's ire than Tem's professional worry.

Nori answered on the first ring. "Craft? What's going on? Where the hell are you?"

"Hello to you too," I said, putting my car in reverse and backing out of the alley. "I'm . . . well, I'll be honest, I'm not exactly sure where I am right now, but I've decided where I'm going. Has there been any chatter about the governor's disappearance?"

"It's not like I have a police scanner in my car, Craft," she snapped. "I did receive a few calls from investigators wanting to talk to you. They were not happy when I couldn't produce you."

No surprise there.

My phone beeped, another call coming in. I glanced down at the number and frowned.

"Why is Tem still calling me? Isn't he in the car with you?"

"No. He took off right after you did at the statehouse. Said it would be his head if he lost you."

Oh. "I'm going to patch him through then," I said, hitting the button to join the two calls.

"Boss, where are you?" Tem yelled over the phone. Wind roared through the line, the sounds of traffic filtering through. Wherever Tem was calling from, he was on the move.

"I'm fine," I said, turning on my blinker.

"That wasn't what I asked." He ground out the words. I'd never heard Tem sound quite so furious. If

I'd been standing in front of him when he sounded like that, I'd definitely be backing away.

I glanced around. I still wasn't sure where I was, but I at least had a general idea of the area, and I was pretty sure I was headed in a direction that would lead toward my father's neighborhood.

"I have an assignment for you," I said, ignoring Tem's fury. I was mostly addressing Nori, but they could both work on it.

"I already have an assignment," Tem barked. "And it is coming from a lot higher up than you. Right now, you're actively obstructing my efforts to do my job."

I sighed. "Fine, then I have an assignment for Nori. I need you to get the word out to all the fae you can reach that I'm working on securing a temporary door to Faerie and they need to be ready to go."

There was silence on the phone for a moment and then Nori said something in that musical fae language I really needed to learn. When she was finished, she said, "Craft, where is this door? How?"

If this worked, every fae in Nekros would know there was a pocket of Faerie in my father's home, but before I secured the door, it didn't seem right to reveal that. It touched too close to my father's well-guarded secrets.

"I'm still working out the details," I said after only the briefest pause. "I need to negotiate with the shadow court before I know for sure it will work, but get the fae ready to evacuate."

Tem cursed, a string of grumbled profanity that aptly expressed how unhappy he was at my statement. "Boss, what are you thinking? You can't go to the shadow court. You're winter."

I was getting so sick of the hard lines fae seemed to set between courts. "I can if it gets us a door. Just get the word out. And the invitation is for anyone. Any fae from any court who is displaced and needs an evacuation route."

In the silence of the phone, I knew they were about to protest, so I added, "Nori said it herself, this isn't winter territory anymore."

A strange sensation passed over me. It wasn't pain, but an awareness of . . . something. Odd and vaguely uncomfortable. I hit the brakes of my car as the sensation intensified, and then a small shadow jumped free of my own shadow. A tiny cat shape landed on the passenger seat. I stared at it, until a driver behind me laid on their horn. Then I jolted, hitting the gas again.

"Just gather the fae," I said and then hit the end button on my cell phone before Nori could answer. I shot another glance at the shadow cat. "Are you here because Dugan has found something, or because he heard I want to talk to the shadow court?"

The cat didn't answer, of course. It turned a circle in the seat and then settled into a shadowy blob, hardly resembling an animal so much as a patch of darkness. I frowned at it, but it was content to wait until I got somewhere I could talk to Dugan.

My phone began buzzing again. I hadn't even had time to set it down yet. I glanced at the display, expecting it to be Nori demanding more information about my proposed door. Instead it was Tem. I groaned, shooting a glance at the shadow cat. "Three guesses on what he wants. The first two guesses don't count."

The cat didn't lift its head. Maybe its ears twitched, it was hard to tell in the blob of shadow it had become. Right, no companionship there. I was definitely more of a dog person. With a sigh, I hit the button on my phone.

"Tem, I'm fine. I don't need a babysitter."

"The king told me to keep an eye on you, and that is damn well what I plan to do. Where are you, boss?"

I did actually know the answer to that question now. I considered holding out, but what would it hurt to take Tem with me? I was going to have a serious discussion with Falin about this whole bodyguard thing as soon as I saw him again, though.

"Okay, fine," I said with a sigh. "I'm near Fairmount Street. I can meet you somewhere, but I am planning a meeting with the shadow court, so if you intend to interfere, this isn't going to work. So, your word you're not going to do anything drastic like drag me out of town for my own protection."

The line was quiet aside from traffic sounds for a moment. Then Tem said, "My oath. I won't drag you off for your own protection."

Well, that had been easier than I'd anticipated.

"Okay then, where should I pick you up?" Because I wasn't sure how he was getting around right now, but I wasn't about to abandon my car.

"Boss, half the state is looking for you. You lie low. I'll come to you. Pull off in an alley or something and give me the name of the side streets. I'm not far from Fairmount."

Ugh . . . another alley. But I couldn't fault his logic. The further delay in reaching my father's was less than ideal, though. Still, I did as he asked, finding a small tucked-away side street to park on. He disconnected as soon as I gave him the address, promising he was only about seven minutes out. At least it wouldn't be a long delay.

While I waited, I texted Caleb. I needed to warn him that the police might show up looking for me, but I didn't want an electronic log of that message, so instead I texted telling him I was working on securing a temporary door into Faerie and asking him to spread the word. Nori would *probably* inform the independents, but I doubted she'd go out of her way to make sure as many as possible received the news and were ready when I had a time and location to share. Caleb had a lot of ties in the independent community, so hopefully he'd help fill in the gaps she missed.

The shadow cat, who'd been content to sleep on my passenger seat while I'd been driving, now stood and paced across the dash of my car. She didn't make a sound, but agitation radiated off her dark form. Because I'd stopped? Or had something else happened? Something on Dugan's side? It would help if the prince had a cell phone, though I guess Faerie having cell towers would be required for that to be useful.

"We'll be on our way again any minute," I reassured the cat.

Her tail whipped through the air, accenting her pacing steps. When that didn't garner the response she desired, she turned and leapt into my lap. Being a shadow, the cat had no true weight, so it was an odd sensation. I was aware of the cat, that she was touching me, but the sensation had no substance. It was an eerie feeling.

The cat stared straight into my face with her featureless one. I frowned at her, unsure what she was trying to tell me. Then she turned, bunched in on herself, and jumped straight into the rearview mirror. Darkness bled over the mirror, and then Dugan appeared—or at least, part of his face appeared. It was mostly just a very extreme close-up of his eyes and the bridge of his nose. From the way the skin around his eyes moved, I guessed he was frowning.

"What am I looking at?" he asked, his gaze darting around.

"Interior of my car. I guess it was the easiest reflective surface your cat could find."

He made a noncommittal grunt, and then seemed to back up, more of his face becoming visible.

"Did you locate the tree?" I asked as his face slowly came into focus.

"Greetings to you as well, my lady," he said and though I could see the smile on his face, there was a sharpness to his words.

I winced. Yeah, that had been a little rude. I cast around in my brain for a suitable greeting. How formal was I supposed to be? I was tired, so I just went with a title I'd heard other fae use. "Hello, Prince of Shadows and Secrets."

Dugan frowned, which wasn't the response I'd expected. "Now you are mocking me."

"I'm not! I—" I cut off abruptly because as Dugan continued moving back so that he was more properly framed in my rearview mirror, the odd oblong shape of the surface revealed the area around him as well. And Dugan wasn't alone.

"Falin!" I surged forward, as if I could jump to my feet in the front seat of the car. That, of course, didn't work. Between the steering wheel and the seat belt, my own momentum slammed me back into the seat. Despite that fact, I was grinning like a loon. I'd spent half a day fearing he'd died until Dugan had told me he was only injured, but then I'd fretted about how badly hurt he might be. He stood tall and strong now, apparently whole. Of course, I'd seen him glamour over wounds that would kill a human, so how okay he actually was might be less clear than appearances.

Falin smiled, a real smile that shone in every part of his face and made his brilliant eyes look impossibly blue, but all he said was "Alex."

My name as greeting, but also said with relief, and affection. I was still smiling and more than anything I wanted to reach through the mirror and wrap my arms around him. I needed to feel that he was okay. To find out if he was still injured under his glamour. To just reassure myself that he was real.

Dugan cleared his throat, reminding me that this wasn't a private conversation.

"Yes. As you have observed, the Winter King has emerged, alive," he said. "And to answer your earlier question, no, I have not located your sapling yet. Ryese . . . is surprisingly difficult to track down."

I wasn't entirely surprised. Ryese's personal magics seemed well suited toward hiding his activity, even from the court of secrets. A month ago, he'd orchestrated a series of murders and managed to conceal nearly all the details surrounding them.

"Do you know if he is still hiding in the light court?" Or was he out here sending me spelled roses?

"I do not know his precise location, but sources suggest he is still inside Faerie. Now you need to make your way to the pocket of Faerie in your father's home," Dugan said after a moment. "We need to talk in person."

I nodded. "That's actually where I was headed. I'd like to discuss a door with you." Because if I could work out the details now, that would give me more time to get the independents in place and get everyone safely evacuated.

Falin's gaze swept across the surface of the mirror. "You're in your car, but you appear to be parked."

"Yeah, well. I had to stop and wait for my babysitter. Which we need to discuss." Speaking of whom, the sound of a motorcycle approaching filled the small street I was parked on. I twisted in my seat.

Tem pulled an enormous black Harley to a stop behind my car. The huge troll still looked large on the bike, but he looked a whole hell of a lot more comfortable astride it than I'd seen him look inside my car or Nori's. I guessed it must have been his preferred mode of transportation, but I had to wonder where he'd snagged the bike from, as Nori said he'd split right after I had.

His eyes met mine through the rear window of the car, and I sent him an abbreviated wave. The look of relief that washed over his face was intense, as if he'd truly believed his head would have rolled if he hadn't found me. Yeah, we were going to have this conversation real soon.

"No worries, the babysitter is here," I said, turning back toward the mirror. "Though I'd appreciate it if you'd call that guy off," I muttered before shifting my focus on Dugan because that was a conversation Falin and I could have later. There were more pressing issues. "About that door? I want to evacuate the fae in Nekros—and any who can make it from farther away, but I'm guessing we are on a time limit with the pocket of Faerie."

Falin frowned, his brows drawing together as he stepped in front of Dugan. "What?"

I returned the frown. Did he disapprove of the door? "You have a different plan? Or do you mean the bodyguard thing? Because if you actually trust me to do this job, then show some trust in me to handle it." Not that there was much job left. The Nekros FIB department had pretty much dissolved unless we found a way to fix the amaranthine tree.

Falin had gone still. The kind of still a large stalking cat can go when it is listening for the sounds of prey. Or danger.

"What are you talking about, Alex? What bodyguard?"

"Tem? Big yellow troll?" I said, but from his expression, I already knew he didn't know who I was talking about. I found myself whispering now, because Tem was right outside the car, already opening the door to the passenger side. "Said the king assigned him to watch over me on the job . . ."

I didn't need to see Falin's cautious headshake; my hand was already moving toward the dagger in my boot. Dugan's warning—"There is more than one king in Faerie"—was delivered a moment too late, Tem already sliding into the seat beside me.

Tem's eyes widened as they landed on the mirror and the not-reflections contained within. The moment his gaze landed on Falin, something hardened in his expression.

"Damn it, boss. Now you've done it," he yelled, tearing the mirror from the car and crushing it in one huge hand.

I jerked my dagger free of my boot, my other hand

flying for the door handle beside me. Unfortunately, I'd never taken the damn seat belt off. Panic flooded through me, and I lashed out with the dagger.

Troll-hide was thick, nigh impenetrable, but my blade was enchanted to slice through anything. The point pierced his biceps, sinking deep, and too hot blood rushed over my fingers, burning my flesh where it touched me.

Tem bellowed in rage, moving fast, too fast. He caught my arm in one huge hand. He was going to crush it. I was going to lose my entire arm. I had only a moment to attempt to wrench my wrist away, to struggle against the impossibly strong grip pinning me. Then I felt the cold sizzle of a spell against my skin. A ready-made charm that held the same sinisterly familiar notes I'd detected in the roses and fire charm.

Then the spell ripped through me, and the world went black.

Chapter 20

The first thing I became aware of was the sound of dripping water.

Pling.

Pling.

Pling.

The sound echoed around my head, making the throbbing pain shatter any attempt at a coherent thought with every resounding drip. I didn't want to open my eyes; my head hurt way too much without adding light to the situation. But my mouth felt like I'd been chewing on cotton, and my throat burned. If there was water, I needed some.

The pain, the sound, and the need for water were my only concerns for a while, as I tried to rouse myself enough to deal with at least one of those issues. Then memories started surfacing.

I'd seen Falin. He'd been alive and well enough to make it to the shadow court. He hadn't sent Tem. And I'd told the troll where to find me.

A new sensation cut through the others, panic flooding me again as I remembered the struggle in the car. I forced my eyes open, bracing myself for more pain.

And found myself in darkness.

I blinked.

I could see absolutely nothing. I could still hear water dripping not far away, and I could feel gritty wet stone under me, but I couldn't see a thing. My first instinct was to thrash and try to jump to my feet, but my body felt heavy, my limbs not responding properly. The spell Tem had knocked me out with—it had worked fast, and apparently was wearing off slow. I couldn't feel my legs, let alone my feet; no way was I standing right now.

But I couldn't just lie in the dark and do nothing.

I took a deep breath, wrinkling my nose at the musty scent of mold that permeated the air. Despite that, I forced down another deep breath, concentrating on the feel of my lungs filling, on my heart—while it was pounding, even it seemed sluggish given the situation. Next I worked on focusing on my arms. I couldn't move them, but I could feel them, though it took me longer than it should have to realize they were bound behind my back. My fingers tingled, a growing feeling of pins and needles stabbing my arms and palms as the awareness in my limbs spread. The small pains were almost reassuring—they meant Tem hadn't dismembered me. It took concentration at first, but I could move each finger, which also meant I wasn't bound in iron. My legs didn't seem to be bound at all. Either that was a pretty big oversight or my captors were very confident that I could not escape from whatever hole they had trapped me inside.

Now that I could feel my body, the piercing pain that had been only in my head now spread everywhere. A deep body ache like I'd once suffered while fevered with the flu. Apparently every cell of my body was fighting off the residual effects of the spell, and it hurt like hell. I clenched my teeth together to prevent myself from whimpering. I had no idea if I was being observed, but it didn't appear anyone knew I was awake yet, and I hoped to keep it that way until I was confident that I could get my feet under me at the very least.

As I lay in the damp darkness, I slowly became aware of a different sensation, one a whole lot more welcome than the pain that was taking its sweet time to ebb. A familiar buzzing sensation, a tickle of magic easily ignored if I didn't focus on it, hummed near the top of my boot. I knew that magic, and the almost alien awareness it contained. My enchanted dagger.

But how could it be back in its sheath?

The dagger had been in my hand—and Tem's arm—when the spell had knocked me unconscious. I had serious doubts that the troll would have pulled the blade from his flesh and then carefully sheathed it in my boot. Which meant the enchanted blade must have found its own way there. Did that mean I was being held in Faerie? The dagger had never moved around the mortal realm on its own. But no, the air here didn't *feel* like Faerie. There was no distant music, no contented feeling of being home, no soft hum of magic. Wherever I was currently smelled of mold and rotted meat, and I could definitely feel the chill of the grave coming off the tiny corpses sharing the room with me. Thankfully, nothing I felt was human, and all the animals were small: fish, squirrels, a raccoon or two, and rats. Lots of dead rats.

I tried again to look around, to pierce the darkness in front of my eyes. Nothing. I wasn't sure if the room I was in truly was pitch-black, or if my damaged vision only made it appear that way. If I had to guess, I'd bet I was being held underground. Maybe a storm drain or a sewer tunnel. Neither sounded like a good place to be lying with my face on the slimy stone, but I didn't have a lot of choice in the matter.

I considered opening my shields so that I could get a better look at my surroundings, but hesitated. Right now, I appeared to be alone, but that didn't mean I was unwatched. The moment I opened my shields, the light show from my eyes would alert anyone paying attention that I was conscious. That would be unavoidable soon, but with each minute that passed, the effects of the spell dissipated. The fog in my head was clearing, as was the pain, and moving my hands was becoming easier. The tingling in my legs suggested they were not yet ready to hold my weight, so I gave it another minute, listening to the water dripping in the darkness, giving my body a chance to shake off the residual effects of the spell.

"She should be awake by now," a deep voice said, the words distant and echoing slightly, like they were coming from down a long hallway.

"She blooded true, but she's not full-blooded. Maybe the spell hit her harder than it would a real Sleagh Maith." The answering voice was female, and sounded like it was coming closer.

I cursed silently.

Apparently I was out of time. I still couldn't see anything, and couldn't guess the size of the room. The air was still and stale, which made the darkness feel claustrophobic, but the echoes of the dripping water made me think the room I was in was fairly large. But was there anywhere to hide? I needed to see, damn it.

I pried open my mental shields, imagining the living vines I used as a wall around my psyche slithering apart and allowing my slivers of magic to peer through. At the same time, I drew one leg up to my chest, rolling up to my knees. A chaotic mix of realities filled the darkness around me, illuminating it with color. I had enough time to notice tall shapes all around me, not far away, as I straightened. Then a jolt of pain and dizziness crashed over me. It felt like a fist slamming into my skull, dragging out my magic, my energy, my very life.

My shoulder collided with the wet stone as I collapsed, my cheek hitting a moment later, but I barely felt the impact, my consciousness slipping.

When my eyes fluttered, the room was brighter, and not from me peering across planes this time—my shields had apparently slammed back into place by reflex. No, someone had turned on a pair of industrial floodlights suspended on a pole several yards away. I squeezed my eyes shut against the sudden brightness, forgetting for a moment I should have probably pretended to still be out cold.

"Oh, so she is conscious," the female voice said at the same time the male speaker said, "Welcome back to the waking world, boss."

Tem.

I blinked, squinting into the light, searching. It took far too long for my bad eyes to adjust to the light. Every one of my crashing heartbeats seemed to take too long as I waited for an attack to land while I was helpless, bound and blind. But no blows landed. As shapes began to resolve, I realized no one was even near me and the room wasn't half as bright as it had first seemed.

I appeared to be in the center of the room, a good five feet of empty space surrounding me. But beyond that cleared space were huge rectangles erected all around me. *What in the world . . . ?*

Mirrors, I realized, after staring at the one directly across from me for a long befuddled moment. At least a dozen mirrors, all facing inward, toward where I was lying. The mirror reflected back my bound form, but also the reflection of me as reflected by all the other mirrors so there were a hundred, maybe a thousand reflections of me bound and confused in the mirror's surface. My head still felt like it was splitting—either from opening my shields while under the effect of the knockout spell or from bouncing off the stone when I'd subsequently collapsed, so I didn't attempt to lift it to look around, not yet. Instead I let my gaze search, though even that much effort made the pain in my head throb harder.

The two large floodlights were bright, but most of

their beams were focused where I was lying in the center of the mirrors. The area beyond the mirrors was harder to make out between the gaps of glass, and the corners of the large space I was being held in were still lost to shadows, at least to my bad eyes. Flashes of silver caught at the corner of my vision as I attempted to peer into the spaces between the mirrors, but it was gone anytime I tried to move my gaze to focus on it. *Magic.* And fae magic, at that, though considering everything, that wasn't surprising. If I made a point of not focusing on the magic, I could almost see it twining between the mirrors, and I gulped as I realized the mirrors formed a complete circle, of which I was in the center.

I started to open my shields again, to try to get a sense of the spell contained in that circle of mirrors, but pain stabbed through my brain as the first crack in my shield opened, and I slammed it shut again. Apparently my psyche was not ready for that yet. My own magic was clearly out of reach for the moment, but what about my body? I lifted my head slightly, just an experimental movement. That didn't cause any debilitating increase in pain, so I craned my neck, still searching for the people I knew were in the room with me.

My gaze finally landed on Tem. He stood, slightly hunched in the low-ceilinged room, just beyond the circle, watching me from between two mirrors.

"You asshole," I said as soon as my gaze landed on him. The words emerged from my throat in a dry rasp, and I coughed before I could continue. "I should have known something was wrong when you made that oath so easily."

The troll shrugged his huge shoulders, but he looked away from me. "I didn't kidnap you for your own good."

No, he certainly hadn't done it for my good.

Tem had been talking to someone, a woman by the sound of the voice, before I'd tried to open my shields and passed out. I scanned what I could see of the room, but didn't see anyone besides the troll. Of course, sprawled on my side on the floor, there was only so much of the room I could see, especially with the mirrors and darkness.

Taking a deep breath, I pulled one knee to my chest again. Then I rolled myself up, over my knee so I was facedown against the stone, but at least my leg was under me. I didn't immediately sit up this time, though, not after having passed out after doing it the first time. I suspected it had as much or more to do with the fact that I'd opened my shields at the same time the first time I did it, but I didn't want to take that chance. So far Tem was hanging back, beyond the mirrors. Did that mean the magic was a physical barrier? I couldn't feel it, so I wasn't sure.

I rolled to sitting slowly, deliberately, testing the position as I moved, ready to stop if dizziness or pain hit. I watched Tem's shadowy form as I did so, but he didn't move as I straightened. He just watched me, his mouth drawn down in a hard frown around his tusks. There had to be a barrier spell in the circle. Why else would he have left me without my legs bound? Of course, my arms were bound, and he was a hell of a lot bigger, stronger, and faster than me, so maybe he hadn't thought it would be necessary.

I'd made it upright without fainting again, so rose on my knees, trying to get my feet under me. That was a little harder, and I swayed slightly, my calves and thighs protesting as they took my weight. I wanted to close my eyes, to breathe and just focus on staying upright, but I didn't dare look away from the troll. He still hadn't moved, but that didn't mean he wasn't about to charge me. I glared at him as I attempted to catch my breath.

"Which king are you working for?" I asked once I was relatively certain I wasn't going to crash back down on my ass. Tem definitely hadn't been assigned to watch me by Falin, and I had serious doubts the Shadow King had sent him. Light was ruled by a queen. So that only left spring, summer, and fall. None of which made a lot of sense. Well, or the High King, but that made even less sense.

"You'll find out soon enough," a female voice said. I jumped, whirling around, and nearly lost my hard-won footing.

I again had to take precious seconds to steady myself before I could trust my eyes to move and search for the source of the voice. I found her a few mirrors over from Tem, squatting low with her knees splayed wide, her tangled hair touching the wet stone ground.

"Jenny Greenteeth," I hissed, my voice emerging from my throat as a hoarse gasp. The fae bogeyman smiled.

"So you remember little Jenny, do you? I'm flattered."

"Hard to forget you trying to drown me."

She flashed a mouthful of sharp teeth and lifted one of her green shoulders. Then she twisted her head in a creepily inhuman manner and fixed her dark eyes on Tem. "I'm not getting blamed for this. You call him."

Tem only glared at her. "She was talking with Winter. It was the only option."

Jenny's lips curled back in what was most definitely *not* a smile. Then she rose from her crouch and turned away from the circle where I stood. "Your blunder. You call him."

With that, she stalked away. I heard metal scrape on stone, and though I couldn't see it, I guessed that must have been the door. I hadn't heard the door open when they'd entered, but I'd apparently knocked myself unconscious again temporarily about then, so I wasn't that surprised. I listened for the sound of a lock turning or a bolt sliding into place, but it didn't sound like Jenny closed the door behind herself.

My legs were free and they weren't even bolting the

door? If my hands weren't bound behind my back, I'd wonder if I hadn't completely misread this situation. But no, Tem had definitely knocked me out with a spell, trussed me up, and taken me to some creepy underground dungeon. It just didn't seem to be a particularly secure dungeon. Which was hopefully a good thing for me.

Assuming I could get past whatever magic I kept catching glimpses of snaking between the mirrors.

I walked toward the edge of the circle, catty-corner to where Tem still hunched. My pace was slow. I would have liked to claim I was faking casual, pretending to ignore that I was a hostage in some creepy mirror-lined circle, but the truth was that my feet dragged and I had to focus on each step. My heart was racing, though. It thudded hard enough that I thought it might be trying to jump right through my breastbone and drag the rest of me out of here.

"I wouldn't get too close to that," Tem said as I approached one of the mirrors.

I frowned at him. His tone wasn't threatening. If anything, he sounded concerned, which was rather ironic since he'd been the one who put me inside this circle. With my hands still behind my back, I couldn't reach out to the magic physically, but this close, I could feel it thrumming through the circle. I had no idea what the magic did—I'd never felt anything like it—but there was a whole hell of a lot of it. I considered sticking the toe of my boot in the space between two of the mirrors, but this didn't feel like a barrier spell. Or at least, not only a barrier spell.

"The last time I saw Jenny, she was working for Ryese," I said, trying to make my voice conversational even as I tried to wrack my brain for a way out of this mess. "But he's not a king. So who are you two working for now? Hell, which court even?"

Tem only frowned at me, then he turned and walked out of sight. When he returned, he held a small orb glowing with silver magic. He touched it to one of the mirrors, and magic sparked, activating glyphs I hadn't noticed in the frame surrounding the glass. One by one, he walked to each mirror, tapping the backs with the orb and making the glyphs on them shimmer. I assumed this was how he was calling the enigmatic *him* Jenny had mentioned. The spell didn't seem to be particularly threatening, and yet I cringed with each glyph that lit up, a cold sweat trailing down my back.

Once he was done, Tem disappeared long enough to put the orb back where he'd gotten it, and then he walked back to the edge of the circle again, watching me. I backed away from the now-glowing mirrors until I was in the center of the circle again. I stared at the mirrors, and they reflected back hundreds of me, my eyes a little too wide and my curls stuck to the side of my head where gray liquid smudged my cheek. I had the ridiculous urge to try to watch all the mirrors at once, as if I expected one of the hundreds of reflections of me to change and prove not to be me at all.

"Did you mean what you told Nori?" Tem asked, watching me watch the reflections.

I was trying to focus on only one mirror, because every time I so much as twitched, all the reflections moved as well, making it look like an army was swarming around me. Yeah, it was an army of myself, but given the situation, it was freaky. If the glyphs were a call, whoever was on the other side apparently wasn't inclined to answer. I could only hope that was good for me. It gave me more time for the spell I'd been hit with to wear off. Not that I knew what I planned to do next, but I wanted to be able to peer across planes again. With my shields locked, I couldn't see through glamour, and I definitely couldn't unravel the spell around me.

"What did I tell her?" I asked, not bothering to look at Tem. I needed to get my hands free. It wasn't metal binding me, and it didn't feel like rope either. I was guessing plastic zip ties, which sucked because plastic was a material that broke down slowly, even in the land of the dead. If I could reach my magic without fainting, I could push the bindings over the chasm, but I was going to have to push the plastic deep for it to dissolve enough to break. Or I was going to have to get to my dagger. That would be a hell of a lot more noticeable, but at least I wouldn't risk passing out again. It would give away the fact that I had the dagger, though.

Tem studied me, his face drawn tight in contemplation. "That you were planning to negotiate a door, and all the fae, regardless of court, could use it to evacuate."

"Of course I meant that. Why wouldn't I have?"

"It's just . . . That's not done. Courts don't help each other unless they've negotiated some deal that makes doing so beneficial to them."

I shrugged, using the motion to cover the fact that I was trying to twist my hands so I could get a finger on the zip tie binding my wrist. I didn't technically need to touch the plastic, but considering I couldn't see it and I didn't want to push all the space around me into the depths of the land of the dead, a touch focus seemed prudent. Also, the tighter my focus, the less magic I'd have to expend.

"What would you get out of saving a bunch of independents?" Tem asked after a few moments.

"Uh, a whole bunch of fae who aren't dead? But I'm guessing you're working for the person behind the doors' destruction, so I guess you don't care about casualties."

He grimaced, looking away from me. "You don't understand."

"You're right. I don't."

The plastic cut at my wrist, but I managed to get two fingers on the zip tie. I cracked my mental shield, just a sliver. Pain jabbed into my mind, but no dizziness this time, and my legs held under me, so I opened it wider. Then I narrowed my focus to my fingers, and the plastic I could feel through my glove. I shoved at reality, and a wave of dizziness washed over me. Too late now to stop. I squeezed my eyes shut, focusing on my tenuous grip on the planes touching the zip tie. This was not how my magic liked to be used. The planes didn't appreciate being shoved around like this. Pain sliced into my fingers, warmth soaking into my gloves as the tips of my fingers split open. My heartbeat tripped over itself, my breath coming in ragged gulps as if I'd just run a mile. Exhaustion rushed through me, as if all my energy were being drained into the ground around my feet.

I slammed my shields closed again. Swaying despite my best efforts. This was ridiculous. I'd used almost no magic, not nearly as much as when I'd shoved the bouquet of flowers out of reality. And yet I felt as magically drained as I did after an hour-long session of practicing manipulating the realities stored in my necklace.

Hopefully that one push at the plastic had been enough, because I wasn't up for another one. I pried open my eyes, forcing myself to focus on Tem. He was studying me, the skin where his eyebrows would have been if he'd been human bunched tight and a frown tugging his lips down around his tusks. Blinking a few times, I met his gaze, both so that I had a place to concentrate, and to distract him from my actions by keeping him focused on my words.

"I don't get you at all, Tem," I said, tugging at my wrists. The plastic stretched. I'd damaged it, thank goodness. But was it enough? I pulled harder, hoping the strain didn't show in my shoulders. "I liked you. Of all the FIB agents, you were actually nice. And I saw your face when you were pulling survivors out of the Bloom. Hell, you stuck your arm in a fire spell. Why?" The plastic snapped, breaking with a soft sound, and the pressure around my wrists vanished. I snatched at the broken plastic, holding it halfway in place so it wouldn't hit the ground and alert Tem to what I'd done. I rambled on, keeping his attention on my face, my words. "How could you have been working for the bad guy this whole time?"

"I'm not working for the bad guy! I'm working for change!" Tem bellowed the words. "Faerie is broken. The High King sleeps through centuries at a time, or maybe he just doesn't care about the fae. The courts are all self-serving. The independents are subject to the whims of whichever court controls the territory where they manage to scrape out a life. The whole system needs an overhaul."

"You talk too much, troll," a new voice said, and I jumped. I'd been staring at Tem and I hadn't noticed my hundreds of reflections fading from the mirrors.

Now the glass reflected nothing, the surface completely empty aside from a soft glow. The emptiness was even more eerie than the hundreds of versions of me had been. The light in the mirrors grew, until they were almost too bright to look at. Then a figure materialized in the brilliance, and the surface dimmed enough that I could make out a dozen cloaked figures surrounding me, watching through the surface of the mirrors. Or maybe it was only one golden-cloaked figure, the mirrors all showing the same image.

"You bound her with plastic and thought that would hold her? She's already free," the figure said, his voice coming from every direction at once.

"Ryese," I hissed, because I'd seen that cloak before, even if it hid his face, and I definitely knew that voice. Then I paused. "But you're no king . . ."

A month ago one of his followers had called him the scarred prince, but he held no court. Was he an upper-level minion for this mysterious king Tem had been trying to call? For his part, Tem cringed at my words. Then he dropped to the ground, falling fully prostrate onto the slimy stone. The golden-cloaked figure ignored him.

I once again found myself unsure where to focus.

Twelve mirrors showed the cloaked figure, watching me from every point in the circle. I again had the urge to spin around, to try to watch all of them and figure out which was the real Ryese. Except was this an illusion? A trick of glamour? It wasn't that one mirror held the real Ryese and the rest were glamour. No, each mirror held the same image of him, all real. And all not. Like a dozen television screens showing the same picture, except this picture was watching me back.

"Oh, dearest Lexi, it has been a hot minute, hasn't it," he said, lifting his hands and pulling back the golden hood. The face below was instantly recognizable, and yet it had transformed since I'd seen him last. The veins of dark scarring from iron poisoning still snaked through half his skin, one of his eyes sightless and clouded over, but where he'd looked sickly a month ago, his complexion gray and sallow, now he radiated strength and inner light. His hair was still short where it had been shorn in his sickness, but even it looked healthy again, once again shimmering like strands of crystals. When he'd moved, he'd used both hands, and while one was encased with a glove, he'd used the hand that a month before had been a shriveled and wasted claw. But most telling was the glowing golden crown resting upon his brow.

I stared at the intricate—and very large—crown. I knew from the brief time since Falin became the Winter King that Faerie always marked her rulers. They could will the crowns to be large and ornate, or simple circlets, but they couldn't remove them, ever. Most of the fae royalty seemed to keep the crowns simple, but not Ryese. No, of course not. I wasn't even sure how the cloak had concealed the huge bit of ornamentation on his head. It positively radiated with light, the golden glow permeating the space around him. Every mirror seemed to be filled with a gentle glow—or maybe that was simply the magic he used in this spell. A magic that was the complete opposite of the spell Dugan used when he communicated through a mirror.

"You've taken over the court of light and day-dream," I said, still staring at the crown.

Ryese smiled. One side of his lips didn't lift quite as much as the other, but the effect was far less noticeable than it had been a month ago. He was healing, maybe nearly fully healed, from his iron poisoning. I hadn't thought that was possible.

"But . . ." I said. "Your own mother?"

The smile fell from his face. The glare in his remaining good eye should have pinned me in place, it slammed against me so fiercely.

"And why not 'my own mother'? She raised me to rule, wanted me to reshape Faerie. She simply failed to see that she would be one of the stepping-stones I'd have to cross. Very shortsighted for a clever woman."

I stared at him. There was no regret in his tone. No mourning. Successions in Faerie were rarely peaceful and almost always deadly. But Ryese wasn't a fighter. Even when he'd been scheming to conquer winter, it had been through underhanded methods. He hadn't challenged the former Winter Queen, but had driven her slowly mad, poisoning her until she could barely hold the court together.

"You didn't win the light court in a duel," I said, because that wasn't Ryese's style, even before he'd wound up crippled from iron poisoning for his treach-ery in winter.

A pale shimmering eyebrow lifted toward his ornate crown. "Of course not. A barbaric form of succession. Leaves the whole court locked down and scrambling for weeks, and then there are all the challengers who think one simply got lucky and that they can take the crown— oh, but you've seen all that in winter, haven't you? How is your little murderous knight? Still managing to hold on to the crown he butchered my dear aunt to gain?"

I bit my tongue, trying not to rise to the bait, but I couldn't help saying, "Dear aunt? You made several attempts to kill her!"

"Touché." He gave me a nod, but a small smile touched half his lips, pleasure that he'd gotten a response out of me. "But as you saw, a messy way to usurp a throne. No, my lovely mother is alive and . . . 'well' is not the correct word, I suppose. She is peaceful, though." His expression turned into a caricature of thoughtfulness. "She is, perhaps, less conversational, her mental facilities lacking what they once were, but she looks as phenomenal as she ever has and that was always more important to her anyway."

"Did you poison her?"

"My own mother?" His tone was all mock outrage as he again repeated my earlier words. He didn't deny it, though.

"What do you want from me, Ryese? Why am I here?"

"Jumping right to the chase, Lexi? I suppose you want me to tell you all my plans and why I destroyed the doors as well?" he said, studying me with that one clear eye. There was something odd about his stance. I hadn't noticed it earlier, too distracted by the transformation he'd undergone over the last month. But he was favoring what should have been his good side, using the iron-damaged hand to accent his words, his weight on that side of his body as well. "Oh, dearest Lexi, don't you know that monologuing is for villains? You heard the troll. I'm the good guy here. The one championing for change in all of Faerie."

"I doubt anyone would enjoy suffering under your rule in your reimagined Faerie."

A wicked smile spread over his face. "And yet they line up to do so. I've never run short of followers."

He had me there. In all his schemes, he always seemed to have toadies eager to run around taking the risks and doing his dirty work for him.

The smile fell from Ryese's face, his expression shifting to something that looked like . . . surprise? Or maybe pain? I wasn't sure. The moment after his eyes widened and his lips thinned, he vanished from the mirrors. Light poured from the surface, making me squint as the room suddenly lit up like a small sun had just risen in the center of it. I tried to peer through the light, to see if Ryese was hiding behind all that brilliance, but it was simply too much, too bright.

I shielded my face with my hand—Ryese already knew I'd gotten free, no reason to pretend I wasn't. With my other hand I palmed the dagger that had made its way back into my boot. Hopefully the light blinding me was doing the same to Tem—I couldn't see him to tell. I doubted he knew the dagger had ended up back in my possession, or he wouldn't have let me keep it. It would potentially be more of a surprise advantage later if I left it in my boot, but there was no assurance I'd be able to get to it later. I could reach it now, so I turned the dagger up, pressing the blade flat against my arm in an attempt to conceal it.

The light was still pouring from the mirrors. Was more than just light coming through? Was that even possible? I couldn't help but think of Alice and her trip through the looking glass. That was fiction, of course, but Faerie had a way of making fiction truth if enough humans believed it *could* happen. So I waited with trepidation, wondering if Ryese would step through the glass. There was certainly enough magic buzzing through the circle that I'd believe it could open a portal. Though Faerie typically required a pretty large price to be paid for wild portals.

A full minute passed, two. I bit my lip, one hand still shielding my eyes, and considered opening my shields again. I needed to glance through the planes, to see what was really going on. My heartbeat crashed in my ears, fast, erratic. I flexed my fingers around the hilt of my dagger. Waiting. Then I took my chance. Opening my shields a sliver, just enough to take a quick glance across planes.

Pain sank claws in my brain and vertigo hit me as hard as a train, knocking me off my feet before I even had time to look up. In less than a blink of an eye, I was on all fours, my stomach twisting and threatening to rebel, my dagger flat on the wet stone beside me.

"Oh, Lexi, Lexi, Lexi," Ryese's voice crooned, the light dimming. "Oh, do do that, my dearest. Do open your magic and let my spell in to drain every drop of planeweaving ability from you. That will speed things up quite nicely."

I gulped, my head shooting up to stare at the closest mirror. That was a mistake as my vision spun with the sudden movement. So that was what this circle did? It drained my planeweaving? I swallowed, blinking, waiting for my eyes to focus again. When they finally did, I found the mirror empty. No Ryese. Not even my own reflection. I frowned, my gaze cutting to the side. That mirror was empty as well, as was the mirror beside it.

"Dear Lexi, what are you planning to do with that little dagger?"

Well, I couldn't see him, but apparently he could see me. My gaze dropped to the dagger where it had fallen beside my hand. No point trying to conceal it now. I grabbed it, enjoying the familiar buzz against my palm as I wrapped my fingers around it. The dagger liked to be used, it liked to slice through things and draw blood. Unfortunately, it didn't have anything to attack currently. Every mirror I glanced at was empty.

Shit, had he really done it? Had he stepped through the glass?

I needed to get off the ground.

I shoved myself upward, climbing back to my knees and ignoring the worrisome black dots that crowded in my peripheral as I moved. They cleared after a moment, and I staggered to my feet, the dagger held in front of me in the best approximation of a defensive stance I could remember from Falin's lessons.

My gaze scanned the circle, searching. But I was alone with the oddly nonreflective mirrors, except for Tem, who was on his knees outside the circle. Then I caught a glimmer of gold in the corner of my eye. I whirled around and saw Ryese pacing, moving from the surface of one mirror to the next, but still inside.

Ryese stopped, glancing back over his shoulder. Whatever he saw made him scowl. Then he turned back, his gaze landing on Tem.

"You brought her here too early, troll," Ryese snapped, his voice annoyed, censuring.

Tem shrank from the edge of the circle, his head low.

"I don't need her yet, and now you can't even knock her back out because you've already activated the circle." Ryese's lip curled in a sneer, and he shook his head, as if disgusted by the entire situation. Then he turned in the mirror to face me. "Lexi dearest, you should probably get some sleep," he said, his tone turning saccharine sweet and so false I was surprised it didn't trigger the fae inability to lie. "You and I, we have a lot to do soon. You're going to want to be well rested."

"Pass. Not interested."

That only made him smile, and it was a scary expression. The kind of smile that held menace but also an assurance that he'd already won. I wasn't sure what he planned for me, but I had no intention of making things easy on him.

"As you wish," he said, "but you might want to at least conserve your magic. Shielded, you should be able to regenerate your magic fast enough to not end up a worthless husk, but I wouldn't push it too hard. Brilliantly burning out right now would still give me enough of your magic to accomplish my goals, but I'd be rather sad to lose my little planeweaver. Besides, you deserve to suffer for a very, very long time for what you did to me." He lifted his hand to the scarred side of his face.

I bit my tongue to stop the retort that he'd caused all that pain to himself. There was no point in wasting my breath. No time either, as with that, his gaze shot to Tem again.

"Try to keep her from killing herself while I finish my preparations here. I'd hate for her to miss my big moment."

Then his figure faded, the light pouring out of the mirrors dimming. My reflection appeared in the mirror again, dozens, hundreds, maybe even a thousand reflections of myself staring back at me. All with the same stunned expression.

Chapter 21

Tem left for a while after the mirrors went dark.

I paced the confines of the circle. I didn't dare open my shields again. While it was possible that Ryese had been exaggerating about what this circle did, it fit too well with what happened every time I tried to touch my planeweaving ability.

I tried slicing through the circle with my dagger—the enchanted blade had accomplished the task before. But Ryese knew too much of my history, and he clearly had caught wind of that particular trick. The magic woven through the circle had been set in layers, like a magical onion. The innermost layer was nothing more than an obstacle, but I had to be able to touch the magic to destroy it, and that meant using my planeweaving. I kept my shields locked, using only the dagger and my innate abilities that made me a nexus point where planes converged, but even that was too much. I made one small slice through the first layer of spellwork and woke prone on the floor some unknown time later.

When I'd first woken in the circle, I'd slowly grown stronger and more alert as the knockout spell had worn off. Now, though, I could feel the drain on my magic,

on my very life force, as time passed. I wondered if
Ryese had taken into consideration that even shielded,
I always touched the other planes. There was no turn-
ing off all of my power.

Tem returned after what felt like several hours, but
he didn't talk to me, just busied himself with something in the shadows of the room. I watched him a
while. It wasn't like I had anything else to do. I had my
dagger, my clothes, and pretty much nothing else. Just
a wet stone floor in a circle of mirrors.

"He doesn't give a rat's ass about you," I said, my
voice more conversational than I actually felt.

Tem looked up, frowning at me. "What?"

"Ryese. You're doing that cretin's dirty work and he
doesn't even know your name."

Tem grunted, going back to whatever it was he was
doing. I wanted to get him talking. I was sure I'd read
somewhere that getting your captor to see you as a person was the best way to survive. But Tem already knew
me, at least a little. I'd only known him a couple days,
but I doubted anything I said now would change any
opinions of me that the last two days of working at my
side hadn't already formed. Still, I had to try something.

"You seem like a decent guy, in most ways. You say
you want change for a broken Faerie. So what did he
promise you?"

Tem glanced at me, his lips pressed tight around his
tusks, making the calloused skin stretch and crack with
his frown. But he remained silent.

"You really think Ryese would make positive
changes in Faerie?" I asked, as much to get him talking
as to figure out why the hell he was doing this. Why
anyone would work with Ryese.

"Can't be worse than a High King who never steps
out of his golden halls and sees what life is like for the
rest of us. One who sleeps through the centuries. Who
just doesn't seem to give a damn what happens to Fa-

erie as long as it keeps existing." His voice rose as he spoke, building in volume until he was shouting the words. Another time I might have shrunk away, but it wasn't like he was going to cross the circle I was trapped in.

"So—what? You guys are trying to get his attention by blowing a bunch of doors?"

Tem scoffed, the sound ugly and hard. "Doubt it even woke him. You think he cares what happens to the independents stuck on this side?"

I did. Or at least I hoped he cared. When I'd spoken to my father, he'd said the king had definitely noticed the doors being destroyed and was already working on the issue. But then my father rarely even went to Faerie. And this wasn't the first time I'd heard fae mention that the High King slept through the centuries. Maybe he was asleep, unaware of the danger Faerie was in?

Tem looked like he was about to say more, building up to another big outburst, but then metal scraped against stone as the heavy door I'd heard earlier opened. I still couldn't see the door in the shadows, but I heard the soft slap of bare feet on wet stone as someone entered.

"What are you doing in here?" Jenny's sharp voice asked as she stepped into the pool of light cast by the two bare industrial lights. She wasn't looking at me, of course. She knew exactly what I was doing here.

Tem's shoulders hitched toward his oversize ears as he sagged under her sharp tone. For a big guy, he sure seemed to be on the bottom of everyone's pecking order.

"I was just keeping an eye on her," he muttered, tossing whatever was in his hand down.

"I don't think he'd like that. You're far too taken with her."

"And what are you doing down here?" he snapped back.

Jenny flashed a smile full of sharp teeth at me as she approached the edge of the circle. "I brought her dinner."

She lifted a small wooden plate. On it sat a dead fish. Not like a fillet of fish, but an entire fish, head, tail, scales, and all. It was clearly raw, and I almost expected its glassy-looking eye to blink.

"She can't eat that," Tem said, his nose wrinkling.

"Then she'll go hungry." Jenny stopped just outside the edge of the circle and placed the wooden plate on the ground. She gave the plate a sharp nudge with one toe, and it skittered across the stone and into the circle with me, the inert wood and dead fish unaffected by the magic in the barrier.

The plate came to a stop a foot in front of me, the fish traveling several more inches to flop onto the grimy stone floor. At least it didn't start flapping its tail, but its glassy dead eye seemed to stare up at me, making my gorge rise.

"Bon appétit!" Jenny called out with mock cheer, turning away with a jeering wave. "Come on, troll."

Tem shot me what looked like an apologetic expression, but he turned and followed Jenny without another comment. To add insult to injury, Jenny cut the lights as she left. Metal scraped on stone as the door shut behind them, but just before the door clicked closed, Jenny called out one last departing quip.

"Try not to die at sunset," she said, her voice dripping acid. "It's been killer."

Then the door slammed, the metal rattling, leaving me alone in the dark with a dead fish and a spell slowly draining away my life.

Sitting in the dark feeling sorry for myself wasn't going to help. The hot tears I felt pricking at the edges of my eyes were no good either. I'd already had my cry today, and while a little voice whispered, *Hey, maybe a hand-*

*some soul collector would come rescue me if I gave in
to my cry*, I wasn't that naive. Maybe someone would
show up at the eleventh hour to help, but I needed a
plan of my own right now.

I blinked in the darkness. What did I have going
for me?

Not much. I couldn't see. I couldn't use my magic. I
was stuck in a circle I didn't understand. And my life
was being sucked out of me by a particularly nasty
spell.

Well, that wasn't all completely accurate. I couldn't
use my *planeweaving*.

I did have other magic. I was a trained witch. I'd
never been good enough to get certified, but I'd spent
years taking remedial magic lessons at the wyrd acad-
emy where I'd spent most of my childhood.

Experimentally, I reached for the raw Aetheric energy stored in the onyx ring I wore, bracing myself for
pain. My magic tapped into the raw energy stored
there, but no wave of dizziness rushed through me. I
drew a small bit of the energy into my psyche, following
the well-worn path I'd used for Aetheric magic most of
my life. No pain. No added exhaustion.

Ryese's spell only affected my planeweaving. It
didn't touch my witchy magic.

I released the Aetheric energy.

It made sense, in a way. The fae largely had little to
no contact with witchy magic and the Aetheric plane.
Ryese had set his trap for a fae, and while I'd blooded
true as a Sleagh Maith, I did have some human in me.
This . . . was actually helpful. But how would I use it?

I sat down in the center of the circle, running a mental inventory on all the spells I knew how to cast from
memory. It wasn't a long list, and most of it wouldn't be
helpful. Tracking charms and silence bubbles weren't
exactly helpful in this situation. A disruption spell
might work, and I did know one of those, but I couldn't
cast one strong enough to take down a spell like what

was holding me. I needed something that would blow a hole in the circle, without killing me in the process.

That thought tickled an idea, spurred on by Jenny's nasty little parting quip advising me not to die at sunset, because with the amaranthine tree gone, the fae here were fading fast. And fae magic, well, it wasn't holding up well. The spell surrounding me was strong as hell, but Ryese had to have crafted it before he blew the doors. That meant it had already been through one sunset and sunrise. Tem and Jenny were likely reinforcing the spells, but at the exact moment of sunset, it would be at its weakest. Maybe weak enough that a disruption charm would create enough of a disturbance for me to slip through.

Maybe.

And that was even assuming I could make such a charm before sunset. I couldn't see my watch in the dark room, but based on the last time I'd looked at it, I was guessing I had maybe half an hour. I also had no materials. Just my dagger and my charm bracelet, but none of the trinkets on my bracelet could hold a spell large enough to bring down the circle around me, even if sunset weakened it to the point of near nonexistence. I needed something big. Something that could hold a lot of Aetheric energy. Maybe I could dig out one of the stones making up the floor or . . . The plate!

I rolled onto my knees, reaching out with my hands, searching for the plate Jenny had kicked into the circle. My fingers landed on the fish first, and I jerked back from the slimy, cold body. A shiver crawled up my arms, down my spine, but I had to keep searching. The plate had been near the fish the last time I'd seen it. I reached out again, cringing as my fingers traced over the squishy, scaled body, but then they brushed against something hard that wasn't stone.

I snatched the plate from the ground, and then scuttled backward, clutching my prize to my chest while getting away from the fish corpse. Then I sat back

down, cross-legged, and ran my hand over the plate. It
had looked wooden when I'd seen Jenny carrying it,
and that seemed to be the case. Better yet, it felt very
simple, only the smallest lip on it and no other ornamentation or carvings. It was about as good of a blank
slate for a charm as I was likely to get unless someone
handed me a gemstone.

I laid the plate on my lap and then drew my dagger
and put it on top, the point aimed away from me in the
hopes I didn't accidentally stab myself when I reached
for it in the dark. I closed my eyes, trying to settle my
thoughts and find the peace I'd need to fall into a med-
itative trance.

Instead my heart raced, and I felt like I could hear
each second tick by, hurtling me toward sunset. My
brain kept providing me with all the reasons this plan
wouldn't work, from simply not getting the charm done
in time, to it not being powerful enough and frying
myself when I tried to cross the circle.

Grinding my teeth, I took a deep breath. Let it out.

I used to have a charm that would create a bubble of
calm in my mind and force me into an artificial trance.
It had gotten destroyed months ago when I'd been
shoving around reality to disintegrate a horde of starving zombies, and I'd never gotten around to recrafting
it. I was seriously regretting that decision now, but I
just hadn't been doing much witchy magic of late.
Spellwork had gotten even harder to craft since my fae
nature had emerged, and it hadn't exactly been easy
before then. I charged the store of raw magic in my
ring, and I kept a few utilitarian spells at the ready, but
that was it these days. Hell, I'd mostly cheated on those
of late, drawing the raw Aetheric with my planeweaving and not in the traditional manner witches did. But
now I needed those old skills.

Another deep breath. I forced all the conflicting
thoughts away and let my consciousness sink lower.
Another breath. My heartbeat finally began to slow

again, my mind clearing with the expanding moments between thudding beats.

It took precious minutes, which I tried not to be aware of, but I finally sank low enough to reach a trance, my psyche sinking down and then floating up, out of me and into the Aetheric. I opened my eyes and light and color danced around me in strings of raw magic. There was a small pull, Ryese's spell tearing at the shields of my mind, as if it could sense I'd sidestepped and had redoubled its efforts. Or maybe here, with my psyche reaching the Aetheric plane, but not my planeweaving, there was enough of a crossover that the spell could get a stronger hold, pull tighter. I'd have to work fast.

Reaching out to the nearest blue strand of pure energy, I drew on it, drinking it down until I glowed with similar blue light. A giddiness filled me, that magical light filling me, lifting me higher into the Aetheric plane. But I couldn't lose focus. I had to gather the energy, pull it back with me, and shape my charm before sunset. I reached out again, grabbing a passing green strand and pulling it in before going for another. The air danced with dozens of colors of magic, but I gathered only those that resonated with me, until I shone like a mosaic of green and blue glass on a sunny day. Then I took the magic I'd gathered and dropped back into my body.

Many witches could take raw magic and craft it directly into a spell. I'd never had any skill at that, which was why I worked primarily with charms directed by runes. My dagger was not an ideal tool to carve runes into a wooden plate, particularly in the dark. But it was what I had. My own skin gave off some light, but not a lot, so I scratched away at the surface of the plate, working mostly by feel and memory, pouring the magic I'd gathered into each line as I worked. Thankfully, the runes to disrupt magic were ones with which I was extremely familiar. When you were not that great at spellwork, knowing how to quickly disrupt an errant spell was pretty important.

As I scratched the last dash of my rune, I felt the first hint of smothering exhaustion that had marked the time between day and night since the destruction of the door. Which meant I was out of time.

I shoved the last of the magic I carried into the wood plate, charging the charm with as much juice as I could give it. The charm practically vibrated in my hands, and I was damn proud of the thing, considering the circumstances. It felt strong, the magic sound.

I just hoped it would be enough.

Sheathing my dagger in my boot, I climbed to my feet and made my way to the edge of the circle. I moved as close as I could to the magical barrier, judging the distance by the amount of magic biting at my skin as I pressed as close as I dared. I wished I could see, at least a little. I couldn't tell if I was in front of a mirror or an opening, but I sure hoped it was the latter.

Then I waited, clutching my disruption charm close.

Somewhere I couldn't see, the sun must have been sinking below the horizon. In this pitch-black room with little sound beyond dripping water and nothing else to sense aside from the magic, I could feel the dwindling Faerie magic in ways I never had before. And then, like a rug pulled out from under the world, the magic was gone.

I gasped, my hand moving to the ball of realities bound above my collarbone. Death had indicated I was carrying strands of Faerie in it, and that they were preventing me from fading as quickly as the other fae. In that moment, as the very air seemed to be ripped from my lungs, with no new air left behind to replace it, I had a hard time believing any magic was left. And yet now, I could feel the thin threads, and as I touched them, I found I could breathe again, though I could still feel that smothering weight of wrongness all around me.

Then I realized I'd used my planeweaving to reach

to Faerie, and it hadn't hurt. The circle was still active around me, I could feel the prickle of magic in it, but it was a flicker compared to the flame it had been. My charm, on the other hand, still buzzed strongly with Aetheric magic.

I shoved the charm in front of me, toward the circle I could feel but not see. I hit something solid—a mirror, no doubt—and repositioned myself. My next waving thrust encountered only magic.

Sparks flew, angry red lines of magic ripping through the air in front of me. It jumped through the charm into my hand, traveling up my arm like fire ants. I jerked back, and the charm hung there, suspended by the competing magic.

"Come on," I whispered, willing the charm to be strong enough. I could barely feel Ryese's spellwork anymore, but it was giving one hell of a fight.

Sparks continued to cascade over the edge of the circle, between the two mirrors where the plate still hung suspended. I found myself counting the seconds. How long before the moment of sunset passed and the spell began to recover?

It wasn't going to work. The charm wasn't enough . . .

Then the charm fell to the floor, the spellwork suspending it no longer strong enough to grasp it. I could see the angry, frayed edges where it had torn through, like a narrow rip in a taut cloth.

I didn't hesitate, but propelled myself through that tear. The spell caught at me, ripping at my body, my magic, trying to entangle me. But it was too weak, too damaged. I crashed through to the other side, my knees slamming down onto the wet stone, my arms barely breaking the fall enough to keep my face from connecting with the ground.

In the next moment the time between ended, the transition over as day became night. There was no rush of Faerie magic back into the world, but the smothering lack of it became considerably less oppressive. The spell only inches from my feet began regaining its strength.

I wanted to lie on the stone floor for a moment, catch my breath, and cradle my smarting knees. But I didn't have time. I didn't know where Tem and Jenny were, or how fast they'd recover from sunset. Which meant I had no time to waste.

I pushed myself up, trying to keep my orientation. I hadn't actually ever seen the door that led out of the room, but I'd heard it and I'd seen the general direction Tem and Jenny entered and exited from. Now that I was outside Ryese's spell, I cracked open my shields. No dizziness, no pain. I was exhausted, but it was the same exhaustion that had been growing for some time now.

I didn't try to hold back the sigh as the planes of existence snapped into focus around me. I don't think I'd ever been so relieved to see a patina of decay suddenly overlay the world. Bright strands of Aetheric magic whirled around, and spaces of color soaked the stone where I'd landed moments before, giving it a temporary stain of pain that faded even as I stared at it. Other planes took shape around me as well, my psyche brushing against them, making them visible to my mental perception. It was a chaotic mess of information, but it was easier to navigate than the pitch dark. It took me only a moment to locate the door. As I suspected, it was unlocked, my captors relying only on Ryese's spell to hold me. I was glad for that.

I raced down the hallway—or was it more of a tunnel?—beyond where I'd been held, and then took the stairs I found at the end two at a time. The stairway led me up and up until I reached a door out into what appeared to be a warehouse. I slowed for a moment as I slipped into an empty storage room. There was no one in this room, but I could hear sounds beyond it. I crept to the open doorway, peering out into the much larger space beyond. It was also mostly empty. Whatever this place had been, it must have been long abandoned. But in the center of the room, a small living area had been constructed with a mattress on the floor, an open suitcase, and a mini-fridge. Tem sprawled on the mattress, one huge arm thrown over his eyes. He gave a pained grunt, but didn't move otherwise.

From the looks of it, he'd been squatting here longer than just today. That made sense, though. He wasn't actually winter court, so he couldn't have been traveling back to winter after work shifts, and I was guessing he'd shown up at the FIB office at least a day or two before I had.

I scanned the area for Jenny, but she wasn't here. There also didn't seem to be a lot of options on doors. I was close to several large cargo bays, but they were sealed tight. An emergency exit had chains securing it, which meant the only door I could escape through was on the other side of Tem's living area.

He hadn't moved, his arm still covering most of his face. I was going to have to risk it.

I crept across the room as fast as I dared, trying to move silently. My big boots? They weren't really made for stealth. I did the best I could, but still cringed, pausing to glance at Tem every time one of my footfalls caused the ancient wood floor to creak. Despite what felt like a lot of noise to me, Tem never shifted. He grunted again once or twice, so I knew he was alive, and from the pained sound, he was awake, but apparently he was still suffering from the effects of sunset.

I was almost to the door when a strange sensation struck me. It started like the kind of electric zing of someone walking over your grave, but then it turned more intense, painful. I couldn't figure out what was going on at first, but then I saw the small shape jump free of my shadow. Dugan's shadow cat. She'd apparently just used my ties to Faerie to move through from a shadow in Faerie to my shadow, and with the amount of damage my magic and psyche had taken over the course of the evening from Ryese's spell, the passage *hurt*.

I must have made some sound, or maybe I'd just run out of luck, because Tem's arm moved as he sat up. His eyes landed on me instantly, his face changing from an expression of pain to one of shock.

"Boss? What . . . ? How did you . . . ?" His words were slightly slurred, confused sounding. But by the end of them, he was struggling to his feet.

I didn't wait around to see how disoriented he still was, but took off for the door, running as fast as I could. The door dumped me into an alley, and I glanced around only long enough to realize that there was only one way to go that wasn't a dead end, then I was running again. Of course, once I reached the mouth of the alley, I had a choice to make.

I glanced in both directions, but I didn't recognize the street. Considering I'd emerged in a warehouse, I wasn't surprised to find myself in the industrial part of town. I didn't recognize the street, but I could hear the Sionan River in the distance. It was a rough area, and more or less abandoned at this time of day.

The shadow cat had followed me when I'd run, but now she turned and took off up the road. Either direction looked as promising as the other—all I cared about was putting some distance between me and the troll who was no doubt giving chase—so I followed the cat. My heart skittered in my chest, my lungs burning, as I pushed myself to keep moving, to run faster. Then I stopped short because just up ahead was a very familiar blue car parallel parked on the street.

My very familiar blue car.

I dashed to it, certain I couldn't be lucky enough that it would really be mine. Except it was, and it was unlocked, with my purse still on the floorboard where it must have fallen during my struggle with Tem. The car had to have been hidden under a glamour all day to have sat unlocked in this part of town and still be here.

I jumped inside, the shadow cat following me, her

tail swishing violently. The interior reeked of fetid troll blood, but I didn't care because the car started when I hit the ignition button, which meant my keys were still in my purse and I didn't have to outrun Tem. The driver's seat had been moved all the way back—no doubt so that Tem could drive it here after he'd knocked me out—and I couldn't even reach the pedals. I hit the button to adjust it, but didn't waste time getting it perfect. As soon as it was close enough that I could reach the gas, I threw the car into gear.

Tem had reached the street. He was staggering, but still making a good pace toward me. I floored it, jolting the car into the street, both hands locked on the wheel. I could hear Tem bellowing in rage behind me, but I didn't stop to look back. I'd escaped, and I was getting the hell out of there.

Chapter 22

There was a very good reason my driver's license listed the restriction that I could not drive at night. I couldn't see.

There was a dotting of streetlamps on some of the roads, but that wasn't near enough light for my bad eyes. So I'd been stubbornly peering across the planes, but the chaotic mess of planes revealed the landscape to my mind instead of my eyes. It was not the best way to navigate a two-ton vehicle traveling at breakneck speed.

I ran two stop signs and a light before the fog of adrenaline-fueled flight thinned enough that I realized that while I didn't want Tem to catch up to me, I also didn't want to accidentally kill anyone, myself included. Thankfully, this part of town was fairly quiet, the streets more or less empty. That wouldn't be the case when I reached a more populated area, though.

I slowed at the next intersection, in part because I was trying to figure out where the heck I was, and because, as I squinted at the traffic light, I couldn't actually tell what color it was. Aetheric energy swirled everywhere, tinting everything with splashes of random color, and the stoplight itself looked like it was about to fall off the wire holding it, the land of the dead making it appear as if all the lights had been busted, the casing around them rusted.

Great.

I inched the car forward, checking that both directions were clear before crossing the intersection, still not sure if the light had been green or red. The next intersection was just as bad, but this one had an odd formless . . . something . . . hanging out at the corner of the street. The other problem about peering across planes? There were other entities that lived on some of those planes, and a lot of them weren't exactly friendly. I sped through that intersection without stopping, but the next one actually had a car, which in my sight was such a rust bucket, if I hadn't seen the soft glow of a soul inside, I wouldn't have realized it was only stopped at the light and not parked.

This was not working.

In the seat beside me, the shadow cat paced, her tail whipping in apparent agitation. "I feel you," I grumbled to her, though I had no idea how much she could understand.

She jumped onto the dash to pace there instead. "Hey. Don't block my view." I was having enough problems without adding a pacing shadow getting in the way.

I reached a major street, one I actually recognized. I could go left to head back downtown or right to cross the river and head toward the magic district. I needed to get off the road. Driving like this was insane. Leaning across the seat, I searched the passenger floorboard for my phone. I found it under my purse, the screen shattered, the plastic casing crushed. For half a heartbeat I hoped it only looked that bad because I was seeing it across the planes. But no. It really was smashed. Tem must have crushed it after spelling me.

Great. So that eliminated the possibility of calling for help. Hell, I couldn't even summon a ride-share to come pick me up. It also meant I had no way to check in and see if the police were still looking for me. I glanced toward the Magic Quarter. I wanted more than anything to go home and curl under the covers with my dog, but that wouldn't accomplish anything useful, and considering I needed to avoid both the human authorities and Ryese's minions, it wasn't a safe option. I could go back to the FIB headquarters; I was pretty sure Nori was loyal to winter, but after the last few hours, I wasn't particularly inclined to take any chances.

Which meant turning left was my best option. I could head to my father's just like I'd planned before I'd been abducted. I'd never told Tem where I'd been headed, so it wasn't like I'd be easy to track, and I still needed to talk to the shadow court about a door for the independents. If Falin was still in shadow, it would be good to tell him what I'd learned about Ryese. The power-crazy fae needed to be stopped, and I doubted the fact that he was now the Light King would make things any easier. I had doubts I'd find Falin in shadow, though. He'd seen at least part of Tem's attack before the troll had ripped the mirror off my car, and Falin wasn't the type to wait around.

A car horn sounded behind me. Apparently I'd been sitting too long. At least that meant the light was green. I flipped on my blinker, pulling forward.

"Well, I guess I'm off to talk to your master," I said to the cat, who was still swishing her tail. "Since you're here, I assume that means he's expecting me, at least."

The cat cocked her featureless head as I pulled into the turn, heading toward my father's mansion. Then she launched herself at the dash of my car. The rear-view mirror was gone—Tem had crushed it before hurling it from the car earlier—so the cat melted into the front windshield instead.

Shadows spread like ink across the glass, blacking out the world beyond. I slammed on my brakes as the visibility through the glass turned to nothing, which, considering I was only partially using my eyes to see, might not have been that bad, but whatever communication spell coated the glass with the cat's shadow also blocked my mind's ability to perceive the road through it.

"I didn't mean right now, you crazy cat!"

The darkness only deepened and another horn sounded behind me. I was still in the middle of the intersection, halfway through my turn. I released the brakes, letting the car roll forward.

A face appeared in my windshield, tilted, oddly distorted, and very concerned. Make that two very concerned faces.

"Alex, are you okay? Where are you?" Falin said.

"Driving!" Or trying to. I hit my window button, rolling it down so I could look out at where I was going. Because this hadn't been hard enough before I had two fae royals blocking the road.

"You need to get to the pocket of Faerie," Dugan said, and I nodded, angling my car toward the shoulder.

"That's where I was headed. If I don't get in a wreck on the way."

"Are you driving at night?" Falin asked, concern thick in his voice.

"Yes. And you two need to get out of my window so I don't crash."

Dugan didn't waste time with good-byes. He and Falin vanished, the shadows dispersing so that I could see through the front windshield again. That was good; now I was back to just the problem that I had to navigate Nekros while peering through the planes.

The drive was excruciating, and I was shaking with adrenal fatigue by the time I pulled into my father's driveway. I wasn't sure how many traffic laws I'd violated during the fifteen-minute drive, but I hadn't killed anyone, wrecked my car, or gotten pulled over by the cops, so I was counting it as a win. It definitely wasn't an experience I wanted to have ever again.

Of course, now that I'd reached my father's, I had a new obstacle: I had to find a way inside. Earlier, there'd been a chance I could have talked my way in before his security or staff was informed about his disappearance. But, unless he'd reappeared while I was being held in Ryese's circle, he'd been gone for hours now. It was almost a guarantee that everyone on the premises knew about his disappearance. They'd likely also been informed that an FIB agent had been his last visitor before he'd vanished.

I glanced at the huge electronic gate stretching across the front drive, an eight-foot wall on either side of it. I tried to imagine myself sneaking around to some dark corner of the property and scaling the wall, and I just couldn't. I was too damn tired for that. I'd been held captive for most of the day, my magic being drained out of me; I'd fought and run, and just navigated through pure madness to get this far. I wasn't an action hero who could bound over walls.

I hit the button on the intercom.

After a few moments a scratchy voice said, "State your name and purpose."

There was almost certainly an APB for FIB special agent Alex Craft circulating. Most likely security here had been warned as well. But I did have another name, one that would have a lot more sway in this house, even if I'd had it legally changed as soon as I'd turned eighteen.

"Alexis Caine," I said, the name rolling off my tongue despite not using it in years. "I'd like to see my sister."

Security left me waiting at the gate long enough that I started to get twitchy. Had Casey refused my visit? Or was security actively calling the cops? I was the unacknowledged child, but I knew for a fact that my father had my real name on an approved list somewhere. My relationship with Casey was complicated, though, to say the least. She might not be my best ticket into the house.

We'd never been particularly close. She'd been a young child when our father had shipped me off to boarding school because I couldn't hide my grave magic. I'd come home during summer breaks, but I'd always been closer to my older brother, not Casey. After he'd disappeared, well, she just became the symbol of everything I wasn't. She was the pretty, perfect daughter my father kept, while I was the one with wyrd magic who he'd hidden away. It wasn't that we disliked each other, we just led very different lives that had little reason to intersect. She hadn't started actively avoiding me until after the events under the Blood Moon when she'd nearly been sacrificed by a psychopath. I'd been the one to stop him and save her, but now I was a reminder of that night. I hadn't thought she'd refuse to see me, though.

Of course, it was possible she hadn't even been told I was here. Maybe my license plate had been run as soon as I'd pulled onto the property and security was only going through the motions.

I was putting my car in reverse, about to get the hell out of Dodge and try to come up with some other way of reaching the pocket of Faerie—not that I had any idea how I'd accomplish that task—when a sharp buzz sounded. With a whirl of gears, the gate rolled open. I eyed the now clear path. So my sister hadn't refused my visit? Or was SWAT en route and security was trying to keep me on the premises until they arrived?

"I can't be skeptical of everything," I muttered to myself, as I let the car roll forward. And I needed inside that house. The shadow cat had returned to the shadow realm after opening the connection in my window. I was sure Dugan would send her back if I didn't get to the pocket of Faerie soon, but I'd rather avoid any more makeshift communication attempts.

The gate shut behind me, and I cringed with the sound of it locking into place. I was committed now. No easy way out. I just hoped I would find Casey waiting for me, not a small battalion of security guards.

It was with more than a little trepidation that I parked and made my way up the front steps. A butler met me at the front door, which I took as a positive sign. Even better, he led me to a small drawing room off the front foyer.

"Miss Casey will be around shortly," he said, gesturing toward an ornate, but uncomfortable, love seat in the center of the room. "Would you care for some refreshments?"

I didn't intend my meeting with Casey to take long, I'd simply needed an excuse to get into the house. I'd probably also need her permission to get upstairs and to the warded and locked suite that now contained a pocket of Faerie. But, I hadn't eaten since breakfast and it had been a very long day.

"Refreshments would be amazing," I said, my stomach rumbling at the thought of food.

He gave a small nod and then let himself out of the room, leaving me inside alone. I didn't sit in the seat he'd indicated, but paced as I waited. The seconds ticked by, turning into minutes, and I fidgeted looking toward the door. Maybe I should try to sneak upstairs and skip seeing Casey at all. Of course, if I did that, there would be quite an uproar and security would be searching the house as soon as someone discovered I'd left this room. I could wait a few more minutes for Casey.

I continued pacing, walking faster as the seconds ticked by. There was a large mirror over the unlit fireplace, and I caught my reflection as I passed it. Then I stopped, wincing as I turned to study my face closer.

I had seen a lot of my reflection over the last few

hours, but my grime-streaked face and curls caked to the side of my head looked a whole lot worse in this pristine sitting room than they had under the harsh lights of the stone room where I'd been held. The butler was clearly worth every penny my father was paying him because he hadn't even blinked at my appearance.

I was scrubbing at the gray smudges on my cheek when the door finally opened and Casey walked into the room.

"Alexis, what is going on?" she demanded before the door fully closed behind her. Then her eyes landed on me and she stopped, whatever sharp words were on her tongue stalling. "Are you okay?"

I dropped my hand, giving up the futile attempt at not looking like I'd just been dragged through a war zone. Casey, of course, looked perfect.

She always dressed like she'd just stepped off the cover of a fashion magazine, and today was no different, though the neckline of her blouse was perhaps higher than it would have been in years past and I could feel the tingle of magic from the concealment charms she wore to hide any remaining scars from that night nearly seven months ago. Her makeup and hair were perfect as she stood in the doorway, looking exactly like the socialite she'd been raised to become. Except that there was a fragility in her blue eyes now, a suspicion and distrust not of me but of the world, that had never been there before.

"I, uh . . ." I ran a hand through my hair, but my fingers tangled and flakes of mud fell from my curls to the very expensive-looking rug. "Hi."

Casey frowned, finally walking the rest of the way into the room and letting the door swing shut behind her. With her initial shock at my bedraggled appearance having passed, her gaze turned to critical disapproval.

"What is going on?" she demanded again.

"It's been a long day."

Her frown deepened. "Do tell. The police were here for most of the afternoon. Daddy is missing."

I'd been prepared to hear that news, and yet I still had to fight not to cringe, to school my face neutral. She studied me for several seconds, her lips compressed in a tight line. Then she walked across the room and settled herself into one of the chairs. Her posture remained perfect as she crossed one leg over the other. That was why the chairs didn't have to be comfortable — you perched on them, you didn't sit and relax.

"Imagine my surprise," Casey said, smoothing the edge of her skirt over her knee, "when the lead detective held up a picture of you and asked if I recognized you. He said you were the last one seen with Daddy."

"And what did you tell him?" Because my relationship to our father was relatively unknown, but not actually secret. Anyone looking hard enough could find it, but if the press caught wind of the fact that the governor's estranged daughter was suspected in his disappearance, it would be quite a scandal. My mind flashed back to the last image I had of my father, blood seeping through his shirt and dribbling from the corner of his mouth, and a sick, guilty feeling twisted my stomach for my first thought being of what he'd think of the damage to his career. Wherever he'd vanished to, he might be beyond caring about scandal.

"I avoided the question, of course." Casey hissed out the answer in a whisper as a knock sounded on the door.

The butler walked in, carrying a tray, which he placed on the small side table to the left of Casey. He filled two cups with coffee from a steaming pot and then looked to Casey, who nodded her thanks, dismissing him without either ever speaking a word.

I didn't exactly rush the tray, but I'd grabbed my coffee before the butler even made it out of the room.

I cupped it between my hands, letting the warmth sink into my fingers as I inhaled the scent. Casey gave me a disapproving look as she meticulously adulterated her own cup with cream and sugar. I ignored her as I examined the rest of the tray, selecting a large shortbread cookie dipped in chocolate before retreating farther away to devour my spoils. The coffee was strong and bitter and the cookie soft with just a hint of sweet. In other words, both were perfect and I made quick work of the cookie, wondering if it would be horrible to grab another, considering Casey hadn't even selected her first yet. It wasn't like I was worried about my younger sister approving of my manners, so I walked over and studied the carefully arranged tray.

"I need to go upstairs," I said without preamble as I snagged a second cookie, this one gingersnap.

The color drained from Casey's face, her gaze moving toward the ceiling as if drawn there against her will. There were two floors above us, and a lot of rooms, but I knew exactly which one painted the thin sheen of horror across her features. I'd had nightmares for months after the events that went down in Casey's old bedroom. From the haunted look in her blue eyes, I guessed Casey still had those nightmares.

She tore her gaze from the ceiling and seemed to shake herself, her composure falling back in place as she took a dainty sip of her coffee.

"Did you know you're glowing?" she asked, watching me consume my cookie with censure in her eyes.

Oh yeah. I'd forgotten she hadn't seen me since that fun little change. Because this wasn't already complicated enough. But I didn't have the time or energy to have a heart-to-heart about all the changes in my life, and I doubted Casey would actually care. I shoved the last bite of cookie in my mouth, considered snagging a third, but decided that might be pushing it. Brushing my fingers off on my pants—which, considering everything those pants had been through today, probably actually made my fingers dirtier—I decided to simply ignore her question and repeat my earlier statement.

"I need to go upstairs," I said again before taking a deep swig of my coffee.

"If there is something of Daddy's you need, you'll have to go through his aides or secretaries. Or the police."

"I just need to visit a room."

"Which room?" The question was so casual it betrayed itself, as did the way her knuckles turned white where she gripped her coffee cup.

I just looked at her.

She slammed the cup back on the tray, coffee sloshing over the rim, onto her hand, but she didn't seem to notice, her eyes hard and fixed on me. "Why? Why would you want to go in *there*, Alexis?" She pushed to her feet and stormed toward me. My sister wasn't a tall woman. Even in her heels she was a full head shorter than me, but right now, she looked fierce, her eyes shiny with tears that sparkled with hot anger. "Where is Daddy? Did you really see him today? What happened? Where is he!"

I didn't step back, but the urge was there. Instead I let my mind travel back to this afternoon. A lot had happened since then, but the horror I'd felt when my father had collapsed was still there, and I let it show in my face. Even if we didn't get along, he was still my father and what I'd witnessed had shaken me.

"I saw him today," I said, again feeling the panic, the fear, the sorrow. I wanted to look away from Casey, to not share those raw emotions as she was more stranger than friend, even if we shared blood. My father had confided recently that he wasn't actually related to Casey, she was just a backup of our mother's DNA for his grand planeweaver breeding program. But he'd raised her, and she deserved to know what had happened to him. So I met her gaze, let her see the emotion in mine.

"I was there when . . . when it happened," I said, biting my lower lip because this was hard, the words resistant to being spoken. "He . . . he was attacked. Hurt. And then he vanished."

She studied me for several heartbeats, and then her eyes narrowed. She shook her head. "That doesn't make any sense, Alexis. What do you mean he was attacked and then vanished? People don't just vanish."

And hadn't I had the same thought? But he had disappeared, not even taking his clothes with him. I had no idea how it was possible, but it was undeniable.

"Look at me, Casey," I said. "Like you said, I glow. This is hereditary. Dad? He isn't human. And he vanished."

There was an edge to my voice, something sharp and cutting. I wasn't yelling. Not yet, but that was a possibility too. I'd had a long couple days. This conversation? It wasn't helping. I needed to wrap it up and get upstairs. To work out a plan to evacuate the stranded fae and to figure out what the hell to do about Ryese.

Casey stared at me like I'd sprouted a second head—or like I'd just stated my glow came from the fact that our father was fae. Wait, yes, that was what I'd just done.

She turned, her heels clicking on the ground. "You should leave, Alexis. I can't have this conversation right now."

Now it was my turn to blink in surprise. She didn't spout denials, proclaiming the purity of our father's humanity. She didn't even seem that shocked by the news, only by the fact that I'd voiced it.

"You knew?" My question was a whisper because I'd had *no* idea until I'd seen the proof with my own eyes half a year ago.

"I *live* here. Daddy is . . . complicated. And then there is you. And you weren't here before Bradley disappeared, but I was and he was doing things humans just don't do, not even witches . . ." She trailed off. I gaped because I'd never known that. Our older brother had vanished when I'd been away at boarding school. I'd only found out when the headmistress called me into her office and let me know that my brother was missing but my father felt it would be best if I stayed at school and kept my normal routine.

"And now Daddy's vanished." Her voice quivered, but it didn't break. "The investigators who were here earlier are questioning if you're involved. There is video of you walking out alone, but they suspect that could be glamour because you look fae." She paused to sweep her gaze over me, and I knew what went un-said was that I didn't just *look* fae, but she didn't state the obvious. "And you're saying Daddy was attacked before he vanished. By who? How?"

I stood there stunned. She stared back at me, eyes shiny like she was holding back tears but also sharp and decisive. I still saw that fragility there, but there was steel in her as well. My sister wasn't half as broken as I'd suspected.

I hesitated a moment before answering her ques-tions. She deserved to know what had happened to our father; the problem was that I didn't have the answers she was looking for.

"I'm not sure. It must have been a magical attack." Though I still hadn't figured out how, as I hadn't felt it and his wards hadn't reacted, but what other explana-tion was there? "As to the who . . . I have a suspect." Ryese was at the top of my list. I didn't know how he'd accomplished it, but the spell in the roses with their sympathy card had carried the same magical signature as the circle he'd created and trapped me inside, and they'd shown up right after the attack. I didn't know why he'd done it, if attacking my father had simply been to needle me or if there was some other plan in the works that involved stirring up the human world with an attack on the governor, but somehow this all came back to Ryese.

Casey bit her lips together, evaluating. "And now you're here and want to go upstairs. That room, it . . ." She paused, a shiver running over her. Then she took a deep breath before continuing. "Is there something up there that will help you solve what happened to Daddy? Bring him back?"

I was rather doubtful of that last part, so all I said was "Before he vanished, he told me to come here." Mostly true. He'd told me to use the space to evacuate the fae.

Again her gaze moved upward. "It's locked."

"I know." I didn't elaborate. Our father had taken me to that pocket of Faerie several times. I knew the wards he kept on the door and which glyphs would unlock it. I'd been back inside that room enough that it no longer haunted my nightmares—or maybe in the months since the Blood Moon I'd simply seen enough worse things that Coleman's attack no longer ranked high enough to be what woke me at night.

Casey looked like she was going to protest, to once again suggest I leave. I wasn't sure what I'd do if she insisted. I needed to reach that pocket of Faerie. How I was going to get the rest of the fae to it once I negotiated a door . . . well, that was going to be its own minefield. First I had to convince Casey to let *me* go up there. After a moment she sighed.

"Come on, then," she said, turning toward the door.

I blinked, not following her. "You're going with me?"

The color washed from her face and she shivered once more before shaking her head. "Never. But I'll walk you as far as the stairs and I'll let security know I've given you permission to head up to the second floor."

True to her word, she escorted me to the stairwell, but she stopped before setting foot on the bottom step. She grabbed on to the banister, as if she could draw strength from the wood, but she made no attempt to follow as I began climbing. I had to wonder if she'd been up to any of the upper levels since the night of the Blood Moon.

"See yourself out when you're done," she said, and then she turned, her heels clicking on the marble flooring as she left me alone.

Chapter 23

❖━═❖═━❖

I made a quick stop to one of the guest bathrooms to scrub the worst of the grime off my face and rinse what I could of the muck from my hair. Without a real wash—or hairbrush—the result left me looking like a drowned rat, but at least less like a filthy one. My clothes, which had several crusted stains I didn't really want to identify, were also pretty much a lost cause. Oh well, it wasn't like I was headed to a beauty contest. I'd have preferred to put my best face forward while negotiating with shadow, but it had been one hell of a long day, and it wasn't over yet. It had taken me longer than I liked already, what with trying to drive with my shields open and then having to get through security and Casey. I needed to make sure the pocket of Faerie had survived the last sunset—which I assumed it had, as Dugan had told me to come here—get the portal negotiated, figure out what to do about Ryese and the bigger issue with the door, and then get some sleep.

I made quick work of the magical locks on the outer door to Casey's old suite, thankful I'd paid attention when my father had brought me here in the past. The magical wards did more than just keep the curious from discovering the hidden pocket of Faerie, they also trapped inside anything that might somehow cross over from Faerie to the mortal realm. I assumed that was the reason Dugan had been sending his shadow pet instead of talking to me in person—the only remaining pocket of Faerie was securely locked down inside my father's rather impressive wardings. I sort of expected Falin to be waiting for me as I rushed into the dark room, but found myself disappointed to discover it empty. I didn't bother wasting any time in the sitting room, which was the first room past the doorway, but made my way straight for Casey's old bedroom.

The moment I stepped over the boundary where the circle had been cast under the Blood Moon, everything around me changed. The air turned sweeter, with soft music drifting just out of earshot, though this music was sadder than I typically heard in Faerie. An enormous sun hung low on the horizon, orange and pink with the shades of sunset even though it was full dark in the mortal realm. The fact that there was another floor above this one had no effect on the open sky above me. The room had outgrown its original dimensions in other ways as well. Once it had been a fairly normal, if large, bedroom. Now the space was considerably larger, more like the size of a ballroom. I frowned. It had been the size of a football field the last time I'd been in here, which meant it had already shrunk by more than half. Would it survive one more transition between day and night? I had to get the fae evacuated tonight, before dawn.

I walked carefully through the space, because Faerie wasn't the only plane manifesting in the room. The land of the dead had been forced into reality in spots and clusters. Other realities as well, though those seemed far less destructive than the land of the dead, which caused anything that passed through it to decay. The planes were scattered about like someone had been inspired by a Jackson Pollock painting, splashing a little land of the dead here and a bit of the plane of residual emotions there.

That hadn't been the case, of course. After all, *I'd* been the one who'd done all this damage. I'd been bound with a soul chain and hemorrhaging power at the time. The results had been chaotic, but hopefully today they would be useful.

I'd still been holding out hope that Falin would be waiting for me in the chaotic pocket of Faerie—possibly Dugan was well. Not that I thought a prince and a king should be expected to wait around for me, but while I'd been more than a little distracted when Falin and Dugan had appeared in my windshield, by the expression on Falin's face, which held some relief at the sight of me, though still riddled with worry, I'd thought that as a boyfriend—not king—he'd be here, ready to sweep me into his arms and find out what I'd been through the last several hours. It was possible I had some unreasonable relationship expectations, especially considering I was the one with commitment issues, but yeah, it stung a little as I walked through the empty space.

"Hello?" I called out when I reached the stone bench in the center of the room.

Nothing. I glanced around. Not even the shadows moved—not that moving shadows would normally be expected, but I was trying to reach Dugan so it would at least be an indication that he was listening, right?

"Dugan?"

Nothing. Had I taken too long to get here? If there had been something time sensitive, Dugan wouldn't have cut off his spell before telling me, right? Or maybe I was still being rather presumptuous and shouldn't expect them to be watching this space close enough to know the moment I stepped into it.

"I'm here to negotiate a portal with the court of shadows," I called out to the dark depths of the room. I glanced at my watch. It was still early evening, but how long would it take to work out passage for the fae and then actually get them all here to this room? While this pocket of Faerie had shrunk, it didn't feel like it was on the cusp of breaking away from reality at the strike of sunrise. Of course, neither had any of the others and they were already gone.

"You do realize he is a prince, not a valet," a deep and not entirely unfamiliar voice said, making me jump as I spun around to scan the shadows.

Nothing in the room moved.

"Down, I believe," the deep voice said. "Check your bag."

My bag? Well, the voice did seem to be emanating from my purse . . .

I pulled open the bag, pawing through the contents until I spotted a small compact mirror I occasionally used for spellwork. I dug it out, flipping it open to find Nandin, King of Shadows, staring out at me from the round, palm-sized surface.

"Ah, there you are," he said with a smile.

He was not who I'd expected to see. "Uh, hello," I said, hoping my voice sounded friendly and not as uncertain as I felt. Belatedly I realized I probably should have added a "Your Majesty" and a curtsy or something as this was a Faerie king I was addressing. Saying it now would accentuate the original slipup, likely highlighting the slight, so I took a different tack. "How are you, Uncle?"

The king's smile broadened, amusement lightening his eyes as he tilted his head. "Reminding me of our familial bond to start negotiations, hmm? A well-played first step."

My smile felt more like a grimace, but I tried anyway. The King of Shadows claimed he was my mother's many-times-removed great-granduncle or some such. We might be distantly related, but there was no emotional bond there. My interactions with him had been recent, brief, and not entirely positive, though they had

arguably been better than those I'd had with most of
Faerie's royalty. In truth, though, I'd have much rather
been dealing with Dugan. While the king had more
authority and was probably the person I *needed* to
speak to if I wanted to borrow the court's planebender,
I at least had a tenuous understanding with the prince.

"As to how I am," the king said, the smile he'd
flashed me slipping, "I admit that things have been better. But then, that is why you are here, isn't it?"

Yeah . . . about that. I had no idea how to begin negotiations with the king, so I just stumbled straight into
it, headfirst. "I would like to utilize your planebender,"
I said, and then grimaced. Utilize? Really? It wasn't
like I was asking to borrow a pair of scissors. The
planebender was a person. If someone said something
like that about me, I'd be irate. Once again I wished I
was having this conversation with Dugan instead of the
king. Also, not having it through a tiny mirror would
be nice. The king's face took up the entirety of the
small surface, and the angle seemed odd. I lifted the
mirror, tilting it slightly, as if that would readjust it. To
let me see around him and if Dugan and—more important to me—Falin were with him. Moving it of
course did nothing to change the king's position in the
mirror.

"Stop that. You are going to make me seasick," the
king snapped and I froze. *Oops.* The king's gaze moved
over my head, or more accurately, over whatever reflective surface he was speaking to me through. He stared
at something out of my view for a moment, and then
nodded, his expression earnest. Were Falin and Dugan
with him? They'd been together when I saw them in the
car window not a full hour ago, but I hadn't seen the
king then.

"Now, a door," the king said, his gaze snapping back
to me. "Everyone wants to talk about a door."

I frowned. The very first thing he'd said had been
about Dugan being a prince, not a valet. That hadn't

really registered at the time. Now I had to wonder who else had contacted him about a doorway. *He does have the only planebender.* All of the seasons had lost doors. Other courts were no doubt also looking for ways to evacuate their people.

That probably meant this negotiation was going to be largely one-sided. I didn't have much to offer and he had the only planebender in Faerie. Of course, his court did owe me a favor. I'd use that if I could. I just hoped it would be enough.

The king stepped back, revealing more of the room he stood in. Not that there was a lot to the room—it was mostly gray stone and dark shadows—but there were people. Dugan, for one, but most importantly, Falin. I smiled despite myself as I caught sight of him, but no huge outburst this time, at least. Where Dugan and Nandin were shadowy figures with their dark hair, oiled armor, and cloaks of pure darkness, Falin was a glowing marble god, all sharp lines and brightness with his pale hair and white shirt.

He returned my smile when our gazes met through the mirror, but there was something else in his features—caution maybe? But about what? Nandin? The door I wanted to negotiate?

"Are you okay?" he asked, his gaze searching, but likely frustrated by the very little amount of me my tiny hand mirror revealed.

"It's been a hell of a day since you told me Tem wasn't who he claimed to be."

"That was little more than an hour ago for us," Dugan said.

Well then, it was a good thing I hadn't needed the cavalry to come rescue me. Though even with only an hour's time, I was still surprised—and if I was honest with myself, a little hurt—that Falin hadn't come after me. He'd more or less seen Tem abduct me, and yes, he'd looked a little frantic when Dugan had established the connection in my windshield, but he hadn't come

for me. That was really getting under my skin, and I
hated to feel that way. And maybe there was another
reason. With only an hour having passed, maybe he
was still trying to negotiate a door. Another thought
hit me, twisting my stomach. Or maybe he was still
badly injured from the duel. He didn't look it, standing
tall and gorgeous in my mirror, but he had a habit of
glamouring over his injuries . . .

"I'll update you on the events of the day, but first—"
I cut off as the image in the mirror jerked. The shadows
filling the edges of the image swirled as the three men
seemed to bounce up and down in the mirror. Except
they weren't bouncing, not of their own volition at
least. Nandin reached out to something outside of the
view of the mirror and Dugan took a step, looking like
he was bracing himself. Falin grimaced, his hand moving to his side as his weight shifted. It was a look of
pain, and Falin was very good at concealing pain, so
whatever injuries he'd hid behind his glamour must
have been bad.

"Ready?" the king's voice called out, the words almost lost in the roar of noise pouring through my mirror as Faerie jolted and rolled.

I thought he was talking to me, though I wasn't sure
what I was supposed to be ready for, but then a voice
answered from somewhere out of my view. "No. It
keeps slipping!"

Someone screamed, the cry frightened, thin, and
very young sounding. The voice cut off almost as soon
as it started, but the scream sent a cold sweat down my
spine. It wasn't any of the men I could see, but it was
impossible to tell if the scream came from the same
person who'd answered the king. Nandin lumbered
forward, stumbling as much as walking out of my view.

The image in the mirror kept jumping and swaying
and I found myself bracing as well, even though the
room around me was still. Silent. Falin took a knee,
and my gaze remained locked on him, watching the

world around him thrashing. My breath lodged in my throat, my lungs burning in protest, but I couldn't breathe. I could only watch Faerie jolt and shudder.

When the image finally stilled, I was looking at the shadow court sideways. Falin, braced with one hand on his thigh and another on his side, was the closest to the mirror. He filled most of the image, so I could see the lines of pain where they tightened around his eyes. He pushed himself up in a swift motion, though it wasn't as effortless as I was used to seeing. *Definitely still injured from that duel.* Of course, once he stood, I could only see him from the waist down. That was true of Dugan as well, though with his dark armor and cloak, he blended in with the shadows so much that I was only sure where he was when he moved.

"What just happened? Is everyone okay?" I asked, and my voice came out in quick gasps even though nothing had happened on my side of the mirror.

"Faerie is unstable," the king said, still somewhere outside my field of view.

A pair of boots stepped up to the mirror, filling the glass. Then the image shook again, moving in an arc as someone righted the fallen mirror on their end. The king's face came into view, his expression grave, his mouth a thin line of worry.

"So, an earthquake?" I asked. There had been far too many earthquakes recently.

"More like Faerie fracturing," he said, his gaze going beyond the mirror. I wasn't sure if he was looking at something I couldn't see or if he was simply thinking. "Things are happening. More doors have been lost."

"More? How many more? Which ones?"

The king's eyes snapped back to me, focusing. He didn't answer, but gave me a searching look. Assessing if I'd trade for the information? Or trying to decide if I should know? Something else?

"Two more," Falin said from somewhere behind the

king. I couldn't see him with Nandin filling the mirror, but that didn't stop the sound of his voice. "South America is cut off, as is Asia. From winter, at least. I don't know about the other courts."

Nandin's face pinched, as if upset Falin had shared what he considered too much. I just blinked, my hand dropping into my purse, and I dug through it by feel, without breaking eye contact with Nandin. We stared at each other, and then Nandin took a step back so that I could see the rest of the room again. Falin was no longer clutching his side, which was a good sign, but I still wondered how badly he was hurt. Dugan was studying me, his thumb running along his jawline.

"The other courts lost the same doors, except spring. Apparently the door in the middle of the Pacific Ocean was a little too tricky to blow, though I've heard whispers that there was an attempt," Dugan said.

I gave him a small nod of thanks, biting my lip as I absorbed the news. Nearly half the seasonal doors were gone. That . . . that was really bad. My hand finally closed on the item I was searching for, and I pulled the map I'd tucked away what seemed like forever ago free, letting it unroll as I lifted it. I ripped my gaze away from the mirror long enough to stare at the map. Sure enough, the color had fled from more of the surface. North and South America were now both completely devoid of color. As were Asia and some of Europe. Finding Nekros on the map, our little folded space didn't unfold as much as it had the first time I'd seen it, the wilds not as wide or dense.

Shit. The folded spaces were sustained by magic, and with Faerie being torn away, magic was leaving the land. Was human magic enough to sustain the cities and towns we'd built in the folded spaces across the globe? Or was the destruction of the doors going to have a rippling effect that would shake the whole world? If the folded spaces collapsed, both human and fae were in danger.

I swallowed hard, looking into the small mirror again.

"When did the latest bombings occur? I had winter's people put extra security on the doors after Nekros's was destroyed. At that time, there were no signs of trouble at any of the other doors." I hadn't had any reports from the other FIB offices, but then again, most of my local agents had jumped ship, taking off for the door in South America—not that it would even be there when they arrived, apparently—and, besides, I hadn't exactly been accessible for reports most of the day, so I shouldn't have been shocked that I hadn't heard about the newest bombings. But why hadn't the increased security helped? Having already lost one door, you'd think they'd be vigilant. Of course, Ryese had planted Tem on my team—he could have plants and sympathizers anywhere. I chewed at my bottom lip. "Could we have this conversation in person? This little hand mirror isn't the best FaceTime device."

Dugan's brows furrowed, and I saw him mouth the word "FaceTime" as if trying to parse out the meaning. Yeah, Faerie didn't tend to keep up with the latest technology. And by "latest," I wasn't even sure most of the courtiers were familiar with the printing press yet . . .

"Answering your first question," the king said. "Around noon in the human realm. As to the second—" The image in the mirror shook again, cutting off the king's words as all three men again braced against Faerie's jolting rumbles.

Two earthquakes in less than five minutes?

My eyes remained riveted on the mirror, waiting for the motion to once again still. An odd sensation at the edge of my awareness dragged at me, but I didn't want to look away from the image in front of me. Falin had braced his legs against the rocking motion of the ground and I felt almost afraid to lose sight of him, though there was nothing I could do to help from the mortal realm. Still that niggling feeling pulled at my senses, calling to my magic. I ignored it, but it tugged at me, a subtle wrongness to it.

The wrongness was what made me finally glance away from the mirror. Ignoring those gut instincts that warned of dangers was a good way to get jumped by really scary things. I thought I was alone in this room, but this was a pocket of Faerie. It was possible that something had crossed from Faerie to this pocket and gotten stuck in here with me, trapped by my father's wards. I glanced around, searching for what was niggling at me without fully taking my attention away from the mirror.

I saw nothing unusual at first. Then my gaze caught on a corner, not because I could *see* anything odd, but because I could *feel* it. The threads of Faerie were dissolving, the pocket surrounding me shrinking. I'd thought I had until sunrise before we were in danger of losing this last bit of Faerie, but now that I focused on it, I could feel it actively dissolving around me.

The sounds in the mirror quieted, and I glanced down as the image stabilized, the men straightening. As Faerie stilled, the fraying strands around me quieted as well. My gaze bounced between the mirror and the corner of the room, but now that the earthquake had passed, the room had stopped shrinking.

"How often is that happening?" I asked as Dugan righted the mirror this time.

"With increasing frequency." Dugan frowned. He was close enough that he took up the entire mirror. "The first one more or less corresponded with the doors blowing. Recently they have been hitting every few minutes. Faerie will tear itself in half at this rate."

I opened my mouth. Closed it. The panic that I'd barely been keeping leashed railed against me, trying to drag my lungs out of my chest. Or maybe it was simply my heart's frantic jumping that knocked the air from me. The pocket of Faerie I was standing in was shrinking, possibly every time Faerie quaked, which meant my window of opportunity to get the locals out was closing. But with Faerie tearing itself to shreds, it didn't sound like any of us were safe in either reality.

"What can be done?" I asked.

"Currently?" Nandin said from somewhere behind Dugan, which I couldn't see as the prince was still filling the entire mirror. I found myself craning my neck, as if that would help me see around him. It did not, of course. "Preventing more doors from falling would be good. We appear to be at some crucial tipping point."

I dug in my purse for my phone with the intention of sending a text to Nori about the fact that more doors had been lost and telling her to contact the remaining FIB offices and get as much security on the remaining doors as possible. But, of course, there was no phone in my purse. Tem had destroyed it, the bits likely still on the floorboard of my car. It wasn't like the initial security I'd ordered seemed to have helped anyway.

"What is being done to secure the doors from Faerie's side?" I asked, wishing I could actually see Falin, as he was the only one here with a door to the mortal realm. The shadow court had little skin in this game, well, except that it sounded like this disturbance was trickling down to affect all of Faerie.

"Faerie is locking down," Falin said and I blinked in surprise.

"You mean all the courts?" I'd known winter had been locked after the bombing, as even the unaffected doors hadn't been able to reach the court, but I'd been under the impression that had been because Falin had been injured in a duel and the court had locked to give him time to recover. I hadn't heard that the remaining doors to the other courts had also locked. Of course, the other courts hadn't exactly been forthcoming.

"All of Faerie, as of this afternoon," Dugan said, his expression grave. "Every door between the mortal realm and Faerie is sealed. Travel between courts on this side is still open, but Faerie has closed herself completely to the mortal realm."

I sank onto the stone bench. That might protect the remaining doors, assuming the explosive spells weren't already in place and Ryese didn't already have people stationed around the remaining doors in the mortal realm. But it also meant all the fae in the mortal realm were cut off. That wasn't too serious for those in areas where the doors still existed, because, while they couldn't travel to Faerie, at least it was still tied to the land at the doors and would sustain the local fae. But for the evacuating fae? They couldn't even bargain their way through the closest territory back to their own courts. Of course, Falin had said the South America doors were gone, so all my agents who'd jumped in their cars and fled toward where the closest winter territory should have been were headed to an equally devastated area instead.

"I need a door," I said, the words coming out surprisingly clear considering how numb I felt everywhere.

Dugan lifted a dark eyebrow.

"Well . . ." the king said and then made an annoyed sound. "Dugan, I know she is a pretty girl, but do let the rest of us see her as well. This is already hard enough with Faerie throwing us around every few minutes and whatever small reflective surface our plane-weaver is using."

Dugan frowned, but backed away from the mirror, opening my view to the rest of the room. Falin had moved closer in the interim, as had the king, so that even with Dugan taking a place beside them, all three men barely fit in the small frame.

"The shadow court owes me a favor. I'd like to trade it for a door for all the fae I can gather." Not that I could gather all the stranded fae in the Americas before this pocket of Faerie deteriorated. Hell, if it were that easy to move fae across such large land distances, this evacuation wouldn't have been an issue in the first place; the locals would have been easily relocated to the closest winter territory before the latest door had been lost. But at least I should be able to rescue the locals, and I'd try to evacuate as many as could reach us until the last thread of Faerie dissolved.

The king frowned at me, but then his eyes once again flickered over toward something out of view of my mirror. What was he looking at? Who was over there? It wasn't just the king either. Falin shot more than one furtive, if weary, glance in that direction. The weariness concerned me, but he hadn't attempted to warn me in any way, so whatever it was, it must be a concern for their side of Faerie, not mine.

"Are you in the habit of reminding kings when they owe you favors? It doesn't seem a healthy trait." Nandin's tone was good-natured, but I bristled at the implied threat. I saw Falin's hand twitch as well, but it was his only reaction.

"I'm simply opening negotiations," I said, keeping my tone flat.

"Ah, my dear—" The king cut off as all three men fell sideways, or more accurately, the mirror they were speaking through fell sideways. From the look of their feet, which was all I could see before my own mirror went completely black, all three fae caught themselves and braced for Faerie's rolling quakes as it shook again. With the image gone, I would have thought the connection broke, except for the awful noise of Faerie rumbling and for the fact that I distinctly heard the king curse, so apparently I still had an audible connection, just no image. Or maybe the mirror had fallen facedown this time.

With nothing to see in my mirror, I devoted my attention to the edges of the room. Sure enough, the threads of Faerie began fraying as soon as the earthquake began. The damage was slow—I doubted the room was losing more than an inch or two per incident—but that would add up. How long would this pocket of Faerie last?

"Find a way to make it work!" the king's voice shouted over the background noise.

I thought he was talking about the mirror, but the voice that answered was younger, not one of the men I'd been speaking to. "I've been trying. Faerie is too unstable."

"Well, it's not going to get any more stable." That one was Dugan's voice, but it didn't sound like he was actually talking to the other two, just grumbling an aside.

I frowned, glancing at my mirror. It was still dark. The sound of Faerie's rumbling was growing dimmer; the angrier shaking must have been quieting to smaller aftershocks. The edges of my room stopped fraying as well, so I guessed the worst of it had passed. Though for how long? There were mere minutes between the last few earthquakes.

I expected someone to right the mirror again, now that the most recent incident had passed. Instead the unknown voice yelled, "I got it. Be quick!"

Without warning, arms wrapped around my waist and dragged me backward, up over the bench I'd been perched on, and into the darkness.

Chapter 24

What the hell?" I yelled as shadows swallowed me. I struggled against the arms locked around my waist, but they were vise tight, dragging me back against an armored chest.

The air around me changed, the darkness filling my eyes turning thicker, more solid. I dropped the mirror as I aimed my elbow into what I hoped was my ambusher's ribs. My other hand reached for the dagger in my boot, but whoever had grabbed me anticipated that move, and his arm slid up, bracing across my chest to grab my opposite shoulder and force me upright.

The bench I'd just been sitting on vanished, a wave of darkness consuming the few feet of space between it and me. The hand mirror, which hadn't even had time to hit the ground yet, shattered in midair, half of it falling to the ground inches from my feet. The other half was gone, still on the other side of the portal. A small cloaked figure dropped to his knees, his breath coming in ragged gasps.

I went still, no longer fighting the arms that had snatched me from my little pocket of Faerie and hauled me into Faerie proper. As soon as I stopped struggling, the arms fell away, releasing me. I stood stunned for a moment, staring at the broken mirror barely a breath in front of my toes. If I had kicked out while being dragged backward, it would have been my leg that had been severed instead of the mirror.

"Are you all right?" Dugan asked as he took a step back, leaving my personal bubble now that he'd released me.

My pulse thundered in my ears, nearly drowning out his words. I turned to frown at him, but my gaze moved slow, unable to look away from the remainder of the mirror until it was physically impossible to see it with the rest of me turning. My eyes finally snapped up, landing on Dugan's dark armor—armor I now knew was warm from his body heat. And very solid, if my smarting elbow was any indication.

"What the hell . . ." I said again, blinking as I forced my gaze to Dugan's face.

His expression was guarded as he watched me but he met my gaze levelly. "I will not apologize for removing you from a realm where you could not safely exist."

"You could have given me a little warning!" And a slightly longer window to make it through the door. I'd been inches from losing a limb. Besides, it wasn't like I'd been in any danger alone in a small pocket of Faerie, and from the sounds of it, as I was carrying around my own pocket of Faerie, I was the fae least affected by the door's destruction. I took a deep breath. I was trembling. Not a lot, just a slight tremor as the adrenaline that had flooded me when I'd been grabbed now drained away. With everything I'd been through already today, I was surprised my body was still up to pumping me full of adrenaline—did that stuff never run out?

Crossing my arms over my chest, I turned my back on Dugan and spun to find Falin. He wasn't far away, and as intently as he was watching me, I was surprised I hadn't felt his gaze like a physical weight. I hurried over to him, but then stopped a foot or so away, unsure. Our relationship was so new, and we weren't exactly advertising it. Of course, we were standing in the court of shadows and secrets, and Dugan had made it quite clear that he knew.

"Hey," I said, feeling awkward. There were so many things I wanted to say, but I didn't even know where to start. Was he okay? Why was he in shadow? And why hadn't he bargained a door with the planebender? I needed to tell him about Ryese, and compare notes about the bombings. To ask about his ideas on fixing the doors.

Falin studied me for half a heartbeat. Then he stepped forward, gathering me in his arms and pulling me toward him. He kissed me, a deep, almost desperate kiss that blasted through my awkwardness. A kiss that communicated relief, concern, and affection all bundled into lips that consumed, breath that became shared, and warmth that surrounded me completely, making me forget about the audience in the room and the fact that our relationship was supposed to be on the down low. I relaxed into his body, returning that kiss with just as much passion, knowing it couldn't last.

When our air finally ran out and we had to break apart, he whispered, "Hello to you too." He was still close enough that the words brushed against my lips and a delicious shiver ran through me, an awareness that tingled over my skin and fluttered in my belly.

I was breathless again, but for a totally different—and much better—reason this time. I closed that inch of space between us, locking my lips on his just because I wanted the feel of him against me, reassuring me he was okay. I didn't let the kiss linger, though, because while this stolen moment was ours and amazing and released a lot of the worry and fear I'd built up since the bombing yesterday, we were not alone and I had a mission here.

I broke off, but he didn't let me get far, his hand in

my hair, cradling the back of my head. "I was so worried," he whispered. "What happened? Dugan couldn't find your shadow after that troll crushed the mirror."

My lips pressed together as I studied him, aware of the taste of him still on my skin, wishing I could save it somehow. "It's a long story. It involves Ryese—he's the King of Light now, by the way."

I was focused on Falin, so didn't see anyone else's reaction to my words, but I heard Dugan's grunt. Was that surprise or . . . ? I stepped back slightly, not far, not out of Falin's arms, but I put some space between us. He didn't try to stop me, his hand falling from my hair to grip me lightly at the waist instead.

I glanced over at Dugan. "You didn't know?"

"That light had a new king?" He frowned, the expression severe on his otherwise handsome face. "No. And I should have. That shouldn't be a secret that could be hidden from us, not even by light, where there are few shadows to overhear whispers."

I turned to see Nandin's take on the situation and found him kneeling beside the planebender. I'd seen the changeling collapse to his knees after closing the rift that I'd been dragged through, but I'd lost track of him after that in the confusion of my abrupt entrance into Faerie proper and my reunion with Falin. He'd apparently collapsed further than his knees, because Nandin was now kneeling over his completely prone form. He had a flask of something he was trying to get the changeling to drink, but I wasn't sure the planebender was actually conscious. It was hard to tell with his hood obscuring his face. His hands were limp at his sides, though one twitched upward for a moment, as if trying to reach for the flask Nandin was attempting to force on him, before falling motionless to his side again.

I opened my mouth to ask if he was okay, but didn't get the chance as the ground lurched.

I'd watched several quakes hit through the mirror. I still wasn't prepared to be in the middle of one.

My legs went out from under me at the first jolting roll of the ground. Only Falin's arms around me kept me from face-planting onto the shadowy floor. He jerked me forward, further into the protection of his body, but I heard him grunt in pain as that movement slammed me against his chest. He guided me to my knees without ever letting go, following me down in a controlled movement despite the way the ground rumbled. My stomach clenched tight, my eyes squeezing closed as I buried my face against Falin, trying not to grab him too tight. He just held on to me.

The noise from the quakes had been bad through the mirror. It was deafening actually being in the middle of it. The room we were in resembled a gigantic gothic cathedral, with gray stone, flying buttresses, and alcoves devoured by shadows. While the ground rolled and jolted, not so much as dust fell from the ceiling and walls, but in the distance it sounded like mountains were cracking apart and crashing down. Somewhere, Faerie was tearing herself apart, stone by stone. The ever-present distant music took on the sound of a wail instead of a song.

With my eyes squeezed shut, waiting for the awful noise and rocking to stop, I realized something else as well. The wrongness I'd felt in the bubble of Faerie, the fraying as the threads unraveled, I felt it here as well.

That realization made my head snap up and I scanned the room, searching for the disturbance in the layers of reality. I couldn't spot any single source. Not like in the bubble in my father's house, where it was clearly the edges dissolving. And the wrongness I was feeling wasn't quite the same either, but it was all around me, in every thread of reality, as if everything that made Faerie was straining, close to snapping.

Shit. If Faerie broke . . .

The noise slowly quieted as the ground stopped lurching and stilled. Falin didn't release me, and I realized I'd more or less ended up in his lap during the quake, his body curled around me like a shield. His breath was jagged where it puffed through my hair, and I didn't think that had anything to do with the quake, not directly at least.

"How badly are you injured?" I whispered, my words so quiet I wasn't confident he'd be able to hear.

"I'll be fine."

I twisted my neck so I could look up at him. The fine lines betraying pain were evident around his eyes again, and while he held me tight, I could feel the smallest tremble in his fingers. He'd said he *would be* fine. Not that he was now. Tricky fae wording going on there. I frowned, but I didn't press him further. When we were alone, I'd have him drop his glamour so I could see how badly he was injured. I could open my shields and check for myself but even though I'd be doing it out of concern, it would be wrong, a violation. I typically didn't think twice about piercing glamour, but I'd checked wounds Falin hid before, and he'd equated it to removing his clothes without consent.

I extracted myself from Falin's lap, trying not to aggravate wounds I couldn't see. He didn't let me go far, though, his gloved hand locking around mine, tethering me. I didn't resist the contact. After everything in the last two days, if I was honest with myself, I liked the reassurance that he was near.

Glancing around, I took stock of the room. Dugan watched us, his expression so blank he had to be making an effort to keep his face empty. The Shadow King was a few feet away, still kneeling beside the small figure of the planebender. The boy no longer looked unconscious at least. He had curled into a ball on the floor, his hands over his head and his thin knees visible through the dark folds of his cloak where he'd pulled them tight against his chest. I couldn't hear exactly what the king was saying, but the tone was gentle, soothing, trying to calm the frightened boy.

"Okay, I know I said we should talk in person, but it might have been a good idea to meet in the mortal realm, instead of Faerie where the ground quakes every few minutes," I said, my legs so shaky that I wasn't sure if the ground was still trembling or if it was just me.

"We were not about to risk getting stuck on that side," the king said as he helped the planebender sit upright. "And I'm not sure he could have fashioned a second door with how damaged Faerie is. You might have noticed that we barely got you here."

"Wait, what? Stuck?" I glanced from the king to Falin, who didn't meet my eyes. "Are you saying I'm stuck on this side? I can't be stuck. I came to negotiate a door for the fading independents and all the other stranded fae." And apparently there were a lot more of them than I'd known when I had made that plan, as more doors had been blown.

"Faerie is too unstable," the king said. "The boy barely succeeded in opening the rift we pulled you through, and it laid him out cold to do it. How would he possibly hold a door large and long enough to evacuate thousands of fae? No. Faerie is intentionally locking down all access to the mortal realm. There will be no more doors. Not by him at least. Not until he has had time to recover."

I wanted to argue, to point out how little time we had left before that final pocket of Faerie vanished forever. But I'd seen the planebender unconscious on the ground. He was a changeling, and I'd never actually seen his face, but he seemed so young, like an adolescent. The door Dugan had dragged me through had been open mere moments. How long would it take to evacuate all the fae in Nekros, I wasn't sure, but it would definitely be too much for him.

"What are my other options for an evacuation door?" Because there had always been temporary

doors between Faerie and the mortal realm. They
tended to be more chaotic, or perhaps simply more
costly. I'd opened one such door once, utilizing overlapping shadows in both realms to merge the space
between them. The door had gotten us where we
needed to reach in time, but it also released living
nightmares on the entire population. I had no idea how
to find such an overlapping point in the realms on my
own, though, especially now that Faerie had lost most
of its connections to the mortal realm. Legends spoke
of other doorways, though the cost for those was usually paid by losing years of your life, by sacrificial
deaths, or by some other extreme payment.

"With Faerie in its present state, no door is likely to
work between here and the mortal realm. Now we
need to move before the interior doors of Faerie start
locking as well." The king turned away from me to focus on the planebender again, who had made it to a
sitting position earlier, but was now braced on all fours.
"Can you walk, or should I carry you?"

"I'll walk. Help me stand." The planebender lifted
his hand toward the king, the tremble in it apparent
even from where I stood several yards away. The rift
he'd opened for me truly had hurt him. No wonder he
hadn't left it open a second longer than necessary.

I stepped closer to Falin, lowering my voice as Nandin grasped the planebender's outstretched hand.

"Why didn't you warn me that they planned to drag
me through that door?" Because it was obvious that
had been the plan, right from the beginning. I'd wondered who the king had kept looking at beyond the
mirror, who he'd been speaking to. He'd had the planebender working on the door from the moment I'd
walked into the pocket of Faerie in my father's house.

Falin grimaced, and there was a lot to unravel in his
expression. Some regret, perhaps, but mostly resolve. I
was reminded of Dugan's words when he'd pulled me
across, that he wouldn't apologize for dragging me

from a realm where I couldn't safely exist. I saw that same sentiment in Falin's face. He'd known what the plan was, and he'd agreed to it even though he'd known I wouldn't have. Which also explained the cautious expression I'd seen on him in the mirror, versus his much more enthusiastic greeting once I was in Faerie. He'd known I'd be pissed, but he hadn't wanted to warn me and risk me not making it to Faerie.

After a moment, he lifted one shoulder. "The window to get you here was narrow. The pocket in the mortal realm is dissolving, Faerie itself is growing more unstable, and then there is the fact that the bender is a shadow changeling, his ability most powerful inside his own court, and we can't stay here. I made a bargain to ensure you were pulled across, though I think they would have retrieved you regardless." He pulled me closer, in a tight hug that I suspected hurt his injuries but which he did anyway, as if he needed more contact, more reassurance I was really there. "When you were taken . . . I couldn't reach you. I tried to renegotiate for another door, so that I could find you, but Nandin would not budge. He feared his bender would be able to create only one door, and he'd risk him only to retrieve you, not to strand a king on the other side."

I glanced at the planebender in question. It had been a risk, the boy dangerously drained from the effort. The king hauled him to his feet and he swayed for a moment, Nandin's hands on his shoulders helping to keep him upright. After a moment, the changeling seemed to steady. He nodded to his king and Nandin dropped his hands, slow, like he was ready to catch him if the boy was not quite as secure on his feet as he thought.

"We need to go now," Nandin said, still watching the planebender as if he was considering picking him up anyway and not risk him walking. "We are too close to the chasm."

Dugan nodded, turning to stride toward the deepest shadows in the room. Falin released me from his tight hug, taking my hand as he turned to follow Dugan. I wasn't going to protest leaving, but I still had so many questions, so I hesitated, my gaze on Nandin and the planebender.

The boy took one uncertain step. On his second step he pitched forward. He would have hit the ground had Nandin not caught him, holding him upright. The sudden motion dislodged the boy's hood, which I'd never seen off before.

Dirty blond hair, not dissimilar to my own, fell into his face, and green eyes went wide with surprise. His hand flew up, grabbing the hood of his cloak, tugging it upward in a frantic motion, his face a mix of shock and horror. He jerked the hood back over his head; the shadows, which were part of a spell, obscured his features again. But it was too late. I'd already seen his face.

"Not possible," I whispered. Because I couldn't have seen what I'd thought. *Who* I'd thought. I stared at the planebender, short compared to me, body unfinished in that way of an adolescent stuck between childhood and teen years. The initial shock of surprise that had slammed into me gave way to a sharper emotion, hotter and angry. I dropped my mental shields, piercing the planes around me as I gazed through them. The shadows under the hood were partly glamour, but the hood itself was real, and without decay in Faerie, it didn't disintegrate so that I could see his face under it. I glared at him. I'd had enough deception and betrayal for one day. I wasn't going to blindly accept more. "Drop your hood."

Falin, who had not been looking at the planebender when he fell, but waiting for me to follow Dugan, turned. His gaze swept over me, no doubt noting everything from my now-glowing eyes to the fact that my hand trembled in his, and then he whirled to face the king. He didn't go for a weapon, but his stance changed, turning defensive and ready for danger.

"What's going on?" he asked.

"The planebender is glamoured, and I don't know why." The words were a hiss because I didn't have any air, couldn't seem to draw any. I'd had too many shocks today, but this one . . .

"My dear, we do not have time for this," Nandin said, stepping in front of the boy. "We need to move."

I just stared at him, my brain spinning, trying to puzzle out all the reasons the Shadow King might want me to believe the planebender was someone I knew. The fall, the cloak slipping, it had looked so accidental, the boy terrified that he'd been revealed. But fae were master manipulators. Did Nandin think his convincing me that I knew his pet changeling would gain extra loyalty from me? Make some favor he planned to request be more agreeable to me?

"Take off the hood," I said again.

Nandin met my gaze, his stern and cold, ready to refuse. But then a small hand wrapped around his wrist. A frown tugged at the king's mouth as he looked down at the planebender. "We do not have time for this," the king said again.

From the movement of the cloak, it appeared that the planebender shrugged. Then he reached up and tugged back his hood. The face below was achingly familiar, even though I hadn't seen it in over a decade. And it didn't change despite the fact that I was peering across planes. It wasn't glamour. Which meant . . .

"That's not possible," I said, sinking to my knees as I stared at a face I'd never thought I would see again.

"Alex?" Falin made my name a question. He still looked like he was unsure if he should be going for a weapon, but seemed to be leaning against it at this point.

Which was good. I didn't want him to attack my older brother.

Chapter 25

B rad?" My older brother's name was more of a gasp than a question.

He gave me a sheepish look and scratched the back of his head as he said, "Hey, Allie."

Allie. I hadn't heard that nickname in years. My mom had called me that, but she'd died when I was five. After that, much to my father's chagrin, my older brother had picked up the habit. But then he'd vanished when I was eleven and the nickname had disappeared with him.

But now here it was. As was my brother.

"You still look twelve," I said, which was probably a stupid comment, but shock was making my brain a bit hard to navigate.

"I am a couple centuries past twelve," he said, curling his nose in the way he always had when we were children and I'd say something he disagreed with.

I stared at him, still not quite believing what my eyes were telling me. But it wasn't just his face; he had my brother's mannerisms, his nickname for me. Everything pointed to the boy in front of me truly being my lost brother.

"How is this possible?" I asked, the question not directed at anyone in particular. Then my gaze narrowed on Brad again. "Have you been in the shadow court this entire time? Why didn't you contact me? I thought you were dead! Hell, I've been in the same room with you a half dozen times over the last six months. Why didn't you ever tell me? At least to let me know you were alive and all right?" My questions grew in volume as I spoke, so that by the time I reached the last one, it was delivered in a squeaky yell.

Brad grimaced, the expression shockingly adult on his young face. He opened his mouth to answer, but Nandin once again stepped in front of him.

"As charming as this awkward family reunion is, we simply do not have the time to waste. We need to get moving before—"

The sudden rumble and roar of another earthquake hitting Faerie filled the air, cutting off the king's words. He cursed, turning to the changeling beside him, but the boy had hit the ground at the first hint of this newest quake.

I was already on my knees, but careened sideways with the jolting floor. I was pretty sure I should just stay there on the ground, riding out the movement, but Falin knelt beside me, gathering me to him. I clung to him as Faerie shook, but my mind wasn't on the chaos around me. It was focused on the chaos inside me.

Every encounter I'd had with the planebender played out behind my squeezed-shut eyes. The first time I'd seen him, he'd helped Nandin pluck me out of the winter court, but the rescue had left me a guest who couldn't leave, aka a prisoner in a very pretty cage. He'd seemed like he'd wanted to tell me something that night, but the harpies who'd been escorting me had reminded him that he'd been forbidden from talking to me. Had he wanted to reveal his identity? Why would the king prevent him? Nandin himself had enthusiastically touted his own distant relation to me—wouldn't he have believed reuniting me with my brother would have earned him bigger points? Or did he fear that discovering my brother was a changeling bound to his court would piss me off? *Can't say he was wrong about that.*

Brad had been there when I'd met Dugan for the first time. He'd opened a hole from shadow to the pocket of Faerie in my father's mansion. Did our father know? It seemed impossible he didn't, and yet it would have been cruel of him to know and never tell me. Of course, my father wasn't exactly known for his kindness or his transparency. I'd seen the planebender a few other times too. I'd even noted that his voice sounded familiar when I'd first heard it, but at the time I had been concentrating more on the fact that Nandin was dying from a magical wasting disease, as was I. I'd never thought any harder about the familiarity of his voice, or tried to place it. Not that I would have come up with my missing brother as a possible match. I'd always believed Brad was still alive, still out there somewhere, but I'd assumed he would be in his midtwenties now. Not a changeling stuck in a twelve-year-old's body.

Faerie ceased her rumbling and lurching before my thoughts settled. My hands trembled, the adrenaline flooding my body making me shake even though Faerie had stopped. Falin drew me up to my feet with him as he rose. The initial surprise had passed and I felt strangely numb, my thoughts slowing, as if my brain had turned off instead of dealing with any more new information. I just stared mutely at Brad, who hadn't made it back to his feet yet, despite the Shadow King's urgings.

"Did you say Brad?" Falin asked, leaning in close as he helped me to my feet.

I nodded absently before saying, "What chasm was Nandin talking about?" My voice sounded odd in my ears, too far away and too empty.

Falin frowned at me, concern flickering in his gaze. Nandin took the segue easily, though.

"The chasm that was created when the realm of dreams was severed from my lands. In Faerie's current volatile state, that chasm is growing." He walked as he spoke, dragging Brad behind him.

Dugan had reached the far end of the room already, and he scowled as he waited for us to catch up, though his expression didn't seem to be targeting anyone in the room. The king crossed the space quickly, Brad having to jog to keep up. Falin gave my hand a squeeze as he turned to follow. I trudged beside him, though our progress was slow, maybe because my legs felt like they'd been tied down with lead weights.

"Where are we going?" I asked, my lips feeling a little too swollen to speak. If I hadn't been fine before Brad revealed himself, I would have believed some latent effects from Ryese's spell were kicking in, or maybe Tem slipped me poison. I doubted either was actually the case.

"Winter," Falin said, the word quick and soft. Not quite a whisper, but almost. Even still, I visibly saw Dugan's shoulders hitch.

"All of us?" I did whisper, not that it made any difference in these halls. The shadows caught my words and echoed them as soft murmurs along the corridor.

"Yes," Nandin said, and his voice wasn't soft at all. His eyes, when he glanced back at me, were tired. Sad. "We are . . . abandoning the shadow court. Temporarily."

The very shadows around us seemed to tremble, and mournful weeping filled the air. I blinked in surprise, and then my gaze shot to Dugan. He was not looking at any of us.

"It's that bad?" My question was quiet, and I wasn't even sure who I was asking.

Dugan nodded, his gaze still fixed on the shadows in front of him. "Our court is taking the brunt, as it was already out of balance and as the chasm where the realm of dreams was severed is more or less an open wound in Faerie."

"We sent the courtiers away while we waited for you to reach the last remaining pocket of Faerie," the king said. "Luckily, you were already on your way."

The shadows we'd entered parted to reveal a large hallway, though I hadn't seen the doorway we'd passed through. Around us, Faerie trembled. Not a violent quake like I'd experienced just moments earlier, but like a shuddering breath between sobs. "She's so sad," I muttered. It wasn't an observation I normally would have voiced, but the heavy numbness my post-shock brain seemed to be stumbling through provided very little filter. I was saying pretty much every thought that crossed my mind.

Falin lifted an eyebrow as he glanced at me. "Who?"

"Faerie."

The land's sorrow permeated the air. It was in the sounds, in the very movements of Faerie. Was it just here, in shadow? The court realizing its king and fae were fleeing? Or was all of Faerie in mourning?

Dugan made a sound somewhere between a grunt and a cough. "With the way the land keeps shaking, I'd say Faerie is more furious than sad."

He had a point. And there were definitely some harsh notes of fury in the air, but the overwhelming feeling I was picking up from all around me was sorrow. I'd always known Faerie had a type of will, but it was strange to think of it as having emotion. And yet it was all around me. Or maybe the land was reflecting something else, like when the winter court had become a chaotic, miserable place corresponding with the former queen's madness.

"So what's our plan?" I asked as I trudged down the seemingly endless halls of darkness. At times we passed through shadows so thick I wasn't sure there were actual walls around us, just darkness. Then we would pass out of that shadow, and while there was no discernible change in the light source, the shadows were thin enough that I could see the rough-cut stone walls.

"We are still working out those details," Dugan said. Then he aimed a speculative glance in my direction. "But I believe we need to hear what you have learned in the last few hours before we finalize our plans. After our conversation was interrupted earlier, you vanished and I could not track your shadow. That is exceedingly rare."

"And yet Ryese and his minions seem to excel at it," I said, wrapping one arm across my waist. Falin still had my other hand, so I couldn't pull that one in without tugging away from him. He noticed my closing body language and drew me closer, putting an arm around my shoulders as we walked.

We reached another of the impossibly dark patches, and I couldn't even see my own hands despite the fact that my skin should have given off enough of a glow to be visible. Then, without warning, the darkness broke and we emerged into sunlight.

I squinted, as this was more light than I'd been in since Dugan pulled me into the shadow realm, but as I blinked, I realized it wasn't actually blindingly bright, just not the gloom of shadow.

We weren't in the shadow court anymore.

I glanced around, instantly recognizing the tree-lined clearing. Honestly, it would be hard to mistake it for anywhere else in Faerie. Four doors stood between the trees at equal distances in the circle, the trees around each door slowly shifting through the seasons. We had emerged from a deep shadow between two large tree trunks, but the trees around us were covered in bright pink flowers with fresh shoots of green leaves. Spring. Those gave way to larger, darker leaves as the trees grew closer to summer's doorway, which looked like a hill of grass and wildflowers between an interwoven ash and oak tree. Once past summer's door, the

circle continued, the leaves changing into brilliant
shades of red, orange, and yellow, and lush ripe fruit
appearing on the trees surrounding fall's large door.
Fall, of course, gave way to winter, those brilliant
leaves turning brown and brittle and then vanishing
from the trees completely as first frost and then snow
covered the boughs until the circle reached a point
where an oak and ash intertwined to form the frame of
a glistening door of solid carved ice. Then, of course,
the trees circled back toward us, the ice melting and
spring blossoms appearing once more. Between the
doors, the gaps in the trees glittered with brilliant light
or deep shadows, which were the paths to those respective courts, though as I glanced around the clearing, I
noticed that there were hardly any shadows left. Aside
from the one we'd emerged from near spring's door,
there were only two other dark trails. Everything else
was golden light. Judging from the grave expressions of
my companions as they also gazed around the clearing,
I wasn't the only one who noticed.

"Let's keep moving," Falin said, leading us toward
the winter door.

As he approached the door, it swung open, greeting
its king back to his court. Inside the icy halls, guards
stood at attention. Under the former queen, the guards
had kept their faces shrouded, all individuality erased,
so I could never tell if the court boasted many ice-clad
guards or just a few that I saw frequently. Falin had apparently opted to remove the guards' shrouds, because
while they still wore their elaborate ice armor, which I
knew would chill anyone who got close to them, the
guards at the door wore nothing to obscure their faces.

They bowed as Falin entered, standing back to attention quickly at his nod. None gave any overt reaction to the king, prince, and planebender following us,
which was much better than the last time I'd walked
the winter halls in Dugan's company—pretty much every guard had attacked him on sight. Now they watched

the shadow nobles with suspicion, but the guards made no move against them.

Falin led us to the court's enormous library. I'd been here only once before, and hadn't had time to really marvel at the sheer quantity of books on that trip. Unfortunately, we weren't exactly on a leisurely visit this time either. I would have liked to walk among the floor-to-ceiling shelves lining the room and see what kinds of books a Faerie library would contain. Old grimoires with long-forgotten spells? Collections of folklore about themselves? Fiction written by fae bards? I had no idea, and this wasn't the time to find out, though I made a mental note to return once life calmed down a little—life would do that eventually, right?

Falin led us to a sitting area in the far area of the library. The furniture appeared to be carved of solid ice, the cushions on the chairs and couches fluffy white snow. Ice furniture was fairly common in the winter court, and I knew if I sat on it, the couch wouldn't actually feel cold, but just looking at it made me shiver. The icy furniture was gathered in a relaxed configuration around a large hearth. The raging fire inside the solid-ice fireplace hurt my brain, but the fire was no more hot than the ice was cold, so I guess it was all aesthetics anyway. Regardless, I gravitated toward the hearth, as if I could imagine some heat radiating off it.

Brad, who had been dragging behind, collapsed onto the closest couch and leaned his head against the frozen-looking back cushion. His eyes fluttered closed a moment later. Had he seriously fallen asleep that quickly? Simply resting? I couldn't say for certain, but I found myself staring at him, his features relaxed and oh so familiar, as if he'd just walked out of the last picture I had of him from when we were kids. I also noted that he hadn't bothered replacing his hood after I recognized him. Apparently his identity wasn't a secret kept from all of Faerie—just from me.

"We need to know what happened," Dugan said,

drawing my attention from Brad. Which was probably good, because I was moments from demanding answers from Nandin, which might not be the best political move nor the wisest use of our time, presently at least. I would get my answers, but they would have to wait. Dugan gave the icy furniture a dubious glance before crossing his arms over his chest and turning to face me. Still standing. "You said Ryese is now the Light King. How do you know? Did you talk to him? Where is he?"

"Did he admit to having anything to do with the bombings of the amaranthine trees?" Falin asked, adding to the list of questions from Dugan.

"And why destroy the trees?" Nandin frowned, brushing his finger and thumb along his chin, idly stroking his beard into a point. "If he has already gained the throne of a Faerie court—the most powerful in Faerie due to the imbalance, even before the most recent damage to the seasonal courts—what is his endgame? Does he plan to overthrow all the courts?"

I lifted my hands in front of me, aiming for a placating expression. "Hold up. One question at a time," I said. "Yes, I spoke to Ryese, but only through a mirror, so I'm not sure where he was. Faerie, presumably, though I guess he could have been anywhere. He was wearing the light crown . . . But I couldn't use my magic at the time. It could have been glamour." I bit my lip as I thought about the conversation. He'd never actually stated he was king. He'd implied a lot, including that he'd mentally damaged the former queen and she'd willingly given him her throne. Or at least, that had been what I'd taken from our conversation, but fae were tricky bastards when left with any wiggle room for lies to be taken as truth. "He didn't actually admit to much. He mentioned the bombings only in passing, but didn't take credit. He . . . he wanted to use my planeweaving ability for something. He had a spell set up that was draining my magic out of me and storing it for his use." I squinted, as if that would let me look back at my conversation with Ryese more clearly. "Whatever he was planning, he was mad that Tem put me in the circle early. He wasn't ready yet."

Falin moved closer to me as I spoke. I didn't realize I was hugging my arms across my middle until Falin's warm arms slid over mine, his fingers lightly interlocking with mine where I was gripping my own ribs tight. I took a breath and forced my body to relax, to lean back against Falin's hard chest.

"I want to hear about all of it," he whispered, leaning down close so the words were just for me. "Later, when we are alone, I want to know about everything from the time you were taken until you escaped."

I nodded. We didn't have time now. There were too many other important things to cover, but he was letting me know he cared, that he wanted to know. I could appreciate that, even if it didn't change anything right now.

"So he is only *probably* the King of Light . . ." Nandin said, pursing his lips.

"Regardless, light is expanding." Dugan took a step forward, toward his king, then seemed unsure. "You saw the clearing. There is no balance. Shadow . . ." He shook his head, apparently at a loss for words.

"So what do we do?" I asked.

"This is Shadow's fight," Nandin said, frowning at me. "Or are you volunteering Winter's assistance?"

"I don't have the authority to do that," I snapped, and Nandin slid his eyes meaningfully to where Falin's arms were around my waist. I ignored the implication. "Besides, this doesn't affect only one court—all have lost doors. And it's bigger than even that. The folded spaces in the human realm appear to be affected." I reached into my purse, digging for the map but not finding it. I frowned, opening the purse with both hands to search. It wasn't there.

Damn it. It had been in my lap when Dugan dragged me into Faerie. It must not have made it.

I made a frustrated sound and shut the purse. "I had a map . . . The wilds are shrinking. I don't know how far it will go if left unchecked. It might just be a side effect, or Ryese's plans might involve destabilizing the mortal realm as much as Faerie. I don't know. He . . . well, that is, I *think* he attacked the governor of Nekros." My voice grew quieter as I spoke, until the last word was nearly a whisper.

Falin stiffened behind me, and then turned me so he could see my face. I wasn't sure the others realized the significance of that statement, but Falin knew the governor was my father.

"How? What happened?"

I shook my head. "He . . . was attacked. I don't understand how. Magic, I think, though there was no trace of it."

"Caine?" Dugan asked, looking thoughtful.

I nodded. "He told me to go to the shadow court. Do you know what happened?" I asked, looking between Dugan and Nandin.

The Shadow King's face was drawn in a hard frown and he stroked his dark beard, pinching it to a point on his chin between two fingers. "I do not, but rest assured, I will look into it. You believe Ryese is behind this attack as well?"

"He'd been taunting me. With roses . . ." That sounded so ridiculous. I hurried on. "Point being, this affects everyone. Every court. Every fae. And even the humans. Ryese has all but declared war."

All three men winced at my last sentence. I lifted an eyebrow, but it was Dugan who volunteered the answer.

"War in Faerie is forbidden. Few things have ever been truly forbidden by the High King, but that is one of them. It's not like we can just gather an army and march into the light court."

"Isn't harming amaranthine trees also forbidden?"

Nandin nodded. "But we have no proof of guilt."

I made an exasperated sound. "Fine. Then what is our plan?"

"The same solution Faerie offers for most problems." Falin's voice was low, and while I couldn't see his face, I could hear the grim resignation in his voice.

"A duel," I said, because that was how all conflicts seemed to be tackled among the fae, but I was already shaking my head. "Ryese doesn't fight his own duels."

"There will be at least one champion to get through," Dugan said, his hand moving to the sword at his waist. "But your king has already slain light's best fighter." He nodded to Falin over my head, and Falin's arms tightened around my waist.

Yeah, but at what cost? I still needed to get a look at Falin's injuries.

"Why would he send his best fighter to duel for the winter throne?" I said, my frown growing.

"A calculated risk to remove one of the more deadly fae in Faerie while also disrupting the court?" Nandin said. "Or perhaps out of a personal vendetta. From what I've heard, Ryese is not a big fan of the Winter King."

That was true. He'd told me he wanted me to suffer for my part in his disfigurement. I'd revealed him, but Falin had been the one who drove the iron dart into Ryese's hand. He probably hated him even more than he hated me. He also knew that if Falin had been killed it would hurt me, so win-win for him, I'm sure.

"The challenge was also nearly guaranteed to at least weaken the king," Dugan said. His gaze moved to Falin. "No offense, but I very much doubt that you will be helpful in a duel in the near future."

Falin didn't move, but it felt like his body turned to unyielding stone. I don't even think he was breathing. After a few heartbeats, he lifted one shoulder, but the movement was stiff. "I wouldn't want anyone's life to depend on me tonight."

It was a lot to admit in this company. Perhaps too

much. I hadn't thought about it before that moment, but Dugan and Nandin were displaced royals whose court was failing. They were, in theory, our allies, but with Falin injured, they could decide the opportunity to claim winter was too great to pass up.

"If Ryese gambled the best-known fighter in light on the chance of taking out Falin before the bombings, then he has something even nastier up his sleeve," I said, the words coming out in a rush as I tried to fill the silence, to redirect the conversation onto the topic of our common enemy.

"Agreed," Dugan said with a nod, and I almost sighed with relief. Nandin was still watching Falin with a speculative assessment, though, and that worried me.

"We should secure some allies. Fighters from other courts willing to stand with us and brave the gauntlet of champions he might have guarding the path to his throne," Nandin finally said after a few moments.

"Could he have more than one knight who would fight for him?" And if that was the case, why was Falin fighting all his own duels?

"Technically? No," Dugan said, lifting one dark-clad shoulder in a small shrug. "But if a challenge is brought before a throne, any number of courtiers may volunteer to fight to defend their king."

"And Ryese seems to have a contingency of loyal sycophants who are likely to jump into danger to protect him," I finished for him. Why was that? What could the smarmy little bastard possibly offer to inspire such loyalty? Tem had indicated he was following Ryese because he believed he would change Faerie . . . Was that the reasoning behind all of his followers?

The ground below me trembled, and I braced myself, but as Faerie began to rumble and shake, the earthquake lacked the violence and intensity of the quakes I'd experienced in shadow. This one was noticeable, but while the books on the ceiling-high shelves shifted a bit, not a single one fell. I remained standing without any struggle, and Brad didn't even wake up, though his chin did fall forward toward his chest, causing him to make a sound somewhere between a snore and a grunt. I realized as the low rumble quieted and the ground stilled once more that considerably more time had passed without a quake than when I'd been in shadow.

Nandin was right, his court was taking the brunt of it; winter was much less drastically affected by Faerie's wrathful sorrow. But how long would that last? If shadow continued to collapse into the chasm, how long before it was destroyed completely, further disrupting the already teetering balance? How long until the rest of Faerie was as severely affected?

As Faerie once again fell still and silent, Nandin rubbed his thumb and finger along his chin again before saying, "So, which of us has connections to the other courts?"

Chapter 26

It turned out, no one had many promising connections to the other monarchs. Shadow didn't interact with the other courts that often, so had never made many efforts to forge alliances as the court tended to be shunned anyway, and Falin was simply too new of a king. Oh, he'd been receiving delegates from the other courts since taking the throne, but actual alliances? Not so much. Add in the former queen's long-declining mental health and that he'd been her bloody hands for decades, and it meant that he had few friends in other courts. *I* actually had what was determined to be the most promising position for approaching summer, and since that was largely based on the fact that the Summer King wanted something from me—and had cursed me when I hadn't immediately agreed to his wishes—it was a pretty good indication of how bad everyone else's interpersonal relationships were.

It did mean I was the one charged with contacting summer.

The hour, combined with an exhausting day full of nasty spells and shocking discoveries, was really starting to drag on me. I did not want to try to play emissary to a lecherous Faerie king or prim and judgy queen, but time was working against us. Nandin lifted a hand toward the mirror over the library hearth and inky shadows crawled over the icy glass. Once the enormous surface was filled with darkness, Nandin turned and nodded to me.

That was my cue.

"The planeweaver seeks an audience with the summer royals," I said, feeling awkward addressing the dark glass, to say nothing of referring to myself as "the planeweaver," but if it got their attention, it was worth the cringeworthy title.

This spell was slightly different from the ones Dugan had been using to communicate with me. Those spells had been direct, his shadow cat bridging the connection on my end. This spell was more of a seeking spell. It would find a reflective surface near the King or Queen of Summer, and my words would travel there, but until they established a connection on their end as well, we would get nothing in return, not even confirmation that Nandin's spell had managed to find a surface in range.

We waited in silence, because our end of the communication was already open and anything we said would be overheard. I fidgeted, tugging at the sleeves of my sweater until I remembered that the crusty black stains on my sleeve were troll blood. Then I wrinkled my nose, dropping my fingers. Not that I could actually get away from my own shirt. I needed to ask Falin if he knew where my castle had ended up. I really needed some fresh clothes.

I'd just surrendered to the yawn that had been threatening for over a minute when the shadows in the mirror cleared and a handsome, deeply tanned face surrounded by soft brown curls appeared.

"Planeweaver," he said, his voice pleasant—but he wasn't smiling and the tightness around his eyes made him look almost like a different man than the jovial and libidinous king I'd encountered a month before.

Of course, I was now in midyawn with my mouth

wide open and my eyes squinted half-shut. Trying to cut a yawn short in the middle is nearly impossible. I snapped my mouth closed, but then I could feel my nostrils flaring as my reflexes tried to finish off whatever impulse makes one yawn. It was probably not a good look. Thankfully, I wasn't the only thing to look at, and I saw the Summer King's eyes scan over the men around me.

"You always keep such interesting company, planeweaver. Are you calling to speak of your return visit to my court?"

As I finally regained control of my face, I fought not to cringe at the mention of visiting his court. I had promised him an extended three-day visit in exchange for speaking to some of his people during a recent investigation. I'd have to follow through on that visit soon, but not right now.

"No. I—" I started when another voice interrupted.

"Planeweaver?" The voice was light and feminine, but with undeniable authority.

The image in the mirror wavered, the king's face becoming less distinct as another image appeared in the mirror as well, this one of a beautiful woman with hair the color of spun gold and features so delicate and perfect a painter would have sold his soul for a chance to capture her likeness. The Summer Queen.

Apparently magic mirror spells included three-way calling. Unfortunately, the spell didn't have any split-screen features, as the two scenes holding the royals were superimposed over each other. Every previous time I'd seen this mirror spell, the reflections were so clear that it looked like I could reach out and touch whomever I was speaking to, but in this case, both royals were slightly hazy, tree branches showing through the queen's delicate shoulders and a pillar running through the king. At least their faces were clear and in focus. Still, it was a little disconcerting, like a double-exposed photograph.

"How lovely to see you, my dear," the king said, and I assumed he was speaking to his wife.

She pressed her full lips together, but only said, "I'm sure." Then her focus landed on me with a nearly physical weight as if I could feel her dissecting everything about me, from my bedraggled hair and stained clothing to the company I kept and the location of my call. "Planeweaver, good of you to reach out to us. Hello, Winter. Shadow." She gave the men tight prim nods. "What is it Summer can do for you?"

I cut my gaze over to Falin, but he was watching the mirror, his face carefully neutral. Not blank, exactly— he looked pleasant, not threatening—but there was nothing genuine or emotive in his features. Which was fine. We had all discussed what needed to be said before we made the call, and we'd agreed I would take lead with summer, but a summarized direction and an actual conversation were a little different.

I cleared my throat and straightened my shoulders before I answered. "We believe we know who is behind the destruction of the doors, and we are seeking allies to challenge him and his people."

"Do tell," the king said, his face growing larger as he must have leaned forward toward whatever surface he was using for the spell.

Dugan spoke up this time, quickly summarizing what we knew and what we'd put together about Ryese and the light court. Both summer royals listened intently until he finished. Then they looked to each other through the mirrors, both silent for a beat.

"There were a lot assumptions and statements hedged with 'we believe' in that summation," the queen finally said, a small furrow appearing in her otherwise creaseless brow.

"True, but the conclusions we've drawn are logical and follow a known pattern for Ryese," I said.

"Perhaps." Her tone was dull, noncommittal. We were not winning the ally we needed here.

"Let us say we believe all your assertions to be correct," the king said, his voice far more jovial than his queen's, but I wasn't fooled by his tone. He was no more convinced than she. "What would we gain by sending our best duelers to the aid of Shadow and Winter?"

"Seriously?" I said, making no effort to conceal my annoyance. Falin, who had been standing to one side of me but not touching me, now grabbed my hand. His touch held a warning, an urging for caution. I tempered my tone before saying, "You would gain the possibility of protecting your remaining doors. How many more can you afford to lose?"

The welcoming and puckish look the Summer King always seemed to wear suddenly froze on his face. His eyes narrowed, ever so slightly, a hint of what looked like anger slicing through, but it didn't show anywhere else in his expression. Of course, my question hadn't really been fair as none of the courts could afford even one door lost, and they'd already lost three. Or maybe it wasn't anger; perhaps that glinty edge to his eyes was a hint of fear.

"An interesting proposition, planeweaver, but there have been a lot of interesting propositions recently. Did you know that not long ago, we were offered a new amaranthine tree for our court in exchange for handing you over?" The king delivered all of this in an off-handed manner, as if discussing something trivial, but his gaze bore into me as he spoke. "Now isn't that interesting, and ever so useful, as I have found myself short a few amaranthine trees."

I went still, and Falin's hand around mine tightened. Not a warning this time, but a reflex. There was a bounty on my head—one it would be hard for any of the seasonal courts to pass over.

"Husband!" The Summer Queen hissed the word, censure in her gaze as it stabbed at the king.

"Are you threatening Alex?" Falin asked, his tone

low, ice-cold, and one I recognized as very, very dangerous.

A flicker of uncertainty crossed the Summer King's face, and I wasn't sure if it was due to him wondering if he'd made a misstep—after all, winter was currently at its strongest and summer its weakest due to the natural progression of the seasonal calendar—or if he simply didn't know my real name and it took him a moment to put two and two together. The uncertainty vanished within the blink of an eye, his features returning to relaxed friendliness as if this was a far more amiable conversation than we were actively engaged in.

"Would I warn her if I were threatening her? Come now, Winter, that wouldn't be in my best interests." The Summer King smiled, and I found myself wanting to believe him. After all, he was a nice guy; he probably did have my best interests at heart . . .

Bullshit.

The Summer King had no reason to look out for me. Glamour. It had to be. He'd tried to bewitch me with his personal glamour before. He was being subtle currently; the warm friendly feelings seeping through me as I stared at him felt natural. But they weren't, and as soon as I realized they weren't, I cracked my shields, drawing on my ability to see through glamour. There was technically nothing to see here—he was just emitting a feeling, a sense of safety and contentment–but my ability to break through glamour still helped insulate me, the happy feelings falling away as soon as I let the first sliver of magic rise.

My darkening glare must have been a pretty clear sign to the king that his manipulation was failing, because he frowned, his gaze moving over the two kings and prince at my sides.

"Who offered you an amaranthine tree in exchange for the planeweaver?" Dugan asked, his hand held nonchalantly on the hilt of his sword. Not that he could

strike the Summer King through the mirror. Or at
least, I didn't think he could, though in all honesty, I
wasn't certain.

The king's frown deepened, but it was the queen
who answered. "I cannot speak for my husband, as we
were approached by two different ambassadors, I believe, but the one searching for the planeweaver sent
only representatives. I did not meet him in person, and
he would not identify himself. He did have the tree,
though, which was . . . interesting."

"Did you see his face? Did he have scars from iron?"
I asked, because I already had a pretty good idea who
she'd spoken to.

"He wore a hood," the Summer Queen said, and
lifted one shoulder in a delicate shrug as if this was a
very unimportant detail.

"A gold cloak and hood?" I asked, and her eyes widened ever so slightly.

"Perhaps." She shrugged again.

"I do believe it was gold when I spoke to him," the
king said, his smile brilliant and his glamour pushing
off a friendly, helpful vibe.

The queen shot him a censuring glare.

"Would you really want to cut a deal for one tree
with the fae who already destroyed three of yours?"
Falin's voice was low and cold. There was nothing particularly threatening in his tone or words. If anything,
he sounded calm and unconcerned, if intense. But I
knew him well enough to hear the danger hidden in the
depths. "Did he offer any reassurances that your remaining trees would be spared?"

"No." The queen's frown deepened. "Of course, had
he done that, it would have confirmed his involvement,
and that would not have been wise. He offered only the
replacement tree. A single one to whichever court
turned over the planeweaver."

So Ryese knew that I'd escaped his trap and fled to
Faerie. Or perhaps he was simply covering his bases.

He surely knew I'd escaped by now, but he couldn't know for certain that I had made it through a door to Faerie, not unless he had a spy among us. I resisted the urge to look around the room. Who would I suspect? Not Falin. I had doubts it would be Dugan, not that I knew him well enough to bet my life on it, but it didn't feel right. Brad had apparently risked his life to get me here, and, well, even if my brother had vanished without a word for more than a decade, I still couldn't see him actively betraying me to my enemies. Nandin? If it suited his purposes I could see him doing it, but it just didn't fit. I doubted anyone who'd been part of getting me here had revealed my entry to Ryese. Of course, we'd walked openly through the winter halls and had been seen by dozens of guards. Who knew how many traitors still lurked in winter. Ryese had spent centuries in the winter court. If he was able to recruit loyal followers from all the other courts, he surely still had sympathetic supporters hiding within these halls.

"Will you pledge your best duelists to preventing the collapse of Faerie and the destruction of more doors?" Nandin asked, redirecting the conversation back on track.

Neither summer monarch answered immediately. I forced myself not to fidget as I waited. At least they weren't refusing outright. That they were considering it was a good sign, right?

Finally it was the queen who answered first. She shook her head, her rosy lips pulling down in a small frown. "No. I will not commit my best duelist or even my second best. Nor will I take such a risk myself, not without more proof that this Ryese you speak of is truly behind it. I have not even seen proof that the Queen of Light has fallen and he is now king. So, no. Bring me more than 'we believe' and 'it can be concluded' and perhaps I will change my mind."

"I concur with my wife," the king said, nodding.

"Devoting such resources and taking such risks when we are already weakened would be unwise. Especially on supposition alone."

I sagged, deflating at the words. So we would receive no help from summer—and they'd been deemed the most promising out of the courts. This did not bode well.

"So, then you will sit on the sidelines and hope someone else saves Faerie," Falin said, his tone that eerie calm, like the stillness of a snow-covered night. "If we succeed, that will be quite a boon your court will owe us."

Both summer royals bristled at the word "boon." They clearly did not like the implication that they would be indebted to winter and shadow.

"I must consult with my wife for a moment," the Summer King said, holding up a hand. The mirror misted over, both royals vanishing from the surface, but it neither returned to reflecting the room nor filled with the shadows of Nandin's spell. So did that mean the spell was still connected and the king had simply put us on hold, for lack of a better word?

"Can they still hear us?" I whispered, glancing at Falin.

He in turn looked at Nandin.

The Shadow King gave the smallest of shrugs. "It would be safest to assume we can still be seen and heard."

Great. I stood waiting and staring at the oddly foggy-looking mirror for at least a minute. When it didn't change, I huffed out an annoyed breath and decided to chance the frozen furniture. I collapsed into the chair beside the couch where Brad was sprawled. His jaw had fallen open and he made soft snoring sounds in his sleep. I stared at him, studying the familiar angles of his face, still hardly believing it could really be Brad.

A glance at my watch showed that it was only a little

after ten p.m. I yawned again, and envied Brad's careless slumber. I was exhausted. My head felt heavy, like it had been stuffed with damp cotton that I was struggling to think through. While it wasn't late, considering that I'd barely slept the night before, added to the emotional shocks of the day and of course Ryese's spell, which had been sucking on my life and power for several hours, I wasn't going to be good for much soon. I gave in to another yawn, as the mirror was still clouded. The day felt like it had been wasted. I'd set out to find a way to evacuate the fae, and failed. I still didn't know what had happened to my father. We hadn't found the amaranthine tree, though I guess we at least knew it was on hand somewhere, as Ryese was apparently using it as trade fodder. We weren't even managing to secure allies against a clear threat.

I sighed, leaning my head against the icy back of the seat, my gaze moving to the fathomless depths of the ceiling, watching the patterns of snow fall above me. My sleepy mind drifted, and I wondered if Caleb had dragged Holly out of Nekros City yet. Did they know more doors had fallen? What would happen if Ryese destroyed more? All of them? The Magical Awakening had radically changed a world that had previously been completely focused on technology. Would the pendulum swing again? Would the folded spaces once again be lost? Magic forgotten? Or was there no putting that rabbit back in the hat, but only human magic would survive? Why would Ryese want either of those outcomes?

My eyelids were growing excessively heavy, my blinks lasting a little too long. Then the fog in the mirror cleared. My head snapped up as a dainty throat cleared.

The queen looked as calm and pristine as she had when the mirror had gone blank, but the king now looked like he'd been running his hands through his hair and his cheeks were flushed, as if he'd been yelling. Or maybe there had been no discussion at all and the king had been up to a very different activity with some fae in the forest with him. I wouldn't put it past him.

"We have reached a decision," the queen said, gazing out at us.

Well, I guess they actually had been talking.

No one on my side of the mirror said anything, but simply waited for her to continue. I smothered a yawn, which was totally unavoidable, but the queen's gaze narrowed and she frowned ever so slightly at me, as if the stifled yawn was commentary on her proclamation.

"We will not be offering fighters," the queen said, still frowning. "But we are willing to offer a truce."

Falin crossed his arms over his chest, his expression unimpressed. "What are your terms?"

"If you challenge light and stop this madness, no fae tied to summer will challenge winter nor shadow for a year and a day. In this way, we will show our appreciation of your potential sacrifice and owe you nothing."

Nandin shook his head. "Not enough."

The queen's scowl moved to him, but the Summer King laughed.

"I did tell you so, my dear," he said. "A truce of five years."

Falin answered this time. "A century."

I blinked, surprised by the demand. Apparently I wasn't the only one.

"You haven't even been alive a century, boy," the Summer King spluttered.

"But I have." Dugan stepped forward. "And for a court who can't muster a single challenger to prevent the destruction of all of Faerie, a century of sending no challengers against our courts seems more than fair."

The way the muscles bunched above the Summer King's jaw made me suspect he was grinding his teeth. His gaze moved, clearly not on anyone in my room, but to his wife. Her lips pursed into a small rosebud, but after a moment she cocked one arched eyebrow. The king's chin jerked upward ever so slightly, like a reverse nod, and then both royals focused on my party again. They might not seem to like each other much, but after their centuries together, they had the silent communication thing down.

"One-century truce, or a truce until all the amaranthine doors are restored. Whichever passes first," the queen said.

Nandin, Falin, and Dugan looked at each other, their expressions all equally unimpressed, but they were considering the offer.

I shook my head. "It's not enough."

All gazes moved to me. The Summer Queen's eyes narrowed, her husband's nostrils flaring in displeasure. I hadn't actually meant to refuse the offer. Hell, I hadn't really thought before I spoke, but now all eyes were on me.

I cleared my throat. Trying to think before I spoke; but I was so damn tired. I wanted them to promise to help us and get this over with so we could move on.

"We are taking all the risk. All you are willing to offer is not attacking us if we are weakened while rescuing all of Faerie? How would that ever be enough?"

"We have no evidence that your accusations are even true. What if we risk our best and this is some double cross from Shadow to grab a healthier court?" the queen said with a sniff.

It wasn't, I knew it wasn't. And yet I couldn't offer her any assurances that shadow wouldn't try to trade up. The shadow court was failing. It had been even before this recent crisis in Faerie. And hadn't I had my own moment of worry that the same might happen to the winter court?

"A hundred-year truce—for every court involved with stopping the megalomaniac destroying amaranthine trees . . ." Because hopefully we'd have more luck with the other seasonal courts and they all deserved that protection if they helped. I paused, trying to let my brain catch up to my mouth. If summer wasn't going to help us directly, they could at least help our people. "And open your borders to refugees stuck in the mortal realm. It may take the evacuees longer than the twelve hours normally allotted with the right of open roads to reach safe territory."

Surprise and maybe confusion registered on the royals' faces. They studied me, evaluating. Then they exchanged more of that silent communication with their gazes. I blinked, trying to keep my eyes open as the silence stretched. This was important. I wished I had some coffee. Hell, even a splash of cold water.

I climbed to my feet, afraid I'd fall asleep if I kept sitting. The Summer King frowned at me. "How long do you want these . . . refugees . . . to be allowed to access our lands?"

"Just long enough to pass through on their journey to reach their own court."

They considered me. Then their gazes slid to the men on my side of the mirror. Falin and Nandin simply stared back at them, but I caught Dugan studying me, looking thoughtful. I hadn't actually discussed any of this with them. I probably should have, before I took over their negotiations. Especially since this condition didn't actually benefit the shadow court. It wasn't like they had any fae stranded in the mortal realm. Not that this would help the fae stranded in the Americas. They weren't going to be reaching winter territory through land travel, but it might help those who'd been stranded in Asia.

The Summer King leaned forward. "Would our fae be offered the same immunity in your lands?"

Everyone looked to Falin. He offered a polite smile. "As long as our truce is in place and you take responsibility for their actions, of course."

The summer royals stared at each other. Then the queen, with her lips pressed tight in a thin line, gave the smallest nod to her husband. The king turned to face us again.

"We are in agreement."

I sank into my seat with a sigh of relief. Of course, with the bargain struck, oaths had to be exchanged, which meant even more negotiations as exact wording had to be agreed upon.

I blinked, and then jerked my head up, as my chin fell toward my chest. My eyes fluttered, and my blink must have been a whole lot longer than I'd thought, for the Summer King was just finishing up the recitation of an oath.

"Then our business is complete," the queen said as soon as the last word fell from her husband's lips. "Fight well in the duels to come. We hope to hear good news from you soon."

"I'm sure," was all Nandin said before lifting a hand and releasing his spell. The summer royals vanished from the mirror as shadows streamed over it. A moment later the icy room we were in appeared in the shiny surface once more.

"Well, that could have gone better," Falin said, a frown tugging at his lips.

"It could have gone worse as well." Dugan turned toward his king. "Do you think we have any better chances with the other two seasons?"

Nandin seemed to consider the question for a moment. "We have to at least try." He turned toward me, studying my undoubtedly sleepy expression. "Clever, finding a path for the stranded independents you seem so concerned about."

I shrugged, blinking a little too rapidly to try to rouse myself.

He gave me the smallest bow of his head. "We will remember that condition in our next negotiations, but we should perhaps not flaunt our dear Alexis's presence. Even if we can convince all the royals that Ryese is behind this, they might consider the chance of securing an amaranthine tree worth dealing with an enemy."

"Fine by me," I said, or tried to. Most of the words came out garbled, as I spoke them through a yawn.

Falin stepped up to the couch where I sat. "Come on, let's get you to bed before you fall asleep."

He leaned forward, but I pressed back into the snowy cushion.

"Don't you dare pick me up."

The expression that flickered across his face was a mix of confusion and hurt. It only lasted a moment, before his features went cold and expressionless, but I caught it. Shit. That had been the opposite of my intention.

"You're hurt," I said by way of explanation, hoping he'd understand.

He grunted under his breath. "I heal quickly." But the emptiness in his expression didn't change. "Come on."

When he held out a hand, I accepted it, letting him help me to my feet, but as he turned us toward the door, I hesitated. "Wait, you can't leave Nandin and Dugan to negotiate with the other courts without you."

He shrugged, still walking me toward the door. "I doubt they need me." When I stopped walking and frowned at him, he sighed. "I'm planning to send Maeve in to monitor winter's interests. In truth, she is a shrewder negotiator than me anyway."

"*You* need to be here. You're the king," I said, digging in my heels when he tried to tug me forward. "Maeve can show me to a room."

He shook his head, the movement sharp and definite. "No. There is a bounty on your head. I'm not letting you out of my sight or trusting anyone else with your safety."

I wanted to argue, but we both suspected there were still traitors in his halls and I'd reached my threshold on betrayal for the day. It was a sweet gesture. He was trying to protect me. But he needed to be here for these negotiations with the other courts. Not only did he need to make sure that the interests of his court were addressed, but as a new king, he needed to be seen as one of the players working toward a solution.

Of course, that was assuming we won and Ryese didn't actually manage to destroy all of Faerie. I was making that assumption, though. I had to. I wasn't willing to consider the alternative.

"Just pull one of the couches out of sight of the mirror. I'll take a nap until you're done," I said around another yawn.

Falin frowned at me, but Dugan stepped up to the closest icy couch.

"It is a sound plan," the prince said, lifting one side of the couch. Then he glanced over his shoulder at Nandin.

The look the king gave his prince said he was not amused by the idea of moving furniture, but after only a moment he joined Dugan. Together they shifted the couch against the wall, where whoever they contacted next wouldn't be able to see it. Falin's frown didn't lessen, but he didn't argue as he escorted me to the repositioned couch. I gave him a quick kiss before I gratefully sank onto the snowy cushions once more.

"Let's do this quickly," Falin said, turning to the two shadow royals.

My heavy eyelids closed before the guys even determined who they would contact next.

Chapter 27

I woke feeling comfortable and warm, my mind drifting contentedly just below full awareness, unwilling to deal with the waking world. A warm body was tucked along my back, strong arms holding me tight. I lay there in that comfortable way as my thoughts slowly surfaced.

I had vague memories of Falin lifting me off the couch and carrying me to bed, helping me remove my boots, and suggesting I take off my sweater, which was covered in mud and troll blood. Now I was lying in an unbelievably soft bed in only my bra and pants. From the firm skin I could feel against my back, I knew Falin was also shirtless. I couldn't help wondering if he was missing any other clothing . . .

That level of alertness also brought back everything else—the bombing, the stranded fae, Ryese's schemes, the earthquakes that had been wracking Faerie, and the upcoming duels. I didn't know the outcome of the conversations with spring and fall. Had we found any allies? Ones that would actually help fight through to Ryese?

I didn't want to jump back into that mess yet. I wanted to close my eyes, snuggle tighter against Falin, and just enjoy this moment without worrying about the fate of all of Faerie. After all, how long had I wanted to be in Falin's arms again? I wanted more than that too. Not the most responsible reaction perhaps, but couldn't Faerie wait a few more minutes? Let me enjoy this just for right now?

Falin's thumb moved, rubbing a slow circle around my belly button, and flutters erupted in my stomach, my skin suddenly hyperaware of all the flesh touching mine.

"Good morning." His voice was husky, deep with sleep, and those flutters picked up in intensity.

"Is it morning?" I whispered, not trusting my voice any louder than that as I twisted so that I could face him. His blue eyes were only half open, sleepy but intense as he stared down at me. I was also correct about him being shirtless; all those pale muscles were bare and begging for my palms to slide over them. Except I was wearing gloves. I always wore gloves now. My scarred hands drew attention in the mortal realm, and blood coated my palms in Faerie.

"No one has come to bother us yet, so I'm assuming it is still morning."

I made a noncommittal sound as I frowned at my gloved hands, unsure what I wanted to do. The blood on my palms was more metaphoric than real. A stain that marked me, that wasn't physical, but it *looked* real. The gloves were preventing me from truly touching Falin. And I *really* wanted to touch him. All of him.

He must have noticed my conflicted expression, as well as where it was aimed. His fingers slid around my wrist, lifting my hand upward. He kissed the back of my gloved hand, then caught the finger of my glove between his teeth and pulled. I winced as the red of my palm appeared, but he freed my hand, and then pressed a tender kiss on my discolored skin.

"There is no part of you that you have to hide from me. I love you. All of you," he whispered.

I swallowed, meeting his gaze. "If my gloves are coming off, yours need to as well."

He hesitated, and I saw the conflict there. The blood on his hands was much thicker, much older, but no less metaphoric. A stain only. And I wanted his hands on me as much as I wanted mine on him.

"All of me. All of you," I said, and the smallest smile caught at the edge of his mouth.

He nodded, releasing my hand to remove his own gloves. I pulled off my second glove, and then gave in to my impulse to touch him, letting my palms trail down his chest and over his tight abs. He wore sleep pants, but the material was soft and thin, the heat of his body passing through it as my exploring hands roamed over his hip and down to his ass.

His now bare hand slid up my spine, leaving a trail of tingly shivers in its wake. When his hand reached the base of my hairline, his fingers trailed forward, feather-light over my jaw, and then gently tilted my face up, so that I was no longer staring at his chest but up into his gaze. There was no sleepiness left in those blue depths. Now they blazed with a heat that threatened to consume me. And oh, I hoped he did.

I wasn't sure if I closed the distance or he did, but our lips met with passion and maybe a little desperation. My tongue darted into his mouth, tasting, exploring. His hand moved into my hair, pulling me even closer as his mouth devoured mine. When we broke apart, it was only long enough to gasp in air, to notice the way my lips already felt swollen, and then my mouth found his again, and that was what I needed because right then, feeling his lips on mine, the brush of his tongue, and his breath mingling with mine, was way more important than air.

His fingers fisted in my hair. My own hands trailed over his shoulders, down his sides, over his ass. I wanted to touch everything. Feel everything. My knee bent, sliding up his thigh as I wiggled closer to him. One of his hands trailed down my bare back, and the pressure around my ribs changed as he deftly unclasped my bra. Then his hand slid under the now loose material.

I moaned as his thumb grazed my nipple, sending a tightening awareness that spread in aching heat through my body. I pressed my hips closer to his, resenting the hell out of my pants, as well as the space still between us. Falin rolled, taking me with him so that I was suddenly straddling his hips as he sat us up in the center of his bed. I groaned at the feel of him pressing hard and ready through our pants.

"Too many clothes." My words came out a throaty gasp.

His responding chuckle was deep and husky. "I can help with that."

He dropped a hand to my hips as I shrugged out of my bra. I expected him to go for the button at the front, but instead his hand just kept sliding downward and back, until he was cupping my ass.

My bare ass.

What the hell? I glanced down. I still had my underwear, but my pants were gone. Just gone. Considering I was straddling Falin with my knees bent under me, that was so not physically possible.

"Did you just glamour away my pants?"

His hand moved to my right breast, lifting it lightly as he dipped his head forward. "Yes."

"You can't just—" I broke off as his mouth closed over my nipple. His teeth grazed the sensitive skin, drawing a small sound from me before his tongue swirled around the peak he'd caused.

He sucked hard, and I moaned, my hands moving into his hair, as if I needed to hold on or risk falling apart. Not that I was going anywhere; his other hand was still clutching my ass, pulling me tight against him. He was still wearing his sleep pants, but neither those nor my panties were thick material and I rocked my hips against his length.

His attention moved to my other breast, and I bit my swollen bottom lip to stop the soft noises escaping me. Then I slid my hands to his shoulders, trying to push him back, push him down, because I wanted—needed—to get his pants off him. I, of course, wasn't strong enough to shove him to the bed, but he let me anyway, his arm sliding around my back to drag me down with him, guiding my lips back to his as his back hit the mattress.

His wince was small. I almost missed it in the chaotic kiss. But with my body plastered to his, I did catch the small jerk of his shoulders. The tiny inhalation of breath that wasn't passion, but pain.

I pulled back. I would have scrambled off him completely, except his hands moved to my hips, keeping me straddling him as I sat upright, him on his back on the bed.

"Shit. You're hurt. I forgot," I mumbled, suddenly feeling awkward even though I could feel the evidence that, regardless of his injuries, he was not unhappy to be exactly where he was.

"I'm healing," he said, starting to sit back up, one hand still on my hip, but the other reaching upward, as if to draw me back in to another frantic kiss.

I shook my head. "'Healing' is not *healed*. How bad are you injured? Drop your glamour." Because I needed to know where he was hurt. Where I needed to be careful of. Geez, my hands had been all over him. Had I been hurting him and he just wasn't letting it show until I'd crashed down on his chest in our tumble down to the bed?

The look he gave me said he would refuse. I placed a hand in the center of his chest, trying to still him even as he reached for me, his eyes still hot with desire. But I couldn't do this knowing I was hurting him.

"Please."

It was such a small word. But it carried a big cost. I could feel it hang between us as the word left my mouth. Falin frowned, letting his body fall back against the soft mattress. We stared at each other. We both knew I could look through his glamour if I wanted. But I hadn't yet. I'd asked.

Falin sighed, dropping his hands from my hips. I'd already been feeling awkward, but now I was pretty sure I'd just completely killed the mood. I should probably get off him. Find some clothes . . . Except he'd apparently magicked my pants out of existence. That was going to complicate things.

"Don't you think about leaving," he muttered, his gaze pinning me to the spot.

I froze. Seemingly satisfied, he let his hands drop to his sides, and then he released his glamour, his gaze never leaving my face as he judged my reaction.

For my part, I gasped, and very nearly tried to scramble off him again. I probably would have, but one of his hands locked on my thigh, ensuring I didn't try to move.

The damage actually wasn't as bad as I'd feared. He was right—he was healing. But it *had* been bad.

The right side of his ribs was one enormous blue and green bruise, a thick pink line of freshly knitted skin betraying what had been a deep gash at least as long as my forearm. Various other bruises marked his arms, but most were small, nearly faded and showing more yellow than purple; they would likely be gone in a few more hours. The most distressing injury, though, was the nearly healed line just to the left of his sternum. It was small, no longer than the first two joints of my finger, but based on my less-than-stellar anatomy knowledge, it was scarily close to his heart.

My hand moved automatically. There wasn't much bruising around that small wound, just the shiny pink line against his pale skin. My fingers hesitated above the healing wound. It was too close to his heart. And if the blade that had made it missed his heart, how would it have missed his lung? It wasn't a big wound, but I was guessing it had been deep.

"I'm okay, Alex," Falin whispered, his gaze still locked on my face.

"How . . ."

"It was a cheap shot. My opponent was a master not only of his blade but also glamour. Plus he had four arms. But he is dead and I am right here."

That hadn't actually been what my "how" was asking. I'd been wondering how he survived the blow. I knew he was resilient, and he healed amazingly fast—and no doubt even faster now that he was king—but that looked like a deathblow.

Shit. Had he died? Was that why Faerie had locked the winter doors temporarily? Death wasn't always permanent in Faerie. With no land of the dead, decay, or soul collectors, master healers could sometimes restore the dead. But death always left its mark. Those brought back could never leave Faerie, or any soul collector who noticed them would collect them. I suspected there were other consequences to entering a plane attached to the land of the dead as well. Was Falin now among those permanently stuck in Faerie?

I'd respected his privacy up to this point. I hadn't opened my shields to examine his wounds. But now I did. It wasn't even a conscious thought. I dropped my shields, looking not at the wounds on his body but deeper, to the silver of his soul. It was still firmly attached to his body, anchored firmly like any living being.

"Alex?" Falin sat up, catching my face gently and tilting my chin so that I was staring into his eyes. "What are you doing?"

"I thought you'd died." I whispered the words, his face turning misty as tears gathered, threatening to spill over. I blinked them back because it was a ridicu-

lous response, but I was almost overwhelmed by the
relief I felt that he was alive, healing. Though it was
coupled with fear, because more challengers would
come. Hell, we were about to go make some challenges
ourselves, and the idea that he could be hurt scared the
hell out of me.

"I'm okay," he said again, covering my hand with his
and pressing it against the healing wound on his chest.
I winced, but he didn't.

"Are you sure you . . . I mean . . ." My gaze flickered
down to the massive bruises covering half his torso.
"Does it hurt a lot?"

Falin made a sound that was half chuckle and half
groan. "Woman, I've been dreaming of getting you
back in my bed for so long, I could be missing limbs
and it wouldn't hinder me." Whatever look I gave him
at that response made him laugh again, the sound low
and masculine. He pressed a quick kiss against my
frown before adding, "Last night it might have been a
problem. This morning, my ribs are a little tender is all.
Nothing else is bothering me. It will be fine. Though
I'm putting back on my glamour. When you look at me,
sympathetic pain and worry are not what I want to see
in your eyes."

True to his word, the bruises and pink scars vanished a moment later, his skin once again pale perfec-
tion. Nothing else changed, though. He hid the wounds,
but I knew that every line of muscle was real—and
fairly earned. My hand was still covering that spot
where I'd come far too close to losing him. His fingers
pressed against mine, holding me there, feeling his
heartbeat strong—though perhaps still a little rapid—
against my palm.

He watched me for a moment, and then his other
hand lifted to cup my face, drawing me closer again.
He kissed me, and it wasn't as frantic as the kisses we'd
shared before, but there was more desperation in it. My
free hand moved to his shoulder, clinging to him as if

afraid he'd be ripped away from me. I kissed him with everything inside me. Relief he was alive, fear of what could have happened and might still in the upcoming duels, a need to keep him safe and terror that I had no idea how, desire because that had not lessened in the least, and . . . love.

That last one hit me harder than the rest because it wasn't something I'd ever admitted to myself. He'd first told me he loved me months ago. At that time, I would have said I cared about him. I enjoyed being with him. I trusted him despite all the reasons I shouldn't. I worried about him. I certainly lusted after him.

But love?

As I kissed him as if he were oxygen and I'd suffocate if we broke apart, I had to admit, while it had snuck up on me, and while we had known each other only seven or so months—most of that time just being friends—it was undeniable. Even to my commitment-phobic self.

And that was terrifying.

"You're shaking," he whispered, pulling back slightly.

Was I? Maybe. I didn't care.

"I love you." The words came out in a single rushed breath, as though if I didn't say them now, I'd miss the chance. Or maybe because I knew I'd chicken out and never say it if I waited. I hadn't said those words since my mother died when I was five. Not aloud. Certainly never with the heat and passion I now felt them.

For half a heartbeat, Falin's eyes went wide, shock and surprise evident in the sudden stillness of his body. Then a smile broke across his face that was pure pleasure. He pulled me tighter to him, kissing me with a devouring ferocity, his tongue claiming possession of my mouth.

"I love you too." The words were a low and sensual rumble spoken directly against my lips, and the desire in me intensified.

His hand grazed over my ribs, down my waist, and over my hips, lighting up my body with heat. I broke from his mouth to kiss a line down his throat, to his shoulders. My own hands explored his body, my touches light. As his fingers slid into the hem of my panties, the skin over my pelvis—and a lot of places a little lower than that—tightened in anticipation. I squirmed in his lap, and he groaned as I rocked myself against the length of him.

"You still have too many clothes on," I said, letting my teeth graze ever so lightly over his collarbone. "Let me fix that."

He probably could have magicked his pants away, like he had mine, but I couldn't do that. It would have been more efficient to let him, but our brief respite had broken through the more frantic, rip-each-other's-clothes-off moment, and now I wanted to slow down and savor this. I'd been blind the only other time we'd had sex, and now I wanted to see all of him. To unwrap him slowly, and take him all in.

I pushed on his shoulders again, letting him know I wanted him to lie back. He resisted only a moment, then surrendered to my request, his heated gaze locked on me as I kissed a line down his body. I kept my touches light, my kisses soft and mindful, as I slid downward, aware of the bruises I couldn't actually see. I reached the spot below his navel, where his pants hung low over his hips. I fisted my hands in the band, and he lifted upward, allowing me to drag the material down. I took my time, letting my lips trace over the flat muscled skin beside his hip bone, down the taut line that led down to his groin. He wore no underwear under the sleep pants, and I paused for a moment as I revealed him, hard and very, very ready.

The pants in my hands, which were still around his thighs, suddenly vanished, magicked out of existence as he sat up, drawing me up with him, back into his lap. His mouth closed on mine and his hand trailed down my body. I knew my panties must have also vanished as his fingers slid down, between my folds, to tease across my most intimate parts.

I gasped, and he drank down the sound, kissing me harder, his fingers dancing over me in a rhythm that made me squirm in pleasure and a need for more, for him, inside me. Which he wasn't doing. I reached down, wrapping my hand around his thick length and stroking hard, but slow. He groaned, the sound sending a shivering delight through me.

My body was on fire with need, his fingers setting a maddening pace of pleasure and desire. I lifted my hips, guiding him inside me. I arched back as he slid into me, filling me. His fingers stilled for only a moment. Then they danced over me again, his other hand at my hip, urging me on.

Our pace was fast, almost frantic as I moved against him. The orgasm that crashed over me hit fast, hard, wracking me with pleasure. I screamed, though I wasn't sure what, my hands locked on Falin's shoulders, my body shuddering as pleasure rippled through me.

He held me close, his lips at my throat, sliding over the soft hollow above my collarbone. But he only gave me a moment to recover. Then he rolled us, his body never leaving mine as he positioned himself on top. My limbs felt loose post-orgasm, but as he moved inside me, that need began burning again, pleasure slowly building, and I arched under him, my hips lifting to meet his thrust for thrust.

My hands slid down his back, cupping his ass as we moved together. There was no more air for long kisses. Our pace increased, my body throbbing with pleasure with each movement, until I once again reached that precipice. I hovered there a moment, on the tense edge of a second orgasm, and then Falin's next thrust sent me hurtling over that cliff. Pleasure pulsed through me in waves, my body shuddering with the release. Falin's fingers curled in my hair, his rhythm faltering as his own orgasm swept over him.

We lay there, clinging to each other, gasping down air as aftershocks of pleasure rippled through me. Then Falin pushed onto his elbows so he could stare down at me.

"I love you, Alexis," he whispered, his gaze ablaze with emotion.

I typically hated my given name, but when he used it, something inside me swelled. I pulled his mouth to mine and kissed him hard, deep. We broke off quickly, both still out of air, but the smile I felt claim my lips was reflected on his. He pressed a quick kiss on the tip of my nose, and then rolled onto his back, pulling me with him so that my body tucked along his side, my head nestled against his chest. We fit like that as if we'd been made as a set, and in that moment, my body heavy and relaxed from pleasure, nothing else mattered. I wished we could stay that way, even as I knew that pretty soon someone would come looking for us, summon us back to the crisis that was likely not waiting patiently.

I sighed, the worries of reality already crawling back under my skin. Then I looked up, and my eyes widened, the worries once again temporarily forgotten.

"Did you do that?" I asked, nodding upward, toward the ceiling, or more accurately, toward the snow-flakes that always seemed to fall and vanish just above our heads everywhere in the winter court.

Falin looked upward, and I knew the moment he spotted what I had by the sudden stillness in his chest, his breath catching in surprise. Above us, the typical geometric shape of the snowflakes had changed. Now it appeared that hundreds of tiny ice roses were drifting down above us.

"I . . . Not consciously if I did," Falin said after a small hesitation, and while I wasn't looking at him, I could hear the frown in his voice.

"Maybe Faerie did it. She certainly sounds happier."
The mournful distant music that had been constant
since Dugan dragged me into Faerie had changed. It
wasn't joyful exactly, but it wasn't sad either. More like
hopeful of future happiness.

Falin reached out a hand, snagging one of the falling
ice roses. "I guess Faerie approves of our coupling."

He held out the rose to me. I managed to get two
fingers on the icy stem before it vanished, like a soap
bubble popping. I laughed and lifted my hand to try to
snag one of my own.

Then I froze, not even daring to breathe.

"Falin . . ." My voice was a strangled gasp, and his
muscles bunched as his arm tightened around me, responding to the sudden terror in my voice. A dagger
appeared in his hand as he sat up, searching for danger.

Danger he didn't spot in his quick sweep of the
room. He twisted to glance at me.

I'd sat up when he had, but I wasn't staring at a
threat in the room. I was staring at my own hand. The
same hand I'd lifted in my attempt to grab one of the
falling ice roses. A hand that suddenly wore a ring I'd
never seen before, with a gleaming band and a very
shiny stone shaped like a snowflake. I couldn't tell if
the stone was a diamond or just really sparkly ice, but
one thing was certain, it wasn't mine, and it was on the
fourth finger of my left hand like a freaking engagement ring.

"What is this? Is this glamour?" I asked, thrusting
my hand toward him.

Falin's eyes widened and the dagger vanished. I
wasn't sure where the blade had come from or gone, as
he was still completely naked in the middle of this
enormous bed, but right now, that was the least of my
concerns. I was too busy freaking out about the ring on
my finger.

Falin took my hand, staring at the bit of jewelry. His
lips pursed, his eyebrows moving toward each other,

but he shook his head. "I don't think I did that either. Not . . . directly, at least."

"Then what the hell is this?" I'd admitted I loved him, but that didn't mean I was ready to get engaged. Hell, didn't he have to ask me first anyway? Not just magic a ring onto my finger.

"Faerie appears to be acting very pushy," he said, which didn't answer anything. "We should probably shower and eat."

He released my hand as he turned toward the edge of the bed. My mouth opened and closed at least twice, my thoughts too jumbled to come out in coherent words. Falin stood and then turned, holding out a hand to help me up. I had the ridiculous urge to grab the sheet and cover myself.

It must have shown on my face, because Falin frowned at me. "I'd let you shower first, but I doubt we have time for you to hide in there for a couple hours, so I'm voting a joint shower."

I cringed, just a little, because it was a fair remark— the last time we'd had sex, I'd fled to my bathroom when we woke the next morning and stayed there as long as possible in hopes he'd leave before I came back out. He hadn't. He'd made pancakes for me instead.

Today I wasn't feeling awkward about the sex, nor regretting that I'd told him my feelings. It was the damn ring on my finger. I was totally not ready for the level of commitment it indicated, though in fairness, he hadn't exactly asked me for any commitment. Faerie, on the other hand . . .

In the last half year I'd faced down zombies, creatures from the depths of the land of the dead, desperate witches, and power-mad fae. I could handle one tiny, unexpected ring, right?

Maybe.

I accepted Falin's hand, letting him lead me off the bed and toward the bathroom tucked away in the far corner of the room. It seemed wrong somehow to be surrounded by ice and yet have the shower deliver the most deliciously warm water, but I wasn't about to turn down the chance to wash up. In fact, as I tried to untangle my curls, I seriously wished I'd showered *before* sleeping with Falin—*I* wouldn't have had sex with me with my hair clumped with splatters of mud. He watched me struggle for a moment, as I seriously regretted not having my usual shower comb, and then his hands moved to my hair. It had to be some form of magic that allowed him to effortlessly work the snarls out of my curls, his fingers massaging my scalp as he rubbed sweet-smelling conditioner into my hair.

"So, what, did Faerie just make me a ring because she was happy we had sex?" I asked as I relaxed into the feel of his hands in my hair. He had it detangled far too quickly—I was enjoying the attention.

"Not exactly," he said, taking a step back and grabbing a bar of soap.

I liberated it from him, because he'd been taking care of me, it was my turn to care for him. I motioned for him to turn, lathering it over his back—and enjoying the excuse to put my hands all over his broad shoulders, trim waist, tight ass, and muscular thighs. In fact, I let that non-answer hang between us longer than normal simply because I was distracted by his body. Eventually, though, my gaze began catching on the glittering stone on my finger instead of his sudsy skin.

I wasn't sure why I hadn't taken the ring off yet. I would soon—probably very soon—but right now every time I caught sight of it, a wave of terror rushed through me, but also some other feeling, something warm and fluttery that I wasn't ready to examine. Both would stop once I took off the ring. And I would do that as soon as I was out of the shower and had a safe place to store it.

"What do you mean by 'not exactly'?" I finally asked.

Falin glanced at me from over his shoulder, his face that careful neutral he tended to show the world. It wasn't an expression he typically wore when we were alone, and I didn't like it. That meant he was hiding his thoughts, his feelings. He turned into the water, rinsing the soap from his back, and then retrieved the bar from me, motioning me to turn so he could return the favor and wash my back. I did, reluctantly, and as soon as I was facing away from him, he spoke.

"I don't think Faerie made it, just retrieved it from wherever she tends to hide it. I believe that is the winter consort ring, but it hasn't been seen in centuries, so I'm not certain. I'd have to consult some texts, or, I suppose, anyone in my council would know. Faerie wouldn't accept any of the consorts the former queen attempted to take. I believe Maeve was the last to wear that ring, before the former queen won the throne." He set down the soap and wrapped his arms around me, drawing me against the length of his body. He leaned down, his lips grazing across my neck, lifting goose bumps on my flesh despite the warm water and steam all around me. "If you remove it, Faerie will likely reclaim it and there is no guarantee it will reappear in the future, if you do decide to be mine one day."

Shit. I trembled, glancing at the ring. The *official consort ring*, apparently. Except I wasn't the consort. Falin's lover? Sure. Without a doubt. But I was still unsettled by the term "girlfriend" at times. I was not committing to "consort." Besides, I was totally not the magical or political backer Falin needed to hold the winter court in peace.

But did I dare take off the ring and lose the possibility forever?

"This isn't a priority right now," I whispered, more to myself than to him, as I dropped my hand. Out of sight, out of mind. Well, maybe not, but I certainly had much bigger issues to worry about. "Are fall and spring sending fighters to help in the duels with light?"

Falin turned off the water and shook his head. "No." He handed me one of the fluffy white towels hanging beside the shower. Wrapping it around me was like being engulfed in a warm cloud. "Both agreed to hundred-year truces with any court who challenged light, as well as safe passage to our fae trapped in the mortal realm, but neither committed any of their people to our cause."

"That's bullshit. Don't they care that their courts are also in danger if Faerie breaks?"

Falin shrugged and then leaned forward to towel-dry his hair. I couldn't help watching him with lustful appreciation. It didn't matter that I was still sated from our earlier lovemaking, or that I was inwardly freaking out about the consort ring, or that I was pissed at the other courts, worried about my father and the independents, or scared of what Ryese might have accomplished since I escaped his trap . . . I still watched Falin's naked body.

"They have no real incentive to send anyone. If we succeed without them, they benefit. If we fail, well, they still have their best fighters in reserve and we've—hopefully—weakened light." Falin straightened and tossed his towel on one of the hooks to dry.

True. Not helpful and rather selfish of them, but it fit with what I knew of Faerie courts.

"And what about shadow? Do you trust them?" Their entire court was staying in winter. That seemed . . . risky, what with Falin being a new king and the shadow court crumbling.

"Trust?" Falin turned, and by the look on his face, he'd totally noticed me checking him out. He smiled, the expression all male and knowingly satisfied. Then he crossed the space between us, wrapping his arms around me. "No. But we have a binding truce between our courts. As long as I am King of Winter and either Nandin or Dugan is King of Shadow, then they will take no malicious actions against me or mine nor I against them or theirs."

I nodded as he leaned down and pressed a kiss against my neck. Which was rather distracting, but something about the truce he'd mentioned bothered me. "So then what happens if the shadow court falls and there is no king?"

His lips stilled, the soft tickle of his breath all that was left on my shower-damp skin. "We had best make sure that doesn't happen."

Right. So it was a loophole, and he knew about it.

Falin straightened, looking into my eyes. "Honestly, I'd gladly cede the winter throne to Dugan—from what I know of him, I think he'd be a decent king and he has the strength to rule. But I can't risk handing him control of you." He lifted a hand and ran the back of his knuckles down my cheek.

I leaned into his touch. "Why isn't running away and leaving all the Faerie drama an option?"

"Magical dependency."

I sighed. Yeah. That. We'd both end up fading.

Falin kissed me, a sweet and deep kiss that eased the weight of our conversation, and as my hands moved to his chest, sliding up to his shoulders, I was reminded of the fact that he was stark naked and I was in only a fluffy towel.

Things might have gotten a little more interesting, but a voice in the main part of the room called out, "Sire, are you available?"

Falin made a small annoyed groan as he broke off from me. "It appears our time is up," he whispered, then he turned toward the opening that separated the bathroom from his bedroom. It wasn't actually a door—likely because doors in Faerie were far too temperamental—but more of a cutout that denoted the separation between the two rooms. "I am here, but do not enter."

"Sire, the shadow royals are awaiting you in your private dining hall." The voice was male and sounded

like it belonged to Lyell, a member of Falin's council.
"The planeweaver has a guest inquiring about her as
well."

My stomach clenched because there were not many
people in Faerie I wanted to see. Really there was only
one person, and he presently had his hands on my
waist. Well, actually, that wasn't completely true. I
wanted to see my brother, but I suspected he'd been
grouped in with the "shadow royals," as I'd never seen
him without Nandin. It seemed unlikely Lyell would
mention him separately. So my thoughts immediately
jumped to Ryese and his minions. By the way Falin's
fingers tightened where they pressed against my hips,
I guessed he was of the same mind.

"Who is it?" I asked.

"I did not ask the young lady's name, but she is a
changeling accompanied by a barghest who assured
me in no uncertain terms that she is a close and personal friend of yours."

"Rianna!" Her name emerged as an excited squeak
as twofold relief rushed through me. One part because
it wasn't an enemy looking for me, and the second part
because that meant she was safe and really had made
it to the winter court. "Where is she?"

"May I come in the room? This is an awkward way
to have a conversation," Lyell said, sounding miffed
from where he stood behind the large privacy screen
just inside the doorway to the bedroom.

"No," Falin said without hesitation. "Answer her
question."

A sigh escaped around the privacy screen. I wouldn't
actually claim to like Lyell, but I tended to like him
best out of the courtiers I knew. He seemed a little
more genuine than most of the courtiers I'd encountered.

"I will show the young lady to the private dining hall
as well, if the planeweaver will be accompanying my
king to breakfast."

"That will be fine," Falin snapped. "You're dismissed, unless there is something else?"

"No, Sire. I will also be awaiting you in the dining hall. In the event you wish the advice of your council during today's deliberations."

As in, the council had caught wind of the fact that we were planning to take the fight to light and they wished to be heard on the matter. Falin's lips tugged downward, just a fraction. He hadn't missed that fact either. It wasn't exactly a challenge to his authority, but it pushed the line. At the same time, he was a new king and advice from more experienced fae was worth at least hearing.

"We will discuss the council's presence when I arrive. Dismissed."

Lyell said nothing else. There was no sound of a door shutting behind him or anything obvious to me, but after a moment or two Falin gave a small nod.

"He's gone," he said, dropping a soft but chaste kiss on my lips before turning to walk into the bedroom proper. "We should dress and head to breakfast."

I followed. I was eager to see Rianna, but there was one big problem . . . "Uh, you vanished my pants. I don't have anything to change into." If Rianna was here, so was the castle, which meant my clothes were somewhere in the winter court. The problem was getting to them. Waltzing around in a towel searching for a missing castle seemed like a bad idea. Of course, I could probably pull the girlfriend card and wear one of Falin's shirts . . .

"If I had to guess," Falin said, stopping in the middle of the room, "that is probably your wardrobe." He pointed to a tall armoire off to one side of the bed.

The armoire wasn't made of ice, which in this court was almost surprising, but then, most of the furniture in Falin's private rooms was constructed of more traditional materials. The wardrobe in question perfectly matched the one on the other side of the bed, both being a pale wood that looked blanched more than painted, just like the bed frame.

"I've never seen that armoire before in my life," I said, frowning at it. I did actually have a somewhat similar armoire in my castle—it had come with the place when I'd inherited it—but mine was dark wood, not light.

"Neither have I. Which is why I'm assuming Faerie added it for you."

Oh. I glanced from the pale armoire to the ring on my finger. Faerie had given me the consort ring. It wasn't a stretch to assume she'd start moving my stuff into Falin's room. I crossed the room and pulled open the two large doors.

I'd expected to find that Faerie had relocated my clothes. Not so much. While I tended toward a lot of jewel tones and black, these clothes were all pale. Blues so light they were nearly white. Soft silver. Pale gray. True white. Several gowns hung in the main portion of the armoire. Not as frilly as what the former queen wore, but certainly fancier than I would normally wear. The built-in shelves held more reasonable clothing, but still in those pale colors. There was even a pair of boots identical in style to the ones I always wore, but these were pure white.

"Uh . . ." I stared at the clothing.

Falin had dressed while I pawed through the clothes, and he stepped up behind me now, surveying the new wardrobe.

"Faerie plans to dress you in my colors, apparently," he said, and I could almost hear the unspoken apology in his wincing words.

I blinked, realizing he was correct. These clothes were all in the palette Falin seemed to prefer. It made sense. Faerie had decided I was the winter consort, and now she was tying me visibly in with Falin and the court. I wasn't sure exactly how I felt about that, but one thing was certain, anything beat wandering around in only a towel. I did open my shields briefly to ensure wherever the clothes came from and whatever they were made of, they were rooted deeply enough in the reality of Faerie that they wouldn't vanish on me—my clothes popping out of existence and leaving me unexpectedly naked the next time I reached across the planes was *not* on my bucket list.

I slid into a pair of white leather pants that were butter soft and fit me like a glove. The top I chose was pale blue with silver threading and while it had some light boning, I could still move freely. Considering I had no idea what the day might hold, clothing that would not constrain me seemed important. I added a long-sleeved white shrug, since the top left my arms and shoulders bare and it was winter, even if it didn't exactly feel like it inside Faerie. There were even gloves in a small drawer, and I pulled on a pair, expecting them to snag on the snowflake gem on the ring, but the magic ring was, well, magical. Despite the fact that I didn't take it off, the ring ended up on the outside of the material, sparkling prettily on my finger.

I frowned at it, but I didn't attempt to remove it. Not yet. If the decision might be irreversible, I wasn't going to just yank it off because I had commitment issues. When we had more time, Falin and I would sit down and have a very long conversation about it.

I glanced at the white boots slouched at the bottom of the armoire, and while I had no doubt they would fit perfectly and be even better quality than my normal boots—everything I was now wearing was finer than anything I actually owned, right down to the lacy panties—I decided to grab my old tried-and-true boots instead. They'd been with me through a lot and I'd earned all of their scuffs. Of course, black boots against white pants made for a rather stark contrast, but I was going with it.

I sheathed my dagger in my boot holster, and then I had nothing left to do to get ready or prepare. We might be heading to breakfast to reunite with Rianna and coordinate with shadow, but I had no doubt this day would lead us to taking the fight to Ryese and the light court.

I totally didn't feel ready.

Chapter 28

A l!" Rianna threw her arms around me as soon as I
stepped through the doorway of the dining hall,
nearly knocking me backward. It was a good thing
Falin was only one step behind me, or her enthusiastic
greeting might have sent me stumbling right back out
the doorway.

"Hey, Ria," I said, accepting her embrace. Like
most people, Rianna's skin was just a touch too warm
for comfort. I hugged her anyway. I wasn't typically a
touchy-feely type, but I'd been worried about her and
she'd obviously had her own concerns.

Technically, Rianna should have dropped into a
curtsy when the king of the court had entered the
room, and over her head, I could see the members of
Falin's council dropping to respectful positions, but
Rianna and Falin had both been living in my castle
with me until he'd become king, and his elevation in
status had apparently been forgotten in her relief at
seeing me. I spotted Dugan and Nandin in the room as
well. They didn't bow, of course, but they inclined their
heads ever so slightly in Falin's direction as he stepped
around me to take in the room. Brad stood beside Nan-

din, his hood down so that I caught a glimpse of his
face before he sank into his own respectful bow. He
looked pale to me. Maybe that was from living as a
changeling in the shadow court, but based on the purple circles ringing his eyes, I got the feeling he was still
weak after the massive amount of magic he'd expended
to open the door that brought me to Faerie. I felt a
twinge of guilt over that but returned my focus to
Rianna.

"I'm glad you're okay," I said, giving her a friendly
squeeze. "How did you find out I was here?" Not that
I was trying to keep it secret, exactly, but considering
Ryese had a ransom on my head, it would be good to
know how far the news of my arrival had spread.

"I knew you must have found a way into Faerie as
soon as I saw the roses."

I pulled back from the hug, staring at her. "The
roses . . . ?" She couldn't mean the snowflake roses,
could she? The ever-present snowfall had returned to
its normal snowflake design by the time Falin and I had
gotten out of the shower. But the flowers had just been
in our room, right?

The look she gave me said *no, not in the least*. She
took a step back, her hand falling to the head of the
barghest at her side, a self-comforting habit she had
when she was nervous about something.

"Uh," she said, dropping her gaze from mine. "Snow
roses falling from the sky about half an hour ago?
Seemed, uh, rather romantic."

Shit. So Faerie had decided to broadcast the news
all across the winter court that Falin and I had finally
had sex. I didn't exactly care if people knew I was shag-
ging my own boyfriend, but still, *awkward*. And did
Faerie plan to announce it every time we had sex? That
would get real old real fast.

"Have you been okay? Getting pulled to Faerie with
the castle didn't hurt you?" I asked, changing the subject. With the sudden awkwardness, I found myself

fidgeting, my hand lifting as if of its own accord to swat at a curl that had slipped into my face.

"I'm fine. I'm no stranger to Faerie, and Desmond has been with—" She cut off, her eyes going wide. Then her hand darted out, catching my gloved fingers from where they'd caught in my curls. "Al, is that an engagement ring?"

I realized a moment too late that I'd lifted my left hand, and that Rianna was now staring at the consort ring on my finger. I hadn't taken it off—yet—but I hadn't expected anyone to notice it, at least not within the first two minutes of me entering a room. Now everyone was noticing because Rianna wasn't exactly being subtle, and I could feel as gazes locked onto me. Inquiring about an engagement ring might not normally have garnered quite so much attention, but everyone in this room knew I was dating the king.

Falin had stepped around me once it was clear Rianna's embrace wasn't going to bowl me over, but now he stopped, turning to glance back at me over his shoulder. He didn't say anything, but cocked one pale eyebrow. I couldn't tell if his expression was asking how I wanted to play this, or just curious to see what I would say, but it was clear he was leaving this ball in my field.

"Uh . . ." *Shit.*

"That can't be," Maeve said, taking two steps toward me before stopping short, still several yards away. "That's the consort ring." Her voice was a harsh whisper, but it seemed to resonate around the large room.

"Sire, this is something you should have discussed with your council—" Lyell started, and then fell silent, as if suddenly remembering this was not a private council meeting and we had two shadow royals in the room.

"It's, um . . ." Well, I couldn't exactly say it wasn't the consort ring. "Faerie did it."

Everyone in the room stared at me, and my cheeks heated. Yeah, that had been a ridiculous thing to say.

Maeve made a scoffing noise deep in her throat and shook her head. "Of course Faerie produced the ring, you twit." She stormed across the room, her hips swaying almost violently with her movements. She all but elbowed Rianna out of the way, snatching my hand from my friend's grasp where Rianna had still been examining the ring. Maeve stared, her lips twisted into a scowl, but her eyes glimmered with something else, something covetous. She'd worn this ring before. And she wanted it back. She might have spent the last few weeks arranging prospective consort meetings for Falin, but there was no mistaking the desire in her gaze as she stared at the ring on my finger. Oh, I doubted she wanted to bind herself to Falin in particular. She just wanted the power that went along with the title. "There had to have been some proposal, some request, for Faerie to produce it. Do not act as if we are fools."

"Maeve." Falin's voice was cold, controlled, and, if you knew him at all, far more terrifying than if he'd yelled. "You are speaking to the woman wearing the winter consort ring. *My* consort ring. And you are precariously close to me deciding I need to defend my love's honor in a duel."

Maeve dropped my hand, jerking back so fast you'd have thought I'd stung her. The blood drained from her face, her already pale cheeks going deathly white as she spun to face Falin. Then she fell to her knees before him.

"I . . . I was shocked, my king. I forgot myself."

Falin stared at her for several tense heartbeats, his arms crossed over his chest and his expression hard. Oh shit. He wasn't seriously going to duel her to the death just because she was acting like a jerk to me, was he? I mean. He was king. He did have to maintain a certain image to hold his throne, but . . .

"It is not my forgiveness you need," he said, his gaze flicking to me.

Maeve's shoulders twitched. Not a full jerk of surprise, but definitely a small hitch. Then she twisted to face me, still on her knees. Her expression was not kind, not apologetic. She didn't like me. She didn't think I could hack it as consort—hell, I agreed with her on that one—but after a moment, a look of resignation fell over her face. If she apologized, she'd be indebted to me. If she didn't, well, that would be a second insult and I'd put money on the fact that Falin would duel her to set a precedent. Maeve was old, and no doubt powerful, but that didn't mean she wanted to try to best Falin in a duel.

"My apologies, Consort," she said, the words hissed out like they'd put up a struggle in her throat.

A debt opened, hanging between us, awaiting my response. It wasn't a large debt, because she wasn't genuinely sorry and the offense hadn't been great, but it was a small bit of leverage. If I was going to survive in Faerie, I probably needed every edge I could gather.

"Apology accepted, but don't call me consort."

Maeve's frown deepened. I wasn't sure if that was because of the weight of the debt locking in place or because of my words. I should have discussed this whole consort ring situation a little more in depth with Falin while we were alone. I needed to be careful. Would the ring vanish if I publicly denounced being the consort? Would I be stuck with the role if I didn't dispute the title?

I pressed two fingers to my temple. A deep throbbing was starting there, a headache I didn't have time for. There were much more important things at stake than my love life.

Turning my attention to the Shadow King, I tried to get the conversation back to a topic other than the ring on my finger. "Falin said the other courts offered truces, but no aid?"

Nandin was frowning, watching me, and I realized there might be more repercussions from this stupid ring than I'd first realized. After all, technically, I was still betrothed to Dugan. Yes, the Shadow Prince and I had both agreed to refuse that marriage, but the original agreement had been created by Nandin and my father, so Dugan and I deciding not to go through with it didn't actually mean the betrothal had been canceled.

"They offered only truces," Nandin agreed, nodding slowly, the frown still affixed to his face. "Which means we are likely in for an arduous day. We should probably dine and determine our next plan of action."

All eyes turned to Falin because this was his court and his private dining table. He gave me one last look, as if silently asking if I was okay with everything that had just transpired. I wasn't, but there wasn't much I could do about it right now. Then he turned and walked toward the large table in the center of the room. It was bare, not even a plate or glass of water on the icy surface, but as Falin approached the head of the table, covered trays appeared, complete with fancy settings and several lit candelabras. He stepped around the chair at the head of the table, pulling out the one on the right and standing behind it before looking at me.

It took me a moment too long—and Rianna elbowing me in the side—before I realized he was holding the chair out for *me*. It was a gentlemanly gesture. Sweet . . . but weird. It wasn't something I was accustomed to. I felt awkward as I made my way to the chair, aware once again of all eyes on me.

Yeah, I wasn't made for this court thing—and this wasn't even the whole court. This was just a few advisors and a couple allies.

"I feel rather overlooked," a voice announced before I could sink into my chair.

I whirled toward the voice. In the time it took me to turn, everyone else in the room materialized weapons. Falin's long daggers were in his hands as he stepped protectively in front of me. Dugan's sword dripped shadows, as did the blade Nandin had produced. Lyell wielded what appeared to be a frozen halberd, Maeve held an icy whip, and Rianna had produced her magical spear. Even Brad produced a small knife from the folds of his cloak, though he stepped behind Nandin, letting the king shield him. I was apparently the only one stupid enough not to immediately grab my dagger. *Totally not made for this Faerie court thing.*

My gaze landed on the source of the voice. The man who'd spoken had propped himself against the far wall in a shadowy corner, one knee bent, arms crossed casually over his chest.

"Wow, check out that aggression. I think I'll sit next to the planeweaver; she's the only one not threatening to gut me just for speaking," he said, flashing a very Cheshire cat–like smile. He tipped his head slightly in my direction, eyes gleaming with mischief.

"What are you doing here?" Nandin ground out the words, lowering but not vanishing his blade.

"A little nightmare told me you were searching for allies against light. I'm hurt no one called me," the man said, not straightening from where he leaned against the wall. He pressed a hand against his chest, feigning injury from the slight of not being called for aid. Did he not care that most of the people in the room still held drawn weapons? "I'm here to join the good fight. To save all of Faerie." That last bit almost sounded sarcastic.

Dugan scoffed under his breath, but his sword vanished. "You, fight?"

The man pushed off the wall and made an exaggerated grimace. "You mean like with weapons, and blood, and pain? No. You're right. I better leave that to a brute like you," he said, flashing a mocking and not quite friendly smile at Dugan. Then he grabbed the long staff beside him and strolled across the room.

Most of the fae in the room still had their weapons drawn, but he didn't seem to care. He was in no particular hurry as he made his way across the space, his focus on where Falin and I stood. If it had been any other fae, I likely would have felt threatened and a little worried about his lack of concern for the dangerous situation he was willfully ignoring. But I knew this fae. Not well, certainly not enough to trust. But I found myself more curious than nervous about his presence. Falin hadn't lowered his weapons, though, so clearly he didn't feel the same. But I felt no need to go for my dagger. Not yet at least.

Lyell stepped forward, his halberd raised, moving to block the path to his king. The newcomer paused, then, looking around the other fae, his gaze found mine. He cocked an eyebrow over an eye lined with dark makeup. He expected *me* to intercede? There were two kings and a prince in this room. I was *not* the top authority here.

I studied him. As Dugan had implied, he certainly didn't look like much of a fighter. He was just as tall as the shadow royals and Falin, but he wasn't nearly as broad or muscular. He wore black leather, but not the fighting armor Nandin and Dugan wore; more of a punk goth style than anything that would protect him. That look was accentuated by the thick eyeliner and his short hair spiked around his face. He carried no visible weapons—not that that seemed to mean much in Faerie—but aside from some black chains dangling from his belt loops, he carried only a long staff. And not a fighting staff. More like a thin pole topped with an hourglass. Sand trickled steadily from the top globe of the hourglass into the bottom, a third having already fallen.

"What is your hourglass counting down to this time, Kyran?" I called out.

He flashed that Cheshire-like smile again, but Dugan visibly startled at my words, and Nandin turned to regard me with dark eyes.

"You know him?"

I nodded. "Self-declared ruler of the nightmare realm? Yeah. We've met."

Nandin's lip curled back in a sneer. "Ruler? More like janitor."

"You always say such kind things, Father." Kyran released an exaggerated sigh. "The planeweaver visits quite frequently. She does so love her guilt-tortured nightmares."

"I told you to stop watching my dreams," I said, but the comment was mostly reflex because I was busy staring between Kyran and Nandin. *Father?* There was minimal resemblance between the two, but now that I was looking for it, I supposed I could see some familial traits. Faerie was such a small place in many ways.

Kyran turned his attention to where Lyell still blocked his path. "Are you planning to let me pass?"

The councilman turned a questioning eye at Falin, who, after a moment, nodded. Falin hadn't sheathed his daggers yet, but he'd lowered them.

"What are you doing here?" Falin asked as Kyran finished his casual stroll across the room.

The slender fae lifted one shoulder in a blasé shrug. "Like I said. I'm here to join the fight against light. To restore shadow. To save Faerie. Blah, blah, blah. So on and so forth."

I frowned at him. "Bullshit. You're here to watch something. What's the hourglass counting down to?"

Kyran's grin grew.

"Enough playing, boy," Nandin snapped. "Answer the consort's question."

The title caught me short, my shoulders hitching at the reference, but I did want—and more than likely *needed*—the answer. The last time Kyran had carried that staff, the hourglass had been ticking down to the moment that a crazed witch using a powerful plane-merging artifact would complete her potentially world-ending spell—or that I would stop her. I couldn't help but wonder if it was once again counting down to some apocalyptic event. The sand wasn't falling fast, but the hourglass couldn't possibly hold more than a few hours' worth of sand. That wasn't a lot of time before . . . whatever was set to happen happened—or we managed to stop it.

"Consort?" Kyran exaggerated his eyebrow lift to a point that would have been comical in another circumstance. "No. Not consort, are you? You haven't agreed to anything."

I glared at him. "We were talking about the hourglass."

"I knew it." Kyran beamed. "You haven't agreed. Faerie must have magicked that ring on your finger. Your commitment issues do leave such nice openings for others still hoping to win your affection."

Now I wasn't the only one glaring at the nightmare kingling.

"Hey, what's with all the aggressive looks?" he asked, his smile never slipping. "I'm not speaking for myself. Planeweaver, you are fascinating, but not my type."

"Nandin said you were the realm of dreams' janitor. Did he mean jester?" I mumbled under my breath, which earned a snorted laugh from Dugan.

Kyran's smile finally dimmed. "You've used that joke before."

"What is the hourglass counting down to?" Falin accented the question by lifting one of his daggers. Kyran was close enough now that the blade touched his throat.

Kyran lifted one hand in a placating manner, palms out—the other hand still gripped his staff. "It is counting down to the end, of course. Or maybe to the beginning?" He frowned. "Or is it more like a semicolon? A to-be-continued."

"Can you be less annoying and more specific?" Nandin growled.

Apparently I wasn't the only one with a dysfunctional relationship with my father.

Kyran gave another one of those lackadaisical

shrugs. "I'm here to help. My oath on it. But there are rules. Don't ask about the hourglass again."

There was a long moment in which no one moved. No one spoke. I didn't even breathe. Finally Nandin shook his head.

"What could you possibly do to help?"

Kyran smiled at his father, and I winced on his behalf, even though no pain at the words showed in his expression. "The realm of dreams is crumbling into the same chasm the shadow court is slipping into. I like the home you've deigned to allow me to establish there. So it is in my best interests to see Faerie restored. I'm offering what aid I can."

"Another ally in this fight wouldn't be a bad thing," I said, my words barely above a whisper.

Nandin shook his head again, but after a tense moment, Falin lowered his arm, his daggers vanishing.

"We will require oaths."

Kyran wiped away the thin line of blood trickling from his throat, the smile never falling from his face. "I expected nothing less."

Chapter 29

⊷═⊷ ═⊶⊷

While Falin and Nandin extracted whatever oaths they required from Kyran, I settled in my seat at the table. I was starving and curious what was under the fancy silver domes covering the food. It smelled like pancakes. I really hoped it was pancakes.

Maeve shot a glare full of daggers my way when I reached for the closest covered platter, but she didn't say anything to me. I hadn't planned to actually eat before Falin made it to the table anyway—not because he was king but because it would have been rude. I just wanted to check what Faerie had served. Instead I settled back in my chair, waiting not so contentedly.

Maeve busied herself assigning seats to everyone present. Despite this being Falin's private dining hall, not the court banquet hall, Maeve attempted to arrange everyone by their court standing. Which meant she didn't want to put Rianna, Desmond, or Brad at the table at all.

I, of course, objected to that plan.

Rianna ended up seated beside me, which put her third from the king of the winter court, to Maeve's obvious chagrin. I'd have insisted Desmond receive the next seat, just to irritate the uppity Sleagh Maith council-woman, but after a look at Rianna's flushed face, I decided not to push it.

Once Falin joined us, we finally got to eat. I was thrilled to discover pancakes, bacon, and eggs hiding under the domes. I dug in with relish, having to remind myself to slow down and actually listen to the conversations across the table as they were kind of important.

Not very productive, though.

"So that's your master plan?" Kyran asked, propping his booted feet onto the table. Even I shot him a glare for that one. Not that he cared. "You are just going to issue a handful of formal challenges against the light throne?"

Nandin set his fork down and turned toward his son. "You have a better plan?"

Kyran shrugged. "No. But yours doesn't seem very . . . time efficient."

"Ryese, if he truly has taken over as the King of Light, will have to respond to an official challenge within a day and a night." Dugan frowned as he spoke, poking at the food on his plate. "Granted, if the first challenger does not make it all the way to Ryese, there will be a break before he has to accept a second challenge, but that is just the way of things."

Kyran didn't answer but shot a meaningful glance at his hourglass. How much sand did it have left? Two hours? Four?

"I don't think we have that kind of time," I said, scraping the last of the syrup from my plate with the side of my fork. "Even assuming Kyran is screwing with us and his hourglass is just counting down when his dry cleaning will be ready—"

The fae in question snorted at my implication, but he didn't interrupt.

"—the fae in the mortal realm are trapped and fading. We need to stop Ryese from destroying any more doors, and we need to secure the amaranthine tree he's

been offering in exchange for me. Summer saw it, so
we know he has it."

"Assuming he is the hooded figure who contacted
them," Nandin said. That was the second ambiguous
comment that had been made about Ryese's involvement this morning. I frowned at him, though I guessed
that if he were the one telling me his long-standing
nemesis was the source of all of Faerie's problems without any proof to back it up, I'd likely be skeptical as
well. Still, I didn't like it.

"Well, the fastest way to secure the tree would be to
turn over the planeweaver," Kyran said, folding his
hands behind his head and leaning his chair back on
two legs.

"No," Falin and Dugan said, simultaneously.

"He has a point." Maeve looked at Falin, her face
open and earnest, without a hint of malice. "It would
bolster our court and allow us to rescue at least some
of our people and independents."

"And it would further the plans of the man trying to
destroy Faerie—which includes our court. Is that the
sage advice you are offering me?" Falin asked, his
voice cold enough that Faerie responded by dropping
the temperature in the room.

Maeve ducked her head, suddenly very focused on
the half-eaten breakfast on her plate.

"Can you at least tell us *where* whatever catastrophic
event you're counting down to occurs?" I asked Kyran,
nodding to his hourglass.

He only gave me that irritating grin, not answering,
and I all but growled under my breath. Then I stood so
I could snag another piece of bacon from the platter
that had ended up just a little out of reach, making me
stretch for it. Nandin, who was sitting directly across
from me, snatched my hand out of the air, his warm
fingers hard where he gripped my hand.

The sudden movement brought most of the people
at the table to their feet, Falin's daggers appearing in

his hands, though he didn't raise them. A truce was in place, but the dark look tugging at the Shadow King's face as he stared at my hand was more than a little frightening. He rose, leaning over the table to peer more closely.

"Where did you get this?" he demanded.

"Uh. I think we covered the consort ring already." I mean, it had been an extended conversation.

Nandin shook his head in one sharp movement. "Not the ring. The key!" He flipped my hand over, making my charm bracelet glimmer as it twisted around my wrist where it showed just above my glove.

"What k—" I cut off abruptly as my gaze landed on a small ornate key dangling beside the other charms from my bracelet. I blinked, frowning at the silver key. "I . . . I've never seen that before." Where the hell had it come from? It was more or less the same size as my other charms, but how had it gotten there? And when?

Without releasing my arm, Nandin lifted his other hand and poked at the small silver key. His finger passed right through it, as if it wasn't there. I just stared.

"Did your father give it to you?" he asked, his dark gaze pinning me to the spot.

"No—or at least, I don't think so?" But he had grabbed my wrist when he collapsed. It was *possible*, but . . . I frowned and reached for the odd key. Where Nandin's finger had passed through it, the silver metal was solid to me, warmed by my skin, and seemed to buzz lightly with magic.

My frown deepened, and I closed my eyes, trying to suss out as much as I could with my ability to sense magic. The key faintly hummed with the magic, so light I wasn't surprised I hadn't noticed its addition to my charm bracelet. It didn't feel spelled like a charm, though, more like the small shape clasped between my fingers *was* magic, the signature both familiar and strange all wrapped up in one. It reminded me of Faerie. And yes, my father.

I opened my eyes. How . . . ? It had to have been when he grabbed me. Unless, maybe Faerie had put it on my bracelet? The same way Faerie had magicked the consort ring on my finger?

Everyone was staring at me, and Nandin still gripped my wrist. His brow furrowed hard as he studied my face.

"You mentioned that Caine was attacked. I tried to contact him last night but was unable to. I think you need to tell us what happened."

Yeah, it was past time to elaborate on that story. I gave a small tug on my wrist, and the Shadow King released me. He didn't sit, though, but continued looming over me.

My mind flashed back to that moment in my father's office, when he'd collapsed to the floor, blood seeping from a hole in his chest. I winced, the memory stabbing at me, twisting my stomach, making my heart pound. "I . . . I'm not sure he . . . I doubt you could contact him. I don't think he survived . . ."

A warm hand encircled mine, fingers squeezing mine gently, offering comfort. I tried to give Falin a smile, but it felt feeble. I did squeeze his hand back, making no attempt to break away from him. Taking a breath that seemed to tremble in my chest, I related the story of how my father had collapsed, bleeding, before vanishing, and how I'd searched but couldn't find any trace of who or what had attacked him. A single tear, hot and treacherous, slipped down my cheek as I spoke, and I squeezed my eyes shut.

"That's not possible," Lyell said from his spot at the table.

I shot a glare in his direction, but my gaze stumbled over Brad on its way. Shit. I hadn't even considered that he was in the room. And I'd just detailed our father's death. Brad's hood was up, his head seemingly hanging low, so I couldn't see his expression.

I bit my bottom lip, shaking my head. "I'm aware it's

impossible. I must have missed something. I just don't know what or how." I turned to Nandin. "Do you have any ideas?"

The king shook his head, but he wasn't looking at me. He was staring at my wrist again, where the small key hung like a charm from my bracelet.

"Do you know what it opens? Does it open something? It feels like magic and Faerie."

Nandin collapsed back into his chair and made a sound that was almost a laugh, except it was dark, and a little scary.

"Finally," Kyran said, removing his feet from the table and standing. Then he began shoveling food in his mouth like his plate would be ripped away at any moment and he was in a rush to eat as much food as possible.

I ripped my gaze from Nandin long enough to frown at the strange nightmare kingling. Then I looked from Falin to Dugan. They both looked as confused as I felt.

After a moment, Nandin nodded, the movement hard and definite. "Yes. I know what it opens. We need to get moving."

"Sire?" Dugan asked at the same time Falin said, "Where?"

The Shadow King didn't answer immediately, and Falin turned to me. "Wait. How is your father involved? He's human."

I cringed. "He's not. I don't know how he was living in winter territory, but he is definitely fae."

Nandin, already stepping away from the table, glanced back over his shoulder at me. "We need to hurry. Girl, I hope you can actually use that key." He let his gaze travel over everyone gathered at the table. "Change of plans. We're headed to the high court. It's time to wake a sleeping king."

Chapter 30

✦━━➣ ⬥

The high court.

I scrambled after the Shadow King, Falin to one side, Dugan at my other. I could hear the others behind me as we reached the doorway to the hall. How long had I been trying to reach the high court? Falin had no idea how to even contact the High King, but my father had apparently slipped me a key to the damn court?

"Is that where it happens—whatever *it* is—the high court?" I asked, glancing over my shoulder at Kyran. "Or do we just go wake the High King and he becomes a major player in whatever you're counting down to?"

The nightmare kingling only grinned, his steps jaunty as we hurried through the icy halls.

"Don't waste your breath," Dugan told me, throwing a dark look at Kyran. "He's not going to answer, and if he does, it will only be with riddles."

"You two don't like each other much," I said, starting to breathe hard from the pace Nandin was setting. We weren't running, but I was pretty sure we could classify the speed as a jog. I couldn't help but notice that neither Dugan nor Falin was breathing any harder, but I could hear Rianna panting not far behind me. Brad, with his child-length legs, was running.

Dugan considered me a moment and then shrugged. "There are only twenty years between our ages. In Faerie, with our long lives and low birth rates, that means Kyran and I pretty much grew up together, the only children in the court at the time. We spent most of our youth as contemporaries. And as rivals. But Kyran never took after his father much."

There was a lot of significance in that last sentence. I glanced from Dugan to the Shadow King, noting their similar armor and remembering their near-identical fighting style. Dugan was prince of the shadow court. Not an inherited title. One given to him because he'd earned it, and the king trusted him to take the court one day, planned to hand it to him.

"And you are like a surrogate son to Nandin." I whispered the words, not wanting them to carry.

Dugan nodded, his expression giving away nothing. Then he turned and studied my face for a moment. "If we are being personal, may I offer some friendly advice?"

I cocked a questioning eyebrow but nodded at Dugan.

"I know that you care deeply for your king," he said. Beside me I sensed Falin tense, and I knew he was listening very closely to this conversation. "You may even believe you love him."

I just blinked at Dugan, hoping he'd say whatever it was he wanted to say before this got weirder and more awkward.

"If you have not accepted the consort title yet, then I suggest a careful contract. One with defined limits and ways out. The summer royals also once loved each other. You see how that turned out for them."

He didn't wait for me to respond, but with his advice imparted, he gave me a small bow and then increased his pace until he caught up with Nandin. I blinked at his retreating back. I knew what he was getting at. The King and Queen of Summer appeared to hate each other and it had divided their court. I paused, my steps faltering until Falin reached back and took my hand, urging me on again.

"We can cross that bridge when we get to it," he whispered, though he was glaring at Dugan's back.

I nodded, because he was right. There was no point talking about it now, not while we had so many more important things to focus on. And yet, now that Dugan had said it, I found myself thinking about it.

Either my slower pace or Dugan's absence gave Kyran an opportunity to catch up, his long jaunty steps bringing him to the spot at my side that the prince had vacated.

"He's a jerk, you know," he said, nodding to Dugan.

"It was logical advice." I wasn't sure why I was defending him, but I couldn't deny the logic behind his words.

"Since when are emotions logical?"

I frowned at Kyran, which did nothing to dim his seemingly unwavering grin. Or was it a gloat? I glanced at the hourglass. The sand seemed to be falling faster now, as if the quicker we moved, the more we hurried on the event it foretold.

Kyran just continued to grin, a bounce in each step. "What an epic tale we're weaving—if enough of Faerie survives to ever tell it. A quest to save all we know. Kings, outcasts, changelings, a planeweaver. A planebender." He glanced around, his gaze moving over Lyell and Maeve. "Those other fae too," he said with a dismissive wave of his hand. "Oh, and a cursed barghest."

I glanced at Desmond. "Cursed?"

"You didn't know?" Kyran made a hmming sound under his breath, though it sounded more amused than inquiring. "I'm not so sanguine about bringing a barghest on this quest. You do know they are omens of death, right?"

I wanted to ask him more—not about the omen of death, but about the curse, because I was fairly certain Rianna was in love with Desmond based on the one time I'd seen them together when he was in his human form. That had been during a revelry, when rules of Faerie tended to be friendlier: taboos lifted, grudges temporarily forgotten, and maybe, curses broken. I'd often wondered why he always remained in his doglike form. Maybe this was the answer.

There was no time to ask, though. We stepped through the winter doors that led to the clearing between courts, and Nandin finally stopped, turning to face me.

"Time to use that key, Alexis," he said, beckoning me forward to the very center of the circle between the doors.

I frowned but walked up to him, glad of the very solid feel of Falin's hand clasped in mine. With my free hand, I unclipped the key from my bracelet. I stopped when I reached the middle of the clearing, turning a tight circle as I looked around. I'd been in this small grove several times before, and I'd never seen the door to the high court—I'd even asked after it the first time I came here and had been told there was no such door. Now I looked around, once again seeing the doors to the seasonal courts as they transitioned through the year in an unending loop. Between them, light filtered through the trees. A lot of light. Only one single path of shadow remained. That was a bad sign.

I saw no other doors. Certainly no secret door I'd missed on any other visit.

"Where is the door to the high court?" I asked, glancing at the Shadow King.

He grimaced, turning a full circle, and then frowned at the packed ground under his feet. "Here, I would think. The seasonal courts are the outer wheel of Faerie. Light and shadow the spokes. And the high court is the center, the hub from where the rest of us rotate. So here, in the center, seems like the right place."

"You've never been to the high court either, have you?"

He gave a small, derisive laugh. "Few have. But unlike most anyone else here, I have spoken to the High King and his representatives. Your father is one of his emissaries. Did he tell you how to open the door? Give you any instructions?"

Emissary of the High King? That might explain a few things. Unfortunately, he hadn't even told me he'd given me a key, let alone how to use it. Though . . . he had mentioned something was key, hadn't he? What had he said? I closed my eyes, trying to remember his exact words. My heartbeat sped up as I mentally stepped back into those moments, again seeing my father bleeding from an unseen attack.

"Blood."

"What?" Falin asked, frowning at me.

"He said that blood was the key. His blood." Shit, how was that supposed to help? Though, I did have some of his blood. The soiled gloves. They were probably still in my purse . . . which was in Falin's bedroom or maybe library. I hadn't seen it since I fell asleep last night. Damn it. I glanced at the hourglass on Kyran's staff, feeling time was literally running out and now we'd have to backtrack.

My whirling thoughts must have been apparent because Nandin cleared his throat and said, "To state the obvious, his blood runs in your veins."

Oh. Right.

Brad stepped forward. "Then I could open the door?" His hood had fallen at some point during our brisk walk and his young face was flushed from exertion, but his eyes shone as he spoke, his excitement evident.

Nandin looked away from him and Dugan seemed to find something suddenly fascinating with the ridge of his knuckles. It was Kyran who spoke up with his blithe tone.

"You share blood with your sister, but she blooded true and you're a changeling. You *might* be able to use the door. But I doubt you could open it."

Brad deflated, his features falling as his gaze dropped to the ground. I glared at Kyran, but he only shrugged and cut a meaningful glance at the hourglass.

Time was short, I knew that. Still, he didn't have to be cruel.

I placed a hand on my brother's shoulder. I remembered him being so tall when I was a kid, but he was far shorter than me now. It was still so weird to have found him. His lips pressed into a thin line before he shrugged off my hand and moved to stand beside the Shadow King.

That stung. Brad and I had always been close, but a lot of time had passed. More for him than me, apparently, even though he looked so much younger. I didn't have time to sort that out. Later, though, definitely.

If there was a later.

I grabbed my dagger and peeled off my gloves. Then I pressed the point of the dagger into the tip of my finger. A small drop of blood welled, and I rubbed it onto the key, just like I would if personalizing a spell. The whisper of magic ringing through the key increased in volume, and my blood swirled over the surface. Then the small smear of red sank into the odd metal.

I looked around. Nothing in the clearing had changed.

"He didn't give you any more instruction than 'blood'?" Dugan asked.

I frowned at the key, shaking my head. "He kind of had a gaping chest wound at the time. There wasn't a lot of opportunity for instruction before he vanished."

I wouldn't have guessed the group around me could frown any harder, but they proved me wrong. No one said anything—what could be said? I returned my attention to the key, wiping another drop of blood onto the strange metal. Again it sank into the key's surface.

The magical whisper pressing against my skin again
increased, but nothing in the clearing changed. My
blood clearly had an effect on the key, but not enough.
I could feel something inside the key waiting, but the
few drops of blood I'd given it hadn't roused the magic.

"Maybe it just needs more blood." I hated blood
magic.

Repositioning the dagger, I moved it over my palm,
already wincing even though I hadn't made the slice
yet. Falin's hand closed around my wrist, pulling the
dagger edge farther from my skin.

"Let me do this. I can provide the needed blood."

"You use twin blades when fighting. I don't think
you should slice up your palm."

We stared at each other, neither backing down, my
wrist—and the dagger—caught in the iron vise of his
grip. Kyran cleared his throat, stepping forward.

"I do believe our planeweaver is the only one who
can open this door," he said, nodding to me, and for
once there was no sarcasm or mocking notes to the
movement. "After all, she is the one descended from
the high court. Now, we should be quick about it. Time
is slipping away."

He shot another meaningful glance at his hourglass,
and my own gaze followed. At least two-thirds of the
sand had fallen into the lower globe now, the sand
seemingly falling at an ever-increasing rate.

"How much time is left?" I asked, trying to judge
how long it would take for the last third of sand to fall,
assuming, of course, it didn't change speed again.

Kyran shrugged. "I'd suggest hurrying."

I met Falin's gaze. He held my wrist locked in place
for one more moment, and then with a frown he released me. He didn't step back, but stayed close. I expected his hovering to annoy me, but I realized, with
more than a little surprise, that it didn't. I liked having
him nearby and knowing he cared.

I dragged the blade across my palm, opening a

decent-sized gash. Blood immediately welled in the long cut, and I closed my fist around the key, pressing the blood into the metallic surface, letting the key drink as much as the magic desired.

And it did. The whisper of magic in the key soared, growing into a song that rang through the clearing. Magic rolled over me, both too hot and too cold against my skin. Then the first drop of my blood escaped and dripped onto the ground at my feet.

And Faerie *moved*.

It wasn't an earthquake, not exactly. It was more like Faerie jolted, startled.

"I think it's working," Nandin said, his eyes wide as he watched me.

Golden vines shot from the ground and wove themselves together, forming an intricate archway that began small, no taller than my knees, and then grew with every pulse of magic from the key in my hand. A pulse, I realized, that synced perfectly with my heartbeat.

The growing doorway had reached the height of my chest when the light in the clearing surged. I didn't look away from the doorway, not until I heard Dugan curse, his sword appearing in his hand as he spun away from the door and toward the outer ring of trees.

He wasn't the only one.

Falin also had his blades in hand as he turned, positioning himself to cover me from attack as he scanned the clearing. I squinted, the light too bright to look at directly. Then a roar of sound crashed over the clearing as fae warriors rushed into the grove from every direction. Fae of every shape and size poured into the space. They raised weapons, shouting as they ran at our group clustered around the growing doorway.

"It's an ambush by the light court!" Nandin yelled, lifting his own blade and charging the fae coming straight at him.

They had us surrounded and outnumbered at least ten to one. Shit. This was bad.

"Protect the doorway," Nandin commanded, his sword biting deep into the neck of the fae in front of him.

Falin grunted something that sounded like "Protect Alex. We can get another door." But he was already engaged with two fae warriors, so I wasn't sure.

I lifted my dagger, but Rianna jumped in front of me, her spear raised as she faced off with the fae who'd been rushing me. Desmond tackled the fae, his enormous black-furred body riding the struggling man to the ground. Rianna drove the tip of her spear into the downed fae's chest, and I spun, looking for the next threat.

"Time for you to go," Kyran said, and then he planted a palm in the center of my chest, shoving hard. I'd been looking for an attack from the charging light fae, not from my allies, and the move caught me off guard.

I stumbled backward, right into the growing doorway. The sound of battle cut off abruptly, the world seeming to swirl around me in a kaleidoscope of colors and shapes as I fell through the door and into the high court.

Chapter 31

❖━━━ ◉ ◉ ━━━❖

I crashed onto my ass on what I would have said was a wooden floor—if wood was cast in gold. *The golden halls of the high court*. The legends had gotten that right, even if few fae had ever seen them.

I scrambled back to my feet and whirled around, searching for the doorway I'd tumbled through. There was nothing around me. No arch. No opening. Not even a pillar or a tree that might mark one of Faerie's more unconventional doors. Just a golden wall, the surface rough and textured like a tree.

No.

Where was the door? Had it closed? Or was it still open in the clearing, just not here? And if it was still open, why hadn't anyone else come through? What was happening in the battle?

I bit my lip, fear slicing deep. My last sight of Falin had been him engaged with multiple opponents, with more closing in. Was he okay? And Rianna. She wasn't a fighter. She'd been holding her own when I last saw her, but why hadn't she jumped through the doorway yet? War was supposed to be forbidden in Faerie, disputes settled with duels, but what I'd just left was definitely a battle; not any stretch of the imagination could call it a sanctioned duel. Ryese and his people might have no respect for the laws of Faerie, but weren't those rules supposed to be magically enforced? Where was the king who was supposed to uphold them?

Well, here, I guess. And Nandin had said I needed to wake him.

I stopped searching for the door I'd stumbled through and looked around. The air here was so still. So quiet. I'd never heard Faerie so quiet, as if the land itself was holding her breath, waiting and watching.

The space was enormous, the curving walls making me suspect the entire room was one large circle. While the walls and floor were that odd textured gold, the ceiling was completely obscured with leaf coverage, like a giant tree hung over the court. Large, lightly glowing flowers hung among the leaves. Hauntingly familiar flowers.

Amaranthine flowers.

There were amaranthine trees here? But no. I didn't see any trees. Just the walls and the leaves and flowers overhead. The only thing actually in the room was a large glowing dome in the center of the room that pulsed with magic, and inside, a shadowy form obscured by the magical glow. The rest of the room was empty. Quiet and still.

Like a tomb.

In fact, compared to the other courts, the high court was oddly plain. Oh, the golden walls were rather flashy, but the more I looked at them, the more I felt they weren't metal. I had a suspicion they were living wood. The court was somehow *inside* an enormous amaranthine tree.

I opened my hand, planning to snap the no-doubt bloody key back onto my charm bracelet. My palm was empty aside from the still-bleeding gash. *Crap.* I scanned the floor, searching. Had I dropped the key when I fell through the door? It wasn't on the floor. I hadn't opened my hand before now. I knew I hadn't. The key had just vanished.

One-time use, apparently.

Panic flared in me again, because I was stuck. No door. No key. No way out. I didn't even see a doorway leading from this room. The high court was a gigantic golden cage. I was reminded of the story my father had told me during the last revelry about the High King and the creation of the courts. He'd finished it by saying that the high court was just the king, bound to his throne, and Faerie. No courtiers, no true court.

The heart of Faerie is his prison.

Hopefully the king could send me back—assuming he wasn't the type to wake grumpy and kill the messenger. But if he was trapped here, would he even be able to help me get back to my friends? He did communicate outside these walls at times, pass and enforce his laws, and he had at least one emissary. Surely there was some way to leave.

So I just have to rouse him . . . And then tell him how much damage had been done to Faerie while he'd been sleeping. Yeah, that was sure to ingratiate me with the king. *Not.*

I crept forward toward the glowing dome and something crashed behind me. I whirled around in time to see a small cloaked figure scramble to his feet.

"Brad?"

My brother glanced up, giving me a sheepish look as he scratched the back of his head. "The door worked," he said, his voice halting. Then he looked around. "But it appears to be gone now."

"Yeah. Will you be able to bend Faerie to get us out of here?" Because a backup plan if the High King woke pissed would be good.

Brad frowned and then closed his eyes. I waited, feeling the seconds tick by. He bit his lips together, his brows furrowing, before his eyes finally flew open again and he shook his head. "Maybe I'm still too exhausted . . . but I don't think I could even on my best day." His gaze moved over the room. "This is the high court? Where is the rest of it?"

"Expecting more glitz and grandeur?" I asked, and he gave me a half shrug.

"Expecting more . . . something for sure. What's that?" he asked, nodding toward the golden half dome in the center of the room.

"The king, I think. I was headed to check it out when you appeared." I turned toward the dome again and he scrambled to catch up with me. As we crossed the room, I asked, "How was the fight when you left?"

"I followed you immediately. Not my kind of scene."

Oh. My brow creased. I'd been here several minutes already when he'd appeared. Of course, time often worked funny with doorways in Faerie.

I didn't say anything else, but studied the shapes slowly becoming clear through the golden dome as we approached it. A throne sat in the center of the circle, a wizened and ancient-looking fae slumped in it. I assumed he must be the king. He was the only person here, and he was slumped, sound asleep on the throne. But he wore no crown, which was odd. Faerie typically marked her royalty in very obvious ways. Of course, the High King might be held to very different rules.

Golden vines grew up from the ground, wrapping around the king's legs and binding his arms to the throne. No, they didn't just bind him. As I stared at the snarled vines securing him to the throne, I realized they were actually growing *into* the king's limbs. Or maybe they were growing out of them, literal roots between him and Faerie. I was studying the strange vines so hard, it took me a moment to realize that the king wasn't just snoozing in his throne, but pinned there by a short sword that had been driven through his chest.

My heart slammed against my ribs, and I rushed the rest of the way across the room, Brad at my heels.

Maybe this was normal. Maybe the king had always been pinned to his throne with a sword . . .

Or maybe he was dead, and that was why Ryese had been able to cause so much havoc.

I stopped short outside the glowing golden dome. It pulsed with magic, and just being near it pricked at my skin. Brad reached out a hand, as if to touch the dome, and I grabbed his wrist, stilling him.

"You don't want to touch that." I wasn't sure exactly what the dome did, but from what I could feel coming off it, at best it would deliver a painful magical jolt, but the magics swirling through it felt a lot deadlier than that. It was a protective circle, one like I'd never seen before.

The king's slumping head lifted as I spoke. So he wasn't dead. Or sleeping.

His eyes opened, his gaze landing on me. Then his lips moved. "A . . . lex . . . is."

Surprise jolted through me. The High King knew me? Knew my name? How?

"Allie?" Brad's voice was questioning as he looked between the king and me. I was just as lost.

I threw open my shields. The room remained the same, the circle in front of me glowing brighter with magics I could now see. I blinked, peering past that magic to a throne that hadn't changed, the vines still growing into the king's limbs, a sword pinning him to the golden chair. But the figure itself had changed. No longer was the king an ancient and wizened fae; now his face was much younger, no older in appearance than mine. A face that was familiar.

My father's face.

I gasped, stumbling backward. My father wasn't an emissary. He was the High-Fucking-King of Faerie.

And he had a sword sticking out of his chest. Right where I'd seen a gaping wound open without apparent cause when he'd collapsed in his office.

"No." I shook my head, still creeping backward, away from what my eyes were seeing, what my brain was putting together. My throat tightened, a hand of panic closing around it. The High King hadn't been sleeping these recent years . . . he'd been in Nekros. Or at least part of him had. It didn't look like this body could move with the way he was rooted to that throne, but some part of him had left. Had been walking around. Acting as governor of Nekros, as his own emissary, and he'd been engineering the return of the plane-weaving trait. *To fix the mistake he'd made by severing the realm of dreams* . . . The creation myth he'd told me at the revelry suddenly took on a whole new weight.

I shook my head again, my fingers pressed tight against my mouth as I stared at the sword hilt emerging from his chest, barely visible in his gold and scarlet robes. I had the sinking suspicion they hadn't been scarlet before yesterday. When he'd collapsed in his office, it hadn't been a magical attack from afar. Not in the way I'd suspected, at least. It had been an attack on his true body. Here, on his throne. Whatever magics he'd been using to be in two places at once must have failed when he'd been attacked. That was why he'd vanished.

But who had attacked him? And how? There was no way in. No way out. I'd thought this place felt like a tomb—and it very nearly was. How was he even alive? And how could I help him?

"I don't suppose you know any healing magics?" I asked Brad.

He shook his head, his eyes too wide, clearly having spotted the sword driven through the king as well.

"What a family reunion this is," a voice said behind me.

I jumped and spun around. Beside me, Brad did the same.

"Ryese." I hissed his name, lifting the dagger still clutched in my hand. "How did you get here?"

Ryese strolled forward, the movement not quite as

smooth as he likely intended due to his limp. His golden cloak covered most of him, but he'd pushed back the hood, revealing his scarred face and the glowing, ornate crown of light on his head. He watched me with his one good eye, drawing closer, but not too close. He stopped a good fifteen feet away, slightly off to the side so he could get a good look at the king in his protective dome. Nothing about the king's condition appeared to surprise him.

"Same as you two," he said. "A door."

My stomach clenched, my heart increasing its barrage against my rib cage. "In the grove between courts?" The question came out too soft. Too quiet. Because if he said yes, that meant the light fae had conquered the grove. No way had Ryese waded into the thick of battle to reach that door. He wouldn't have risked his own neck. So if he'd reached the door I'd opened, every one of my friends and allies in that clearing must have been killed or captured.

Ryese flashed a cruel smile, lopsided where one half of his lips didn't fully work. "Is that where you opened yours? Not a good location. Didn't you know? There is a very deadly battle raging there right now."

I looked away, not wanting him to see the relief in my eyes. If the battle was still ongoing, then hope wasn't lost. My grip tightened around the dagger in my hand, and I scanned the room. No army had followed Ryese, not even a single lackey or bodyguard. I bit my bottom lip. It was just him. Currently at least. That meant Brad and I outnumbered him. I took a cautious step forward.

I was no fighter, but Ryese . . . Well, even before he'd suffered iron poisoning, he'd never been one to fight his own battles. Plus, there were two of us. Brad had drawn his knife, though I noticed he'd edged behind me. If my dismal skills were deemed to be the better out of the two of us, he likely wasn't going to be much help. Still, maybe I could end this right here. Right now.

"No closer, Lexi," Ryese said, lifting a hand—the hand that he'd favored a month ago because it had been twisted by iron poisoning. Now it was his formerly strong side he was keeping hidden under his golden cloak. I'd noticed that when he'd captured me in his mirrored circle too. Was he injured?

I took another step forward, keeping my weight balanced between my legs like Falin had taught me. I was only about twelve feet away now. Reaching out with my magic, I unfurled the ball of realities I carried. Layers of reality flowed outward with my magic, creating an overlay of planes around me. The effect was invisible to most, but it let me manipulate realities not normally found in Faerie. I'd been practicing, pushing my limit further, and Ryese was just inside the boundary of my influence. I took another sliding step toward him.

He scowled at me. Then he flexed his hand.

I was prepared for him to try to use glamour against me. Or perhaps a spell. I thought I was ready.

I was wrong.

Golden vines burst from the ground around my feet. I yelped, jumping back, but it was already too late. They weren't glamour vines. Ryese had commanded Faerie herself, and the very fabric of Faerie had obeyed him.

The vines snaked around my ankles, with more lifting from the ground to crawl up my calves, and up, over my knees. I hacked at the growing vines with my dagger, squirming and struggling. Ryese just tsked at me under his breath.

"None of that now," he said, and with another wave of his hand, vines uncoiled from the leaf coverage overhead, lashing out to encircled my wrists. The vines snapped tight, pulling my arms up, over my head. Effectively immobilizing me.

Brad charged forward, his knife raised. Ryese didn't bother capturing him in vines, but made a swatting motion with his hand, and a thick vine jutted out of the ground and slammed into Brad. The blow knocked him across the room, into the dome protecting the High King. Brad seemed to stick to the dome for a moment, like a bug in a fly trap, and his eyes flew wide in pain before rolling back in his head. He slid from the dome to land in a heap on the ground. Then he didn't move again.

No! Not Brad. I'd only just found him again. Was he still breathing? I couldn't tell. I jerked at the vines holding me, but I couldn't move.

Ryese made a mildly curious sound, watching the reaction the dome had on the changeling. "That was informative. I had been wondering what that dome would do," he said casually to Brad's unmoving body. Then he turned his attention back on me. "Hmm, those lovely vines remind me of someone." He shot a glance at where the High King sat rooted and bound to his throne. "A family resemblance."

The blood drained from my face, but I glared at him. "How did you know?" Because I hadn't even known until I'd seen the face below the High King's glamour.

"I've known for a while. But even if I hadn't, my dearest Lexi, his blood running through your veins is a requirement to step foot in the high court. Which, by the way, means if you were hoping the cavalry would come riding through the door you made, you can stop holding your breath. Your allies cannot join you." His smile was cruel, cold.

My mouth opened. Closed. Opened again, but all I managed was a sputter that didn't come out as coherent thoughts. "Then . . . how . . . ?"

Ryese leered at me. "How did I enter? Have you not figured that out yet?" He gave a mocking shake of his head. "Faerie is such a small place in some ways. You run into family everywhere you turn."

I gaped at him. Then my gaze slid to the slumped figure on the throne.

Ryese let out a laugh that was as pleasant as broken glass grinding against my eardrums. "I see daddy dearest never spoke of me, little sister."

"Sister?" I shook my head, the refusal as much shock as disbelief. "But . . . No. I met your father. The winter councilman the former queen killed. Blayne."

Ryese's expression darkened. "Blayne was my mother's consort at the time of my birth. He raised me, but he wasn't my blood. No, that part of my DNA was contributed by a man who never came to visit me after my birth. Of course, I was more fortunate than most of his offspring through the centuries—they were never allowed to reach maturity. My mother was a clever little vixen who knew how to use her beauty and charm to extract the most binding of oaths."

"You . . . you're my *brother*? But . . . you tried to marry me when we first met."

"That isn't unheard-of among the fae, but, in my defense, I didn't realize you were the High King's spawn until you shook off his spell concealing you."

"Yeah, and then you tried to kill me. More than once." Hell, I was pretty sure he *still* planned to kill me.

Ryese gave a dismissive shrug, the movement oddly lopsided. "Well, that is even more common among the fae. Sibling rivalry is strong here. Now, Lexi dearest, sit tight a bit. I have use for you, but not here. We'll head to my ritual site as soon as I'm done." He turned his attention to the figure inside the protective circle, and then took several shuffling steps forward, his limp more pronounced than before. "He can't hold out much longer," he said, his voice oddly conversational, as if we were old friends discussing nothing of importance. "You alone, my dear Lexi, will have the honor of watching me ascend to High King. It's time to give in, old man. You're only harming Faerie by resisting. I will fix your mess once I'm ruler."

"Bullshit," I muttered.

"Language, Lexi," Ryese said, but he didn't look away from the dying king pinned to his throne.

I jerked at the vines pinning my arms, to no avail. The vines were still growing, my arms now encased to the elbow and held painfully tight over my head. The vines encircling my legs coiled all the way to my hips. I could move little more than my head at this point. How the hell was I going to get out of this?

My gaze slid to Brad. He still hadn't moved. I was on my own.

I tried pushing the vines into the land of the dead, to force them to wither and decay. But the vines were alive; they'd have to be dead to wither. There was no ambient Aetheric energy here, in the heart of Faerie, even with the plane I'd unfurled. I tapped into the small amount of Aetheric energy stored in the ring I carried, drawing it into myself. There wasn't much. I hadn't had time to refill the ring after my escape from Ryese's circle. Once again I wished I could use more offensive magic. A fireball would come in handy right now. That was out of the question—not only did I lack the skill to craft a fireball, but I didn't have enough juice to try to jumble something makeshift.

But maybe a small spell? Something simple? I twisted my neck so I could gaze at the vine holding one of my wrists. Then I concentrated on the spot a few inches above my hand, crafting a first-year-academy spell used to light a candle. Of course, a candlewick was meant to catch fire. That was its purpose. A wick more or less *wanted* to catch fire.

A supple, living, magical vine?

Not so much.

After what felt like far too many of my crashing heartbeats, a blackened scorch mark formed on the golden surface of the vine. Acrid smoke wafted from the growing dark spot. I was close . . . Just a little more. I was almost out of Aetheric energy too. *Come on. Just catch.*

Pain erupted along my scalp, my head violently jerked forward by a hand clasped tight in my hair. I winced, which was why I missed Ryese's lifted hand until the back of his knuckles slammed into my cheekbone, knocking my face sideways and sending pain throbbing from my teeth to my eye. Considering he hadn't released me, the force of the blow also tore out hair.

"Stop," he said, a finger pointed inches from my nose.

I clenched my jaw, swallowing the pained sound threatening to leak from my throat. I also swallowed some blood where my own teeth had sliced into my cheek with Ryese's blow. I'd been so engrossed in burning the vine, I hadn't even heard Ryese move close. *Stupid. So stupid.* And now I didn't have enough Aetheric energy left to try again, even if I did get a chance when he was distracted.

Ryese glared at me, one eye clouded over, the other so pale, it nearly matched the blind side except for the black of his pupil. When I didn't say anything, but also didn't offer any other fight, he released my hair and took a shuffling step back. He tucked his hand under his cloak again, but not before I caught sight of it. His hand—actually his entire arm—the one that should have been his "good" arm, was red, the skin raw and crusted over.

He saw my gaze and shot me a leering grin. "Killing a High King has some consequences." He patted my cheek, and I cringed, I couldn't help it. "Not to worry, dearest Lexi, I'm sure I will heal quickly enough once I'm High King. I mean, look how much just being king of one court has done." He lifted his iron-damaged hand. The skin was still dark, but there was strength in the limb again—I'd certainly felt that. He ran his fingers over the elaborate glowing crown he wore, and his gaze moved toward the magic dome again, his eyes hungry, greedy. "Imagine how much more I'll gain being king of all courts."

"And bound to that throne? Yeah, that sounds *fun*."

He rolled his good eye—the cloudy one not moving. "I have no intention of repeating our father's mistakes. Now, shut up and don't cause trouble. This is a big moment for me. I don't want you tainting the memory."

He limped back to the edge of the circle. "Stop delaying the inevitable, old man. Your time has passed."

The High King, my—our—father, lifted his head. His eyes fixed on Ryese for a moment, and then moved to where I was slowly being encased in golden vines. "This . . . was not . . . my plan." The last word was nearly lost as he coughed, the reflexive movement making his entire body shudder.

When his coughing fit passed, the king wheezed in several breaths that sounded too thick, too wet. A fresh dribble of blood trailed down the corner of his mouth. He squeezed his eyes closed, and I knew Ryese was right. My father wasn't going to make it much longer. The fact that he was still alive at all was a testament to how powerful he was, or perhaps how much Faerie wanted to preserve him, but even that time was running out.

He opened his eyes again, his gaze finding me.

Magic rushed over me. Into me. Filling me. Overfilling me. It dove under my skin and expanded until my body felt like it couldn't contain one more drop. But the magic just kept coming.

My father's eyes fluttered closed, his head dropping, but his words reached me, even through the onslaught of magic. "All hail . . . the High Queen."

Chapter 32

I quivered, my entire being quaking. It felt like I'd grabbed a magical live wire—which was not far from the truth as I'd just been forcefully plugged into the full magic of Faerie. It was too much. It poured into me until I felt like every cell in my body would break apart. And it just kept coming. I could feel the land. Feel an intelligence, a presence, press against my mind. It was huge, so big it threatened to crush everything that was me right out of my body. It filled me until I felt like I would shatter, and then it paused, as if it hovered over the last part of me it hadn't yet claimed.

"Do you accept?" The words were not exactly a voice in my head as much as they were a feeling. A rising awareness of thought that wasn't mine.

I shuddered where I hung from the vines holding me, but managed to pry my eyes open. The world around me seemed stuck, as if I'd been ripped out of time. My father's mouth was still wrapped around the word "queen." Ryese appeared to be frozen in mid-movement, his face caught between shock and outrage. Brad's eyes were now open, his hand flat on the ground in front of his face as if he'd been about to push up from the floor when time had stopped.

"What?" My question came out a pained gasp.

"Do you accept?" Again, the question was more feeling than words.

"Accept what?"

"Me."

I blinked. The world around me was still frozen. "Are you Faerie?"

A warmth filled me; it felt like pleasure, though it wasn't mine. *"Accept, and we would be Faerie."*

I swallowed, the small movement hard with the pressure of magic still filling me. If *we* would be Faerie, I would be High Queen. That seemed like a really bad idea.

Displeasure cut through me with the thought, but again, it was a feeling coming from outside of me, not mine. A discordant music rang out in the distance, accenting Faerie's unhappiness as she reacted to my thoughts.

"My king has held out as long as he can. I can do nothing more. We both agree you are better than the alternative, but you must accept."

The alternative being Ryese. If I refused, he would become High King. I couldn't dare refuse. And yet if I accepted . . . I squeezed my eyes closed, already knowing I couldn't say no, but not wanting to agree.

"Will I be chained to that throne?"

"You didn't conquer me, so I will not conquer you."

Well, that was a relief.

"But you would be mine, wholly."

The relief evaporated. I bit my bottom lip. In front of me, Ryese's shoulders moved, twisting as if in slow motion as he whirled in my direction.

"I cannot hold this. We are out of time. You must choose."

My father's eyes fluttered, his head sagging forward.

Ryese finished his turn, the movement speeding up, time crashing back into place as his good eye landed on me, rage making his pupil expand.

"I accept." The words barely escaped my lips before the torrent of magic crashed into me again.

I'd already been filled with the magic, my skin too tight under the pressure of it. Yet now even more rushed into me. Through me. The last barrier in my mind that had held my sense of self ruptured as Faerie flooded me.

I screamed and Faerie cried out with me.

The ground shook, knocking Ryese to his knees. Brad, who'd gotten both arms under him, collapsed again, and my father hung from the sword pinning him to his throne.

Still I screamed, the sound ripping from me as more magic rushed into my mind, my body, my very soul. I screamed until my voice broke.

And still the magic poured into me. It felt like it lasted hours, but I returned to my senses to the sound of Ryese laughing as he climbed back to his feet, so it couldn't have been that long. I blinked hard, sagging in the vines restraining me.

Ryese shook his head, still laughing, the sound mirthless. "You stupid, prideful old man." He stepped forward, closer to the golden throne.

A throne no longer surrounded by a magical barrier.

"Give away the crown before I take it by force. I get it." He limped up to the throne. "You could have picked any fae inside Faerie. But you kept it in your bloodline, even though that meant handing it to a child who has no idea how to use the power and who will die oh so easily. And then I'll have it anyway."

I gasped in air, unable to breathe around the magic flooding me. Was Ryese ranting at the High King's corpse? He wrapped his hand around the hilt of the blade and pulled it from my father's chest. My father arched backward, sucking down a pained-sounding breath. Ryese flashed his teeth in a malicious smile. He lifted the blade, pulling his arm back across his chest.

No. If he swung out—he'd take my father's head.

"Ryese!"

He hesitated at my scream, turning that lopsided smile on me. "Wait your turn, Lexi. I'll be there soon. Sadly, I think we'll have to waste your potential as a planeweaver. Your prompt death is now required."

He turned toward my father, his sword rearing back, ready to swing. For his part, my father sat slumped, but rooted, in his throne, staring up at Ryese with only partially focused eyes.

"No!" Brad launched himself forward. His knife flashed and then sank into Ryese's side.

Ryese bellowed in anger and pain. Brad tried to backpedal, but he wasn't quite fast enough. Ryese might not be a fighter, but he was still faster and stronger than a changeling stuck in the body of an adolescent. He lashed out, slamming the hilt of his sword into the side of Brad's head.

Brad crumpled and I screamed, thrashing against the vines binding me. Ryese ignored me, sneering as he pressed a hand against his bleeding side.

"Annoying gnat," he snarled, kicking Brad's unconscious body.

"Stop!" But I could do nothing to back up the command.

Ryese turned toward me. He flashed teeth, but it was more grimace than smile. "Oh, Lexi. You are about to lose a lot of family, aren't you? If only you could do something with all that power you've been undeservingly handed." Then he lowered the point of his sword, pointing it at Brad's unprotected throat.

No. I couldn't let this happen. I had the full potential of Faerie's magic burning under my skin. But Ryese was right. I had no idea how to use it. Hell, I'd never even been able to manifest my own glamour.

But I had to do something.

I pushed on the edges of my extended realities. It was already the widest circle I'd ever made, but I had a lot more magic to push behind it now. I fed the magic rushing through me into my unfurled ball of realities, and the edges glided across the room, sweeping all the way to the far wall. Then I focused on Ryese and the sword in his hand. I wrapped the land of the dead around the sword as it thrust forward.

The blade crashed into my brother's throat with an explosion of red. But it wasn't blood. It was rust, the blade shattering into oxidized flakes.

Ryese stared as the hilt of the blade disintegrated in his hands. Then he whirled on me.

"What did you do?" He shouted the question, wiping the remains of his blade from his fingers. Then he took a breath, as if calming himself. His voice was back to a normal volume when he spoke again. "Fine, Lexi. I can deal with you first, if that's what you want."

"Don't move," I shouted, but the words were all bluff and, judging by the gleam in his eyes, not a convincing one.

He lifted a hand, and the vines that had been slowly entombing me picked up speed, squeezing tighter as they grew. A new vine dropped from the ceiling, wrapping around my throat.

No.

I struggled, but the vines only tightened. I twisted, trying to focus on the vines, pushing the magic roiling inside me at them. They squeezed, blocking off my air. Black dots exploded in my vision. No. Damn it. I had all the power of Faerie, and I couldn't even stop a few magical vines!

Ryese laughed. "I can't draw this out the way I desire, dearest Lexi, so as a consolation gift, I'll impart to you this promise: Once I'm High King, I will wipe

out the dark smudge that is the shadow court. Then I
will decimate winter, making sure anyone you ever
cared about is destroyed in the most painful way I can
imagine."

No. Rage boiled in me, combating the fear, and I
forced my spotty vision to find Ryese. I couldn't use
Faerie magic to stop him. I didn't know how. But I had
my own magic. The magic I'd always had. And I
reached out with that.

I reached for Ryese the way I would a corpse. He
wasn't dead. Had never died. My grave magic couldn't
reach him in the land of the dead. But I could touch
more planes than just the land of the dead. I could
reach the crystalline plane where soul collectors existed. Where souls existed.

I reached into Ryese's still-living body and wrapped
my magic around his glimmering soul, still firmly attached. I'd always avoided touching living souls. It felt
wrong, my magic trying to recoil from the hot, living
energy of his soul. I didn't stop. If I died now and Ryese
lived, he'd destroy Faerie and everyone I loved. I
wouldn't let that happen. I couldn't.

So I sank my magic into him, digging into his soul
with claws made of myself. Then, as the darkness
pressed harder on me, I pulled. Hard.

Shock registered on Ryese's face. He stumbled forward, as if he could keep his soul in his body simply by
occupying the same space. I pulled again, and Ryese
went ashen. Heat and warmth rushed into me, the life
I was draining off him filling me. And it was wrong. It
hurt. I could feel it in my own soul. Faerie cried out
around me. I didn't stop, but pulled again, harder.

My vision went black, my last sight the horror on
Ryese's face. I kept pulling, dragging the living life out
of him. The pain in my body was gone now. The panic
buzzing away behind a haze of nothingness. But I kept
pulling, not even sure why.

Somewhere, far away, I heard a thud. Then I became

aware that I was falling a moment before I slammed into the ground.

I gasped in air. It hurt, like daggers being dragged down my throat. Everything hurt. But right at that moment, hurting was good.

Hurting meant I was alive.

I sucked in more air, each breath stronger. The darkness fled from my vision, and I pushed away from the ground.

The vines were gone. Ryese lay crumpled on the ground, his body empty. Soulless.

I'd not just killed him. I'd consumed him. Like a monster.

I shivered.

My hand moved to my shoulder, where my soul had mostly healed from a malicious spell. It was still the weakest point, and as I looked at it now, I saw through the planes that the old wound was open again, the fissures deeper and longer than they'd ever been. I didn't know if it would heal—what I'd just done . . . it was the kind of act that destroyed a person.

I did what I had to do.

And I believed that. But it still had damaged me to the core of my being. Not that I had time to focus on that fact.

Brad was a few yards in front of me. I crawled to him and pressed my fingers to his throat. A strong pulse beat against my fingertips, and he groaned at my cold touch, his eyelids twitching but not opening. Unconscious, probably had a concussion, but if I could find a way out of here, I hoped he'd be okay.

My father made a noise, a sucking, wheezing cough, and I hurried to him next. The wound in his chest oozed blood. Oozing instead of pulsing probably wasn't a good sign. It likely meant he was nearly out of blood. I was surprised he was still alive at all.

"How can I help?" I asked, kneeling down in front

of him. His skin was ashen, lips bloodless. "We need a healer."

He shook his head. Reaching out, he took my hand, patting it lightly. He opened his mouth, but no sound came out, whatever words he planned to say remaining lost in the hiss of his labored breathing.

"Damn it. I need a door out of here to get some help," I yelled, frustration warring with desperation.

Golden vines sprang from the floor right beside me. I scuttled backward, afraid they'd reach for me, but they wove around each other, forming a growing arch. An arch identical to the one I'd taken to reach the high court.

I'd asked for a door, and I'd gotten one.

"Okay then," I whispered, pushing up to my feet and approaching the doorway. I couldn't see what was on the other side, didn't know where it would take me. To help, presumably, as that was what I'd requested, but I wasn't sure Faerie's version of help would match mine. I hadn't heard Faerie inside me since I'd accepted being High Queen, but I could feel her around me, and in my mind, alien and strange.

A soft wind fluttered through the room, and I could have sworn I heard laughter in it. Was . . . was Faerie laughing at my internal dialogue? The laughter in the wind grew louder, the breeze ruffling my curls.

Right. Well, that was weird. But I didn't have time to examine it. I needed to find a healer. I started toward the doorway but then stopped. Only those of the king's bloodline could enter the high court—how likely was I to locate a healer who met that requirement?

Considering that Ryese had said my father typically didn't allow his progeny to reach adulthood, pretty damn unlikely.

I walked back to the throne and stared at the dying king. I wasn't sure how he was still alive, maybe just too stubborn to die, or Faerie might be keeping him alive through the roots she'd planted in him. They didn't look like new additions, something she'd done since he was stabbed, but old, long since healed and adapted to. But if I couldn't bring a healer back here, I was going to have to take him to the healer.

Not that I could carry both my father and brother out. I moved beside Brad and shook his shoulders. He groaned, eyes half opening and then wincing shut again.

"Wake up. We need to get out of here."

Again he groaned. His eyelids fluttered, eyes slitting open. His gaze didn't quite focus on me, his pupils mismatched. Definitely a concussion. Crap.

"I'm going to drag you closer to the doorway," I told him, and then grabbed him under the shoulders and pulled him across the golden floor.

He blinked at me as I released him to slump beside the golden vines. At least he was somewhat conscious. Hopefully he would be mobile by the time I retrieved our father, because I didn't think the former High King would be moving of his own volition anytime soon.

I knelt beside my father and pulled out my dagger. Then I carefully but quickly cut away the vines and roots binding him. Some fell away harmlessly. Others dripped thick red liquid that was almost certainly blood. Above me, my father moaned and shuddered, his breathing turning shallow.

"Don't die from this," I muttered, moving to his leg, the last limb I needed to free.

He was barely breathing, his head falling listlessly to the side when I slung his arm over my shoulder and hauled him up, out of the chair. With his arm held over my shoulder, and my arm around his waist, I carried him, his feet dragging across the golden floor. He was heavier than he looked, and I was struggling by the time I reached the doorway. Brad, at least, had managed to get to his knees, though he held his head in his hands and swayed, like the room spun around him.

"Ready?" I gasped out as I stopped beside him.

Brad nodded, and then winced from the movement. He didn't stand, but wrapped an arm around my leg, the touch ensuring the door took us all to the same location. The doorframe widened to accommodate us, and I stumbled through it, plunging my father and Brad through the door with me.

And stepped out back in the middle of the battle I'd left who-knew-how-long-ago.

Directly in front of me, Rianna pulled her spear from the neck of a fae as Desmond faced off against the warrior attempting to flank her. Bodies littered the ground around Falin; I spotted at least half a dozen dead or maimed fae, and yet, that seemed wrong, like I'd spent far longer in the high court than the few minutes that seemed to have passed here.

"Perfect timing," Kyran whispered in my ear, his Cheshire grin in place and no sand left in the upper globe of his hourglass. "And nice crown."

I frowned at him, reaching up to wipe the sweat from my forehead, and my fingers brushed something hard and warm. I froze, confused for a moment, until I realized it was a small circlet. Right. I'd killed Ryese. That had earned me the light court. I hadn't even noticed, all things considered.

I didn't waste time, but stepped forward and raised my voice as loud as I could. "Everyone cease fighting!"

My command bellowed across the clearing, as if Faerie had picked up my voice and magnified it. And maybe she had. I could feel Faerie as I never had before, and I had an awareness I couldn't quite explain of every fae in the clearing.

Weapons hit the ground as if the fae could no longer hold them, and all eyes turned toward me. The murmurs began immediately. Whispers from the light warriors.

"Is that the crown of light?"

"Is that . . . Who is she carrying?"

"Is she a queen?"

Falin stepped toward me. His weapons were also gone—apparently I'd disarmed everyone. "Alex?"

"Help." I mouthed the word, not daring to speak it aloud.

I didn't need to.

Falin rushed to my side, reaching out to help me lower the king to the grass. Nandin was there a moment later, helping Brad to his feet.

"Girl, that's the High King," Nandin hissed, staring at what appeared to be a body and no longer a living fae.

"I'm aware. We need a healer."

Nandin nodded. I expected him to delegate the task to someone else, but he handed Brad off to Dugan and then he himself took off toward the door to winter.

I'd never recalled my ball of realities, and it had followed me here, filling the clearing. Collectors appeared in the grove, moving among those who'd fallen in the battle. Death nodded to me, and I spotted the Raver as well. Two other collectors, ones I didn't know, also moved among the dead. Fear spiked through me, and I looked at my father. He wasn't dead, not yet, but I could sense the life fading from him. Today, in this field, whoever died here would remain permanently dead.

Because I'd brought death to Faerie, at least for the moment.

I'd been High Queen less than ten minutes, and in that time, I'd cannibalized a living soul and then brought true death to a field of warriors. Yeah, this was going well.

I could have reclaimed the layers of reality, given the collectors nowhere to exist, but then I'd be forsworn and the Mender could accuse me of reneging on the debt I owed him. He'd called it in for me to collect the battlefield dead of Faerie. And this had been a battle.

I pushed away from the ground, glancing around. Maeve had fallen—this would be her second and final death. Lyell looked badly injured, but should survive. Rianna had a few lacerations that might need attention, and Kyran looked like he'd taken a pretty good blow, but while Falin and Dugan were both splashed with blood, it didn't appear that the blood belonged to either warrior.

Light had fared far worse.

"All hail the Queen of Light!" a voice called out from somewhere in the clearing. Suddenly the call seemed to come from every direction as the light warriors fell to their knees.

"I don't have time for that right now," I snapped at them. "I need a healer. Probably more than one. The best healers in Faerie." Nandin had already gone to find one, but he wasn't back yet. And besides, there were enough injured in this field that we needed more than a single healer.

One of the light warriors jumped to his feet and took off for a path of light at a run.

"I take it I missed something," Dugan said, approaching me slowly, his gaze moving from the dying king at my feet to the crown of light on my forehead.

"Yeah, understatement." I fingered the crown again, frowning. "Dugan, what do you think about the title 'King of Light'?"

Chapter 33

——◦—⟫═◦═⟪—◦——

I stood beside the amaranthine tree we'd planted in the center of the grove between courts. Dugan had found it stashed away in the light court within hours of accepting the throne. There were a lot of unquiet murmurs about how I'd handed the crown of light to the—now former—Shadow Prince, but it felt like the right choice. Faerie agreed with me, which was an odd sensation, but I was now very aware of the mercurial moods of Faerie.

She was hurting, the balance badly damaged and in need of time to repair. Dugan was sympathetic to the plight of the shadow court, which made him the ideal person to rule the court that was meant to be its counterbalance. I'd already visited the chasm between the realm of dreams and the shadow court once. I hadn't been able to repair the rift and rejoin dreams to shadow, even with the magical boost from Faerie. But I'd made a start. It would take time, perhaps a few years of visiting several times a week and reconnecting a thread or two at a time as I could, but I'd repair it.

Falin placed a hand on my waist. "Now what?" he asked, nodding to the sapling.

I wasn't sure. I looked around the tree to the ancient-looking fae on the other side. My father, wearing the glamour of an old wise king, stood with his arms crossed, staring at the tree. The healers had arrived in time, and he was recovering remarkably fast. It had been less than two days since I cut him from his throne, and he probably needed a longer recovery, but we had to start this now. The doors that had survived Ryese were open again, and with the truces in place, displaced fae were beginning to trickle back into Faerie, but the Americas were cut off. We needed a permanent door. A connection to the land so we could reach the stranded fae.

"You're sure about this?" my father asked, staring at the sapling we'd planted. "It will be decades before the other seeds I planted will be large enough to take root in both mortal reality and Faerie and form a door. This is our only shot."

I nodded. "We only have the one tree. All the courts will have to share it to maintain balance."

My father smiled, as if that were the right answer, though I had the feeling it wasn't the choice he would have made. He'd refused to take the high throne back, despite his rapid recovery. There had been quite a bit of arguing over that one, which led to him calling me a petulant child and me pointing out that was exactly why I shouldn't be High Queen of Faerie. It might not have been his plan for me to wind up as High Queen, but he'd spent more than a millennium bound to Faerie, her ruler but also her captive, and he wanted freedom. I tried to abdicate, but while Faerie had allowed me to hand off the light court without any resistance, she wouldn't let me opt out of the high court. I'd accepted. I was hers now, and she intended to keep me.

At least she hadn't physically bound me to the throne.

My father had agreed to advise me as well as to continue to act as the official face of the high court. I'd also taken Falin, Dugan, and Nandin as my advisors.

They were the only ones besides Brad who knew I was High Queen, and I planned to keep it that way. I had a lot to learn, and like Ryese had said, I had no idea how to use the power I'd been handed, so I was vulnerable. I had no desire to fight endless duels. So the current plan was to keep my position secret. My council of kings were bound by oaths to protect my secret as well as some pretty unbreakable truces that would keep them from challenging me for the crown. It was the best I could do.

They surrounded me now, as we stood in the center of the clearing with the small sapling. A whole lot of hope was bound in its thin branches. We were about to try something that had never been done, but if it worked, it would help restore some balance to Faerie.

Ryese must have slipped into the high court at least a century ago to have stolen a seed that grew into this sapling. Then, from what we could gather, he'd used the sapling and his bloodline to gather followers through all of Faerie. We didn't know how many he had, or how much trouble they might still cause now that he was gone, but I was trying to repair what damage I could.

The first step was tethering this tree to mortal reality.

Dugan, Nandin, Falin, my father, and I had debated all night over where its mortal connection should be established. North America had been the easy decision, as it was North and South America that were the most cut off from Faerie. I'd argued for Nekros because it was home. Somewhere slightly more south and central would have been more ideal, but in the end, my sentimental attachment to Nekros decided it. Besides, the folded space holding Nekros was one of the largest on the continent.

It took both my father's and my magic—as well as Faerie's contribution—to establish the door. By the time we finished, I was swaying on my feet. Apparently the last time my father had attempted this, he'd had a whole team of planeweavers.

"Should we check it out?" I asked in panting breaths.

Only my council was with me presently, the clearing sealed and the doors to all the courts momentarily closed. Later, my father would make the official announcement about the tree to the courts. He'd been pretending to be his own emissary for centuries. Now he would legitimately fulfill the role of emissary of the high court.

"Are you up for it?" Dugan asked, giving me a skeptical look.

That look was reflected in Falin's eyes as well. He had his arms tight around me, and I might have been leaning against him for more than just emotional support.

Straightening, I took a deep breath and nodded.

I wanted to make sure the doorway really worked, and worked the way I'd intended. The fae in the mortal realm had been fading, cut off from Faerie for days now. By placing the door here, in the center of Faerie, connected to all courts, I was not only allowing the belief magic that would be collected from these territories to nourish all of Faerie, but, in theory, the territory in the mortal realm that this door covered should belong to all courts and to none. That meant independents, regardless of court affiliation, should be able to exist there without fading.

The Americas had just become the first truly neutral territory for independent fae.

I walked hand in hand with Falin around the tree, Dugan, Nandin, and my father following in our wake. I expected to emerge in the fire-ruined remains of the Bloom. Instead we stepped into a room that looked identical to how the Eternal Bloom had appeared prior to the bombing, except that the massive tree that once stood in the room was now a small sapling bearing only a few of the ever-blooming flowers that gave the tree its name.

"Nice work," I whispered to Faerie, gazing around the room, because I knew the land itself had refashioned this place. It was an exact replica, missing only the fae who typically frequented it. But they would come. More than had ever been here before would now come.

Faerie buzzed happily in the back of my mind, pleased by my appreciation.

We wove through the tables until we reached the VIP door. Nandin and Dugan stepped through without a backward glance. They'd never been able to move freely through the mortal realm before, but this tree was tied to light and shadow as well as the seasonal courts, so their courts had access to the mortal realm for the first time. No surprise that they were anxious to explore. Falin stepped through next, still holding my hand, but my fingers encountered a solid invisible barrier as they touched the doorway, and I stopped short.

Falin stepped back inside, frowning. I pressed my palm flat against the barrier that prevented me from walking through the door. I couldn't see it, but it didn't give an inch.

"I did warn you," my father said, his arms crossed over his chest. "Honestly, I'm surprised Faerie let you get this far. We might want to make sure no natural disasters hit the courts while you've been in this blended space and outside Faerie proper. She can be rather . . . possessive."

"Faerie's not unhappy," I said, because I could feel Faerie in the back of my mind. She didn't mind me coming to this pocket she'd created, but she wasn't going to let me leave her influence completely. I was the High Queen. And I belonged to Faerie.

At least I'm not rooted to a throne, I reminded myself again. It was cold comfort.

"Let's head back," Falin said, turning me toward the small amaranthine sapling.

I shook my head, but it was my father who said, "No, kingling, you need to go find that Agent Nori of yours and start working out the relocation of winter's fae to Nekros. Alexis's plan will extend this territory more than normal, but it is still only one tree, and a sapling at that. There will be a lot of areas that are very thin on magic. Nekros just became the magical hub of the Americas."

Falin frowned at him. I placed a hand on his arm. "And I need you to find Holly and Caleb to make sure they're okay. It's going to be really hard to explain why I can't leave Faerie." At least without telling them why, but I couldn't tell anyone why, not even my friends. "And Tamara . . ." Geez, what was I going to do about Tam? She wasn't fae or a changeling, so Faerie was a dangerous place for her. I wouldn't even trust asking her to meet me at the Bloom. I gave Falin a small smile. "Let them know I'm okay and hope to see everyone soon. And PC. Would you bring him here?" Because Faerie wasn't going to deny me my dog.

He nodded, but he didn't return my smile.

"I'll escort you back, Alexis," my father said, walking toward the amaranthine tree. "I need to contact the other courts to explain the new conditions to them and get them on the task of relocating their independents as well."

I didn't follow him. Instead I stared through the doorway. Outside I could see mortal sunlight, deceptively bright and inviting, though I knew it would be cold—after all, it was winter in Nekros. The mortal realm wasn't particularly kind—I was half-blind there, and the weather tended to be extreme. But it was home.

Around us, the distant music of Faerie turned sad, reflecting my mood. Or perhaps it was her sorrow at my homesickness.

"You sure you don't want to make those proclamations on your own behalf?" I asked my father, still gazing out the doorway.

He stopped and turned to look at me. "Alexis, you have all of Faerie. I had a golden prison. No, I don't wish to return to it. It took me centuries to figure out a way to tear my soul in half so I could walk somewhat free, but it was never the same as true freedom. I don't intend to relinquish this freedom so soon after acquiring it. Now, stop moping and let's go."

Right. I sighed. Then I lifted onto my toes to kiss Falin. He wrapped his arms around me, deepening the kiss to something more than the simple good-bye I'd intended.

"I'll return soon," he promised when we broke apart.

I nodded and watched him go, my hand still on the barrier that stopped no one but me.

Faerie and I were going to have to have a serious discussion about this.

Epilogue

Three months later . . .

I stood in the hospital room, the newborn curled in my arms staring at me with large dark eyes.

"I don't think I look enough like your mama," I whispered to him as his little nose started to scrunch, the precursor to the cry I knew would erupt from him any moment.

"He's probably hungry," Tamara said, pushing herself into a sitting position in her hospital bed.

"Probably. Oh, Tam. He's precious," I said as I handed him back to her. And he was. The pregnancy may have had some rough patches, but he was healthy and perfect.

Tamara nearly glowed as she gazed at her son. The small baby settled as soon as her arms closed around him, turning his tiny face into her.

"Yep, hungry," she said with a small chuckle as the baby rooted, his mouth opening as he searched for milk.

I smiled, but gathered my purse. "I'll give you two some privacy." After all, he was a day old; they were still figuring everything out. Also, I could see Ethan hovering outside the door. He'd stepped out for my visit, but I knew he was anxious to get back to his wife and newborn.

Tamara, already fiddling with her hospital gown, looked up, as if she wanted to argue, but then she smiled. "I'm glad you could make it, Al."

"Me too," I said before ducking out the door. And I was. Faerie and I had reached a compromise we could live with, but my trips into the mortal realm were still rare. This was a special occasion, but I didn't dare stay long.

My planeweaving meant I carried realities with me. I was never actually apart from Faerie, even in the mortal realm. I was more or less a walking embassy, everything I touched becoming part of Faerie while I was in contact with it. Even still, Faerie might have denied me leaving her lands except that, High Queen or not, I was a grave witch, and wyrd magic couldn't be denied, even by Faerie. I could only raise shades and release my ever-refilling wyrd magic in places where the land of the dead existed. While I could merge planes in Faerie, she liked death in her halls even less than letting me leave.

So we compromised.

It gave me some autonomy, and I could feel the small thrill Faerie got from exploring the mortal realm through me, but Faerie interacting directly with the mortal realm could occasionally have unpredictable results. So I spent most of my time outside of Faerie proper in pockets of blended space.

And Faerie had created quite a few such pockets for me. My castle was back in its private pocket behind Caleb's house, my friends once again in residence. I also now had a very nice and very large office in FIB headquarters created from a small pocket of blended reality. I wasn't agent in charge of winter anymore, though. I was now director of the FIB of the Americas, each season's agents as well as the newly established branches for light and shadow reporting to me.

The fact that these two continents belonged to all courts, and thus none, was very new territory. I was working on turning the FIB into a unified organization, and in the Americas it was going . . . okay. The fae were slow to change, even when change was thrust upon them, but I did have several kings and Faerie itself at my back, so I was making some progress, though it often felt I took one step back for each two forward. Still, that was a net gain of one.

Driving through the streets of Nekros, the top of my convertible down in the early spring air, and headed toward Caleb's house and the castle hidden beyond, I almost felt normal again. Not a secret queen. Not the embodiment of a magical land. Not a planeweaver. Just Alex Craft, grave witch.

Of course, that was only an illusion. Everything had changed, though not all of it for the worse.

Brad being back still seemed surreal three months later. He was familiar, and yet so different. We'd actually all gathered at the Caine estate for dinner one night. That had been weird. Casey took it well, all things considered—my little sister was more resilient than I'd ever given her credit for. My father was still my father, though, and we bumped heads a lot. And avoiding each other wasn't really an option anymore. Not only was he one of my advisors, he also was my primary teacher on using the magic that came with the high throne. He'd also stepped right back into his life as Governor Caine—and I had no idea what kinds of spells or bribes he used to cover up his brief disappearance, but within a week of his return, it had no longer been news—so in addition to dealing with him as an advisor in my life as a secret queen, I interacted with him regularly in my professional capacity as director of the FIB. We saw a lot of each other. It was . . . tense, but workable.

Falin met me in the front room of the castle. With pretty much all of Faerie locked in binding truces, there were no more duels to fight, so his schedule had opened up a bit. There were, of course, still hours of negotiation meetings to attend and delegates to entertain, and as a whole, the royals were still a sneaky bunch trying to get as good a position as they could for their own court while inside the truce, but Faerie was at a more stable peace than she'd been outside of a revelry since the first time she shattered and was formed into the current court system. It afforded us more time together, of which I was grateful.

Falin kissed me breathless as greeting before asking, "How was your visit?"

"It was nice. Tamara is doing well and her baby is adorable. Are you staying for dinner?"

He nodded, and I dumped my purse on the table beside the door before heading toward the castle's large dining hall. He couldn't always meet me for dinner—hell, I didn't always make it to dinner at the castle as I didn't really live here—but we both tried to stop in as often as possible. For both of us, it offered a note of normalcy.

Voices drifted from the room up ahead of us, and I picked up my pace, Falin at my heels.

Holly was standing in front of the large dining table, making wild gesticulations and speaking in a voice pitched much lower than her normal tone so I guessed she was doing another impression of the defense attorney she'd been facing off with in court all week, her antics delighting those gathered around the table. She turned as I entered, a huge smile breaking across her face as she called out, "Al, did you get to meet the baby?"

"I did. I even got to hold him," I said as I claimed my normal seat.

"Isn't he cute?" Rianna chimed in, which made Desmond huff loudly at her side, his large doglike jowls blowing outward.

We discussed the baby as Falin and I loaded our plates. Then Caleb relayed several stories from his day.

While he was still taking some commissions for art and wards, he'd joined the new department I'd created in the FIB to assist in the relocation and adjustment of the huge influx of fae who'd moved to Nekros following the neutral door opening.

Dugan joined us before dinner was finished, which wasn't unusual. Nandin and Brad would even occasionally drop in, though not as often as Dugan. It had been odd the first time the former Shadow Prince, now Light King, sat down with the bulk of my friends for what was basically a family meal, but he actually fit in among my friends quite well. His humor tended to be a little drier, and he didn't always understand modern slang, but he'd told me once that he thought friendship might be valuable enough to work for, and he'd made quite a few friends here.

We were in the middle of dessert when Falin glanced at his watch and the smile on his face dimmed, his arm tightening around me in the smallest of squeezes.

"We have to go meet with summer now, don't we?" I asked with a groan, already knowing the answer. "I so need more chocolate cake first."

That earned a chuckle around the table, but keeping royals waiting was never a good idea, even with a hundred years of a truce stretching out in front of us, so I took one more large bite and then made my good-byes.

At least the commute time wasn't bad. While the amaranthine tree was the only official door, and it was Faerie's tether to mortal reality, I could use any doorway to step into Faerie. It was certainly convenient, but I tried to only use it in the pockets already containing Faerie, as not even my father was sure of the long-term effects of using it in doorways existing solely in mortal reality.

Court was still one of my least favorite things to attend. It always seemed to be a lot of double-talk or circular conversations that never accomplished much. Still, I was High Queen, so I attended when I could.

Not that most attending knew my actual station. The winter consort ring had never vanished, so on advice from my council, I did nothing to dispel assumptions that I was only a seasonal consort. Tonight's court meeting was another irritatingly long session that ended with nothing actually being said, at least from what I took away.

Hours later, as I lay in the center of Falin's enormous bed, curled against his naked body, exhausted but content, I stared at the small snowflake ring. The idea of committing to be his consort had seemed so enormous when the ring first appeared. I laughed, shaking my head.

"Mmm, what's so funny?" Falin asked, letting his fingers trail down my bare back, the light touch sending happy shivers through me.

"Oh." I shook my head. "It's not really funny, I guess." I lifted my hand so he could see the ring too. His fingers went still on my back. "I was so scared of the changes commitment might bring. It seems trivial now, after having committed to all of Faerie."

He'd gone so still, I didn't even think he was breathing. I twisted so I could look at him and found him watching me, his face unreadable.

"Faerie never took away the ring when I became High Queen. Can one hold two titles at once? Or would they have to abdicate one to take a new title?"

He lifted an eyebrow, but the edge of his lips turned up, the first hint of a growing smile. "You briefly held both the high and the light court."

"True."

He rolled onto one elbow, his free hand sliding up my body to my face. He traced a finger down my chin before leaning down and kissing me. It was a sweet kiss, gentle and loving.

"Are you finally ready for me to ask, Alexis?" He whispered the question, his icy blue eyes bright as he studied me.

Was I? Just the idea made my heart flutter wildly in my chest, but it wasn't such a bad feeling. I loved Falin. I knew that without a shadow of a doubt.

"Hmm." I trailed my fingers over the muscles of his arm, a teasing smile playing over my lips. "Consort to the Winter King kind of sounds like a step downward when I'm already High Queen, doesn't it? Wouldn't it make more sense," I whispered, leveraging myself closer, so that I was a breath away as I whispered, "for you to become consort to the High Queen?"

His eyes widened, just slightly, and then his lips sealed with mine. While the previous kiss had been sweet, this one was deep, demanding. I surrendered myself to it completely. Snowflakes shaped like amaranthine flowers were falling all around us by the time we broke apart, both breathless.

Falin gazed at me, drinking in my features with his eyes. "In that case, will you be my Queen?"

"Yes," I whispered, even though the word scared me. The smile that broke across his face was more than worth the twinge of nervousness, because I was already his, I just hadn't admitted it aloud.

"I love you," I said, leaning up to kiss him again. He pulled me in tight against him and I surrendered to the joy in it.

I was High Queen, and I'd take care of Faerie the best I could, do my part to help repair the balance, but I couldn't make all my decisions as High Queen. I still needed to be Alex and make some choices that were for me, not Faerie. And this one? It was all for me, and it made me happy.

ACKNOWLEDGMENTS

Wow. I've now written "The End" on Alex's story. It's hard to believe, a little sad to say good-bye, but very exciting. There are a lot of people who helped me get to this point and I wouldn't have made it alone, so I want to call out a big thank-you to those individuals and groups.

First, I'd like to thank Jessica Wade and her team. Her guidance and all of their hard work have helped shape each book in this series into a final form that could be released to those who would enjoy it.

A huge thank-you goes to Lucienne Diver, who has always believed in the series and who takes care of so much behind the scenes so that I can focus on story-telling.

Also, I wouldn't have made it this far without the amazing support of my friends and family. Friends who read for me—a special shout-out here to Nikki and Xandra, who read early drafts of *Grave War*, but many more have read for me throughout the series—and family who helped in other ways, from distracting little people to being there for emotional support when things got tough or just being an amazing encouragement, thank you. To Mom, in particular. And to Jason. I can't thank you enough.

And, of course, thank you to all the readers who have made it this far in Alex's story. This tale literally would not have ever been able to be fully told without you. Thank you for reading. Thank you for wanting more. I hope you enjoyed this final story.

Ready to find
your next great read?

Let us help.

Visit prh.com/nextread